Gabbey,

TWISTED ROCK

A STONEPORT MANOR MYSTERY

JILL SANDERS

Merry Christmas
Jill Sanders

GRAYTON

SUMMARY

Someone to watch over Rose.

Losing her husband in a small plane crash last year has forced Rose to get on with her life. But when a storm rolls in, her world is shattered with the discovery of a body buried deep within her own walls. Now, as all fingers point in her direction, a mistress steps out of the shadows, along with a dark family scandal that might shed some light on motive. As people around her drop like flies, the real killer gets too close, and Rose seeks the help of the police officer who knocked on her door one rainy night a year ago.

Royce Sawyer is the cop who'd had to tell Rose that the love of her life was gone forever. Seeing the pretty blonde's struggles for the last year has been heart-wrenching, but when everyone starts to suspect the quiet wife has a dark side, Sawyer finds it hard to keep his personal feelings separate from his professional ones, especially when it's obvious that someone's out to stop him from getting to the truth.

To Jody...
You know why...

ONE

Rose falls in love...

ROSE MAY HAVE ONLY BEEN ten years old, but she knew, just knew, that Isaac Clayton was the boy she was going to marry when she grew up. He was everything she had ever dreamed of, her very own prince. He was tall, or taller than her, anyway, but most boys in her class were at this point. He had blond surf-style hair that she found cute and deep blue eyes that reached into her soul. Most important of all, he was the smartest boy in her class. Rose was enamored of him, a word she had just had on a spelling test the week before.

She'd been happily surprised when, during recess shortly after her tenth birthday, he'd sat with her on the monkey bars to talk to her. Her heart had raced and her palms were so sweaty, she had to wipe them on her jean shorts. By the end of that week, they were holding hands on the swings and spending all of their recess time together.

Just looking into his blue eyes did funny things to her insides.

It took a year for Isaac to plant a chaste kiss on her cheek—her first. She hadn't thought it could get any better, but five years later their first fumbled sexual encounter behind the bleachers during a school dance proved her wrong. Her entire body had exploded when he'd used his fingers on her lady parts, as her mother had called them. A year later they'd had their first "real" sex in the back of the new car his father had given him for his sixteenth birthday. She'd known then that no other man could ever make her feel the way Isaac had.

When they were eighteen, he asked her to run away with him when he went to college. It had been hard to say no to him, but she'd had her own college plans and wanted to follow through with her own life goals before settling down with him for good.

Watching Isaac head to Boston for law school as she went in the opposite direction, to California, for art school had been devastating. Still, they had called each other almost nightly and, even though she doubted him, he promised her that he had stayed true to her, just as she had to him. She had flirted occasionally and, once, she had made out with a guy at a party. But it had never meant anything to her, not like it meant with Isaac. She had only done it to confirm that Isaac really was the only man who could make her knees weak and cause her heart to vibrate in her chest. After testing the waters, she knew Isaac was the only man for her. He was her soul mate and she couldn't imagine being with any other man for the rest of her life.

Seven years after graduating high school, they were both on the same side of the continent again. He'd finished law school and had immediately been hired at his father's law firm in New York City. Rose moved into a small apartment with Isaac. New York was bigger than anything she'd ever imagined. It was shocking to know that Isaac still held such power over her mind and body. It was as if no time had passed. They easily picked up where they had left off and she could tell, just by looking deep into his blue eyes, that he'd stayed faithful to her.

Less than a year later Isaac proposed and in five months she was walking down the aisle surrounded by family and friends in her hometown of Twisted Rock, New York. Her perfect dream wedding with her very own prince. Life couldn't have gotten any better.

Isaac surprised her with a honeymoon in Italy, and the weeklong vacation was the most romantic she'd ever experienced. Isaac had been the boyfriend of her dreams and now he was the husband of all the fairy tales.

That first year of their marriage, Isaac purchased a three-thousand-square-foot loft for her after he got a raise at his father's law firm.

She had turned one of the four bedrooms into an art studio and spent her days painting. In the evenings they attended the many social events that his job and family obligations required.

Over time she became less satisfied in the city. Her art suffered, her social life was nonexistent, and, since Isaac traveled a lot for work, she found herself becoming very lonely.

After expressing her concerns to Isaac about it, he'd surprised her by purchasing a house in Twisted Rock for their one-year anniversary. They quickly sold their loft and moved back home.

Isaac had worked hard and, like his father before him, he'd gotten his pilot's license the year after graduating high school. For his twenty-fifth birthday, his father had given him a brand-new Gulfstream plane, so he could fly back and forth from Twisted Rock to the city on an almost daily basis. She worried about the commute, but Isaac assured her that he enjoyed the hour and a half trip much more than being stuck on a train or in the back of a cab.

But still, a month after moving home, Isaac purchased a small two-bedroom loft in the city for when he had to stay overnight. This became an almost weekly occurrence because he'd made partner at the firm, thanks to his father's influence and pull in the company. Isaac now had a bigger paycheck, but less time at home.

The house he'd purchased for her was more of a mansion. She'd driven by the old place lots of times when she was younger, but it was bigger than she'd imagined. Stoneport Manor had sat empty for as long as she could remember.

The old mansion had been given the name long before she'd been born. It boasted six bedrooms, four and a half bathrooms, a full-sized office with an attached library, a great room, a formal dining room, a kitchen that was larger than her childhood home, and a full cellar. There were several outbuildings on the property including a boat house down a steep set of rocky stairs and an old gazebo that was falling in on itself, which sat at the highest point of the eight-acre property. At one point, there had been two or three other good-sized homes that sat on the Stoneport Manor estates, but those homes had been sold off many years earlier. There was also a large flower garden with high stone walls and old fountains filled with dirt and grass. She hoped to start repairing them that spring.

The second she stepped through the heavy wood front doors of the house, she understood why no one had taken on the giant task of fixing the place up. It was not only going to take a lot of time but a lot of money, which Isaac assured her they had plenty of.

That first night, she couldn't have been happier as Isaac carried her across the threshold. They spent that evening in a sleeping bag in front of the fireplace, making love the entire night.

Rose spent her days cleaning or guiding the contractors Isaac had hired to help fix the place. She found plenty of time to focus on her art in the lonely evenings when Isaac was stuck in the city. Most of the weekends they spent either working on the place together or driving through the countryside, shopping at antique stores for furniture to fill the giant home. She'd never enjoyed herself more than when they spent time together.

Isaac took her on a short weekend trip to California's wine country for her birthday, and she fell in love with him all over again. They had talked about starting a family, but he wanted to wait until the end of the summer when his schedule wasn't so busy. She understood, even though it broke her heart to wait any longer. In the end, they had agreed to wait a few months longer before trying for their first child.

Happy-ever-after was no longer just around the corner; she finally had everything she'd ever dreamed of. The perfect husband, the soon-to-be perfect home, and, soon, their first child. Life couldn't get any better.

A STRANGER COMES CALLING...

It was one of those winter evenings when Rose wished it would snow. It felt cold enough, but thunder continued to rattle the walls and the rain kept falling.

Their home sat along a low bluff on the northeast side of Lake Erie. It was a beautiful spot come spring and summer, but in the fall and winter, the place was a reminder that scary things moved in the nighttime. Floorboards creaked, and the lights flashed every time the fuse box was taxed. Every room had cold drafty spots and some of the windows had cracks or slivers of glass missing from them, letting the chill in further.

They had lived in the manor for four months now and still most of the work hadn't even begun.

The home was quiet that evening since the workers hadn't been able to return to work due to the rain. Luckily, they had finished pouring the new foundation wall two days prior to the rain starting. The new wall was required on the west side of the manor, where the old stone wall had fallen in.

It had taken almost a month for the workers to remove all the old stones from the wall. They'd had to place two large steel support beams to hold up the foundation until the cement could be poured.

They had brought in several truckloads of dirt, and several more were due to arrive after the cement cured and the rain stopped.

The rain had started the very evening the cement was poured, but she was assured by RJ Gamet, the foreman Isaac had hired, that the cement had already cured enough to withstand the moisture.

As the rain continued, she feared that the west side of the house would soon slide into Lake Erie far below. The manor sat almost fifty feet from the nearest downslope towards the water, but that didn't stop the worry.

Isaac was returning home that night and she knew that

he would probably head out there with a flashlight after dinner to check on the wall for himself.

She was making one of his favorite dishes: pork tenderloin with a caramel rub and wine sauce on a bed of green beans with brown spiced rice. She'd spent the first year of their marriage learning to cook his favorite meals since she'd had a lot of time alone in the loft.

Cooking, to her, was like art. She enjoyed every aspect of it, from planning and preparation to making the final plate look like a masterpiece. Isaac always told her that he enjoyed every bite.

Shortly after moving into the home, Isaac had turned a small storage room in the basement into a wine cellar for their growing wine collection. She enjoyed making meals that would complement the wine he'd chosen before heading out to work each day. Since he'd spent the last few days in New York City and on travel, he'd picked out a bottle for the day he'd return before leaving.

He'd chosen a rich Chardonnay they had picked up in Italy on their honeymoon. She'd searched all weekend and had finally found the perfect meal to go with it.

With the meal underway, and his arrival getting closer, she couldn't stop the excitement she felt that tonight they might officially start making a family together. She'd checked all the charts and knew that she was ovulating. Tonight was the first time they would be together after coming to the big decision.

As she put the finishing touches on the table and lit the tall white candles on the crystal candlesticks they'd gotten for their wedding, she tried to contain her excitement at seeing him again. Would it always be like this? She hoped so. Almost a year and a half into their marriage and she was still finding new ways to fall in love with her husband.

From his little text messages during the day to the flowers he had delivered to her on a regular basis when he was stuck in the city, everything Isaac did brought her closer to him.

She had built a fire in the massive stone fireplace that opened to the dining room and the grand living space. Since the old house was always drafty, there was usually a fire going in the hearth. The HVAC system hadn't been updated yet and the old boiler sat silently in the basement until it could be replaced.

The workers wouldn't get to the inside work until they were sure the foundation, roof, and electric in the most-used rooms were sound.

They still didn't have power in more than half of the house, but she didn't complain. She knew they were working as fast as they could. Isaac had made sure the crew had started on the kitchen and bathroom areas first. Unlike the first two months they'd lived there, at least now she could cook and dry her hair. They had spent a lot of time eating at local diners and bumping into old school friends. The small town of Twisted Rock was a fifteen-minute drive from Stoneport Manor and sat along a very small cape. Its name came from the first settlers along the rocky shoreline. Seeing the massive sweep of colorful rocks that the wind and waters had carved out which rose from the edge of the riverbed, twisting around as if some child's playthings, had given the town its name and its character.

Since Rose's graduation, her mother had moved to Pittsburgh with her second husband, Bill, to be closer to her only grandchildren. Rose's sister Jenny had moved there after marrying her high school sweetheart. Jenny was four years older than Rose and had three kids now, two boys, Regan and Cole, who were nine and seven, and a six-year-old girl named McKenna.

Rose had a stepbrother, Hunter McDonald, who lived less than an hour away in Buffalo. She'd gained him as a brother when she was nine and her mother had married Bill. Her father, Glenn Browning, had died when she was very young, and she didn't remember him. He'd died in the line of duty as a local police officer, but her mother hadn't shared the details with her. Every time Rose asked about him or how he'd died, her mother would tear up and say it was too hard to talk about.

At first, she hadn't known how to act with a brother, but in time, she and Hunter became inseparable.

Now, there wasn't a week that Hunter wasn't up at the house helping them out with one thing or the other. Hunter and Isaac had been best friends growing up. Wherever she and Isaac went, Hunter was usually a few steps behind. She'd missed seeing him when they'd lived in the city and enjoyed having him closer again.

Rose took every chance she could to visit the rest of her family, but lately, she was tied more and more to the house. Not that she minded, but it would be nice to fill her time with children soon.

She checked herself in the mirror one last time and glanced down at the crystal-encrusted watch Isaac had given her as a honeymoon present.

She ran her hand down the red chiffon dress she'd purchased in the city. The short sleeves and skirt allowed the chill in the air to hit her, but she knew Isaac would enjoy the view.

He should be walking through the door any minute now. She moved towards the kitchen, her red heels clicking on the old wood floor. The sound changed as she stepped onto the classic black-and-white tile flooring in the kitchen.

Two new restaurant-quality gas ovens and stovetops sat along the far wall of the kitchen. They had been a gift from Isaac shortly after they had moved in. A beautifully decorated antique copper vent sat over the stoves. The vent was original to the home and had needed almost a full day's worth of work to clean it up to a shine. There was a small shelf just under the vent and above the stoves where she kept her spices. An old marble-topped chop block with a sink in it sat in the middle of the room. She had plans to purchase barstools for the island area soon. Glancing around, she could just imagine how the place must have looked when it was built and how it would look when they were done with it.

There were two ornamented wood hutches built into the wall opposite the stoves where they kept all their china and appliances. In between, them was the entry to a large walk-in pantry.

A new doublewide stainless-steel refrigerator and a smaller wine fridge sat on the end wall, with one of her favorite features of the manor, a dumbwaiter.

A small sitting area was right next to a glass door that led out to a small deck and what would become her herb garden, come spring.

They hadn't picked out a table and chairs yet for the area, so the space sat empty.

Her dream kitchen was almost complete. The only thing left to do was restain some of the woodwork, put new copper ceiling tiles over the cracked and broken ones, and replace some of the lighting. She had plans to hang the copper pans she'd received for their wedding over the chopping block but hadn't found the right hangers yet.

Checking the oven one last time, she decided to keep the pork warming until she heard the bell informing her that Isaac's BMW had come through the old iron gate and was pulling up the long drive.

The gate mechanism hadn't been repaired yet, so the large iron gates sat open. Isaac had wanted to know when someone was driving up the driveway and had installed the small security-type doorbell at the gate area himself.

She walked into the living room and glanced around. So much work still needed to be done here. They had a small leather sofa set directly in front of the fireplace. A large Italian baroque-style mirror hung over the Italian marble hearth. They had lucked out that the hearth had been undamaged and only needed a day's worth of elbow grease to clean it.

Checking herself in the mirror, she applied her lipstick and smiled at her reflection. She'd grown her hair out because Isaac loved to run his hands through the long blonde tresses.

A few minutes later, she returned to the kitchen and checked again on the food, anxiously glancing down at her watch every few minutes. When an hour passed, she pulled out her cell phone and texted him. She guessed that he was probably flying home and didn't want to distract him.

-Did you get delayed?

She thought of texting him fifteen minutes later after no reply came but didn't want to bother him if he was in the air. She knew that he was cutting across the state and that his cell service dropped several times during the hour-long flight. He normally didn't call when he was away on business trips since he didn't have a lot of time to himself. Still, he made a point to text her when he could.

She hated being out of contact with him, but every now

and then, he'd send her a text message or flowers. Every time the delivery truck showed up, she knew he'd been thinking of her. Yesterday's flowers had been yellow roses, her favorites. He had texted shortly after they had arrived, but it had been just a quick one.

"Thinking of you. Always yours... IC"

Almost two hours after she'd expected him home, the bell finally chimed, signaling a car in the driveway. Rushing to the kitchen, she pulled out the pork and set it on the table, hoping it wasn't too dry. She relit the candles.

Since the fog and rain were still so bad, she couldn't make out his car as it came slowly down the long driveway towards the four-car garage where her own SUV was parked. She stood in the hallway waiting for him, excited to see him and start their new family together.

She frowned when the doorbell chimed. She'd expected him to walk through the doors and wrap his arms around her like he normally did. Hearing the bell, she wondered if she'd locked the front doors and quickly reached for the heavy metal handle. Pulling the thick wood doors open, she smiled brightly, but the smile died instantly when she saw a tall police officer standing on the front porch in the dim light. He looked familiar, but she couldn't remember his name. He was roughly her age, tall, good-looking with a chiseled chin covered lightly with dark stubble from a long day. His jet-black hair was wet from the rain, making him look dark and dangerous, the kind of man Rose had always avoided. However, it was his green eyes that stood out to her most. The look in them told her instantly that something was wrong.

From the darkness, another officer stepped forward and she turned her eyes away from the first man. She'd known Rodney Carson most of her life. He was roughly the same age as her father would be if he was still alive. The man's silver hair was thick and in desperate need of a cut. Still, his blue eyes had always looked at her with kindness and a hint of sadness that she always related to the loss of her father.

Both of the men's hats and coats were soaked as they stood under the cover of the long porch that ran the length of the front of the house.

"Evening, Rose." Rodney tilted his head slightly, then nodded to the other man. "This is my new partner, Sawyer." Rodney took another step forward, twisting his hat in his hands. "May we come in?"

"Is there something wrong?" she asked, surprised she could get the words out. She was feeling a little light-headed.

"It's best if we come in," Officer Sawyer, replied. Her eyes moved back to him and she noticed that his green eyes were pleading with her.

She moved back and, without a word, the men stepped into the foyer. Their shoes and her heels echoed off the stone flooring that covered the entryway to her home.

"Rose, it might be best if we talk in there." Officer Carson nodded towards the fireplace.

She moved as if on autopilot towards the warmth. Standing by the old mantle that Isaac had helped her clean, she turned on the men as they followed her towards the fire.

Officer Carson motioned towards the sofa. "Why don't you—"

"Just spit it out," she broke in, her shoulders held high.

Officer Sawyer set his hat down on the end table and moved closer to her.

"We're sorry to be the bearers of bad news." Sawyer took a deep breath. "Your husband's plane disappeared this afternoon somewhere over the Atlantic coast. There's a search party currently out looking..."

The man's words faded away and she could hear her heart beat loudly in her ears just before a ringing noise consumed her. The room spun quickly and the last thing she remembered was Officer Sawyer reaching for her, his green eyes hovering above her as all else went dark.

TWO

Sawyer's fresh start...

He'd spent most of the last two years trying to forget Ann. She'd stomped on his heart hard when she'd left their short-lived marriage of two weeks for his best friend, Nick. The divorce had been quick, and she'd emptied out half of his savings account to move to California.

Leaving Cleveland had been a given for him after being left raw. His partner had retired, putting him in charge of training a rookie, something he didn't feel he was any good at.

He'd packed what few belongings Ann had left him and driven to his new job in Twisted Rock. He'd spent a few summers visiting his grandfather's farm in the picturesque town.

Having only good memories of the place, he'd submitted his resume at the local police station on a whim. When he'd gotten the call, he'd jumped at the chance to get out of the city and start a new life.

He'd sold the small condo he'd purchased the first year on the force and turned a tidy profit, enough that he'd been able to purchase a small converted-barn home. He'd fallen in love with the little place at first sight, from the bright blue barn door that opened up from the dining area onto a covered stone patio to the thick wood beams that held up the master bedroom loft.

It was the ultimate rustic bachelor pad, complete with a classic claw-foot bathtub and an open kitchen with wood shelves for his glasses and dishes. The wood countertops, steel sink, and cast-iron fireplace made the place even cozier.

Just beyond his patio was a small lake that was stocked with pike and trout. Half his weekends were spent sitting on the dock with either his wired-haired mutt, Ozzy, or his new partner, Carson, who'd taken to him right off.

He'd enjoyed the first few weeks on the job and was thrilled at the slower pace of the town. Instead of calls about shootings, robberies, or domestic violence, he went out on calls for barking dogs, flat tires, kids vandalizing the school, and even a loose horse. He'd had to rush home halfway through the day to change his uniform after that one.

He enjoyed getting to know the people in town and remembered a handful of them from his summer trips visiting his granddad.

He'd stopped by the old man's grave on several occasions and had even driven by the old mansion a few times.

The day had started just like every other day, with Ozzy jumping on his chest to wake him up five minutes before his alarm went off.

Eyes half-closed, he made his way like a zombie down the narrow wood steps and opened the back door so the dog could rush out and do his business. He stood there and watched as the sun rose over the lake. He really had to install the damn dog door he'd purchased last month so he didn't have to get up so early each day.

Leaving the door open, he pulled out a mug and poured a cup of coffee. Thank god for programmable coffee makers. Taking the cup with him onto the back patio, he sipped the hot liquid as he watched Ozzy chase birds in the yard. He laughed at the small mutt as he tried to catch birds who were, without a doubt, way smarter than he was.

He checked his watch and then snapped his fingers to call Ozzy back to his side.

"It's time to get ready for work, boy." He scratched the dog's chin when he jumped into his lap. Getting Ozzy was the first thing Sawyer had done after things had ended with Ann. She'd had a firm no-animal rule because she hated cleaning up after them.

For the two years they'd been together before marriage, she'd controlled everything about his life, including who he hung out with and what he ate.

It wasn't until he was free of her that he realized how much of his life she'd controlled. He promised himself he'd never fall for a woman like that again and Ozzy was his daily reminder.

Taking the dog with him, Sawyer went inside and showered. He got dressed, pulled his service weapon from the hidden wall safe, and strapped it to his hip.

When he left the house, Ozzy watched from his spot on the back of the sofa. His sad eyes almost broke him, even though he'd be back for lunch to let the dog out again.

He parked his truck at the police station and was greeted by his partner, Rodney Carson.

"Carson." He nodded to the older man. He was thankful they'd been made partners. There were several officers on the force that he didn't get along with. Two of them, Rick Brown and Sue Madsen, were your classic know-it-all types. They felt it was their right to "show him the ropes." He'd spent almost seven years on the force in Cleveland and had seen and done more than the backwoods cops had even dreamed of, including getting shot twice. There were times that he doubted the two officers had ever fired their service weapons at an actual person. And still, out of respect, he kept his mouth shut when they insisted they knew more than he did.

"Morning." Carson fell in step with him. "We've got a call already this morning." He pulled out his phone as they made their way towards the back door of the building. "I received a text half an hour ago."

He sighed, waiting for it, knowing it was coming. "Goldsteins again?" he asked.

Carson chuckled and nodded. "They say that Dan has parked his truck and blocked their driveway again. We'll head out there after we clock in."

He nodded and followed Carson into the building.

The Goldstein and Tibbs families had been feuding for generations, or so he'd been told. It had all started when the Goldsteins purchased a piece of land from the Tibbs's great-great-grandfather, long before the county roads were put in. The land hadn't been anything special. However, when the county cut a road directly through Tibbs's prime real estate, he'd demanded the Goldsteins sell back their lot of land to him. When they refused, court battles had ensued. The Tibbs family was left on the brink of bankruptcy, which had caused even more strife between the families.

When the court ruled in the Goldstein's favor, the Tibbs family had taken to harassment tactics. Nothing illegal, and nothing anyone could prove, but tactics that were meant to annoy.

Why the Goldsteins hadn't sold the land years ago was the question on the minds of everyone in Twisted Rock.

After clocking in, Sawyer and Carson drove out to the Goldstein property on the edge of town.

The older Goldstein met the patrol car at the edge of their long drive, which was indeed blocked by Tibbs's beat-up pickup truck.

The county road ran directly in front of the old house and as Sawyer got out of the car, Carson motioned for him.

"Why don't you go knock on Tibbs's door and wake him up so he can move this eyesore. I'll go deal with them." Carson nodded towards the older couple.

Sawyer didn't mind dealing with Tibbs since he was far more reasonable than the hysterical couple, who liked to shout and rage on.

He stepped up on the broken porch and was about to knock on the door when he noticed it was cracked open. He peeked inside, squinting his eyes in the darkness, and called out.

"Dan?" It took a moment for his eyes to adjust. When they did, he rushed in as he called out to his partner, "Call an ambulance."

Dan Tibbs was lying face down in a pool of blood and vomit. Sawyer rolled him over and felt for a pulse. It was weak, but he was alive. Sawyer grabbed a fresh towel from the kitchen and held it firmly over the large stab wound on the man's shoulder blade.

Carson stepped in and looked around, blinking to adjust his eyes.

"He's been stabbed," Sawyer said. "Did you call it in?"

"Yeah, they're on the way." He knelt beside him. "Does he have a pulse?"

"Yes, it's faint, but there." He nodded to the knife sitting next to the man. "Stabbed in the shoulder blade."

An hour later, after questioning the Goldsteins, who acted as each other's alibi, he went back home to change out of his blood-covered uniform. He normally left a spare uniform in his locker at the station but hadn't yet taken it back to work after getting it cleaned after the horse incident.

He tossed the soiled uniform in the laundry bin and was buttoning up the last button on his new shirt when his phone buzzed.

"Yeah?" he answered after seeing Carson's name on the screen. His partner was sitting out in his driveway in the car, waiting for him to change.

"Got another call." Carson sighed. "Better hurry, there's an accident on the highway."

Sawyer strapped on his gun again as he made his way towards the door. Ozzy stood at the door with a ball in his mouth, waiting to be let out so they could play, something they did every day during his lunch break.

"Sorry, buddy. I'll be back for lunch, and then we can play." He scratched the dog's head, locked up, and rushed towards the car.

The patrol car raced towards the highway and, when they came upon the wreck, Sawyer instantly knew there'd be a fatality. He'd seen enough accidents in the city to gauge how bad it was at first glance.

Brown and Madsen had arrived before them, and Sawyer noticed that there was a white sheet covering the driver-side window on a small sedan, which was upside down. Madsen directed traffic around it and the other vehicle that had been in the accident.

Brown was hovering over a man that was leaning against the other car, near the edge of the road. The way the officer was standing, Sawyer knew he was interrogating the man.

"I'll deal with Brown." Carson nodded towards the two men. "Why don't you go see if there's anything you can do to help out Madsen."

It was a huge relief to have a partner who could keep himself in check.

Sawyer made his way towards the upside-down car and, while Madsen watched, he nudged the sheet aside to make sure the person inside was deceased. He'd read reports about officers calling a death and then having the paramedics discover that the victim wasn't actually dead.

Reaching in, he felt for a pulse on the woman's neck and held in a sigh when he felt stillness there.

"I've already checked her," Madsen said dryly behind him. "She's gone. DOA." Sue Madsen was a thick woman with muddy brown hair and a chip on her shoulder bigger than the state of New York.

"It's standard practice to have two of us check..." He reached in and touched the woman's wrist. When she flinched at his touch, he jumped slightly and held in a curse this time. "We've got a live one," he called out. "Get those EMTs here fast!" He yanked the sheet aside and started first aid on the middle-aged woman.

A little over an hour later, he once again tossed a soiled uniform into the bin. He pulled on his last clean one as Ozzy waited patiently with the ball still in his mouth.

"Okay, buddy, this time I'll take a few minutes and play with you." He sat out on the back patio and tossed the ball as he ate a cold turkey sandwich.

Gathering up his soiled uniforms, he dropped them off at the cleaners in town before heading back to the station.

There was a standard one o'clock meeting every day and

as he walked into the room, the entire office broke into cheers.

"What's this all about?" he asked Carson who quickly got up and made his way towards Sawyer.

"Wendy Green is alive and recovering at the hospital thanks to you." His partner was the first in the room to shake his hand. He noticed that neither Brown nor Madsen were present.

After the room settled, the chief of police, Matthew Deter, stepped in and quieted everyone down. The man was a bear of a person. He looked like an ex-lineman who'd seen too many hits in the game, but he was one of the nicest men Sawyer had ever worked for. The man was fair as well as very tolerant of some of the officers working under him that tended to goof off too much. He had a wicked sense of humor that most found too dry. He and Sawyer got along really well.

"As you've all heard, Sawyer is a hero for doing his damn job." Everyone in the room chuckled. The chief held up his hands to quiet everyone again. "The fact remains that two of our officers failed this morning. They've been placed on admin leave until they attend further emergency training." The room was quiet. "Which means we're two short and we'll all have to pull extra hours in the coming weeks until they're back on duty." Several people in the room groaned. "Yes, thank you, Officer Sawyer, for showing us just how far we've fallen from grace. I'll be expecting everyone to sign up for extra medical training within the week as well." Another groan went through the crowd, and the chief held up his hands once more. "Which is mandatory."

By the time Sawyer walked out of the room, he was pretty sure everyone on the force hated him.

The rest of the day he and Carson drove around town and answered petty calls—shoplifting at the local grocery store, high school kids throwing rocks at the cars on the highway, and even a woman who needed help breaking into her car after locking her keys and her ancient, blind Chihuahua in her sedan at the gas station.

Half an hour before he was due to clock out for the evening, he and Carson were called into the chief's office.

When they stepped in, the chief got up from his desk and shut the door behind them. Whatever it was, it was serious.

"We've received a call from the state PD. A small plane carrying one of our elite townsmen has gone down over the Atlantic coastline. We don't have much detail at this time, but"—the chief handed Sawyer a piece of paper— "they're searching. We'll need to inform the wife."

Sawyer read the printout.

Isaac Clayton 24 years old. Lawyer for Clayton Law firm, New York, NY.

Rose Clayton 24 years old. Artist. Wife.

21 Sorrow Cove Bend, Twisted Rock, New York.

"Have they found anything?" Sawyer asked, handing the printout to Carson, who immediately sighed and shook his head.

"Not yet. The plane's tracking device last had him in the eye of a pretty bad storm over the Atlantic. He's supposed to be a pretty good pilot, but... these things happen. There was no mayday call and he maintained radio silence until the plane disappeared. They're waiting for clear weather to send the search planes out but have boats out searching now." The chief walked over and sat down. "The Clayton family has lived in these parts for a while now. His old man has donated more money to our little town than I'll make in my lifetime. So, this is a priority and I want my best officers knocking on the woman's door. She needs to be handled with kid gloves." The chief's eyes turned to his. "Kid gloves. Got it?"

Sawyer nodded. "We'll drive out there now."

He'd driven by the massive mansion called Stoneport Manor—named because of an old stone sign with faded letters that sat at the end of the long driveway—more times than he could count, as it was only a mile down the road from his own place. They'd also been called out to her nearest neighbor's house, which sat across the street from Rose's place, a few times. Boone Schneller was a drunk, a troublemaker, and a downright pain in the ass. The man stockpiled weapons and shot at anything that crossed onto his land.

As Carson pulled the patrol car through the iron gates, Sawyer whistled.

"Yeah, I would've thought that someone would tear this place down rather than move in," Carson remarked. "It's been empty for as long as I can remember. I think the last residents were the André family." He glanced over at him as he parked behind a BMW SUV. "Three generations ago." Carson leaned forward to look out the car window at the massive house, then he turned towards him. "I've known Rose and Isaac since they were kids. Damned if I know how to handle this."

Sawyer shook his head. "There's no easy way. Have you had to perform a death notification before?"

"Nope. Well, once, but they knew he was going. Cancer. The man was as old as the hills." Carson sighed and looked up at the massive mansion again. "Looks like she's waiting to welcome him home." He nodded, and Sawyer followed his gaze.

Sure enough, the downstairs of the house was lit up like a beacon in the darkness as the rain continued to fall steadily. Smoke billowed out of the chimney and he could vaguely smell some sort of meat cooking in the wind that blew the rain sideways towards the car windows.

"Better get it over with," he suggested.

"I'll let you take the lead on this. She's about your age, sweet girl. I knew her father really well," Carson added.

"Knew?" he asked before getting out.

"Her dad was on the force. Died in a shootout long before she was old enough to remember him. Her mother remarried and moved with her new husband to Pittsburgh to be closer to her older sister and her kids."

He reached for the door handle. They made their way quickly to the cover of the front porch. Removing his hat, Sawyer rang the doorbell and was a little surprised when it opened quickly.

There was a soft glow behind the woman. Sawyer's breath instantly caught at her beauty. The red dress fit her thin body perfectly, its low cut showcasing the most perfect pair of breasts he'd ever seen. Her blonde hair was tied up in a low loose bun at the base of her neck. Her blue eyes searched his.

A memory surfaced quickly of a younger girl with blonde hair and steel blue eyes. She wore a bright red swimsuit. He was at the local swimming pool the first summer he'd visited his grandfather, which meant he must have been eleven or twelve. The girl had just jumped off the diving board when he finally worked up enough nerve to approach her.

He'd admired the way she moved in the water, so naturally, so smooth. Driven by hormones, he'd made his way across the pool to talk to her.

She'd been laughing with a blond-haired boy as she sat

along the side of the pool.

Sawyer sat next to her on the ledge of the pool and smiled over at her.

"Great dive," he'd said, kicking himself for not thinking of something better to say to her.

The blond-haired boy splashed water at him and told him to get lost.

"I wasn't talking to you," Sawyer said, his eyes still glued to the girl's face.

"She's with me." The boy had moved up to sit next to the girl on the opposite side. The girl turned towards him.

"Sorry, I'm with him." She had smiled at him and he'd felt his heartbreak for the first time in his life.

Shaking off the memory, he opened his mouth to speak, but his partner beat him to it.

"Evening, Rose." Carson stepped into the light of the porch. "This is my new partner, Sawyer. May we come in?" he asked.

The woman's blue eyes darted between them.

"Is there something wrong?" she asked. Her voice was low and smooth, but he could hear the concern.

"It's best if we come in," he said gently. Her eyes moved back to his and he could tell she saw the sorrow in them. He hated this part of the job, telling someone their loved ones wouldn't be home for dinner, or ever. It was harder than anything he'd ever done before, even being shot at.

She moved back, and, without a word, they stepped into the foyer. The place was bigger than he'd imagined. It needed a lot of work, but he was surprised at how solid it felt.

"Rose, it might be best if we talk in there." His partner nodded towards a room with a fireplace.

They followed her into the warm room, which was lit by

the glow of the fireplace and candles set on a table full of wonderful-smelling food. The sight of the table she'd set for her husband's homecoming caused an ache to spread in his chest. Here is what he'd always dreamed of having with Ann, he thought somewhere in the back of his mind.

"Why don't you—" Carson started saying as he motioned towards the sofa.

"Just spit it out." The woman straightened her shoulders and braced herself. Sawyer could see in her eyes that she had guessed something bad was coming.

Setting down his hat, he moved closer to her, just in case she passed out.

"We're sorry to be the bearers of bad news." He took a deep breath. "Your husband's plane disappeared this afternoon somewhere over the Atlantic coast. There's a search party out looking..."

He didn't make it any further before the woman started slipping. Reaching out, he easily caught her and gently picked her up.

"Set her down here." Carson motioned towards the sofa. "I'll go get her a glass of water." He disappeared into the back hallway.

Sawyer held onto the woman for a moment. She was smaller than she looked and weighed next to nothing. Her dark lashes lay on her pale cheeks and his eyes moved to her red lips as he laid her gently down on the leather cushions.

"Here." Carson handed him a glass of water. He set it down on the table as he gently nudged the woman to wake up.

When her blue eyes opened, he saw raw and pure sorrow fill them as realization struck her. He vowed then and there that he would someday be loved half as much as this woman had loved her husband.

THREE

Life goes on... almost one year later...

The hardest part about losing Isaac was the looks that everyone gave her whenever she went into town. She'd filled the lonely days and nights by throwing herself into work on the house or into her art, and she'd managed to subdue the ache that sleeping alone had caused. But seeing her friends and the people she'd known her entire life look at her with pity had almost been too much to bear.

Here it was, a week before the year anniversary and she was still treated as if Isaac had just died yesterday. The way people talked to her brought up the old hurts again and again, like pouring lemon juice on a paper cut. She winced inwardly every time someone asked, "How are you doing?" in that tone that really said, "Your husband is dead, and I feel sorry for you."

It drove her mad. It was one of the reasons she found herself going into town less often and having things delivered to the house instead.

She'd taken a few calls from Sean, Isaac's father, but for

the most part, up until this point the man was giving her a cold shoulder. His calls were short and to the point, all business. Isaac's will had been signed months after their marriage and was solid since Sean had witnessed the signing himself. All assets had been quickly and neatly transferred into her name after the standard waiting period when a person goes missing was up. In this case, Sean had filed for the certificate of death himself. He'd conveyed his reasoning to her via a very short phone conversation three months after Isaac's disappearance.

"I've filed for a certificate of death for Isaac," Sean had said briefly after she'd answered the phone. She noted that he hadn't even asked how she was doing.

"You..." she'd stammered.

"It's important for us for closure to tie up any loose ends. This will clear the way for the firm to execute Isaac's will quickly."

"His..." At that point she hadn't even thought about money.

"I know this is difficult on you, which is why I've moved forward on your behalf. You should see the documents come via currier soon, and the bulk of Isaac's life insurance will be automatically deposited into your account. If you have any questions, you know how to reach me."

She had swallowed and closed her eyes as more tears rolled down her cheek.

"For what it's worth..." Sean's voice had softened and changed. "I couldn't have asked for a better daughter-in-law. Isaac truly loved you."

When the line had gone dead, she'd lain there on the hardwood floor and cried until morning.

For those first three months after Isaac's death, all work

on the large manor had stopped. She'd called the foreman and told him not to bother since she was pretty sure she was going to sell the place and move out of the drafty old mansion.

Family came and went. Not even Isaac's father stayed long after Isaac's funeral. Fake funeral is how she thought of it since they had buried an empty coffin.

Sean Clayton had been his normal charming self during the entire ordeal. He'd always presented himself as if an audience was in the wings waiting to applaud or boo at a moment's notice. She'd brushed it off most of the time since Isaac had assured her that he was very important and had to uphold his reputation for some of his more important clients. But she would have liked to have had a private moment alone with the man at the funeral, if just to feel some sort of closure in the mess that was her life.

At first, she'd been so stuck in depression that she'd been on the verge of a nervous breakdown. She never left the house, didn't see anyone, and had even turned Hunter away when he'd showed up to visit her. Then, one evening, she'd had a wakeup call when Officer Sawyer had stopped by. He claimed that he'd driven by the place and, seeing all the lights off, had stopped in to see if she was okay.

He had stood on her doorstep, his hat in his hands, much like he'd done the night he'd come to tell her Isaac had disappeared. The memory had flooded her mind and she'd been in a haze, so much so that she'd hesitated in asking him inside. Then she had remembered that the lights were off because the fuse had flipped, and she hadn't wanted to go down to the basement to fix it herself.

She'd invited him in and had instantly felt embarrassed at the state of the house. She'd taken to sleeping on the sofa next to the fireplace, and her blankets and pillows were piled up on the cushions. There were dishes, used tissues, and clothing strewn all over the room. She hadn't cared one bit until Sawyer had stepped into her home.

Embarrassment hit her hard and fast. What had she become? She'd allowed herself to sink into the worst kind of depression.

Even Hunter had stopped coming around after she'd yelled at him when he'd complained that there was no food in her refrigerator and that she was starving herself to death. Her brother had tried to talk her out of her depression by bringing her flowers and food, but she'd just let the flowers die and the food had all spoiled when she didn't eat it.

Sawyer walked in that night and acted like nothing was wrong as he chatted and avoided all her dirty clothes. He crouched down to stir the fire and added another log to the dying embers. She hadn't even realized she'd been cold until he gently set a sweater over her shoulders.

"You'd better wear socks or slippers. This old floor is probably cold." He'd nodded to her bare feet. She looked down at them and gasped at the fact that she hadn't painted her toenails since the day before Isaac had crashed into the Atlantic Ocean. Her toenails were long and colorless, and she quickly found a pair of socks and pulled them. "I'll go down and check the fuse box if you show me the way."

She walked towards the basement door and opened it. A burst of cold air rushed up the dark stairs and he turned towards her.

"Is there an open window down there?" he asked.

"No." She frowned, trying to remember what the basement looked like. She hadn't left the main floor of the house since the days following Isaac's funeral. That thought had tears slipping down her cheeks.

"Hey." Sawyer had touched her shoulder lightly. "It's okay, I'll check it all out while I'm down there," he'd assured her before disappearing into the darkness.

She turned and glanced around while she waited for him to return. It was as if she were opening her eyes for the first time in months.

The place was a disaster. When she spotted a pair of silky underwear that Isaac had purchased for her on their honeymoon sitting on the floor by the fireplace, where Sawyer had just been, she gasped and rushed over to pick them up. Tucking them into the pocket of her sweater, she moved around and quickly tried to hide the mess before he came back upstairs.

She happened to catch a glimpse of herself in the mirror above the fireplace and gasped again.

She'd lost weight, almost ten pounds, she'd wager. Her once shiny hair was tied in a ragged knot on the top of her head and crazy wisps hung in every direction. Her face was bare of any makeup, and the dark rings under her eyes were so blue, she swiped at them, thinking that it was dirt.

Pulling the clip from her hair, she redid the bun to the base of her neck and straightened her sweater to cover herself more. No wonder he'd placed the sweater over her shoulders. She'd only been wearing a thin white camisole and a pair of Isaac's pajama bottoms. She had, at one point, worn a couple of his dress shirts, but now they were piled on the sofa. She was using them as a pillow and burying her face in them each night, so she could be surrounded by his scent.

The lights flickered and suddenly the power was back on in the house. She groaned as the light showed her just how far she'd slipped.

It looked worse in the light, and she immediately wished for the darkness again and closed her eyes.

A pair of strong hands gripped her shoulders and pulled her against a hard chest. For a moment, she allowed herself to imagine it was Isaac who held her so close and so gently. Then Sawyer spoke and broke the fantasy.

"Easy, it's not as bad as it looks." His voice was lower than Isaac's had been. His chest reverberated with each word spoken. It was a soothing sound, but it disturbed her just the same. She pulled away and wrapped her arms around herself.

"I hadn't realized..." She turned to him. "Thank you." Her chin rose, and she straightened her shoulders. "I appreciate you fixing the power."

"It was no problem." His green eyes ran over her and she could tell he wanted to say more, but instead, he swallowed. "There's a broken window in the basement you might want the workers to see too soon."

"Thank you, I'll call them tomorrow about it." She mentally berated herself for stopping all the work on the place. Isaac wouldn't have wanted her to give up on the place or herself. She made a move towards the door and he picked up his hat and followed. She closed her eyes when she noticed the silk bra that went with the underwear she'd stuffed in her pocket sitting underneath it.

His eyes remained on the red bra, then slowly moved up to her eyes. She could tell he was avoiding lowering his eyes to where her nipples poked through the thin sweater she wore over the silk camisole.

"You might want to dress a little warmer until they get your heat back up and running. Winter is still officially here, and I'd hate for you to catch a cold," he said smoothly.

She tucked her sweater closer and nodded. "Yes, I'll take your advice, thank you, Officer Sawyer."

"It's no problem. Please, just Sawyer."

She frowned. "Isn't that your last name?"

He smiled for the first time and she felt her heart skip at the transformation it caused in the man. He had a dark and mysterious look about him, but when he smiled, he became sexy as hell.

"Yes, it is, but in the police force, everyone goes by their last names."

"What is your first name again?" she asked, unsure why she wanted to know.

"Royce." His smile wavered slightly. "But, as I said, feel free to call me Sawyer."

She nodded. "Thank you again, Sawyer."

"You're welcome, Mrs. Clayton." He stepped past her.

"Rose," she corrected. It was too painful to hear the Clayton part of her name. "Just Rose," she repeated.

She leaned against the doorframe as he stepped outside and turned towards her. The light from the front porch shone down on him, causing his green eyes to shine as the pitch darkness behind him accented the jet black of his hair.

"If you need anything else..." he started to say.

"I'm sure the workers can manage. But thank you again."

He nodded, and a slight irritation crossed his eyes. "It was no problem. Night." He turned, then stopped. "I met you once." He turned back to her. "And your husband. I think we were twelve. I was visiting my grandfather for the summer. You and Isaac were at the local swimming pool." He shrugged. "I don't know why I'm saying this." He sighed and glanced into the darkness. "I just wanted you to know that, even back then, I could tell you two were meant for each other."

She swallowed the hurt and shut the door on him, unable and unwilling to show him the tears. Leaning her head against the stained glass of the door, she allowed more tears to fall.

When she heard his car start, she straightened and swore that those tears would be the last. From here on out, she would only permit so many more tears in her life.

She needed to get a handle on herself. Standing at the entrance of the great room, she decided that there was no time like the present.

She sent off a quick text to RJ to see if the workers could start fresh in the morning, and then she'd pulled on an old T-shirt and jeans along with her tennis shoes and had gotten to work turning the place back into a home. Her home.

Now, nine months after that night, she stood in her great room and smiled. Gone was the old rotted wood flooring. In its place, for the time being, was brand-new plywood. Stacks of the new hardwood flooring sat just inside the front doorway. Sweat rolled down her back through her tank top as she pulled on the thick gloves.

"Are you sure about this?" Hunter asked her.

Her brother stood by her side, frowning down at the massive pile of wood they had just hauled into the house from the flatbed truck she'd rented.

Hunter had helped her get out of the house in the past months. Sawyer may have helped her wake up on that night long ago, but it was Hunter who'd gotten her to breathe again. He came down as often as he could and would force her out of the house for meals or shopping sprees to find furniture to fill the mansion. They had been close as kids, but they were growing even more so now, and she felt closer to him than with her sister, Jenny. Seeing Jenny with the kids was very painful. She'd really been looking forward to becoming a mother, to having Isaac's children. Seeing her sister's happy life opened the wounds all over again.

Hunter tried to come down to visit every other weekend, but his new job in Buffalo kept him busy. But when he was there, she always enjoyed his company and his help around the house.

The workers were still working hard on the house, as well. Most of the major things were done now and all that was left to do was some painting and some minor work on the basement.

She'd convinced Hunter to help her replace the flooring and some of the wood planks on the back patio she enjoyed so much. She loved to get her hands dirty and enjoyed accomplishing something huge like this herself. As she looked around the house, she could see several projects she'd done over the past year all by herself and was even more proud of the work than she would have been if the men she'd hired had done it instead.

"I'd better be sure." She chuckled. "Otherwise I shouldn't have spent a week tearing out the old flooring."

"Not that." Hunter sighed. "I mean about staying here once you're done with this place. You could always move up to Buffalo and be closer to me."

After losing Isaac, she'd wanted nothing to do with the big place. But now her sweat, blood, and tears were in each room. Now, this was home. Her home.

She smiled over at Hunter. Her stepbrother was on the short side, but he still towered over her five-foot-five frame.

His sandy blond hair had thinned sometime in high school. His blue eyes and round face had at one point been very attractive and, to some, still were. He was the closest family she had now. She'd leaned on him heavily. Him and Sawyer.

The officer had made it his mission to check up on her on a weekly basis. Each time he stood on the doorstep, she was reminded of the night almost a year ago when he had told her about Isaac's plane. Still, it was nice having someone to talk to other than her brother. And that someone being as attractive as Sawyer was didn't hurt.

"Of course, I'm sure." She glanced around and smiled. "This is my home." She slapped him on the shoulder. "Ready to get to work?" She took a step to get started, only to have the doorbell ring behind her.

Spinning around, she pulled open the door and felt her heart skip when she noticed Sawyer standing on the front steps in worn jeans and a black leather jacket with a dark green T-shirt underneath. It was the first time she'd seen him out of uniform and, somehow, he looked even more dangerous.

"Hi," she said, wondering if seeing the man on her doorstep would always make her heart jump with sadness.

"Hi." He glanced past her. She looked back to where Hunter stood over her shoulder. "I... uh, heard that you were installing new flooring and came to offer some help."

Her eyebrows shot up. Small towns had their own methods of getting the news around. She figured he'd heard from either the hardware store or from one of the workers in town.

"Do you know anything about installing hardwood?" she asked, leaning against the door jam.

"I've installed it a few times," he answered, his eyes still behind her.

She sighed and opened the door. "Sawyer, my brother Hunter. Hunter, Officer Sawyer." She motioned between them. "Come on in. We could use the expertise since neither of us know what the heck we're doing."

Sawyer walked in and removed his jacket. She'd never seen him in short sleeves before and couldn't help but appreciate the thick arms full of muscles as he placed his coat on the hooks by the front door.

"Nice to meet you." Sawyer held out a hand to her brother, who hesitated for a moment, then took it.

Rose swore the men were comparing muscles as they shook hands. Not wanting to get in the way of a testosterone battle, she opened the first box of flooring. She glanced up at Sawyer. "So, show us the ropes."

Four hours later, she opened the last box. With Sawyer's help, they had finished the flooring much more quickly than she'd planned. She'd expected that she and Hunter would be working on it longer than one day.

Her back, knees, and neck hurt. But as she looked across the brand-new hardwood flooring, pride outweighed the pain she was feeling.

The dark wood matched the doors, railing, and windowsills perfectly.

"Good call on the flooring," Hunter said, wiping sweat from his brow. "This place looks amazing."

She handed another board to Sawyer, who was on his knees, placing the last row of flooring down.

She'd spent the last four hours trying to avoid appreciating every ripple under his shirt as he worked. The cords of muscles in his arms were distracting enough, but the way the T-shirt stuck to him as he worked and the way his worn jeans hugged him was something she'd never had to deal with before.

Desire had been a given with Isaac. If she'd wanted, he'd been there to provide a release for her. Wanting and not being able to touch was a completely different animal.

"Would you like to put the last board into place?" Sawyer looked up at her. She'd been watching his butt as he bent over the flooring. When he glanced back, her eyes snapped to his and she felt herself blush.

"Sure." She jumped in quickly. Kneeling beside him, she took the rubber mallet from his hands and laid the last cut board into place.

"Just tap it here." He touched the board and she noticed how strong and long his fingers looked. Her entire mind was focused on his hand, and when she swung the hammer, she missed the board completely and had to try again. This time, concentrating, she hit the mark and the board slid into place smoothly. "All done." He glanced over at her with a smile.

She still hadn't gotten used to seeing the relaxed look on his face and each time he smiled at her, she examined him as if seeing him for the first time. It was like watching a full-grown male lion cuddle up to a tiny human baby instead of eating it. You just couldn't take your eyes away.

"Are you okay?" he asked softly.

It was then that she realized she'd been staring at him. Her eyes had been locked on his lips, so she tore them to his eyes and blurted out the first thing she'd thought.

"Your eyes aren't really green." She mentally kicked herself as he chuckled.

"Tell that to my driver's license." He shifted, gripping her wrists and pulling her off the floor.

"You have a speck of brown just here." She pointed to

his left eye then was horrified that she was pointing at him and dropped her hand quickly. His smile grew.

"Yes, it's called heterochromia iridum." He blinked and moved slightly closer. "My mother has it."

She moved closer and looked at his eyes better. Sure enough, his right eye was a vibrant green while his left eye was half green and half hazel. They were beautiful. She'd never seen eyes so clear, so stunning before.

"Well, I'm starved. How about we order some pizza?" Hunter broke into her inspection of Sawyer's eyes.

"Can't," Sawyer said. "Ozzy's waiting for me." He glanced down at his watch and hissed.

"Ozzy?" she asked, dusting off her hands. She couldn't wait to sweep and mop her new floor.

"My mutt." Sawyer smiled. "I heard you might need some help replacing your back decking as well?" He gathered his leather jacket.

"You seem to hear a lot," she joked. She knew he'd heard it from Carson, who had stopped by the other day. She'd told him what she was up to that weekend.

"I think we can handle things..." Hunter jumped in.

She shushed him quickly. "I'm not turning away free help," she said with a smile. "Why don't you bring Ozzy tomorrow? I'm sure he'd enjoy running around and I'd enjoy meeting him. That is if he's a nice dog."

Sawyer chuckled. "Ozzy loves everyone." She watched him pull on his leather jacket and mentally imagined what it would feel like to run her fingers over those muscles on his chest.

"Good, then it's settled. We'll pick the wood planks up first thing, around eight in the morning." She turned to Hunter. "How about you run into town and get the pizza while I sweep and mop?"

"Sure." Her brother grabbed his jacket and followed Sawyer out.

"Thank you again, Sawyer." She waved as Hunter shut the front door behind them.

As she started to sweep the new hardwood flooring, she daydreamed about unique green eyes and very muscular arms holding her.

FOUR

SOMETHING GOES BUMP IN THE NIGHT...

Sawyer stepped out into the warm evening and enjoyed the sweat that was dripping down his back. His knees, back, arms, and shoulders hurt from the manual labor he'd done in the past few hours.

He stepped off the porch as Rose's brother fell in step with him.

"I don't know what kind of game you're playing, but my sister can't take the weight of a relationship right now," Hunter warned him.

Sawyer turned towards the man. Hunter was almost a full foot shorter than he was. It appeared that he lifted weights but didn't always eat the right things since he gauged he was a good ten pounds overweight.

Still, this was Rose's brother and he looked very concerned and guarded.

"I'm not looking for a relationship at the moment," he said smoothly. "I'm just helping out a friend."

"Is she?" Hunter asked. "Your friend?" he added when Sawyer just looked at him.

"I'd like to think so." He turned towards his truck.

"I don't want to sound like a big brother, but... just know that I'm watching."

He smiled. "I would think worse of you if you hadn't said something," he called back as he slid into his truck.

Hunter climbed into his car and shot out of the driveway before him. He made a mental note to warn the guy about the speed limit next time he saw him. As he pulled out of the driveway, he had only a split second to react as an old truck swerved directly towards him.

He jerked the wheel so that his truck slid into the ditch. Rose's neighbor Boone Schneller crashed his old truck into a tree less than a foot from him.

Pulling out his phone, he sent a message to Carson before rushing over to give aid.

When he opened the truck's door, the smell of alcohol hit him.

The old man was hunched over the wheel, chuckling.

"Are you okay?" He touched the man, who came up swinging. Sawyer took the surprise punch to his left eye, then caught the man's fists before he could swing again.

"What a ride!" The man laughed again as he leaned back in the seat. "I've got to do that more often."

"Come on." He hauled the man to his feet and had to catch him from falling on his face.

"Are you okay?" Rose called from the end of her driveway. "I heard the crash." She'd run outside in her bare feet and hadn't bothered putting on a jacket. Even though the fall days were still sultry, the evenings had started to chill.

Pulling off his jacket, he handed it to her. "Go sit in my truck. It's cold out here." He nodded towards his truck and turned back to the older man.

"Now, Mr. Schneller, how many times have we told you

not to drink and drive? This will make your second DUI." He checked the man's pupils.

"I'm not drunk," the man practically screamed at him.

"Sure, you aren't." He sighed and walked the man a safe distance from the wreckage. "Carson will have to come and read you your rights. I'm off duty."

"I told you"—the man swung out again, but Sawyer was waiting for it and easily caught his fist— "I'm not drunk."

"Okay, I'll play along. What are you then?" he asked, setting the man down on his truck gate.

"I'm high." He giggled like a teenager. "Tried it for the first time. That guy was right, it's way better than booze."

Sawyer rolled his eyes and groaned inwardly.

"Is he okay?" Rose asked from the driver seat of his truck. She had his leather jacket wrapped around her. She was swimming in it and he found it oddly appealing.

In the months after her husband's death, she'd gone from skinny to frail. That night he'd stopped by and fixed her electricity had almost broken him.

She'd looked so lost, he'd wanted to pick her up and take her home to nurse her back to health. But when he'd come back up from the basement, he'd seen the change in her eyes.

He'd watched her closely, stopping by on a weekly basis and seeing her progress each time. She'd gained back some of the weight she'd lost those first months after Isaac's death.

"He's fine," he answered.

"Should I call..." She stopped when her eyes landed on him. "What happened to your eye?" She frowned and moved to get out of the truck.

"He punched me." He nodded to the old man, who was on the verge of passing out.

She got out and rushed to his side, then reached up and gently touched his eye. "It looks bad."

He shrugged and watched the man slide down into the back of his truck bed. When he let out a loud snore, Sawyer relaxed.

"I'm fine. I've had worse." He glanced down at her feet. "You're going to bruise the bottom of your feet." He gently picked her up and set her back in the front seat of his truck. "Stay put until I can drive you back to the house. Carson should be here to take care of him soon."

At his last words, they both heard the siren coming down the road.

Instead of Carson, Brown and Madsen parked behind his truck. He groaned inwardly—at least he thought he had —but when Rose touched his arm, he realized she'd heard him.

"Stay in the truck," he said softly as he went to meet the other officers.

He went over what had happened with them twice. Brown hauled the unconscious man into the back of his patrol car while Madsen called the tow truck.

"I'm taking Rose back home." He nodded towards his truck. "If you need anything else, you know where to find me."

He slid into the front seat of his truck. Rose had moved over and sat in the passenger seat.

"Seatbelt," he said softly.

She looked at him. "We're just going to the end of the driveway." She chuckled.

He dropped his hands from the steering wheel. "And I was almost killed just now, at the end of the very same driveway." He smiled.

"Fair enough." She nodded with a smile and slid on the seatbelt.

"How did you run down the driveway without any shoes on without cutting your feet?" he asked as he pulled up to her front door.

"I didn't." She sighed and glanced down at her feet. "I guess I was so concerned someone was hurt, I didn't feel the pain."

He glanced down at her feet and when he saw the trickle of blood on his floorboards, worry flashed quickly in his mind.

After parking, he got out of the truck and gathered her in his arms to haul her back inside the house.

"You don't have to carry me, I'm perfectly —"

"Shush." He glanced around the entryway. "Bathroom?"

"Over there." She nodded. "But I have medical supplies upstairs in my bathroom." She nodded to the stairs on the left.

He took them two at a time as she chuckled.

"What?" he asked when he reached the top. "Where?" He glanced around. There were six closed doors around the landing area.

"The farthest door on the left." She pointed. "I'm not bleeding to death," she hinted. "There's no rush."

He was already in what he assumed was her master bedroom. Not sparing a glance around the space, he headed towards the open doorway and gently set her down on the bathroom countertop.

"The Band-Aids are under the sink." She pointed.

He set the first aid kit on the counter next to her, took out the antiseptic, and began cleaning the cuts on the bottom of both of her feet.

When she hissed at the sting, he softly blew on the area to ease her pain.

"I don't think Band-Aids will help. They usually don't stick to the bottom of your feet," he supplied.

"No, I wouldn't think they would. I'll be fine, really." She wiggled her feet and for the first time that day, he noticed the bright pink color on her toes.

"See." She jumped from the counter and gripped his shoulders and winced when she stood. "Okay, so I may have to invest in some slippers or boots to leave by the front door."

His hands were on her waist, holding her still. In one move, he set her back on the countertop. "Looks like you'll have to stay off your feet for a while."

"I can't, I have to sweep and..."

He stopped her by chuckling. "How about I run home, get Ozzy, and come back to help you?"

She twisted her lips as if she was thinking. "Hunter should be back soon with the pizza. I can just have him..."

"Okay." He took a step back and helped her down slowly. This time, she stayed on her feet and looked up at him.

"My turn." She reached for a wet cloth and wiped his face. He was a little surprised when the cloth came back with blood on it.

He glanced past her and winced as he saw the cut under his eyes. "He must have been wearing a ring."

"It doesn't look like it needs any stitches, but you're too tall for me to get a good look at it."

He bent down until they were eye to eye and held still as she examined his face. He winced as she dabbled some antiseptic over the cut.

"Sorry," she whispered, but she continued to clean the

wound. Her breath fell over his face and he closed his eyes to keep her from seeing what was behind them. What she was doing to him. "There," she finally said, and he straightened up. "I don't think a Band-Aid will stay put there either."

"I'm fine." He glanced at himself in the mirror and knew that come morning, he'd have a shiner. "I've got to give props to Mr. Schneller. He sure has a mean right hook."

"The man scares me." She shivered visibly and wrapped her arms around herself.

"Oh?" He turned his attention to her. "Why?"

"When we first moved in, he would leave us notes in the mailbox, claiming that this was his land. No one had lived here for over thirty years and he'd been using the land to hunt on. I've caught him cutting across the property to make his way to the beach to fish as well."

"Did you call it in?" he asked.

"No. Isaac and I agreed that he'd done it for so long, there wasn't any harm in it. Isaac had a talk with him and the hunting stopped, but every now and then I still see him crossing the land to fish."

"I'll have a talk with him." He thought about it. "Trespassing is trespassing."

She shrugged. "He never bothered me before, but now that I'm alone…. Especially now that I know he's exploring other… recreational pleasures"—he chuckled— "I think it's best he stayed on his own land."

He nodded. "Agreed, I'll talk with him. He may be stuck in the hold for a while after this last stunt while waiting for sentencing." He started to follow her out of the bathroom, which he realized was quite impressive now that he'd had a chance to look around.

The bathroom was bigger than the entire downstairs of his house.

There were marble floors and countertops, and an open shower with only two tile walls to close it in. Her claw bathtub was twice the size as his and sat in front of a large arched window that faced out to the lake.

He stepped back into her bedroom and whistled. "Wow, you know, I thought the downstairs was impressive."

She glanced over her shoulder. "I'll give you a tour."

He looked at his watch. "Tomorrow. Ozzy is waiting for me at home."

"Right. Thanks again for... my feet." She giggled.

"Thanks for the eye." He was smiling down at her when they heard the front door open.

Hunter called out, "Rose? Why is Sawyer's truck still here?"

Rose sighed. "I'll let you go. I'll see you tomorrow?"

He nodded. "I'll be here to help you pick up the lumber."

"Eight," she supplied, and he nodded.

"See you then." He followed her down the stairs.

When Hunter spotted him coming out of her bedroom, the man's eyes narrowed.

He figured he'd leave Rose to the explanations and without another word, stepped outside and left.

As he figured, Ozzy had left him a little reminder of why he shouldn't take so long to get home. Letting the dog run free, he cleaned up the mess and threw a meal into the microwave. He sat on the back patio watching Ozzy chase birds and thought of what being close to Rose had done to him.

Climbing the stairs an hour later, he crawled into bed with Ozzy and quickly fell into a Rose-filled dream state.

Ozzy's low growl woke him, his entire body coming awake in a split second.

"Easy," he said softly and listened as the dog vibrated next to him.

He grabbed the knife he kept behind the headboard and tiptoed to the edge of the loft. Looking over, he immediately knew that the house was empty. Going to the window, he saw the dark figure dart from behind his truck.

Using his thumbprint to unlock the hidden safe, he pulled out his weapon and rushed down the stairs.

"Hold it," he called out, but it was too late. Whoever had flattened his tires was long gone.

Using a flashlight, he walked around his truck and cursed. At least he'd spooked them off before they could get to all four tires.

Pulling out his cell phone, he called it in.

At eight o'clock that next morning, he parked his motorcycle beside Hunter's car as Rose and her brother stepped out onto the front porch.

"Where's Ozzy?" she asked as her eyes ran over his bike.

"He had to stay home. Car troubles." He decided to leave it simple.

"That's too bad." She frowned. "We're ready to go." She nodded to the flatbed rental truck.

"I've got to be back in town at noon." Hunter turned to Rose. "I tried to reschedule the meeting, but..."

"What is it, exactly, that you do?" Sawyer asked. He hadn't heard much of the guy in town. To be honest, he didn't even know if the man lived in Twisted Rock.

"I'm a lawyer," Hunter said, his chest puffing out slightly. "In Buffalo."

"It's a long drive to come all this way," Sawyer commented.

"Rose has enough spare rooms that I can stay over when I come down." He smiled and tossed the keys to the truck to him. "I'll have to follow you since I need to head out soon."

Rose hugged him. "Go, we can handle this. Like I said, it's just a few boards that need replacing."

Hunter looked down at him, his blond eyebrows raised. "You got this?"

"Sure." He smiled. "Like she said, it's only a few boards."

Hunter was silent for a while. "Okay. If you need any help, give RJ a call."

"I will." Rose got on her toes and placed a sisterly kiss on Hunter's cheek. "Go, be a lawyer and sue someone."

He chuckled. "Thanks." Hunter waved at him and got into his car.

"Ready?" he asked once the car disappeared.

"Yes." She smiled up at him. "Maybe on our way back, we can swing by your place and pick up Ozzy, so he won't feel so lonely."

He nodded. "Sure, I'll just have to think of a way to get him home again."

"I can drive him in the truck," she said as she slid into the seat. He glanced over at her.

"You don't have to do that."

"You only live a mile from here."

"How do you know that?" he asked.

"Simple." She leaned closer to him. "I asked around." She laughed. "Small towns." She rolled her eyes. "Go, I don't want to miss all the good pieces of wood."

This time it was his turn to laugh.

"So, are you going to tell me what happened?" she asked once he was on the road.

"What do you mean?"

"Something happened. I could see it in your eyes. Car problems?" she hinted when he remained silent.

He sighed. "Someone slashed my tires last night."

She gasped. "Oh no!"

"Yeah, I was thinking it was..." He shut his mouth and shrugged. "Kids," he lied.

"You live pretty far from the road. Why would kids go to the lengths of hiking back there to do such a thing?"

"Not everyone likes cops." He pulled onto the highway. "I've arrested a lot of people in the year and a half I've lived here."

"I'm sure that's true. Still, do you think you'll catch who did it?"

"No. But my insurance is paying to have the truck towed and new tires put on. They only got to two of them, since Ozzy woke me up."

"Then he deserves a treat," she jumped in. "I always wanted a dog." She sighed and looked out the window.

"Why didn't you get one?" he asked.

"Isaac didn't..." She grew silent and didn't finish the sentence.

"You know, the local shelter has some great dogs. We can always swing by there and check them out," he suggested.

She turned back to him and the sadness behind her eyes was replaced with possibility.

FIVE

A TSUNAMI OF FEELINGS...

Sawyer laughed at Rose as a group of dachshund puppies surrounded her.

"They're all too cute to pick just one." She giggled as the puppies ran around wildly trying to lick her face.

"That's why I picked Ozzy. He was a year old and already house trained." He stood outside the fenced-in area and leaned against the railing, watching her.

She had to admit, he looked even better than the puppies at the moment. Her libido was working overdrive. Could you blame her? It had been a year since the last time a man had touched her.

Standing up and trying to clear her sex-deprived mind, she made her way slowly through the mass of excited ankle biters—as Hunter had always called small dogs—and exited the kenneled area.

"Okay, you might have something there. I don't have time with all the construction to train a puppy. Besides, they chew on wood." She turned to him, frowning. "Don't they?"

"All dogs can. You'll have to do some training to get

them to change any unpleasant habits they may have," he answered.

She thought about potty training a puppy, then thought about simply training an older dog and nodded. "Okay, take me to the older dogs."

The wood planks they had purchased earlier were in the back of the truck. When Sawyer had suggested they make a quick stop at the shelter before getting Ozzy and starting work for the day, she'd jumped at the opportunity.

They walked through the rows of kennels and a small terrier mix caught her eye and melted her heart. The little girl shivered and cowered in the corner, but when Rose picked her up, she snuggled to her chest and almost purred.

"This is the one." She turned to Sawyer. "I'll take this one."

He chuckled. "Not much of a guard dog." He gently stroked the dog between the ears with one fingertip. Rose couldn't help but watch the movement and daydream. Her libido again.

"Still." She broke her thoughts and snuggled the dog against her chest. "She's the one."

"Okay, I'll go find someone to start the paperwork for..." He glanced down at the sign hooked to the kennel door and laughed. "Mrs. Tinkles?" He chuckled as he went and found someone to help them.

"Don't worry about him. The first thing we're going to do together is change your name." She held the small dog up until they were nose to nose. Her eyes squinted, and the small dog followed suit. A wave of love hit her like a tsunami.

"That's it." She hugged the dog to her chest. "Tsunami..." She didn't like the sound of it and ran a few variations through her mind as they waited for Sawyer.

"How about Tsuna?" she asked Sawyer when he returned.

"What?" Sawyer looked at her funny and she laughed.

"You know, for a name. Short for tsunami." She turned the small dog his way and he laughed uncontrollably.

"You're going to name that small, gentle, scared, little dog after a large, overwhelming wave that terrorizes millions and destroys everything in its path?"

She looked down at the dog and smiled. "Yes." She touched her nose to the dog's and felt the wave of love hit her again.

Less than half an hour later, they walked out of the shelter. Tsuna needed two days to get ready. She had to be neutered and chipped, not to mention updated on all her shots before she was able to go to her new forever home.

Rose hadn't known there was so much involved in adopting a dog, but she found it all very fun and enjoyed the new experience.

She leaned back in the truck and relaxed as Sawyer drove. When he pulled onto a small dirt road, she sat up slightly. She was curious to see what kind of place he lived in. The rustic feel of the quaint refurbished barn home made her smile.

"I like your place." She leaned towards the dash, so she could see the place better.

"I'll give you a tour." He parked the truck and got out. "They must have come to get my truck." He motioned towards a parking area in front of a detached garage. "Come on, Ozzy's excited there's company."

She could hear a dog barking now and followed Sawyer to a small blue door on the side of the house.

She was happily surprised at a few things. The first was that Ozzy wasn't the massive beast that she'd imagined from his name. He was a wire-haired dog almost as small as Tsuna. Second, she fell in love the instant she stepped into his home.

The entire first floor was open space. She could see from one end of the house to the other. The kitchen sat at the far right of the space, with a dining room in front of a massive bright blue barn door. There were shelves instead of cabinets over each countertop in the kitchen. Every single cup or plate was perfectly in place as was each container of food. They were all perfectly labeled in crisp handwriting on the small black chalk area on the front of each container. She'd seen homes like this in the magazines but had never imagined it belonging to a bachelor.

The stairs were tucked at the back of house. It was steep, and each step was made of half logs. There was a small sofa and TV area just beside and under the stairs. A massive iron stove sat between the sofa and a recliner.

Glancing up, she could see that the entire floor above was a loft.

"I've got to let Ozzy out before I show you the rest." He made his way towards the large blue barn door.

He unlatched the door and slid it open. The view he exposed was breathtaking.

She followed him and stepped out onto a patio area. There was another table and chairs, but this set was made to bear the brunt of everyday weather. Beyond the patio was a small green field and only a few yards away was a beautiful lake with a dock hanging over its peaceful waters.

Ozzy had followed Sawyer out and now that he was done with his business, the dog came sniffing around her.

She sat down in one of the chairs and gave him her attention until he lost interest.

"See?" Sawyer chuckled. "He likes everyone."

She smiled. "Okay, finish showing me around." She nodded back to the house.

They walked back into the house and he motioned for her to head up, then he followed her up the narrow stairs.

"Have you ever bumped your head on this?" She tapped the low beam that seemed too low for even her to fit under.

"The first few months I lived here, I thought I was going to go brain dead." He easily maneuvered up the rest of the way. "Now I have it down pat."

He raised his arms and motioned for her to look around.

Okay, she was really impressed. He was extremely tidy. There wasn't even a pair of shoes sitting on the floor.

As she suspected, the entire top floor was open as well. A small half-wall blocked the view from the downstairs. The bed sat directly against it. Along the back of the house, there was a small window with a small claw-foot bathtub under it. To the right was a very narrow shower, and there was a toilet and small sink area next to them.

"So much for privacy up here." She motioned to the toilet.

"Ozzy doesn't mind since I watch him go too."

She chuckled and shook her head as she walked towards his bookcase. She was surprised that it was full of fiction books.

"Sci-fi?" She glanced back at him after picking up one of the novels she'd read herself.

He shrugged. "You've got to read something, right?"

"Most men don't." She ran her fingers over each novel, wishing silently to borrow a few of the titles.

"What else is there besides books to fill a dark, rainy night?" he asked.

She turned to him, her eyes running up and down his fit form. "Some would claim sex is a good time filler."

"It can be..." he said in a deep voice, his eyes locking with her own.

"With the right partner," they finished together.

She turned and glanced at a picture he had hanging up in a frame until she could get herself back in check.

"You?" She ran a fingertip over the image of a young boy who looked a lot like Sawyer. Leaning in, she vaguely remembered the summer at the pool. "I think I remember you." She turned and squinted her eyes in his direction. "You complimented my dive?"

He smiled. "Yup, that's me, Mr. Smooth."

She laughed and walked over to the window. "You left an impression on me. What about your parents?"

"Dad passed when I was ten, which is why my mother decided to start shipping me up here every summer to spend time with my grandfather, so I could be around a man." He rolled his eyes. "Really, it was because she had a new boyfriend and they liked to travel without a preteen boy tagging along." He shrugged.

"Siblings?" she asked, a little more curious.

He shook his head. "Never got lucky in that department."

After a moment of silence, she turned and sighed. "We'd better get to work. This deck isn't going to repair itself."

He nodded and followed her down the stairs. Ozzy sat in her lap as he drove them towards her place. It took less than five minutes before they pulled into her driveway. As Sawyer pulled the truck towards the back of the house, she gasped.

"Oh!" She felt shock and anger at what she saw and quickly set Ozzy aside and jumped from the still moving truck.

"Rose!" Sawyer called after her, but she was already stepping onto the small deck area that jutted off the back of her kitchen. The small deck was her biggest joy come spring since she hadn't gotten the walled garden repaired and planted yet. She'd set up the area with a table and chairs and several large pots full of herbs that she used when she cooked.

She and Hunter had moved a lot of the massive pots aside so that several of the deck boards could be replaced.

As she stood there, tears rolled down her cheeks at the destruction.

All of the pots lay in shards surrounded by heaps of dirt and wilting greenery. Her lawn furniture was twisted or broken in pieces. Even the decking that hadn't been destroyed now had what appeared to be ax marks in the once-smooth wood.

"I'll call it in," Sawyer said behind her.

"Why? Who?" She sighed as she bent down and hugged Ozzy, who had come up to her and scratched at her leg for attention.

Rose sat back and let Sawyer do most of the talking. He knew what time they had left, how long they had spent looking at dogs and at his own place, picking up Ozzy. She rarely even kept track of lunchtime and frequently forgot to break through the day to grab some food.

She was thankful when Sawyer's partner, Carson, offered to help them clean up the mess. He swept the dirt and old plants into a bin. There were several plants that could come back, and she set them aside in the temporary plastic jars that she'd purchased them in last spring.

She had planned on buying a large cart to wheel the plants into the sunroom and out of the cold this winter.

Now she was looking at purchasing more pots and even a few new plants as well.

"Hey." Sawyer got her attention again. "I made us sandwiches." He set the plate down in front of her.

He'd already hammered the table back together and had fixed two of the four chairs.

"Oh." She blinked and looked around. "Where is Carson?"

"He left a few minutes ago." He touched her shoulder lightly. "Maybe after eating, you should go lie down. I can work on replacing these boards."

"No, I..." She shook her head. "I'll help." She smiled. "We'll need more boards."

"I don't think so. Remember, I suggested you buy a few extras. I think we purchased enough."

"Good," she said.

"Rose." The way he said her name had her looking over at him. "Eat. Whoever did this obviously wanted to get to you. Don't let them win."

He was right. It had obviously been someone out to hurt her. Someone who knew how much her herb garden meant to her. Raising her chin, she nodded and picked up her sandwich.

"So," he said after she took a bite, "want to tell me who hates you?"

She sighed. "I was wondering the same thing." Her mind played over several names.

"Before you say anything, I should tell you that Schneller made bail late last night."

"You don't think..."

"My chief had a talk with him about crossing property lines."

"Oh." She set her sandwich down and glanced around. "Yeah, I could see him doing this."

Sawyer nodded. "So could Carson. He's over there now taking his statement. As well as talking to him about my truck tires."

"Right." She frowned and looked towards the property line. "Should I expect more of this?" She motioned to the area where the mess had been.

"Possibly. You might want to install cameras. There's nothing we can do unless you catch him in the act."

She sighed. She didn't want to always have to listen for her crazy, strung-out neighbor breaking something of hers.

"Okay, cameras it is," Sawyer said. "I'll do some research and let you know the best ones out there."

She leaned forward and smiled at him. "Thanks."

"Now, eat the rest of that. You're going to need your strength to get all this work done."

He wasn't joking. They tore up the old damaged and rotted boards and found they had miraculously purchased just the right number of pieces.

Since they had bought the right length boards, there wasn't any cutting required. Sawyer nailed the boards in place while she sat back to watch him work, once again enjoying the way a simple T-shirt and worn jeans fit him perfectly.

They completed the entire deck in just over an hour, leaving plenty of daylight to enjoy.

"I plan on painting and sealing the entire thing." She smiled down at the new decking. "Maybe next weekend."

"We're supposed to have rain all week into the weekend," he mentioned.

"Then maybe the following week. The men are working

on replacing all the windows this week." She glanced up at the side of her home. From here, the place didn't seem so massive. Maybe that's why this was one of her favorite spots.

"All?" he asked. She turned to him.

"Yes, the ones in the basement too." She smiled. "Come on, I'll give you that tour now."

After seeing his place, she once again felt self-conscious about the tidiness of her own place. Not to mention the heat that was still coming off Sawyer every time they brushed against one another as they moved.

On the main level, she walked him through the kitchen. "The kitchen." She motioned like she was Vanna White, causing him to smile. "Pantry." She opened the heavy wood door and when he leaned in to get a look, his shoulder brushed her arm and she felt her breath catch. So, instead of focusing on him, she glanced over and noticed that the shelves were almost bare. She hadn't really enjoyed cooking since Isaac... She turned away from the dark closet.

"This is a dumbwaiter." She slid open the wood doors in the stone archway. There were two rows of shelves. "The cooks used to send up meals so that the staff could feed the owners." She leaned in. "Can you imagine what it must have been like back then." She rolled her eyes. "Breakfast in bed every day..." She shut the doors and continued on the tour. "The back stairs lead up to a doorway in the main hallway upstairs and to the attic." She turned and walked into another room she hadn't used since Isaac's death. "The formal dining room." She used to really enjoy this space, but now she ate most of her meals at the smaller table and chairs in the kitchen area. "The living or great room, which you've seen already." The new flooring was clean, and the wood gleamed in the light that came in through the large windows. She had hung thick curtains over the windows to give some sense of privacy and to keep the chill out, but now that the windows were going to be replaced, she was thinking of changing to a lighter material.

He was silent as he followed her through each room. The office where Isaac used to work when he was home that now only collected dust. The library, a room she used often and enjoyed a lot. There was a smaller fireplace there, and on cold nights she could often be found snuggled up in front of it. The den, another room she rarely used since it reminded her of Isaac. There were two bathrooms downstairs, a full one between the den and the library and a half bath in the hallway near the kitchen.

They climbed the front stairs and she showed him the guest rooms, each with their own bathroom. She had decorated them after Isaac's death. She'd taken her time stripping the old wallpaper off each wall, choosing paint colors, and hunting down the right furniture for each room. The work had been her saving grace, filling her time with movement so she didn't have time to wallow in self-pity and loneliness.

Now, at the closeness of Sawyer, it was hard for her to control the steamy thoughts that kept sliding into her wicked mind. She tried to stay focused on showing him around and making mental lists of things that still needed to be done to the place as she continued down the hallway and showed him the door that led to the back stairs.

"Go down and you'd end up in the hallway between the kitchen and the dining room. Going up leads to the attic room." She imagined at one point the space had housed the maids for the home. Since moving in, she had turned the massive room into her art studio. There was a small bathroom up there, which still needed some work done to it.

Sawyer's dark eyebrows shot up and she motioned for

him to climb the wide wood stairs. Here, she hadn't yet gotten around to painting the walls. The dark cream color was in desperate need of a lighter shade and maybe some colorful art to brighten the climb she made every day.

Stepping into her favorite space, she stood back as Sawyer looked around.

There were two large windows on either end of the room that let in the natural light. The windows would be replaced with double-paned windows and their larger size was the reason for the delay in the window order. RJ had indicated that the manufacturer had to specially make the windows in order for them to fit perfectly.

In the room, canvases, easels, and art supplies of every kind filled shelving along one windowless wall. Stacks of finished pieces leaned against the opposite wall.

Since she hadn't been focused on selling her artwork since Isaac's death, there were close to a hundred finished pieces overrunning the space.

"So, you *are* an artist," he said, looking around. The fact was, she hadn't let anyone up there since Isaac. Not even Hunter had stepped foot up here yet.

"Yes." She twisted her fingers behind her back, hoping to hide her nerves as he walked around and studied the pieces she'd done in the past year.

"These are great." He turned and studied her. "Do you sell them?"

"I... used to." She sighed. "I haven't for a while."

He turned to her. "Since Isaac?"

She nodded. "When I feel ready, I'll call Julie, my agent. Until then"—she glanced around and smiled— "they stay in my cave."

He moved over to a stack of paintings. "May I?" he

asked. When she nodded, he started going through them slowly.

Her heart skipped when he came upon one of the first pieces she'd done after Isaac's death.

The mirror image of Sawyer stared back at its subject with obvious desire behind the matching green eyes. He reached down and pulled out the canvas and set it on the empty easel, so he could study it further.

She walked over and stood next to him. She'd learned the best way to deal with situations like this was head-on.

"What do you think?" She kept her eyes on the painting.

"I think it's incredible." It was a low rumble. "I've never been captured so... perfectly."

She turned to him, her heart in her throat. "Not everyone sees the same things."

He turned to her, his eyes searching hers. "No, they don't."

SIX

T*HERE ONCE WAS A MAN*...

Sawyer couldn't stop the pull towards her. Rose's blue eyes beckoned him until he was a breath away from her. His hands moved up to her shoulders and he closed the short distance separating them. Her chest pressed into his as he lowered his head. She reached up on her toes and met him halfway.

The feeling of her soft mouth under his had his fingers tightening on her skin. A soft moan escaped her, sending his body into overdrive. He pulled her closer until she was pressed against him completely, wrapping his arms around her. Holding her to him, he nudged her back until she bumped into the massive work table that sat in the middle of the room. It was covered with paints and supplies.

He placed his hands on her waist and lifted her until she sat on the edge of the table. He nudged some of the items aside, making room for her.

"Sawyer," she said as he rained kisses down her neck. Her fingers dug into his shoulders. "I need..." She moaned as he tugged her shirt over her head.

"I know." He almost growled it out. He had known each time she'd looked at him with desire. Every single instance had caused his body to react and his desire to spike.

Seeing the soft lace covering her, he dipped his head and tasted her skin. She was sweeter than honey and he desperately wanted—no, needed—more. A wave of pleasure hit him when her fingers dug into his hair to hold him in place and guide him to where she wanted his attention.

The soft moans she made were driving him crazy. He didn't know how much longer he could hold himself back.

His hands had stilled on the waist of her jeans, but when she wrapped her legs around his hips, he moved closer and traced the line. Her breath hitched as he circled her navel.

His lips returned to hers as his finger dipped below the seam of her jeans. She arched back, giving him better access to more of her skin.

"Yes," she cried out when he leaned back to jerk the buttons open, exposing a matching pair of panties. He stepped closer again and dipped his fingers beneath the soft material. When he plunged a finger into her softness, she arched and cried out. She leaned back on the table, holding herself up with her arms as her eyes closed, and she threw her head back.

Dipping his head, he enjoyed her breasts as his hands worked on pleasing her, exploring the smoothness of her skin everywhere not yet exposed to his view. Her hips moved in sync with his motions and he sensed she was close to coming. He vaguely heard his cell phone buzzing but tuned it out. She cried out in release as he watched her, enjoying the site of her letting go.

Slowly removing his hand, he pulled her closer until he felt her heart settled next to his. Then she wrapped her legs around him and rubbed her still jean-clad pussy against his hard-on.

"My god," he sighed. "There is nothing I'd like to do better than slide into you right now." He rested his forehead against hers.

"What's stopping you?" she purred.

"The fact that my cell phone is buzzing, and I fear it's work. I'm on backup duty starting..." He glanced at his watch and groaned. "Half an hour ago."

"Oh." She leaned back and frowned. "I..."

He stopped the awkwardness by leaning in and kissing her again. "My god, if it wasn't for work, I'd spend the entire night making love to you."

She smiled and nodded. Just then they both heard Ozzy bark downstairs as a car pulled up outside.

She rushed to pull on her T-shirt and snap her jeans.

He took out his phone and groaned. "That's Carson. He knew I was here with Ozzy and on the bike. He's going to take Ozzy home for me."

They walked down the stairs together, and at the base of the stairs, he turned to her and kissed her once more. "Night."

"Night." She smiled back at him. "Be safe," she added before he scooped Ozzy up and walked outside.

The bike ride home allowed him to cool down some. Still, as he pulled on his uniform, he couldn't get the sight of Rose opening for him out of his mind.

The call was about an overturned semi on the state highway, which took up most of their night. Most of the crew was out there directing traffic or taking statements from the people involved in the four-car pileup that had ensued after the semi had crashed.

Before he could take a break, the sun was coming up.

Carson dropped him off at the house when they were done. He let Ozzy out just as the heavy rain started. Then he climbed the stairs, peeled off his uniform, and slid between the sheets in just his boxers.

Ozzy jumped up and, after circling a few times, lay down in the middle of Sawyer's legs, one of his favorite spots.

He didn't wake again until his cell phone buzzed, and Ozzy barked to wake him up.

"I hear it," he told the dog, reaching for the phone. "Hello?"

"There's been an incident at the Clayton place." His chief didn't bother with hellos.

He ran his hand over his face and tried to clear his mind. Then it dawned on him. Clayton. Rose Clayton. He sat straight up. "Is Rose okay?"

"All we know at this point is that there is a body. We're heading out there now. Meet you there. Carson's on his way to pick you up."

His heart actually stopped. He'd never felt light-headed before, even when he'd been shot. Now, however, everything went white and he could hear his own heartbeat pounding in his ears.

He dressed quickly and was out the door waiting for Carson to pick him up.

He tried calling and texting Rose several times, with no reply. He thought of searching for Hunter's number, but Carson arrived quickly, and his energy was better served making his partner drive as fast as he could.

When they pulled into the long driveway, there were police cars, ambulances, and even a fire truck, all with their lights flashing. It was almost like a damn disco as he rushed past all the vehicles towards the front porch.

He pushed through the half-closed front door.

"Chief?" he called out.

"Back here," someone said.

He was rushing through the living room towards the basement door when he heard her voice.

"Sawyer." It was a small sound he'd almost missed.

He stopped in the middle of the room and looked down. She was sitting on the sofa, softly crying into a tissue.

Not thinking clearly, he pulled her up into his arms and held onto her. "My god, when they said..." He broke off, unable to finish the dark thoughts he had.

"It's... I think... Sawyer, it's Isaac." She cried and buried her face into his shoulder.

"What?" Was she saying that her husband's body was in her basement?

He glanced around and spotted his chief, who motioned that he wanted to talk to him privately.

"Sit." He nudged her back onto the sofa and then knelt in front of her until her eyes met his. "Can you hold on just a little while? Then I'll have more answers for you." She nodded and wiped her eyes with a tissue. "Carson." He turned to his partner who was standing by the end of the sofa. "Stay with her, will you?"

"Sure thing." His partner sat down and pulled Rose into his arms.

Sawyer had forgotten that they knew each other so well. Then again, everyone in town knew everyone else.

He made his way to the top of the basement stairs and followed the chief downstairs. His tour the other day hadn't extended to the basement, but he'd been down there once before when he'd helped her turn her power back on.

With the lights on now, he could see so much had changed in the past months.

Someone had cleaned out more than half of the old junk that had been down there. There was still a fancy wine room with a glass door near the base of the stairs, but the rest of the basement sat almost empty and there was a massive hole in the west wall.

"What happened?" he asked, walking towards the destruction. Rain streamed into the basement through the large sheets of plastic someone had set up outside to keep the area dry.

"It looks like the rain did a little foundation damage. Mrs. Clayton..."

"Rose," he corrected.

Deter nodded. "She heard the noise and came down here to see what had happened. When she used the flashlight to check out the damage..." He moved his flashlight and Sawyer saw the body. The tarps were put in place to keep the rain off the body, not the damage.

Being stuck in cement had kept the decomposition to a minimum. He recognized Isaac Clayton almost immediately from the pictures he'd seen. The man's head, left shoulder, and chest area, along with parts of the man's hips and legs, were exposed, while other parts of him remained buried behind thick concrete.

"Looks to me like it's Isaac Clayton. So, the question is... How did her husband end up in a four-foot cement wall in her basement instead of at the bottom of the Atlantic?"

"I'll handle..." He turned to go but Deter stopped him.

"Actually, since your partner has informed me that you've been spending some time with"—he nodded to the body—"the wife, I'll need you to step out of this one, at least until we rule her out as a suspect."

"Out?" He glanced back at the body and saw what he

hadn't at first—a large piece of rebar sticking through the man's chest. "Murder?" he said under his breath.

"Yeah," Deter answered. "We'll need to bring her in for questioning. I'll need your word that you won't say anything. I need you to step out of this, or I'll set you out of it." The warning was soft, but Sawyer got the man's meaning.

"You have my word," he promised only because there was no doubt in his mind that Rose had nothing to do with the horror still laying half buried in cement.

He followed Deter up the stairs. When he met Rose's eyes, she must have read the truth in his, since she started crying again.

"It is him. How?" She shook her head.

"That's the question we're going to get to the bottom of. We'll need you to come in for some questions." Deter stepped forward. "You may want to get dressed."

"What about..." She glanced towards the basement door.

"Don't worry about a thing. The crew is going to take a few hours down there. They'll do what they can to stop the rain from coming in to the basement, but you might want to schedule repairs as soon as the rain stops," Deter answered.

Carson stood and pulled Rose up with him. "Officer Madsen here"—he pointed to the female officer—"will take you upstairs and help you change."

Sawyer hated leaving Rose in the other officer's care, but he knew he had to keep his distance, at least until the chief cleared Rose of any wrongdoing.

Rose glanced back at him as Madsen led her out of the room.

He tried to keep all emotion from his eyes as he watched her leave.

"So?" Carson turned to him.

"It's Isaac Clayton." Just saying it made his stomach roll.

"Thought he went down in the Atlantic," Carson added.

"So did everyone else. We'll need to make a few calls."

Deter stepped in. "I want Sawyer as far from this as possible, Carson. You seem to know the woman pretty well. Is there going to be an issue?"

"No, sir. I only know her as well as I know most in town," Carson answered.

"Good, you'll make the call to New York City and find out who took off in that plane. We'll need to talk to the construction crew who put in that damn wall." Deter ran his hands through his thinning hair. He turned to Brown, who was leaning against the fireplace. "You'll take lead on that. Get with them, find out when they poured the cement and why not a damn person saw a dead man with a piece of rebar sticking out of his chest. Then we'll have to deal..." Just then the chief's phone rang. He held up a finger as he answered it.

They all waited while he talked, listening to the one-sided conversation.

"Damn it. fine, I'll deal with it. Yes, set it for..." He glanced at his watch and rolled his eyes. "Nine. Yes, that's nine o'clock in the damn morning. Fine, sorry." He took a deep breath. "Yeah, okay, see you then."

He tucked his phone into his front pocket and rolled his shoulders. "Well, things just got worse. The press has gotten a whiff of this." His eyes moved around the room. "Anonymous source called it in that Isaac Clayton's murdered body was found in his wife's basement."

Sawyer's entire body went rigid. Rose hadn't even

talked to the police yet and he knew that the press would spin it as if she was already being painted as a murderer.

"Looks like the father is flying in. He's a hot-shot lawyer who's donated a lot of money to this town." The chief was running his hands through his hair again. "He's demanded a meeting with me. I've put him off until tomorrow morning. So, let's get going and see what information we can find out before then. I'd like to clear the wife as soon as possible." He nodded towards the stairs as Rose and Officer Madsen were walking down.

Sawyer hated seeing how pale Rose was, how fragile she looked. It reminded him of the night he'd shown up and turned on her power. She'd been so frail, and he didn't think she'd survive going through something like that again. But with everything that had already happened, he figured finding her husband's body in her basement was going to be a lot worse for her than the man going down in a plane over the Atlantic.

Rose rode in the back of the chief's patrol car to the station as he and Carson followed close behind them.

"I just can't see her doing something like that. I mean, she's a tiny thing and from the looks of it, Isaac Clayton wasn't a small man."

"No." He sighed. "The question isn't if Rose had anything to do with it. The question we should be asking is who murdered her husband and why did they try to hide it by flying Isaac's plane into the Atlantic?"

Carson nodded. "Think you can keep your personal feelings for her away from the job?"

He glanced over at his partner. "I'm going to make a point of it. I don't want anything getting in the way of clearing her name quickly."

"Good," his partner said as he parked at the station.

"Looks like we have trouble. Local news, from the looks of it."

"Damn." Cameras flashed as Rose was led out of the back of the chief's car and rushed inside.

"Yeah, you know what this means. Chief is going to be in an even sourer mood. He'll have to make a public statement."

Sawyer nodded. "We'd better get in there and get to work."

Carson stopped him by placing a hand on his arm. "For what it's worth, I think you two are great together. I don't have an ounce of doubt that Rose didn't have a thing to do with this. I saw her after... that night. You can't fake that kind of love for someone."

"No," he agreed, "you can't fake it." He didn't know why those words didn't soothe him. But as he got to work clearing her name, they kept playing over and over in his mind.

SEVEN

BEYOND DOUBT...

Rose couldn't control the shaking. She sipped a cup of terrible coffee someone had handed her as she sat in the room she suspected was for questioning. She'd seen enough cop shows to know that they'd try to get something from her to either pin the murder on her or clear her name.

She hoped it was the latter. Chief Deter was a good man, or so she'd always thought. She didn't really know him personally. All she knew about him was that he'd been chief for more than a decade, he had a wife and three kids, and he was an honest man.

Still, when he and another officer walked into the room, she felt sweat roll down her back.

"Mrs. Clayton, I'm Chief Deter, and this is detective Anthony Anderson."

"Hello." She nodded to the middle-aged man as he sat across from her. "Do I need a lawyer?" She looked between the two men.

"Not at this time. Unless you'd feel more comfortable with one present," the detective answered. "At this point, we just need to establish a timeline. Basics. You know, when you saw your husband last, your whereabouts, those kinds of things."

She nodded and set the coffee mug down, then took a deep breath. "Where do I start?"

"I'll leave you in the detective's capable hands," the chief said before leaving the room.

"I'll be recording this conversation," Detective Anderson said.

"Yes, okay." She nodded as he clicked the recorder on the table.

"Please, state your full name."

"Rose Marie Clayton."

"Your husband's name?"

"Isaac Clayton."

"The date of his death?"

The date should have been embedded in her memory, but for some reason, it didn't come to her quickly.

"August eight, of last year," she finally answered. The detective made a note in the file in front of him and gave her a look.

"How did you find out about his death?"

For the next hour, she answered basic questions. Where was she before the cement was poured? Who had poured it? Was she there when it was poured? When had her husband left? When was the last time she'd seen him?

These questions still ran through her own mind as she tried to determine how the love of her life had ended up inside the basement wall.

When the detective was finally done questioning her, she was exhausted. She'd downed four cups of the foul-tasting coffee and had, because of it, taken several bathroom breaks.

The entire time she'd sat in the stale room, she hadn't seen Sawyer anywhere. When she went to the bathroom, a female officer accompanied her.

She'd lost track of time and was shocked to see light as she stepped outside, thinking it was already morning. But that was short-lived when it quickly became apparent that the lights were coming from the news crews that were set up on her front stoop. As questions were thrown at her, bright flashes went off from all the cameras that were turned in her direction.

The same female officer that had helped her change drove her back home almost six hours after she'd found Isaac's body.

"Someone will be stationed outside your gate"—the officer nodded to a parked patrol car— "to make sure you stay put and for your own protection."

"My own..." She shook her head, unable to fathom why she needed protecting. Too tired to think clearly, she sighed. "Thank you." She got out of the car and slowly made her way up the stairs.

She pushed open the front door, but a full minute passed before she finally stepped inside her home.

A wave of the shakes hit her as she closed the door behind her.

What had they done with Isaac? Where was he now? She closed her eyes and rested her head against the door as tears streamed down her cheeks.

Why was it even harder now than it had been a year ago? Losing him in the ocean had been difficult, but knowing he'd been under her feet all along? This was somehow worse.

Sliding down the door, she tucked her head into her knees and cried harder.

Minutes later, somewhere in the house, her phone beeped, causing her to jolt out of the stupor she was in.

When she got up, her body felt like she'd just run a marathon. Her legs ached, her head was pounding, and her eyes were blurry as she tried to locate her phone.

Finally finding her phone on the kitchen counter, she checked her text messages. They were all from Sawyer, from late last night, shortly after she'd found... She closed her eyes and took a breath before reading his texts.

-Are you okay?
-Where are you?
-Oh, god, please answer
-Please, be okay, just be okay

Tucking the phone to her chest, she climbed the back stairs and, without removing her clothes, lay down on her bed and responded to him.

-I'm sorry I didn't see these, I left my phone in the kitchen last night. I can't believe it.

Instead of hitting send, she deleted it and just typed:
-I'm home now

She waited for a response, but when one didn't come, she set her phone down as her eyes slid closed.

She woke with a start when her phone rang. Fumbling awake, she picked it up without looking at the screen.

"Is this Rose Clayton?" The woman's voice sounded muffled.

"Yes," she answered, sitting up and holding the phone closer to her ear. "This is Rose."

"You killed him. I'll make sure you pay if it's the last thing I do." When the line went dead, Rose glanced down at the phone. It was from an unregistered number. She was about to see if she could trace where it had come from when the phone rang again in her hand, causing her to jump.

This time, a local number displayed on the screen.

"Hello?" she answered, expecting another threat.

"Mrs. Clayton, this is Police Chief Deter."

"Yes?" She relaxed slightly.

"I thought I should be the one to tell you, there's going to be a press conference this morning at eleven. We're going to give some basic information about your husband's case. I just want you to know that, as of right now, we've moved your name down on the suspect list."

"What does that mean?" she asked, closing her eyes and rubbing her temple as a headache started spreading there.

"It means you're not our top suspect," he answered.

"Can you tell me who is?"

"At this time, I can't. We don't want any interference with our investigation."

"I understand." She glanced around and realized that the sun was fully up. Looking over at her clock, she noticed that it was ten minutes until eleven. "Should I... come down there?"

"No, it's probably best if you keep a low profile. We've cleared the site, so you can get workers in there to fix the damage. If we need anything else, you'll hear from us."

"Thank you, Chief."

The man made a small sound, then said his goodbyes and hung up.

She checked her phone for messages from Sawyer, but she hadn't received anything. She plugged her phone into the charger, peeled off the slacks and sweater she'd pulled on quickly last night, and stepped into the hot shower.

Leaning her head against the cool tile, she played over everything that had happened to her in the last twenty-four hours—Sawyer pleasing her in her art studio, hearing the massive crash and going into the basement to see what had happened, the questions the detective had asked her.

She wanted to watch the press conference, so she kept her shower short.

She pulled on a pair of leggings and a long sweater, slipped on some socks, and turned on the television hanging in the corner of the bedroom.

Instantly, the chief's face filled her screen. She sat on the edge of her bed and watched him make a statement about finding Isaac, where he'd been found, and when he'd disappeared. He mentioned that they had several suspects and that she was not their primary one. Then he went on to answer questions.

She was surprised that most of them had to do with her. Why weren't the police looking at her? Where had she been when he'd disappeared? Where had the body been found exactly?

The chief answered all of the questions quickly and accurately.

Then the question about Isaac's plane came up. The chief paused and said that some parts of the investigation couldn't be discussed.

It hadn't dawned on her about Isaac's plane. Pulling out a notepad from her nightstand, she started writing down a list of questions she had for the chief.

Who had taken Isaac's plane from the hangar in the small private airport just outside of Twisted Rock where Isaac had kept it? Clearly, if his body was in the wall, he'd never left Twisted Rock. What about New York City? Why hadn't someone from his work told her that he hadn't shown up for work those two days he was supposed to be there?

By the time she was done, she had almost two dozen questions. Seeing that the local news had moved on, she hit the chief's number on her phone and waited for him to pick up. She told him she had questions, and he assured her that someone would be by her place later that day to discuss the case further with her.

Then she called RJ to schedule him and his crew to repair the damage. When he didn't answer, she shot him a text.

She was shocked by his reply.

-I'm sorry Mrs. Clayton, I can no longer work for you. I've been informed by the police that I'm under investigation for the murder of your husband. You'll have to find a new foreman.

She looked at his text, reading it over and over before it finally sunk in.

Of course, the police would look at him and his crew. After all, they were the ones who'd poured the cement. How had they not seen Isaac? Had it been on purpose?

She wrote a few more questions on her list.

She thought about how much RJ had helped her for the last year and shook her head. No, RJ Gamet couldn't have had anything to do with Isaac's death.

She punched out a message to him quickly.

-I understand. I'm sorry for this mess. For what it's worth, you've been a big help to me over the last year and I truly appreciate all the hard work you've done around the place.

There was no reply.

Twisted Rock was a small town, so she had to hire an out-of-town crew from Fredonia to the south. The crew couldn't make it out there that day, but she was assured that they could have the cement trucks there the following day.

Making herself some toast, she took a cup of coffee out onto her new back patio and sat in the shade as she tried to build up enough courage to go back into the basement and assess the damage.

Instead, she replanted her herbs in temporary plastic containers and then carried them into the sunroom.

By the time she was done arranging everything, there was a sheen of sweat over her skin. She grabbed an apple for lunch and ate it while she did her normal cleaning around the house. Laundry was something she actually enjoyed, since it was just her, the one load a week she normally did only took up about half an hour of her time.

Dusty, however, was something she didn't enjoy, and with the larger house, it took up almost a full hour each week.

Grabbing a soda, she climbed the stairs, thinking she'd enjoy some time in her studio.

She'd forgotten that Sawyer had pulled out the painting of himself she'd done shortly after that night he'd fixed her power. The painting had been her first after Isaac's death. Somehow, looking at it now made her feel strange, so she tucked it back behind the other paintings.

Just seeing her work table reminded her of the other day, what he'd done to her. A little over two hours later, she still couldn't get him off of her mind and was too flustered to concentrate on work. Frustrated, she paced, looking back to her workbench and remembering that moment. Less than an hour later, she descended the stairs without having lifted a single brush.

She needed to focus on something other than Sawyer. As she passed the basement door, she stopped and slowly reached her hand out towards the doorknob. She had just worked up enough courage to open the door when her doorbell rang, causing her to jump.

She made her way to the front of the house and took a deep breath before opening the front door.

Sawyer and Carson stood on the other side, much like they had the night they'd come to tell her that Isaac's plane had gone down.

"Rose." Carson stepped forward. "Can we come in?"

She nodded and stepped back, keeping her eyes from Sawyer's. He hadn't responded to her text and, by the look in his eyes, she got the hint that he was trying to distance himself from her for some reason. That hurt worse than if he'd just admitted that he'd made a mistake in getting involved with her.

She motioned for them to sit on the sofa, but they remained standing by the fireplace as she sat. She kept her focus on Carson as she tucked her hands in her lap to keep from fidgeting.

"The chief wanted us to stop by and fill you in on a few things we've discovered," Carson said, pulling a little notepad from his pocket.

"Go ahead." She nodded.

"First, it appears that your husband's plane was removed from the airfield just outside of town on the seventh."

"Not the sixth, the day he left here? Or rather, the day... he was supposed to?" she asked.

"No."

"Do they know if it was Isaac who took it out of the hangar?" she asked.

"No, it appears that it's pretty much a self-serve type of situation. Anyone with a key to his hangar could have gotten in. There isn't a check-in or check-out. His flight plans were filed and confirmed, but anyone could have called those in or signed in online if they had his passwords."

"What about his work? He had meetings scheduled," she asked.

"They confirmed that he didn't have any meetings scheduled that week. The last they saw of him was the day before, when he left to come back here. He only had the evening off and wanted to spend it at home."

"Yes." She remembered a little more detail of that time. "He came home on that Thursday evening because they were going to pour the cement the following day. He was scheduled to have Friday off, but he had gotten a call that evening. Isaac was needed in the office first thing the following morning to handle an emergency."

"What did he do that night, before the call?"

"We had dinner, I made chicken." She frowned, trying to remember the meal.

"Anyone else there?" Carson asked.

"My father-in-law, Sean, had come up from the city. He only stayed until the following day. He has, or rather had, his own place on the water a few miles from here. He sold it shortly after..." She shook her head. "Hunter had stopped by earlier in the evening and stayed on for dinner as well. We were celebrating him passing the bar exam. He left shortly after Isaac's father left, before Isaac went down to inspect the footings."

"Then?"

She glanced quickly at Sawyer before revealing the next bit of information.

"Isaac came upstairs and went to bed."

"Were you still awake? Did you see him?" Carson asked.

"Yes." She blushed, remembering the last time she'd

made love to her husband. It had been one of the most passionate nights in their life together. She had expected that it was because he'd finally agreed to start working on having a baby the next time he came home.

"About what time was that?" Carson asked.

"Ten." She shook her head. "Eleven?" She shrugged. "It was late."

"Did you see him in the morning?"

She closed her eyes. "No, he left me a note on the pillow."

"Was that the last time you heard from him?" Carson asked.

"No." She pulled out her phone. "He sent me a text message the following day, just after the flowers arrived." She showed him the message. Over the last year, she'd looked at it more times than she could count.

"Did you go down to the basement with him?" It was the first time Sawyer had spoken since arriving. Her eyes turned to him.

"No, I'd had two glasses of wine, and I was feeling tired, so I went up to bed when Hunter and Mr. Clayton left."

"And he went downstairs alone?" Carson asked.

"Yes, Hunter and Sean had left shortly after dinner."

"How long was your husband down in the basement?" Sawyer asked.

She shrugged, trying to remember. "Ten, fifteen minutes. Long enough for me to shower, dress for bed, my normal nightly rituals."

"How long were... you two together once he returned upstairs?" The tone of Sawyer's voice was flat and when she searched his eyes, she stiffened at the lack of emotion behind them. She knew he had guessed what they had been doing upstairs and was asking how long they had made love that evening.

"Less than ten minutes." She straightened her shoulders.

"Did you fall asleep right away?" Carson asked.

"Yes, it had been a long day. I'd stripped the rest of the paint off the stairs by hand. I was tired."

Carson nodded, then jotted in the notepad.

"When is the time of death?" she asked when he was done.

"They're estimating before midnight on Thursday night, the fifth," Carson answered.

Her head felt light and she had to take several deep breaths before she could ask her next question.

"Then, who sent me the flowers and the text messages? Who flew his plane from the airport? Then flew it into the Atlantic?"

"We're looking into it." Carson wrote something down. "Was your husband's cell phone gone when you woke that next morning?"

"Yes, so were his bag and his briefcase. His keys, his car, which they found parked at the airport." She closed her eyes. "Hunter had to drive it home for me," she said softly, remembering the anguish she'd been in after the funeral.

Then she opened her eyes. "Isaac was dressed. Why would he leave me in bed in the middle of the night, get dressed, and go down to the basement?"

"We're not sure, but that's just one more question we're looking into," Sawyer answered.

EIGHT

Amour...

It was hard watching Rose struggle with the details. He wanted to wrap his arms around her and hold on as realization struck her that her husband hadn't flown to New York that fateful day, but had in fact been lying dead in her basement, waiting for the cement trucks to encase his body in what would be his tomb.

"If there's anything else you can think of..." Carson started to say but was interrupted by their radios going off.

"Carson, Sawyer, Chief wants you to call in."

"I'll get it." Sawyer stepped out of the room as he pulled his phone from his pocket.

"This is Sawyer," he said when the chief answered.

"Where are you two?"

"We're at the Stoneport Manor like you requested."

"Good, stay there, there's been a new development. I'm on my way." The chief hung up before he could ask any questions.

Walking back into the room, he nodded to his partner. "Chief wants us to stay put."

Carson's eyebrows shut up, but then he nodded. "Maybe, if it's not too much to ask, could I get a glass of water?"

"Oh." Rose jumped up quickly. "I'm sorry, I should have asked if you wanted something." She started to rush out, then turned to him. "Officer Sawyer, would you like anything?"

Hearing her speak so formally to him tore him in two. "No, thank you, Rose." He made a point to call her by her first name and a slight smile played on her lips before she left.

"What's up?" Carson whispered once they were alone in the room.

"Not sure. Chief says there's been a new development. We are to stay put until he gets here."

"Damn, I was hoping for a nice quiet dinner tonight." Carson sighed.

Sawyer glanced down at his watch and cringed. "I was supposed to pick up my truck half an hour ago." He pulled out his phone and texted the mechanic to request they drop the truck off at his house and leave the keys in the mailbox. An instant reply came confirming they'd have someone do it. "Now if I only had a sitter for Ozzy."

"Why?" Rose asked, walking in with a glass of water for Carson.

He turned towards her. "It looks like it's going to be another late night."

"You should install a doggie door."

"I have one, I just haven't had time to install it yet." He motioned for her to sit down. "The chief is on his way over. We'll wait around until he gets here."

Just then there was a knock on the door and Rose stood back up. He followed her into the foyer, and when she opened the door, he jumped into action as questions were thrown at her.

"Rose, did you kill your husband?"

"Rose, why bury Isaac in the basement?"

Flashes blinded them both as a small group of paparazzi snapped pictures from her front porch. More than a dozen pictures were taken in the seconds it took him to slam the door shut. He didn't get it closed before the last question rang out clear as a bell.

"What are your thoughts about your husband's mistress coming out with a statement? Is it true you killed Isaac because of the child...?"

He turned and snapped the lock, then glanced over at Rose, whose face had turned an even paler shade of white.

"Mistress?" she said, turning slightly towards him. "Child?"

He held onto her shoulders, afraid that she was on the verge of sliding to the floor.

"Isaac's mistress. Someone asked what I thought about my husband's mistress coming out and that Isaac had a..." Her hands went protectively over her belly as if she was holding her dead husband's child deep within. Her eyes snapped to his and he watched them fade before his eyes as she pitched at an odd angle. He swooped her up quickly into his arms.

"Well, hell," Carson said behind him, "better bring her in here,"

Sawyer gently laid her down on the sofa and Carson placed a blanket over her.

"Seems like we were just here..." his partner mumbled. "I'll get her some water." Sawyer heard him disappear down the hallway.

"Rose?" His worry for her grew when she didn't move at

first. Last time, she'd woken quickly. This time, he had to lightly slap her cheeks and sit her up before her eyes fluttered open.

"Is it true?" She searched his eyes.

"I don't know," he answered truthfully.

Just then, the doorbell rang again.

"I'll get it this time." Carson held up his hand to keep them in place.

A minute later, the chief walked in, followed by Detective Anderson.

"I think you're too late. The paparazzi already spilled the beans," Carson said softly. Sawyer heard him and nodded at the chief when he glanced in his direction.

"Mrs. Clayton." The detective sat across from Rose. She was sitting up again, the blanket wrapped around her legs and the glass of water gripped between her hands like it was a life vest. "We've been contacted by a woman in New York who claims that she had a five-year affair with Isaac."

Rose buried her face in her free hand as tears rolled down her face.

Carson reached over and took the glass of water from her hands and set it down on the table.

Sawyer had moved away from her when the chief had walked in, but now, he wished he could hold her, comfort her.

"She says that Isaac Clayton is the father of her son," he continued.

Rose's eyes snapped up to the detective's and her lips opened and closed several times, as if she was trying to speak. Her hands were gripped together over her belly as she rocked slowly. "No," she finally said, "it can't be."

"Did you know about your husband's affair?" the detective asked.

Just then, the front door burst open and Hunter rushed in, slamming the heavy door behind him. At the same time, Rose whispered, "No."

"Don't answer that." He pointed to Rose, then stopped between Rose and the detective. "My client has nothing further to say to you at this time."

Rose closed her eyes and continued to rock back and forth slowly.

"You're the stepbrother... Hunter McDonald?"

"Yes, and as of this moment, Mrs. Clayton's lawyer. If you wish to question my client further"—Hunter produced a card and handed it over—"you have my number."

The chief nodded. "We'll be in contact." He tapped the detective's shoulder. "We'll clean up the mess out front. Our patrol car will stay put." The chief's eyes moved over to Rose. "For your client's safety."

He followed everyone to the front door but turned as he walked by Hunter. "Keep her safe."

The man's eyes narrowed at him, but then he nodded, and Sawyer turned and walked out.

Back at the station, he searched out the chief before heading home.

"Is it true?" he asked. "How did we miss a mistress?" Sure, they had only had a few hours to find out everything they could on Isaac Clayton and his past, but all the same, a mistress shouldn't have been too hard to miss. Especially, when the victim had been deceased for a full year. Why was the woman coming out of the woodwork now? Why not a year ago when the news spread about Isaac Clayton's plane going down?

"I'm asking the same damn question." Deter's eyes narrowed at him. "Shut the door." He waved to his office door.

Sawyer stepped in the small space and shut himself in with the chief.

"Sit." He motioned towards a chair. Sawyer had a quick flashback to the time he'd spent in the principal's office.

"Hell, we all missed it." Deter took a deep breath.

"And the kid?" Sawyer asked.

"That too. The birth certificate is under..."—he glanced down at a stack of papers on his desk— "Owens. Kristy Owens."

The name sounded familiar. "Kristy..."

"Owens, the actress." Deter was reading off the fax that had come in. "B movies apparently. If my memory serves me right, *Night of the Bees*." He glanced up from the sheet then back at it and nodded.

Sawyer vaguely remembered hearing about the scandalous woman. She'd had affairs with some of the wealthiest men in New York. It had been rumored that she had tried to blackmail a senator after taping their liaison a few years back.

"Now she's claiming she had Isaac Clayton's love child." Deter sighed.

"What does Isaac's father have to say about it?" Sawyer asked.

"The old man has lawyered up. I got about two seconds with him before five lawyers wearing fancier suits than I've ever seen followed him into the room. It seems that dear old father-in-law is covering his own ass but screw his daughter-in-law." The chief shook his head. "When I asked about her, the man seemed very uninterested. Like he had someplace else to be or something he was trying to hide."

"Why would he need a group of lawyers?" Sawyer asked.

"He was there that night, left after dinner. He used to

own a house a mile or two down the road, and that's where he spent the rest of the night his son was murdered, alone. Now he owns a house in Buffalo. Sold the place shortly after Isaac went MIA. Plus, he has his pilot's license."

"Right." Sawyer leaned back in the chair.

The chief looked down at the folder. "Now a mistress shows up. It shuffles the list of suspects around some. Kristy Owens is rumored to stoop to blackmail and we all know there isn't a whole lot of steps from blackmail to murder."

"What do you need me to do?" he asked.

"Go home, you look like shit. Sleep, shower, eat, walk that funny-looking mutt of yours, and then I'll see you bright and early tomorrow. We can't afford to not keep this one professional."

He nodded and got up. "I won't fuck this up. It's too important."

"Yeah, I figured as much when I walked in and your face was as white as Rose's." He waved him out of his office.

Sawyer headed home to do just what the chief ordered. However, when he found himself staring at the ceiling instead of falling asleep, he flipped on the television. The news was playing, and he listened for a while about world events. His eyes began to shut but then popped wide open when he heard Rose's name.

"We have an exclusive interview with Kristy Owens, who claims that her lover—the father of her three-year-old son, Ash—was murdered by the man's wife, Rose Clayton. Stay tuned."

The station went to commercial, and Sawyer picked up his phone to text Rose. He'd read her last message but knew that any further communication with her could look bad on his part.

Now that the entire world was watching, he couldn't

chance sending a text to her. He set the phone back down and turned up the volume when the commercials ended.

The interview started like any other. They ran over the woman's career and her past run-ins with both the law and with scandal, while the woman looked on, smiling as if the introduction highlighted her in a positive view.

"Thank you for joining us tonight, Kristy. I'm so sorry for your loss."

"Thank you." Kristy's smile had instantly disappeared, and her eyes pooled with giant tears that almost instantly flowed down her painted cheeks. "Isaac was my life. He was an amazing father to my Ash. And it's such a shame that my son will never get to know his father because of that woman."

"The woman in question is Rose Clayton, Isaac's widow," the broadcaster said.

"That woman is no widow, she's a murderer," Kristy jumped in. The camera zoomed to her eyes and Sawyer shut the screen off.

Now pissed, he jumped up from the bed and paced his small bedroom.

"Fuck it." He picked up his phone and dialed Rose's number. It rang three times before she answered. Her voice was a whisper and he worried that he'd woken her up.

"Where you asleep?" he asked softly.

"No," she answered.

"Did you catch the news?" he asked, fearing.

"Yes." He heard it now, the sadness, which caused his heart to wrench.

"Don't let it bother you. Remember, she's an actress," he added quickly.

"She has Isaac's son. Something he..." She stopped and

took a deep breath. "Hunter has advised me not to talk to you."

"Yeah, I'm not supposed to talk to you either." He sighed. "Want to hang up on me?" he asked.

"Do you want to hang up on me?" she returned softly.

"No, what I want is..." He decided he didn't care anymore. "I want to hold you in my arms and assure you this will all blow over soon." She was silent. "Are you still there?"

"Yes, tell me again," she said.

He smiled and leaned back against the bed frame and filled her in on everything he wanted to do with her, to her.

When he woke the next morning, he had a new spark and purpose. He'd play it by the books, but he wasn't going to let anyone tell him he couldn't keep his private life and his professional life separate.

He walked into the station ready to get to work. When he noticed all the people standing around outside the chief's office, he pushed through the crowd and glared at several people until they all went back to their own desks and jobs.

He knocked on the chief's door.

"Come in," Deter called out.

Sawyer opened the door and instantly knew why everyone had caused a scene.

Kristy Owens sat in the chair opposite Deter.

Deter stood up, looking slightly uncomfortable. "Good, you're here. I was just telling Miss Owens that you'd be happy to give her a police escort to her rental home."

"Rental?" He stepped into the room and the woman turned around and ran her eyes over him slowly. The instant interest that flooded the woman's eyes almost made Sawyer recoil. She practically purred like a kitten or, rather, a lioness.

The woman might not live in Hollywood, but she sure knew how to dress the part. The bright white jumpsuit she wore screamed for attention. The top was no more than a vest, exposing far too much skin for this time of year in upper New York state, as her very full double Ds hung out the front of the vest for anyone to see. Her bright blonde hair fell over her shoulder in a stylish hairstyle. She was beautiful, easily one of the prettiest B movie stars he'd ever seen. Okay, the only one he'd seen in person. Still, there was something behind her eyes that made his skin crawl.

"Yes." Kristy stood up and almost purred the next words. "I figured it was best that I stay close during the investigation. She stepped closer to him. "After all, I need to know what happened to my dear Isaac."

"For your son's sake?" he asked. Surprise flashed behind her eyes.

"Why, yes, of course." She shook her head slightly and smiled, and he could see the lies behind the crystal blue eyes of hers, which were hidden behind heavy black eyelashes.

"Is Carson in yet?" Sawyer asked Deter.

"Called in sick. He said that both he and Brigit got it at the same time," Deter answered.

Sawyer nodded, then motioned for the woman to follow him out.

"Sawyer," the chief called. He glanced over his shoulder. "Make sure to take care of Miss Owens and remember what I told you last night." He added the last part as a whisper, meant for his ears only.

He nodded, then left.

When he stepped out of the chief's office, Kristy instantly took his arm as if they were strolling down the Thames in the middle of spring.

"So, your name is Sawyer?" she asked.

"Officer Sawyer." He pulled her hand from his arm and opened the outer door for her. "Where's your car?"

"Oh, over there. The driver is waiting for me." She waved, then noticed a few paparazzi hovering near the limo. "See, I can't even step outside." She sighed but straightened the hem of her vest top as she licked her lips. "Walk with me." She wrapped her arm through his again.

He wanted to push her off but knew that the media was watching, and besides, he was in uniform.

She smiled and waved as they walked closer to the flashing cameras. Several questions were shouted at her and she threw back a few answers, making sure to include the line from last night's interview.

"That woman is no widow, she's a murderer."

He opened the back of the limo for her, then nodded to the driver. "I'll follow you." The man waved and stepped into the car.

Turning on his red and blue lights, he followed the limo out of the parking lot. He wasn't surprised at the house she'd rented. It overlooked the lake and was one of Twisted Rock's most expensive rental places.

He pulled in behind the limo, intending to quickly disengage himself from the property, but Kristy waved for him to roll down the car window.

"Why don't you come in, you know, check the place out. My security hasn't arrived yet." She frowned.

Taking a deep breath, he mentally kicked himself for falling into her web.

Getting out of the car, he nodded to the limo driver, who was already retreating towards the garage area.

He stood back as she opened the glass doors with a code from her phone. "It's always such a pain to do all this myself." She glanced at him over the rims of her black sunglasses. "My assistant just had a baby." She smiled, and he wondered if she had an assistant at all. He remained silent as she opened the door and motioned for him to go in.

The second the doors were shut, he started walking around the place. "I'll check everything out. Once your security detail gets here, you may want them to check in with the chief. He'll need their information."

She nodded and tossed her purse and sunglasses down on a glass table.

"Well, I suppose this will have to do," she said in a disapproving voice loud enough for him to hear how bored she sounded.

He ignored her and moved around the massive three-bedroom place, checking every closet and room and even the garage.

When he returned to the living area, she was reclining on a white leather sofa, glancing down at her phone as if she was bored.

"All clear," he said, heading towards the door.

"Oh, Sawyer, I mean..." She giggled. "Officer, could you stick around until my security gets here? They say they're only half an hour away."

"I'm sorry..." he started but she sighed and tilted her head.

"Your chief did say to take care of me." She patted the spot next to her on the sofa. When he remained standing, she frowned. "How about a drink?"

"I'm on duty," he said.

"No, you silly, for me." She got up and walked over to the bar area.

It had been a very long time since he'd been called silly. Junior high maybe? He watched her while she poured herself a martini. She looked like she'd spent quite a few nights behind a bar.

She walked over to him with the drink in hand and tugged on his hand until he sat down. Since his weapon was by his side, he had to adjust it as he sat on the low furniture.

"There, now isn't this better?" She sat next to him, leaning closer until her breast brushed his arm.

Then she leaned down and slowly sipped the martini, making sure to lick her lips as her eyes met his. She reached over and set the drink down, causing her vest to fall open and expose her full, round, puckered left nipple. He kicked himself instantly for looking at it, for being a total man and letting desire well up instantly at the sight of tits. Even if they were really nice tits, his mind screamed at his body for the gut reaction.

"Miss Owen, I understand you're used to how things are done—"

He didn't get any further because she plastered herself to him. Her long-manicured fingernails raked over his crotch, causing his cock to jump at her demands. When her bright pink lips descended to his, he jumped up quickly, bumping the coffee table and causing her drink to spill.

She laughed, actually laughed at him.

"I'll wait outside," he said firmly.

"Don't be ashamed. I'm sure it happens to some men. The next officer they send my way will know more about pleasing a woman," she called after him.

He stopped, his hand on the fancy door handle, then he turned back towards her, his eyes narrowed.

"You can think whatever you want about me, but the men on our police force are not here to please you. We're here to serve and protect, and there is nothing in the rules that says I can't haul you in for assaulting an officer if you jump on another Twisted Rock officer like you just did me."

She chuckled. "Don't be sour." She stood up and walked closer to him. "I won't tell anyone." She ran her finger over his lips slowly and he gripped her wrists to pull her back a step. "It's our little secret." Her hand escaped his and she slowly ran it over his crotch as a low moan vibrated from her chest. "You do have such powerful... tools." She winked and turned away. "It's too bad you're afraid to use them. Go." She waved, dismissing him. "Wait outside."

NINE

A PICTURE IS WORTH EVERYTHING...

Rose was going stir crazy. She needed to get out of the house. But ever since the news of Kristy Owens's affair with Isaac had broken, she'd feared to step foot out of her front door.

There were normally several cars parked at the end of her long driveway, and she was afraid that whatever she did, she'd be followed and harassed.

Hunter had arranged for another meeting with the detective for tomorrow since he had to drive back home for the night, he'd promised her he'd return long before the meeting tomorrow. Which had left her alone in the big mansion again that night. Trapped.

Last night, she'd dreamed the entire night about finding Isaac's body again. At one point, she'd imagined him standing over her bed, looking down at her with such a lost look, such desire as if they were stuck in two different realms and he understood they could no longer be together. When she woke, she'd been crying for him, which had given her another headache.

When her cell phone rang, she was surprised to see the animal shelter's name on the screen.

"Hello?"

"Hi, Mrs. Clayton, Tsuna is ready for you to pick up. If you want, we're open until five today."

"Oh." She smiled instantly, remembering the small dog. She glanced down at her watch. "I'll be there in... half an hour."

"No rush, she'll be here for you."

"Thanks." She hung up and looked for her keys.

She picked them up from the mantel and was halfway to the door before she actually looked down at the set of keys in her hand.

It took her a moment to realize what was wrong with them. The tiny four-leaf-clover keychain she'd given Isaac on their short one-day trip to Ireland stared back up at her.

She hadn't seen these keys since... Isaac had disappeared. She'd always believed that Isaac had the keys on him when his plane had gone down. Steadying herself by placing her hands on the back of the dining room chair, she set the keys down on the table. She looked at them as if they'd jump up and bite her as her mind whirled.

With shaking hands, she pulled her cell phone out of her back pocket and dialed the first number she thought of.

"Hi." Just hearing Sawyer's voice settled her world.

"Isaac's keys. I found them. They were..." She turned her eyes to the mantel and frowned. "They were on the mantel." It sounded silly when she said it, but there it was.

"Okay..."

"No, I'm not crazy. They were lost, or so I thought, at the bottom of the Atlantic with my husband. Don't you see? The keys are here. The keys to his car, his hangar, the jet."

She felt her breathing hitch and her head grew light. She was instantly afraid she'd pass out again.

"Are they the only set?" Sawyer asked, sounding interested finally.

"To the hangar and the jet, yes. His car, no, we had two sets."

"We'll be right over." He hung up and she sat down on the chair until her breathing settled again. She watched the keys, as if afraid that if she took her eyes from them, they'd disappear again.

When the doorbell rang, she stood up, keeping her eyes on the keys and walked backward to open the door for Carson and Sawyer.

"There." She pointed to them across the room.

"You're sure these are your husband's?" Carson asked.

"Yes, I bought him the keychain in Ireland on our honeymoon. We had a layover and spent the night there before coming home. He never removed it from his keys."

Carson bagged the keys. "Where did you find them?"

"The mantel. I was running late." She turned to Sawyer. "Tsuna's ready and I was so excited to pick her up, it didn't register that they weren't my keys until here." She motioned to the spot she was standing in. "Where have they been? How did they get here?" She shook her head.

"We'll have to find out. You said you held them?" Sawyer asked.

"Yes," she sighed. "I suppose my fingerprints are all over them now." She closed her eyes. "God, I'm so easy to set up. Just like all the stupid people in those CSI shows and movies."

She heard someone chuckling and opened her eyes to see Carson smiling at her. "I'll have to remember that one.

As long as you didn't touch every single key, here," he tossed her his keys. "Show me how you held them."

She gripped the bundle of keys like she had earlier. "Like this."

"See, in your fist. I doubt there'd be more than one good print of yours on here. We might get lucky and get someone else's as well." She handed him back his keys.

"Thank you." She touched the man's arm.

"We'll follow you to the animal shelter," Sawyer jumped in. "It's kind of... crazy out there."

"Oh?" She turned to him with a frown.

"Yeah, ever since Kristy Owens arrived yesterday, the entire town is flooded with news stations and paparazzi vans."

"She's... Is that woman in Twisted Rock? Why?" She sat down in the chair.

"Why else? To get her three seconds of fame," Carson said. "Sawyer spent some time with the woman yesterday. What's she like in person?"

"Scary," she thought she heard him mumble. "Come on, let's go get Tsuna. I'm sure she can't wait to get home."

With a police escort, she drove to the shelter and waited for the worker to bring out the little dog who'd stolen her heart.

Tsuna was carried out, and the little dog's entire body shook with pleasure when she spotted her.

"I've never seen this little girl so happy before," the woman said as she handed her over to Rose. Tsuna instantly wiggled in her arms, crying happily, and kissed her face as Rose laughed and held the little dog tight. Tears streamed down her face and she closed her eyes as emotions overwhelmed her.

When she opened her eyes, the woman was smiling at

her. "Like I said, I've never seen her this happy before." She touched her arm.

"Thank you." She smiled.

"We'll get this paperwork finished quickly so you can take her home." She motioned for her to follow her into a small area.

Less than half an hour later, Rose walked out holding the little dog in one arm and a packet of paperwork in the other.

Sawyer and Carson stood leaning against the front hood of the patrol car.

"Who's this?" Carson walked up and gently scratched Tsuna between the ears. The little dog did a happy shake and looked up at her for approval.

"This is Tsuna. Tsuna, this is Carson." Tsuna licked his hand.

"Cute. I've been thinking of getting another dog since my Gus died last year." His eyes turned to the shelter.

"What's been stopping you?" Sawyer asked.

Carson chuckled. "The fact that if I walk in that place, I'll probably come out with more than one animal."

Sawyer chuckled. They all turned when a car pulled into the drive. Instantly, Rose tensed.

"We'd better go before they have a chance to..." Carson started, but it was too late. The van stopped, and a camera crew jumped out, already filming.

Sawyer grabbed her arm and quickly rushed her back to her car as she tucked Tsuna tight against her chest for protection.

"Straight home," he warned her as she got in the car.

"I need supplies for Tsuna." She nodded to the small dog who was now shivering from fear in her lap.

"Home. We'll grab what you need after we make sure you get there safely."

She nodded and started her car. The drive back home was stressful, since the van and a few others followed them back, as far as her gates. She continued up the drive, but the patrol car stopped, blocking the entrance. She knew that Sawyer and Carson would keep anyone from entering her property and she thought that it was past time to get the gate fixed.

Parking in the garage, she snuggled Tsuna to her chest and walked towards the back porch. Stopping only a few feet from the garage, she gasped.

Every board that she and Sawyer had hammered into place the other day was destroyed. Some of the large pieces were completely missing, leaving gaping holes where they once sat.

She gripped the small dog to her chest as if, somehow, she could make it all better. Tears streamed down her face.

"Hey," Sawyer said directly behind her. He was pulling her into a hug, and she buried her face into his shoulder. Tsuna gave a little squeak between them, waking her up. She jumped back and checked the dog.

"She's okay," he assured her. "Carson will fill out a report for all this and file it." He nodded to the destruction. "I know we talked about it the other day, but it appears that your neighbor Boone Schneller is stirring up trouble after making bail."

"Do you really think he did this?" She motioned to the mess. "Just because I won't let him cross my land anymore?"

"He's known around town for holding a grudge. He was top of my suspect list for piercing my tires, but since we didn't have proof..." He sighed.

She had forgotten about that and nodded. "I'll just have to be more diligent." She moved towards the door.

"You can't become a prisoner in your home. How about those security cameras? I looked into a few brands and have some information I can send you."

She nodded. "I'll have the new contractors look into it, as well as fixing those gates." She looked back down the long drive at the vehicles still parked on the street.

When she spotted a few cameras pointing in her direction, she carefully stepped over the destruction and opened the back door.

"I'll wait here. Carson's going to go get Tsuna a few supplies." He stepped in after her as the patrol car disappeared back down the driveway.

"Thank you." Setting Tsuna down on the rug, she busied herself by pulling out a bowl and filling it with water for the dog. "How about a cup of coffee?"

He nodded, and she turned to complete her task. It was strange, being alone with him again for the first time after what he'd done to her upstairs.

Her body ached for him to touch her again, but now there was all this... Isaac mess between them and she doubted he would ever look or touch her again the way he had before.

Setting the mug down on the table, she motioned for him to sit. "How about some crackers..." She turned to go, but he reached out and grabbed her hand lightly. He held it until she exhaled and met his eyes.

"Rose, nothing has changed between us," he said softly.

"Hasn't it?" She tilted her head slightly as she studied his eyes. She was mesmerized by what she saw there; it was so hard to look away.

"Not as far as I'm concerned. Unfortunately, I have a job to do and I can't let this... get in the way of clearing your name. Not when there's a possibility someone could use it against you."

She thought about what he was saying and nodded after a moment. "Then, until after this is settled, friends?" She twisted her hand in his until they were shaking.

He smiled and nodded. "Friends," he said softly and just the way he said it caused her knees to almost buckle.

"I have a cherry pie I made the other day. Would you like—"

"Yes," he answered quickly and smiled. "Pie is my kryptonite."

She laughed. "Good to know. I may need that knowledge in the future."

He dropped her hand and she turned to head back to the kitchen. She smiled down as Tsuna followed behind her and sat at her feet while she cut them each a slice of pie and dabbled cream over the top of each one.

That night, she and Tsuna snuggled in her bed and watched the news. Once again, Kristy Owens filled her screen. Only this time, she wasn't alone. There were images, snapshots of her with Isaac at an event, two months prior to his death. Images of the younger couple, who had apparently met at college in Boston. Isaac seemed so young and so happy as he held onto a very young Kristy Owens, known back then as Kristina Renaldo. Anger flooded Rose as more and more shots of the couple appeared, shots that, according to the dates shown, had been taken after she and Isaac had married.

There was one from less than two weeks after they'd returned from their honeymoon when they were living in

New York City. But the image that totally broke her heart was the image of Isaac holding a small baby boy. The child couldn't have been more than a day old, and Isaac smiled up at the camera like a proud father.

Tossing the blankets from her legs, she jumped from the bed. Tsuna watched her as she paced back and forth in front of the television set.

"Owens, for her part, has been seen recently playing host to a very hot cop in the small town of Erie." An image of the blonde seductress on the arm of Sawyer made Rose sit on the edge of the bed. Her heart felt like it had just burst in her chest. She covered it with her hands as she watched a few more images of the pair flash by. They were all from the same day, but while one was clearly at the police station, the other was at a private residence were Sawyer was stepping in the front door behind Kristy. The jumpsuit the woman wore hugged every curve on the busty blonde. "It's rumored he's been on private security duty since the actress arrived in town. Could this be the beginning of a new scandal as the town's police force continues the investigation into the death of Isaac Clayton?"

There was a quick commercial break and Rose sat there, replaying her conversation with Sawyer earlier that day. Had he been backing off for more reasons than not wanting to bungle the investigation? Maybe it was just an excuse to break things off with her so he could pursue Isaac's lover.

Obviously, Rose hadn't even known how to keep the man she'd loved for most of her life loyal. How was she expected to keep the interest of a man like Sawyer? What did she really know about him anyway, other than he'd been in Twisted Rock for a little over a year? He'd lived in Cleveland before moving into town.

The next report started and caught her attention again.

"Our next segment is about the financial gains that are possible for Kristy Owens from pursuing Rose Clayton. Could Kristy Owens's motives be the financial turmoil she's been in the past six months? After signing a lucrative contract with Fuller Films earlier this year, Owens breached the deal a little less than two months later. Fuller Films successfully sued Owens and won back almost double the amount of the advance. It's been rumored that Owens has struggled financially since then and is on the brink of bankruptcy. Could Owens be pushing Rose Clayton's guilt in the murder of her husband in order to get her hands on Isaac Clayton's fortune? The fortune has been estimated in the high millions, left to him by his mother after her suicide when Isaac was only five years old. The fortune was left to Clayton's late wife upon his death. If Rose Clayton is found to be guilty of her late husband's murder, just where would the vast fortune go? Could Kristy and her son with Isaac actually get Isaac Clayton's father and the courts to reverse the will implemented almost a full year ago?" The newscaster turned towards another camera. "Here to answer that question and more is Owens's lawyer..."

Rose shut off the television, unable to listen to any more. Walking over to her dressing table, she looked down at the ring on her finger. The ring Isaac had placed on her hand when he'd promised to be loyal to her. Pulling it off, she shoved it in the bottom of her jewelry box and turned to look at the room.

It was lies, all lies. Sure, Isaac had left her comfortable after his death, but there was nowhere near what they had hinted at. The house and cars were all paid off, and his life insurance check had come six months after his death had been ruled an accident. There had been their checking and savings accounts as well as a few bonds and stocks. The fact was, before his death, she'd been a rising artist in New York. Some of her paintings had sold for six figures, money she hadn't had to touch.

She continued to pace as the small dog watched from her spot on the bed.

Carson had gone a little overboard purchasing things for Tsuna. The man had gotten two dog beds, food, bowls, treats of every kind, and even several toys for the girl as well as a leash and a new collar.

Rose couldn't imagine not having the small dog up with her in the bed at night.

"I have to do something." She turned to look at Tsuna, who tilted her head as Rose spoke as if she was trying to understand what she was saying. "I'm so mad right now, I could..." She kicked out and her bare toe hit the soft ottoman at the base of the bed. "Ugh!" She groaned with frustration. "How about we tackle hanging the new shelves in the sunroom?"

When the little dog stood up and barked, Rose took it as a yes. She snatched her up and descended the stairs.

She was halfway down them when she heard the noise. Every fiber in her body froze. Her breath stuck in her throat as she watched a dark shadow cross at the base of the stairs.

She'd been so determined to get to work, she hadn't bothered with turning on a light. She reached for her cell phone, but it was back on her nightstand upstairs.

Glancing back, she wondered if she could make it up there and lock the door before whoever it was jumped her, or worse.

She took one step back, thinking that stealth was the

best chance she had. The old stairs had a different idea as the floorboards let out a loud creaking sound.

Without waiting for a better chance, she darted up the stairs as Tsuna barked in her arms. She was just about to open the door when she heard her name and froze.

"What the hell are you doing here?" She turned on Hunter, who stood at the top of the stairs, a little breathless and laughing at her.

He reached over and flipped on the light, casting the entire upstairs into brightness. Rose had to blink a few times before she could see.

"I told you I'd be back for your meeting in the morning." He smiled at her, then his eyes fell to Tsuna and his smile disappeared. "What is that?"

She looked down and laughed. "This"—she held the small dog up and kissed its nose— "is Tsuna. My new dog."

"I'm allergic to dogs." He frowned.

"I know, but she's so small, I didn't think it would be a big deal. Besides, you're only here every other weekend now. I figured she could stay out of the room you stay in." She shrugged.

"Still." Hunter shook his head as Tsuna made little growling noises at him. "It's a dog."

"Shush, this is Hunter. He's family." She held onto Tsuna, whose entire body vibrated with growls. "You've scared her." She rolled her eyes at Hunter. "You scared me."

"Sorry. I thought I'd drive back tonight, sneak in, and you'd be none the wiser. What were you doing up?"

"I was pissed." She motioned back to her room. "Isaac's mistress is all over the television. Pictures of them together." She felt the anger return.

"How about we head downstairs? I'm starving. I was

heading to the kitchen to make a sandwich when you scared the hell out of me."

"I scared you?" She walked over and wrapped her arm around her brother, tucking Tsuna under her free arm. "What do you think you did to us?"

TEN

S0, YOU'RE BEING INVESTIGATED...

The small room was packed. Since he couldn't officially take part in the questioning, Sawyer stood behind the one-way mirror with Carson and a few other investigating officers. The chief had tried to keep them out, but Carson had persuaded him that they might need to know some answers and see how Rose answered them.

Rose sat next to Hunter, looking very nervous as the detective sat across from her.

"As you know, there's been more information come to light since the last time we talked," the detective started. "With your lawyer's permission, we'll continue the line of questioning."

Hunter nodded and gave Rose a reassuring smile.

"I'm ready." Her shoulders were straight as if she was trying to project courage, but he could tell she was nervous.

As the detective started his questions, Sawyer watched Rose closely. She'd chosen a soft rose-colored blouse with a slight V neck. She wore delicate silver necklaces over the softness of her neck with matching bracelets on each wrist and several rings on each of her fingers. For the first time since he'd known her, she was without her wedding ring, which caused something deep inside him to stir.

He watched the scene and wished he could punch something when the questioning turned harder and more direct. He'd been on the other side of the glass plenty of times. Hell, he might even have pushed her as much had he not been so sure of her innocence and so damn attracted to her.

Turning away, he decided he couldn't take anymore. "Take notes, will you?" he asked Carson. "I've got to get some fresh air."

"Sure," his partner said, slapping him on the back lightly.

He stepped outside, expecting a few minutes of quiet. Instead, it was his turn to be bombarded with questions from the media. Microphones and cell phones were shoved in his face as cameras rolled or snapped pictures of him.

"Is it true you're involved with Kristy Owens?"

"How long have you and Kirsty Owens been seeing one another?"

"Is your affair with Miss Owens going to hinder the case against Rose Clayton?"

He blamed himself for freezing up. But, upon hearing Rose's name, he spun around and stormed back into the station.

"What was that all about?" someone asked him.

He turned to see Rick Brown and Sue Madsen walking towards him.

"Media frenzy." He stormed past them and thought he heard them chuckle.

He stepped into the break room to pour himself a cup of coffee and spotted his face on the television set that was always running. Walking over, he turned on the sound and watched the news report. Apparently, it was common knowledge that he and Kristy Owens were having an affair. Even more shocking was when a fuzzy image of him holding Rose with Tsuna tucked between them as he comforted her at the destruction of her back deck flashed on the screen and the newscaster actually said the words "deadly love triangle."

He marched into the chief's office without knocking.

"I am not having an affair with Kristy Owens," he blurted out.

The chief narrowed his eyes at him, then motioned for him to shut the door. Sawyer slammed it.

"Contrary to what every news station is saying right now, I didn't—"

"I know," the chief broke in, almost laughing. "Sit." He motioned to the chair across from him.

Sawyer was too pissed to sit, but when the chief asked you to sit, he didn't ask a second time.

"We think Owens started the rumor herself to get the media off her financial problems."

He remembered the report mentioning something about it. "How deep is she in?"

"Bad. I've just been going through it all." He turned his screen around. "She's dollars away from heading into bankruptcy. She dumped her son off on her mother a few months back because she couldn't afford childcare while she worked."

"They mentioned something about breaking a contract?" he asked.

"Yeah, Fuller Films signed her for a remake of some classic film, but the contract had a gag order clause. One of the first things Owens did was to sell an interview and do a tell-all to one of those entertainment magazines. You know, the kind at every check-out stand?"

"Yeah." He shook his head. "Not the brightest one there."

"No," he agreed. "I'm sure the entire Owens thing will blow over, but for now, my concern isn't your relationship with the actress." He punched a button and the fuzzy image of him holding Rose popped up on the screen. "Is this going to be a problem?"

"Does it have to be?" he asked, already knowing the answer. "No." He shook his head. "No problem."

"Good." The chief turned his screen around again. "For now, you're off the case. I can't afford the time I'd waste on an investigation into one of our officers."

He nodded. "What about Carson?"

Deter's eyes moved to his. "For now, I need him where he is. You can switch to evening shifts. Go see HR to arrange everything." He waved him away.

Sawyer walked out of the office feeling defeated. He'd come to Twisted Rock to make a fresh start, maybe even climb the ladder and someday become chief himself, later in life, when he wanted to sit behind a desk. Now, thanks to some movie star with financial problems, he was off the first real case that the small town had seen in almost a decade.

An hour later, he was letting himself into his house while Ozzy danced around him, as if he had surprised him with a midday visit on purpose.

He stripped off his uniform and pulled on a pair of worn jeans and a T-shirt, grabbed a cold beer, and walked out onto his back patio barefoot to watch Ozzy run around the yard. It was reported to be one of the last warm fall days for a while. They were expecting the first snowfall later next week and the temperature would be on a steady decline starting later that evening.

He had just finished the beer when a car pulled into his drive. The late model rental parked behind his truck. When Kristy Owens stepped out, he frowned.

"Miss Owens." He nodded to her as she stepped onto the back patio.

"What a quaint little place you have here." The tone of her voice was pleasant, but he reminded himself that she was an actress.

"Thanks. What can I do for you?" he asked as Ozzy rushed up to sniff the newcomer's feet.

"Oh, how cute." The woman knelt and gave attention to the dog for a moment before straightening again.

Today's outfit was just as revealing as the previous one. The white suit was replaced with a pair of tight cream-colored pants the color of her skin and a bright yellow blouse that hung off one shoulder, almost exposing her left breast completely. She wore high-heeled boots that made her almost the same height as him.

"What can I help you with?" he asked again.

"I just came out here to talk, you know." She rested her hand on his arm. "About what everyone is saying on the television."

"There's nothing to it..." he started, but she broke in.

"So, you're not seeing Rose Clayton?"

"No." He sighed. "She's simply a friend."

A smile played on her lips. "I was thinking about the other day." She moved towards him and he held up his hands to stop her.

"The chief took me off the case." He saw the change in her eyes as her smile fell.

"What has that got to do with us?" she purred.

This time it was his eyes that narrowed.

"There is no us," he said clearly. "I know that you're probably used to men falling at your feet, but I can't afford to get tangled in the web right now." He stepped back.

Her bottom lip actually quivered as she frowned at him.

"Everyone deserves a little fun." She moved closer to him.

He took her wrists in his hands easily, holding her away from him.

"I've got somewhere to be." He snapped for Ozzy to come.

She pouted again. "If you change your mind…" She ran a finger down his chest. "You know where to find me."

He waited until she climbed back in the rental car and drove away before shaking his head. He'd been hit on plenty before, but never by someone so… driven before.

He locked the house and helped Ozzy up into the truck. A nice long drive would settle his mind.

He hadn't planned on ending up at Carson's place, but when he pulled into the driveway, his friend met him on the front stoop.

"Evening." Carson handed him a beer. "Did you come to sulk?" He bent and scratched Ozzy's head.

"No, I came so you could fill me in on the rest of the interview." He sat down when Carson offered him a spot.

Carson sipped his own beer and sat across from him. Ozzy jumped up next to his partner and enjoyed a snuggle. His dog was on a friendly basis with most people in town. He'd brought him over to Carson's place on numerous occasions over the last year.

"Not much happened after you left. Anderson asked her the same questions over and over. Rose didn't slip up once and answered everything the same as she had before."

"Have you found out anything more?" he asked, getting to the heart of why he was there.

"No." Carson sighed. "I'm not supposed to share anything I do find out." He looked at him. "Chief's orders."

"Right. You still think she's innocent?"

"Rose?"

He nodded.

"Hell, yes. I saw what losing Isaac did to her. Even the best movie actress in Hollywood couldn't fake that."

Sawyer ran his hands through his hair. "Who's on the top of your list?"

"Hell, I'm not a detective, but after hearing more of what's been going on, there are a few people on the list."

"Yeah, just promise me one thing..." Sawyer started.

"Sure."

"If you find something that might... tip things in her direction, you'll let me know first?" he added.

His partner was silent for a while, then nodded his head quickly.

Driving home, he thought about what he knew about the case. He laid out the suspects and ran over the reasoning. He hated to admit it, but Rose was the one with the most to gain from Isaac's death. She'd gotten all his assets, stopped the affair—if she'd known it was going on—and got her freedom. Still, the lost look in her eyes for those few months after Isaac's disappearance ensured him that she had no clue her husband's body was rotting in a wall under her feet.

He pulled into his parking spot and let Ozzy out. The dog sprinted between his legs, barking. Thinking the dog had spotted a rabbit, he started walking towards the front door. He heard Ozzy let out a squeal of pain and then go silent.

"Ozzy?" He sprinted in the direction that he'd seen the dog run, calling his name.

Using his cell phone as a flashlight, it took him almost five minutes to find the unconscious dog. Blood seeped from a nasty cut on the top of Ozzy's head.

With shaky hands, he bent and caught up the dog, holding him close to his chest as he sprinted towards the truck.

Holding Ozzy in his lap, he drove fast towards the vet while he dialed the emergency number on his phone.

When he pulled into the parking lot, the vet and a staff member met him outside with a small gurney. Laying Ozzy down gently, he followed them into the clinic and answered any questions they had.

No, he didn't know what had struck the dog.

Ozzy had been unconscious for almost five minutes before he'd found him.

He sat in the waiting room when told to. His clothes were covered in blood, Ozzy's blood. He stared down at his hands and thought he might lose it if someone didn't come out soon and tell him his dog was okay.

Half an hour later, Carson walked in.

"Barb called." He nodded to the woman behind the front desk. "What happened?"

"Hell if I know. We left your place, and he jumped out of the truck when we got home. I thought he was chasing a rabbit, then I heard him cry out. It took me too damn long to find him." He ran his hands through his hair. He'd washed the blood off, but the memory was still there. He rested his head on them.

Carson slapped his hand on his shoulder. "Did you see anyone?"

"No, I didn't see or hear anything. Just Ozzy yelp out in pain."

Carson nodded. "I'll wait around and see how he's doing, then go and check out your place."

"Thanks." He looked up as the vet walked out.

"Ozzy's fine." She held up her hands. He liked Dr. Kelly. She didn't BS and always cut to the chase. "He has a nasty bump on the head. I've had to put in a drain to allow some of the bleeding and swelling to go down. I'll want to keep him for a few days to watch over him."

He nodded, not sure what she was talking about, and only focused on the fact that his dog was going to be okay.

"Do you know who hit him?" Dr. Kelly asked.

"No. Are you sure he was hit?" he asked.

Her eyes moved to Carson's and she nodded. "I'd wager by the butt of a weapon, most likely a rifle. I've seen it a few times before. You can almost make out the shape of the stock. Plus, there was a scrap of jean material in his teeth. Looks like he was on protection mode before he got hit."

"Can I get the material, and do you think you can get an impression of the mark?" Carson asked.

The woman held up a small baggie with a small chunk of dark jean material in it. "I can try for the impression. I'll call you tomorrow if I get something. Until then, Ozzy's resting comfortably."

"He's awake?" Sawyer started to move past her, but she rested her hand on his.

"I don't want him to get excited. I've given him something and he's resting. I want to keep him as still as possible to allow the draining. You can come back and see him tomorrow." She smiled up at him.

"Okay." He swallowed, then took a deep breath. "Okay," he said again. "You've got my number if anything changes."

She nodded. Sawyer turned towards Carson. "Let's go look for the asshat that did this to my dog."

They spent almost two hours scouring his land without finding any clues. There were some tire tracks on the main road about a mile from his place, but they could have been there for days. Still, he snapped a picture of them along with a few others.

By the time he crawled into bed, he was exhausted. He was a little surprised when his phone chimed with a message from Rose.

-I saw you on TV today.

He groaned. -Don't believe everything they say.

-You weren't taken off the case?

-That part you can believe, yes. I'm sidelined.

-What part were you talking about?

He felt like kicking himself for thinking about the report about him and Kristy.

-Nothing.

-The part about you and my husband's ex-mistress?

-I'm not supposed to talk...

He started typing, but she beat him to it.

-You're off the case now, so don't tell me you can't talk about it.

He groaned. She was right.

-I'm not seeing and have never seen Kristy Owens in any form other than to serve as protection by the chief's orders.

She didn't respond so he added.

-For the record, she's not my type. My type leans

towards a softer blonde-haired beauties with haunting blue eyes the color of the lake during a storm.

He frowned when the phone was silent. Then smiled when her last message came through.

-Thank you.

ELEVEN

Legal ease...

She woke to a little dog licking her face. Smiling, Rose pulled Tsuna closer to her as Tsuna wiggled and whimpered.

"Do you have to go out?" she asked and got her answer when Tsuna danced around and made happy little sounds.

She pulled a long sweater on over her T-shirt, slid on her slippers, gathered the dog, and made her way down the stairs.

Hunter was already awake and sitting at the kitchen table, glued to his laptop.

"Sorry, did I wake you?" he asked, looking over his computer screen.

"No, Tsuna has to go out." She opened the back door and the little dog rushed out. Too late, Rose remembered the missing boards and rushed after the dog, who had gracefully maneuvered over the missing pieces like it was an obstacle course.

She chuckled and leaned against the doorjamb to watch her.

"Why did you get a dog now?" Hunter asked from his spot at the table.

"I've always wanted one. I couldn't get one when we lived at home because of your allergies, and Isaac had always said no because they were a big responsibility." She shrugged remembering several of the arguments they'd had.

She'd tried to persuade him that if they got a dog, she wouldn't be so lonely all the time. Isaac's only argument was that they made messes and were a huge responsibility. Since she'd wanted to please him, she'd held off.

"It's small enough to be a rat," Hunter joked. But when Tsuna entered the house again, he still held back slightly. She instantly worried about his allergies. She'd never seen him have a fit before and wondered how bad they were.

"Is she going to bother you?" she asked, setting the dog down in her bed by the back door.

"No, I don't think so." He shrugged. "We'll see." He turned back to his computer. "There was a new report out this morning." He nodded to the muted TV and hit the remote. "It's about to play again. It should help our case."

"Our... case?" She frowned as, once again, Isaac's face filled the screen.

"We are following new reports that have surfaced overnight that the late Isaac Clayton, the lawyer from Twisted Rock whose body was found in his wife's basement, had taken part in an extortion plot along with his father, Sean Clayton, CEO of Clayton Law Firm, a prestigious New York law firm that boasts big clients such as..."

Rose turned to Hunter with a frown. "Extortion? Who? What are they talking about?"

Hunter hit the mute button. "It appears that Isaac's father has been blackmailing some of his more famous clients," he answered.

"That's terrible."

"There's even a new angle that says Isaac went to his father and told him he wanted out, and Mr. Clayton killed him for it."

She shook her head. "No, I can't see that... Sean loved Isaac. He was the best father." She turned to watch the TV again as images of Sean Clayton flashed, several that she had taken herself and had shared on social media long ago. Sure, the man had been MIA since Isaac's funeral. Since Isaac's body had been found, she hadn't spoken or seen Sean Clayton once. She didn't even have an updated phone number for him. The number she had in her phone went to a pizza delivery company now.

After Isaac's death, she'd closed her social accounts, unwilling to deal with all the well-wishers. She'd remained offline ever since, which meant she hadn't stayed in touch with most of the people from Isaac's past.

"Do you think it's true?" she asked Hunter.

He shrugged. "Who cares, if it gets the media and the police off your back."

She thought about it. "Yeah, but... you know Sean, the relationship he had with Isaac. Do you think he could do..." Her eyes went to the basement door. She had yet to go down there. Even when the new workers wanted to ask her questions, she remained at the top of the stairs.

She knew they would be there again today, trying to close the massive hole that had been her husband's grave. The crew had been working for the past few days repairing the wall in the basement as well as replacing all the windows in the house. She tried to avoid the basement and thinking about what she'd seen down there, so she'd allowed the new contractor, James Dylan, to do what he wanted so far.

"Anyone's capable of murder if pushed enough." Hunter went back to work on his computer. "I'm sorry, I still have work to do..." He nodded to the screen.

"Oh, sorry. How about I make you some pancakes?"

He glanced up and smiled. "Blueberry?"

"Sure." She chuckled and got to work. It had been over a year since she'd cooked for someone.

Whenever Hunter came down to visit, they would go out to eat or get takeout. She knew it was his way of getting her out of the house.

Making the simple breakfast was like breathing for the first time in a year. She had cooked simple meals for herself and occasionally baked, but it wasn't the same as cooking for someone. She'd missed it.

After they'd eaten, she cleaned up, showered, and went up to her studio. She carried Tsuna's bed upstairs with her and the small dog settled in the corner of the room to sleep. She glanced around the space.

There were easily over a hundred new paintings. So many new ones that she'd done after Isaac's death.

She started going through them, setting aside the better ones.

When she had more than a dozen, she called her agent to see if she could arrange a showing soon.

Julie Cromer had been her agent from day one. She'd gone to school with her in California. Julie's career as an agent had shot off quickly after moving to New York and securing several bestselling artists, which had at one point included Rose.

"Oh my god!" Julie answered her phone. "Please tell me you're doing okay."

"I am." She smiled.

"What's all this craziness I see on the news?" Julie asked.

She sighed. "I don't want to talk about that now. I want to talk about the stacks of art I have for you. Please tell me that you can help me unload some of these, so I can make room in my studio?"

Julie was silent for a moment. "How about I make a trip up there this weekend to see what you have?"

The possibility of Julie visiting again made her smile. She had come for Isaac's funeral and had stayed for a few days after. She'd come back once a few months later after Rose had recovered from her breakdown.

"I'd love it." She was already mentally planning the meals she knew Julie enjoyed.

"I'll head up first thing Friday morning," Julie said.

"I can't wait. See you then." Rose hung up and went through the stacks of art once more, making sure she agreed with what she'd set aside.

"Hey." Hunter knocked on the door. "I thought..." He stopped and looked around. "Wow. I've never been up here." He stopped and smiled at her. "Nice."

"Thanks." She waved him in. She hadn't let anyone else see the place, other than Isaac and Sawyer.

The memory of when Sawyer had been up there surfaced, and she turned away to hide the blush the memory caused.

"Julie's coming up this weekend," she said, moving the stack of paintings she had set aside.

"Thinking of selling these?" He helped her set them on her workbench, the same bench where Sawyer had pleased her like she couldn't remember Isaac ever doing.

She needed to get her mind off the sexy cop.

"Yes," she said, keeping her eyes down until her mind cleared.

"Cool, can I see?"

She stood back as he went through the pieces. When he came to the painting of Sawyer, he focused on it for a while, then glanced back at her.

"The cop?"

She nodded. "He has unique eyes." She focused on Sawyer's eyes in the painting and tilted her head as she looked at them.

Hunter moved on to the next painting.

"You shouldn't have any problem selling these. You've always been so talented." He touched her shoulder.

"Thanks." She jumped when Tsuna rushed over and started barking.

"Someone's here." Hunter nodded to the large window. "Looks like she's a good little guard dog." The doorbell chimed, and Rose scooped up the still-barking dog and headed down the stairs.

When she saw Carson and Detective Anderson on her doorstep, her breath caught.

"What is it?" she asked.

"Can we come in?" Carson asked. She motioned for them to step in, but Hunter stopped them.

"Do you have a search warrant?" he asked.

"Hunter, please, I will always cooperate with the police." She motioned for them to come in. As Carson passed by her, he reached out and scratched Tsuna's head.

She showed them into the sitting area and stood next to the fireplace. She hadn't lit a fire yet, but with the darkness of the sky outside, she knew she would need one later that evening. She set Tsuna down in her dog bed, but the dog went over and jumped onto Carson's lap to get attention.

"As you may have heard, there's a new theory going around about Sean Clayton," the detective said.

"Yes. I'm sorry, I can't give you any information about that. Isaac and his father never talked about work when I was around."

"We were hoping," Carson jumped in, "that is, we know your husband kept an office here."

"He did. I haven't really touched it since the last time he was in there." She motioned for them to follow her.

Opening the office door, she stood back as the two men entered. "You're welcome to look around. I'm not sure what you might find. I only go in there to dust." She stayed outside the doorway. It was too hard for her to cross the threshold, especially now.

"Thanks, we'll let you know if we find anything." Carson nodded to Hunter.

"My client has no knowledge of the law. Anything you find…"

"Yeah, we know." Carson interrupted and waved him off.

"How about some lunch?" she asked, hooking her arm through Hunter's arm. She could tell he was going to hover over the men and attempted to distract him.

"Actually, I was thinking of heading into town to pick up some more boards. I noticed you haven't replaced the ones that were torn up yet."

"Don't bother. I talked to my new contractor and he said he'd be happy to do it. He was picking up the boards at lunch today and should have the deck back to normal by the end of today." She smiled.

"New contractor?" Hunter frowned as they walked into the kitchen.

"RJ quit when they started investigating him. I think his

pride and his concern for his reputation got the better of him. I had hoped he'd come back after his name had been cleared, but..." She shrugged.

"Who'd you hire this time?"

"Someone from Fredonia, a James Dylan." She walked over to the fridge and got out the makings for grilled cheese sandwiches. She pulled out the chili she'd made a while back and heated it up while she grilled the sandwiches.

"Are you sure about this contractor?" Hunter asked her.

He continued to question her as she cooked. Finally, she handed him a beer and told him not to worry, she could take care of herself.

They had just sat down to eat when Carson walked into the room.

"We've taken a box full of papers. I've got a receipt for all of it here." He handed her a piece of paper.

"Why do I need a receipt?" she asked.

"It's for legal purposes. It shows what they took and where from." Hunter reached over and took the paper from her. "I'll hold onto that." He nodded to Carson. "Anything interesting we should know about?"

Carson tilted his head at Hunter. "We'll keep you posted." He turned to Rose and nodded. "You might want to check in on Ozzy. He's at the vet. Someone attacked him last night."

"What?" She jumped up, leaving her food untouched. "What happened?" She walked with Carson towards the front door.

"We're not sure. Sawyer had just returned from visiting me and someone attacked Ozzy. Knocked him out. The vet has him for the next few nights."

"Why didn't he tell me last night when we talked?"

Carson shrugged. "Not sure, but when I left him, he was still pretty shaken up."

"I'll go and visit Ozzy and see how he's doing. I have to get a few more things for Tsuna while I'm at it." She glanced down at the small dog, who was begging Carson for more attention.

The man bent down and picked Tsuna up and snuggled with her for a moment before handing her over. "Take care of this one." He scratched Tsuna again. "See you later."

"The cop again?" Hunter asked from the doorway.

"What?" She turned. "Oh, yes, someone attacked his dog. You remember Ozzy."

"Sure." Hunter frowned over at her. "It won't look good if you're seen with one of the lead officers in your case."

"Sawyer was removed from the case." She walked over and got her jacket from the hook. "I'm going to head into town. There are a few more things Tsuna needs. Do you want anything?" she asked.

"No."

Tsuna loved riding in the car. The little dog lay down in the seat and slept the entire trip to the veterinary office.

She turned to Tsuna. "Do you want to stay in here or would you rather—"

A knock on her car window caused her to jump. Her hand went to cover her heart as she squealed.

The sound of Sawyer's chuckle made her heart jump again, but for other reasons.

Rolling down her window she glared at him. "Did you do that on purpose?"

He smiled. "No, I was coming out of the vet's after visiting Ozzy and saw you pull into the parking lot. It's not my fault you were engrossed in a one-sided conversation with Tsuna."

She smiled. "I've heard you talk to Ozzy like this too."

He nodded, his smile falling slightly. "Is Tsuna okay?" His eyes moved to the sleeping dog.

"Yes, we're actually here to see Ozzy. Carson was just up at the house and told me what happened. Why didn't you tell me last night?"

"I didn't want you to worry. The thought of you trying to drive down here last night wasn't a pleasant one."

She nodded. She could see herself dropping everything last night to come check up on the dog.

"How is he?" she asked after getting out of the car.

"He's resting. The doc says I can take him home tomorrow."

"Oh, wonderful." She leaned against her car door. "Any clue who did it?"

He shook his head and leaned his hip next to hers against the car. "No, but when I find the guy…"

His eyes moved past her as a van pulled in.

"Damn it, why won't they leave us alone?" He nodded to the photographers.

"How about some lunch?" she asked out of the blue. Now that she knew Ozzy was okay, her stomach was reminding her that she'd left her lunch sitting untouched on the kitchen table. She was sure Hunter had finished it off, along with the rest of the pie she had in the fridge.

"I doubt we'd have any privacy around town. How about my place? I can make us some sandwiches and Tsuna can run around while we talk."

She nodded and quickly got back in the car. "See you there."

TWELVE

SIDESWIPED...

Sawyer followed Rose's car to his place. The van continued to follow them, so he made a call and about a mile from his turnoff, the van was pulled over by a patrol car.

When he parked beside her car, she got out and let Tsuna down on the ground.

"It pays to have friends." She smiled up at him as he walked towards her.

"Yeah. It's bad enough that the town has been invaded by paparazzi, now they're following my every move as well. Why don't they go back to stalking movie stars? I'm sure Owens loves the attention."

He took her elbow and led her to the back patio. Tsuna followed them, tip-toeing slowly through the tall grass.

Chuckling, Sawyer leaned down and picked the dog up.

"She doesn't look like she likes the tall grass." He set her down in the well-manicured lawn closer to the house.

Rose laughed and sat in the chair Sawyer pulled out for her.

"I'll step in and make us some sandwiches." He glanced back. "Keep an eye out for her. We have hawks and she's small enough to get scooped up." He was thankful Ozzy was big enough he didn't have to worry when the dog took off to chase wildlife.

Rose rushed to scoop up the dog and held her tightly as her eyes turned skyward.

He made them a couple of turkey sandwiches, threw a bag of potato chips into a bowl, and grabbed two sodas before heading back outside.

When he returned, Rose was leaning back and enjoying the sunshine, Tsuna fast asleep in her lap.

"Better enjoy the sun while it lasts." He set the food down. "We're supposed to get rain soon, then our first snowfall shortly after."

She nodded and shifted the sleeping dog. "I was just thinking about having some more firewood delivered this weekend. Stoneport Manor has a lot of things I need to keep track of. It's a pretty big responsibility."

"Why hold onto it then?" he asked, opening the soda and handing it to her. "Why not sell once you're done fixing it up?"

"Its home," she answered without a pause. "It's the place I want to raise a family someday." She nibbled on a chip. "What about you? You can't always live in the... How did you put it? The ultimate bachelor pad?"

"Why not?" He looked around the place. They were losing the sun already and he saw Rose shiver when a breeze crossed the deck and yard. He estimated they had less than ten minutes before the rain would start.

"I mean, haven't you thought about marriage?" she asked.

"I've been married. It didn't work out." Her eyes widened slightly, and he shrugged.

"What happened?" she asked between bites of her sandwich.

"Ann, my ex, decided I wasn't the man for her and ran off with my best friend from grade school, Nick," he said quickly. His theory was, the quicker he said it, the less the chance of the pain surfacing again. He was slightly surprised when, this time, with her sitting across from him, the old hurt didn't return at all.

"Ouch." She shook her head. "It looks like we both stepped into that pile."

He chuckled at her analogy. "We'd better head in, it's starting to rain." He grabbed up the plates and opened the barn door leading into the dining area.

Less than a minute after they stepped inside, a wall of rain started to pour down. A cold wind blew with it, so he shut the big door. He loved sitting there watching and listening to the rain with the door open when it was warmer.

"Just in time." He laughed when Tsuna walked over and lay in Ozzy's bed like she owned it. "She makes herself right at home, huh?"

"She's come a long way from the scared dog she was at the shelter." Rose smiled down at the dog like a proud mother.

"Have you had security cameras installed yet?" He motioned for her to sit down at the table inside as he went and grabbed a couple beers. "Sorry, I don't have wine."

She smiled and sipped the beer. "That's okay. I like beer, too. I ordered an entire security system. The company that's coming out next week to install a new gate controller will install almost a dozen cameras while they're at it. I'm having the best package installed—cameras, alarms, remotes, and passcodes for the gate."

"Good." He took a deep breath.

"Sawyer," she said after a minute of silence, "why did you invite me out here?"

He glanced around. "The house is quiet without Ozzy." She smiled and set her beer down. His eyes moved to hers and he blurted out, "I've been thinking about you."

She swallowed slowly; the movement was hypnotizing.

Just then, his phone went off and he cursed under his breath as he pulled it out of his pocket and frowned at the emergency message.

He stood. "I've got to go. The chief is calling me in."

"I hope it's not about... us, this." She shook her head as she stood up.

"No, he's got a job for me. I was supposed to have the day off, since I start the night shift tomorrow, but..." He walked towards the door. "I've got to change and head in."

She scooped up the sleeping Tsuna and followed him to the door. "Thank you for lunch."

He nodded. "I've got an umbrella." He opened the umbrella he kept by the door and started to walk her outside.

"No, I've got this, go to work," she urged him.

"I... Hell." He pulled her close and covered her lips with his. "There, now I won't be thinking about it all night."

She smiled. "Now I will. Until I see you again."

He smiled. "Go, before I convince myself to call in sick."

She rushed to her car, holding Tsuna like a football. He watched as her taillights disappeared down his driveway.

He headed upstairs, pulled on his uniform, and strapped on his weapon. When he stepped outside, he saw that the rain had caused a thick fog to settle over the field surrounding his house. The mist came floating off the water and drifted around the house.

He was a few steps from the grey blob he imagined was his truck when a dark figure rushed him from the left side and slammed him on the side of the head. The first blow hit him just below his left ear, knocking him face first into the tailgate of his truck. His face connected with the metal and he went down on his hands and knees.

It took him a moment to recover, but then a steel-toed boot connected with his left kidney, sending pain shooting throughout his entire body.

He quickly freed his weapon, but by then, the figure had drifted back into the thick fog. He thought about shooting into the darkness, but years of training forced him to lean against the tire rim and pull out his cell phone instead.

Carson answered. "Yo, what's up?"

"I've been attacked." He coughed and cursed when blood came out of his mouth. "Better get here fast. I don't know if he's gone."

"Home?" his partner asked.

"Yeah, son of a bitch jumped me as I was heading out." He listened to the noises around him as Carson told someone he was with what was happening.

"We're on our way. Hold tight. Do you have your weapon?"

"Yes," he said, feeling everything going fuzzy. "Better hurry, I'm fighting off passing out."

"Just don't shoot us when we drive in."

"Got it," he said as everything went white. He bit the inside of his lip and felt himself focus a little more. The pain in his back was almost as bad as the pain when he'd been shot in the thigh a few years ago.

"Damn it," he sighed. "Don't make fun of me if I pass out. I think he busted my kidney."

Carson replied. "Just don't die on me and I promise not to mess with you."

He could hear the sirens and fought to stay conscious until they arrived.

As if in slow motion, he watched Carson rush through the fog, the smoke swirling around his partner's body as if getting out of the way. He blinked, and when he opened his eyes again, he was strapped to a gurney as they loaded him in the back of an ambulance. He blinked again and was being rolled into the hospital, the bright lights blazing into his eyes. His stomach revolted, and he had to turn his head, so he didn't choke on the sandwich and the beer he'd just had with Rose.

A tray was put in front of his face and the straps on the gurney were released so he could roll slightly. When he moved, pain shot up into his ribs and stomach. Once he stopped throwing up, he answered as many of the hospital staff's questions as he could.

He was taken to X-ray and then rolled into a private room where he waited for a doctor to come in to visit him.

"You're pretty lucky," the doctor said a few minutes later. "It could have been worse."

"Really?" Carson said sarcastically from his spot in the corner of the room. Sawyer glanced over at him and he shrugged. "Sorry, go on."

The doctor turned back to him. "You have a concussion, a moderate one, and a lacerated kidney, not a burst kidney." His eyes moved to Carson, who nodded. "We'll want to watch you overnight, then you'll be on bed rest for about a week and off work for six."

"Six weeks?" He moved to sit up, but winced and felt his stomach roll again, so he held still.

"At minimum. You'll have to come in and let us check you out before we agree to let you go back to work."

Just then, the chief walked in. "What the hell." Deter walked over and shook his hand. "I've heard of crazy plans to get out of working, but this..." The man sighed and smiled down at him.

"Six weeks," Sawyer repeated.

"I'm sure you'll cut that in half," Deter said.

"I'll want to see him in two or three weeks. We can gauge it from there. Until then, he needs to rest if he expects to keep his left kidney."

"That bad?" he asked, feeling all the energy drain from him. The doctor nodded as an answer. "I'll be back in an hour to check on you. Rest," he said before leaving.

Deter turned to him. "Tell me you saw the bastard that did this."

Closing his eyes, he shook his head. "It was too foggy to see his face, but he was big, bigger than me, I'd wager. Steel-toed boots, like they use on construction sites."

The room was silent, and he opened his eyes again. "What?"

"Nat Willis?" Carson asked the chief. "He lost his job after that last DUI you gave him. He's out on bail as of last week."

"It's worth checking into." The chief nodded to Carson, who started to leave the room.

"I'll be back soon," Carson called back to him before leaving.

"What did you call me in for?" Sawyer asked, trying to

get comfortable, since he knew he wasn't going anywhere soon. They had stripped him of his uniform and his chief had his gun in his hands.

"We can deal with that later. You need to rest." The chief held up the gun. "I'll check this into the locker. You can get it back when you come back to work."

"Thanks." He glanced around. "Tell me they didn't cut me out of my clothes."

Deter chuckled. "No, they're there." He nodded to a bag on the nightstand.

"Good. I'd hate to have to get another uniform." He felt his head drifting. "Damn, did they say anything about my head?"

He closed his eyes and tried to focus.

"You've got a concussion. That's why they're keeping you overnight. The doctor just told you that."

"Right." Everything was foggy, and he'd already forgotten what the man had said five minutes ago about his kidney.

"Rest." The chief touched his arm. "Someone will be here, watching out for you."

He nodded and closed his eyes. When he opened them again, the room was dark.

Reaching for a light switch, he winced with pain and grabbed his side.

"Easy." Rose's voice was like nectar from the heavens. He reached out to find her, to touch her, but only found air.

"Rose?" he croaked out, surprised at how dry his mouth was.

"I'm here." A low light turned on across the room. "I didn't think you'd appreciate the bright lights."

Even the low light was causing pain in his head, and he nodded in agreement.

"What happened?" he asked as his memories of the afternoon escaped him. He remembered sitting on the patio eating sandwiches with her, then... nothing.

"Someone attacked you shortly after I left." She took his hand in hers and ran a finger over his palm. "You have a lacerated kidney and a concussion."

He heard the concern in her voice, and he glanced up at her and met her eyes.

"Hey, it could be worse." He gripped her hand tighter.

"How?" The tears that were streaming down her face caused his heart to hurt.

"You could have been hurt." He tugged her down until she laid her lips softly over his. "See, I'm feeling better already."

She smiled down at him and wiped the tears away with her free hand.

"Besides," he added, "now I get a vacation."

She shook her head. "Don't joke. I can't..." More tears rolled down her face. He reached up and gently wiped them away, ignoring the pain the move caused.

"Come down here." He patted the spot next to him on the bed. She gently moved to sit beside him.

"This is all because of me, isn't it?" she asked.

"No," he answered, unsure whether what he was saying was true or not. Then he remembered something.

"Carson?" He glanced around.

"He went to get some dinner. He said he'd be back in half an hour. He's the one who called me." She smiled. "I think he's trying to play matchmaker."

"Too late." He took her hand up to his lips. "I wanted you the moment I laid eyes on you." He kissed her soft skin again.

She shook her head and smiled. "That's the medicine talking."

He didn't have the energy to argue with her. "Ask Carson when he gets back if he found out if it was Nat Willis. I'm not going to be able to keep my eyes open much longer." He'd heard the beep on the machine and knew that the new pain meds flowing through his system would have him snoozing soon. "Stay with me if you can."

"I'm right here," she said as he drifted off.

This time when he woke, it was to the sound of arguing.

"What the..." He stopped when he realized Rose was in the room. "What is going on?"

"Will you please tell these... men"—Rose's eyes narrowed at Carson and the chief— "that it's the smartest move for you to come stay with me for a few days so you have someone watching over you twenty-four seven. I have plenty of rooms. Besides, my agent is going to be here tomorrow, so if it's Sawyer's reputation you fear for, then don't worry, we'll have a chaperone."

Sawyer laughed and so did Carson and the chief.

"It's not, and you know that's not the issue," the chief said. "It's the damn press in town. If they get wind that one of us is staying in the house with the woman under investigation in the murder of her husband..." He sighed. "Things could turn ugly."

"And they aren't already? It's been splattered all over national news that Sawyer is seeing my husband's ex-mistress and that we are in some twisted love triangle. Besides, you could always paint it that I'm under house arrest or that he's there for my safety, like security."

The chief was silent for a while and he looked over at Carson.

"Gee, I wonder what Sawyer think about all this? Too bad we can't ask him," Sawyer said with a smirk.

"What do you think?" Rose asked softly.

"I think I can ride this out by myself at home."

Three voices rose as they continued to argue about where he was going.

"Why must I go somewhere?" he finally asked.

Rose walked over and sat next to him. "You need someone there to watch out for you. You won't be able to put on your own shoes, let alone cook for yourself."

"The doc says it's best someone be with you at least for the first week," Carson answered.

"Then I'll call someone and have them watch out for me," he said clearly.

"Who?" Rose asked.

"I don't know. I'll hire a nurse if it will make everyone stop shouting over me."

"I think it's best if you have Rose look out for you." Carson stepped forward. "I can swing in daily and check up on you myself, as well."

"Whatever. Just stop yelling."

"We aren't," Rose said softly. "It just sounds like it because of your concussion." She smiled down at him. "Rest, I'll take care of everything."

THIRTEEN

A HELPING HAND...

Ozzy was enjoying the back seat of Rose's car as they drove away from the vet's the following day, but with every bump the car hit, Sawyer would make a strained and painful sound and hold his side.

"Sorry," she said each time.

"Why didn't I notice all these potholes before?"

She giggled and apologized again.

"How are you feeling?" she asked as they pulled into her driveway. There was a police cruiser sitting across the street and, thankfully, no media vans in sight. They had stopped off at his place before picking up Ozzy from the vet. The dog had a small cut on his head with three stitches. The fur around it had been shaved to the skin.

Rose had packed a bag of clothes for Sawyer along with a few books and his laptop. He'd tried helping her load everything up, but when he turned white as a sheet, she'd forced him to sit. He hadn't argued, and she wondered if it would be this easy to watch after him all week long.

When she parked by her garage, he got out and tried to pick up his bag.

"You take Ozzy." She handed him the leash. "Go introduce him to Tsuna. I'll take your stuff up to the room you'll be staying in."

He took the leash from her and made his way slowly towards the back deck.

The workers had finished replacing all the boards and the deck was back to normal. They had secured them with thick screws instead of nails, which she had been told would stop whoever had ripped them up from doing it again.

Hunter had left that morning after sharing breakfast with her. He said he'd try to make it back down sometime next week, but he was due in court and had a lot of preparation to do.

She'd often wondered why he'd chosen Buffalo, but after seeing how successful his business was, she understood.

She set Sawyer's bag down on the bed in the room directly across the hallway from her own. Hunter always stayed in the room at the end of the hallway and she wanted to keep it available if he made it back.

She would put Julie in her favorite guest room, the one she thought of as the robin-egg blue room.

She unloaded Sawyer's clothes and set everything in the dresser, making sure the attached bathroom had everything he'd need for his stay.

"There you are," he said from the doorway. He was leaning on the doorjamb, watching her. She noticed that his face was still pale, and he was a little winded. "The dogs are best friends. They're already snuggling up by the fire I built."

"You shouldn't have exerted yourself." She set his bag in

the bottom drawer and walked over to him. "I'll make us some dinner."

"I can help." He followed her down the stairs. When they reached the bottom, both dogs jumped up as if they had been caught doing something bad.

"You can watch." She smiled over at him.

"When is your friend supposed to be here?" he asked when he sat at the kitchen table. She had to nudge him into the chair, but he went without argument.

"Tomorrow midday sometime."

"You've known her... how long?"

"College. I went to UCLA and majored in art with a minor in business."

She'd come home from the store and put the fixings for boeuf bourguignon in the slow cooker before heading out to pick up Sawyer from the hospital. She'd enjoyed planning their meals for the week. The kitchen smelled wonderful already. She estimated another half hour and the meal would be ready, so she started on the homemade bread. Flipping on the oven, she pulled out the bread pan.

She'd made the dough a few nights ago and had almost a dozen loaves of it frozen in the large standup freezer just inside the mudroom.

She'd set out the frozen dough that morning and, now that it was thawed, rolled it once more. Taking a stick of butter, she greased the pan, covering the loaf with melted butter and some seasoning.

"What is that?" Sawyer asked from the table.

"Bread," she answered as she put the pan in the warmed oven.

"Homemade bread?" he asked, trying to see the roll.

"Yes," she smiled. "I make the dough ahead of time and freeze it so I can simply thaw, season, and cook."

"Real homemade bread?" he said again.

She chuckled. "Yes. Haven't you ever had homemade bread?"

"No, who has? I mean..." He shook his head. "No."

"Your mother didn't bake or cook?"

"Sure, things like spaghetti and mac and cheese, but not homemade bread. No one that I know had homemade bread growing up."

She glanced at the basement steps and frowned. She wanted a red wine to go with the meal but still hadn't brought herself to go down the stairs. The small wine fridge at the end of the island was empty.

"What's wrong?" He turned and glanced at the door.

"Nothing." She walked over to the door. "I'll go get some wine." She hadn't realized she was standing there, her hand on the doorknob, until Sawyer's hand rested on her shoulder.

"I'll go with you." He said softly, "Have you been down there since..."

She shook her head. "I... don't think..."

"Together." He took her hand. "You can do this. Remember, this is your home. You've nothing to fear."

She nodded. "It's not fear, it's the memory that kicks me in the gut." She opened the door. A cool blast of air hit her.

"Didn't they fix the hole yet?" he asked.

"Yes, but they haven't put in the glass door I requested. Since there was already a hole there, I thought I'd add an exit from the basement instead of just another wall." She glanced over at him. "It was the new contractor's idea to put in a large sliding glass door. He says that if I ever decide to finish the basement, it would be a big bonus."

Sawyer nodded. "Good idea."

They made their way down the stairs. Her heart

jumped when she noticed the new cement wall. There were large wooden planks over the space where the glass doors would be, which was where most of the cold air was coming in. She was thankful the workers had installed door sealing around the basement door so that none of the cold would escape into the upper rooms.

Still, as she looked across the empty space, she remembered the rainy night last week when she'd heard the rocks falling and felt the entire house shake. Her first thought had been that it was an earthquake. Then she'd remembered the basement wall and her worry about its safety the nights before Isaac had disappeared.

She'd grabbed her flashlight and headed down the stairs, expecting to see half of the house caved in. Instead, as she'd assessed the damage, the light had shone on a shoe. Shoes, she remembered. When she'd turned slightly, the light had landed on Isaac's face, still half-encased in cement. She'd screamed, dropped her flashlight, and rushed upstairs. Almost five minutes had passed before the panic attack had ended and she had composed herself enough to call 911.

"Here." Sawyer distracted her and stepped between her and where she'd last seen Isaac. He opened the wine closet door and nudged her inside.

She stepped in and instantly felt warmer.

"It's warmer in here than out there." She chuckled to cover the fact that her entire body shook with the memory.

He pulled her close and she realized nothing could hide the fact that she was shaking. "It's okay, I'm here," he assured her.

She wrapped her arms around him loosely, afraid to hurt him if she held on too tight. Her face rested on his shoulder. When she looked up at him, she smiled at the black eye he had. Reaching up, she touched it lightly.

"Here you are, bruised and hurting after someone attacked you, and I can't stand to walk into my own basement." She took in a deep breath.

"For good reason," he added softly.

"Still." She straightened her shoulders and dropped her arms. It was hard walking away from him, but she backed up a step. "Wine." She looked around. "Isaac knew more about it than I did, but I'm sure we can find something to go with the boeuf bourguignon." She started looking.

"I could help you if I knew what boeuf bourguignon was." He chuckled.

She smiled. "Beef stew. Red wine would go great, something dry maybe." She glanced at the labels.

"How many bottles do you have?" he asked, his eyes scanning over the storage area.

Isaac had put in the custom wine shelves himself the first month they'd lived in the house. Since it was on the north side of the manor and the outside walls were covered completely by dirt, they hadn't even needed a cooling system in place. The room, when the door was shut, stayed at a chilly 55 degrees Fahrenheit.

"I'd say close to two hundred." She pulled out a Merlot. "You do like wine, right?" He was standing with his hands tucked behind his back, as if afraid to touch the bottles.

"Some of it. I'm willing to try others," he answered honestly, and she smiled.

"If you don't, I'm sure when Julie gets here we can finish this off together." She held up her choice.

She tucked the bottle under her arm and opened the door. She avoided looking in the direction of the wall and practically sprinted up the stairs.

Sawyer shut the door behind him and the warmth of the

upstairs and the wonderful smells of baking bread and cooking beef soothed her instantly.

"I'll open this." He took the bottle from her. She wanted to argue, but the look in his eyes made her nod instead.

"I'll set the table." She disappeared into the formal dining room and busied herself with putting out the good place settings. Out of habit she pulled out the candles and was about to light them when she remembered who she was having dinner with and why Sawyer was here. This wasn't a romantic dinner like she used to have with Isaac.

Her face heated. She quickly put the candles away before Sawyer could see them and walked back into the kitchen.

"The bread smells wonderful," Sawyer said from the table. He'd poured her a glass of wine and she walked over to taste it.

"Perfect." She opened the oven, and the room filled with the smell of warm bread.

She dished up the stew and sliced a few pieces of the bread.

"Let me help." He reached for the bowl, but she nodded to the wine instead.

"You carry the wine and glasses in. I'll get the rest." She took the bread in first, then came back for the stew.

She sat down and smiled when Sawyer took the seat across from her.

"To a slow recovery," he joked, holding up his wine glass.

"To recovering." She smiled and sipped the wine. "Please, dig in."

"This looks amazing." He picked up his spoon and began eating. She was surprised at how much food the man could put away.

After dinner, Sawyer tried to help her clean up, but he was out of breath and turned white again, so she strong-armed him into going into the living room to relax. When she walked in half an hour later, he was fast asleep on the sofa. Both dogs were laying across his lap, snuggling together.

She gently nudged Sawyer and his eyes slid open quickly.

"You'd be more comfortable in bed," she suggested. "I'll watch Ozzy tonight, so you can get some sleep."

He nodded and stood up. She watched him sway slightly and reached for him.

Wrapping her arm around him, she took him upstairs. He walked like a zombie, slow and purposely.

"Do you need any help?" she asked as he sat on the edge of the bed.

"Shoes." He nodded to his feet. "Bending is a bitch." He ran his hands over his face. "I feel drugged."

"You did eat three bowls of stew and half the loaf of bread."

"Good food," he mumbled and smiled. "I can't remember the last time I had a meal so wonderful."

"You'll have plenty more this week. As long as you promise me you'll take it easy." She pulled off one shoe, then reached for the other.

"I'll try, but as soon as I feel better..." His eyes darkened. "Rose, someone has to figure out who's doing this."

"Carson seemed to think it was Nat Willis." She set his shoes at the end of the bed. "The man worked under RJ before he quit on me."

"Was he around the night Isaac...?" he asked.

"I'm not sure." She sat next to him on the edge of the bed and tried to remember. "I know the workers had finished the pre-wall work and left early before Sean and Hunter arrived. I can't imagine them sticking around and waiting until after we'd eaten dinner." She shrugged.

"Still, if he had issues, he could have come back that night and caught Isaac off guard." He reached up and rubbed his head, then winced.

"Are you okay?" she asked.

"Yeah, it hurts when I raise my hands over my shoulder." He rolled his shoulder and looked down at himself. "Dressing and undressing is going to be fun. Not to mention showering."

"There's always the bathtub." She smiled when he gave her a face that clearly said, 'not a chance.' "Come on, then." She stood and reached for his shirt.

He chuckled. "I think I can—" He shut his mouth when she gave him a look. Then he smiled. "Nurse Rose. I'm in your very capable and sexy hands."

She nodded. "Lift your arms as high as you can."

She slowly tugged the T-shirt the nurse had helped him into earlier that day over his head.

When the shirt was off, she gasped at the massive bruise over his ribs and his side.

The bruising covered his left shoulder and back, as well, and there was a nasty red scratch just above his hip where the toe of the boot must have connected with his skin.

Her fingers played gently over the area.

His breath hitched, and she stopped.

"It only hurts when I breathe," he joked.

"I'll start a bath." She got up, but his hand on hers stopped her.

"Rose, I can take care of myself."

"I know, but this is a lot more fun." She touched his

face. "Besides, I'd like to repay you as much as I can for helping me put in the flooring."

He nodded. "Bath it is then." He dropped her hand and she moved out of the room.

She poured some Epsom salts into the water to help with the swelling and left him to soak in the tub as she went downstairs to let the dogs out. The floodlights the workers had installed lit up the entire side yard and she watched both dogs rush out, do their business, and then come back in.

After they came back inside, she poured herself another glass of wine and took it upstairs. She settled in the window seat and pulled out her tablet to read a little. The dogs settled in the dog bed, snuggling close together as if they had been best friends their entire lives.

She had read for almost a full half hour when something caught her attention from the corner of her eye. Looking into the darkness, she thought she had probably just seen a snowflake fall and was about to turn away when the beam of a flashlight shone in the backyard.

Her entire body tensed as the light made its way closer to the house. Then she realized that whoever it was must be heading towards the hole in the basement wall.

Not sure what to do, she jumped up and rushed towards Sawyer's room. Without thinking, she barged in, calling his name.

He was standing in the bathroom door, a towel wrapped low around his waist.

"Someone's out there." She tried not to shout. "They're heading towards the basement." She turned as both dogs rushed into the room behind her.

"Stay here." He reached into his bag and pulled out a gun which looked personal since it was different than his service weapon she'd seen many times before in the holster on his hip.

She frowned, remembering that she'd emptied that bag and hadn't felt a gun in it earlier.

"Wait," she cried out, gripping his arm. "It's snowing. You can't go outside like that." She motioned to the towel. "Besides, you look like you're about to pass out." His coloring was off, and she could tell that he was drained.

He groaned and walked over to pick up his phone.

"Carson, someone's sneaking around here. Normally I'd take care..." He was silent. "Yeah, on the west side of the basement near..." He looked at her. "You know."

He hung up and turned to her. "He's five minutes away."

FOURTEEN

Twisted...

Sawyer pulled on his jeans quickly while Rose stood in the doorway watching him. Then he tossed the wet towel over the back of the chair and reached for his shirt, only to hiss with pain as his kidney reminded him that he was supposed to be taking it easy.

"Let me." She placed the shirt over his head carefully.

"Shoes." He nodded to them on the floor. He didn't want Rose to know that he was already winded just from putting on his jeans and would probably pass out if he had to bend over again.

"You're not going out there." She held his shoes away from him.

"Yes, I am. Carson's on his way." He reached for the shoes, only to have her jerk them high above her head. She knew that lifting his arms was pretty much impossible at this time.

"Rose," he warned.

"We'll wait for Carson. You are barely standing up as it is." She tilted her head as if challenging him.

Just then, they heard a shot from far away. It was more instinct than anything, but he grabbed her and threw her on the bed, then quickly covered her body with his.

Their breathing was the only sound as they waited for what seemed like minutes even though only seconds had ticked by.

"That was outside," she whispered, looking up at him. She'd dropped his shoes and both of the dogs were now cowering on the pillows of the bed.

"Damn it." He picked up his phone and punched Carson's number.

"Was that you?" Sawyer asked when Carson answered.

"What? I'm about a minute out."

"Shots fired." He relayed the details as he slipped on his shoes without tying them.

When he went to move, Rose was standing in the doorway, arms on either side of the doorjamb, glaring at him.

"Rose won't let me go check it out," he finally conceded.

"Alone?" Carson said in his ear. "Sit this one out until I get there. I'm pulling in the driveway now."

Since he was finding it hard to focus on her face, he tossed the phone down and sat down on the edge of the bed. "Happy?" he asked.

She smiled and nodded. "Yes." She turned to go, but he stopped her.

"You are not going outside," he growled. A wave of energy spiked at the thought of her outside and in danger.

She glanced back at him. "No, I'm turning on the front floodlights so that Carson can see clearly."

"I'll go down with you." He stood again and followed her downstairs. They turned on the lights as they went until almost every bulb in the house was lit up.

The knock on the door made Rose jump. One hand covered her heart and the other her mouth.

"It's Carson," his partner called from the other side of the door. "I'm freezing my butt off out here," he added.

Rose rushed to open it. "Did you find anything?" she asked.

"Haven't fully looked yet." His partner eyed him. "I knew you'd want to go out with me. Do you think you're up for it?"

Sawyer nodded. "I'm game." He started, but again Rose stopped him.

"You are not leaving me alone in the house by myself. Haven't you seen any horror movies?" She grabbed her jacket and slipped on a pair of mud boots. "Stay." She snapped her fingers and both dogs sat on their butts.

Sawyer already had his jacket on and an extra flashlight Carson had handed him.

"Let's go." He waited as Rose locked the front door.

"In the movies, they wait until you're outside, then sneak inside." She shrugged and tucked the key in her pocket.

Sawyer wanted to laugh, but he had to admit, playing it safe was smart at this point.

They walked around the massive manor, shining their lights in every dark corner as the interior lights and floodlights lit up the night. When they reached the place on the west side where Isaac's body had been found, she stopped.

"If you want, you can stay here," Carson said to them both.

"No." She held up her chin and marched quickly around the spot.

Their flashlights shone around and when they spotted fresh footprints in the snow, Carson pulled out his weapon.

He reached for his, but his partner shook his head. "You're not on duty. Besides, all anyone would have to do is blow on you to push you over and take that weapon."

He wanted to argue, but Carson was right. He was having a hard time just keeping up with the man at this point.

They followed the footprints away from the house towards a group of trees near one of the entrances to the beach area. When Sawyer's flashlight beam hit a pair of boots in the grass, everyone froze.

"Take her inside," Carson said, but it was too late. Rose gasped at the site of the body.

He pulled her into his arms, sheltering her eyes from the worst of it.

"Who..." She tucked her face into his shoulder. "Who is it?"

Carson walked over and reached down.

"I'm not sure. We'll have to wait until the coroner tells us." Carson shined his light where the man's face used to be.

Sawyer turned away and started walking back to the house. "I'll take her up."

"Watch out for anything," Carson called after him. "I'm calling this in."

The entire walk back to the front door, his eyes scanned the darkness. The only set of footprints were that of what he assumed was the victim. Could it be suicide? Why would someone kill themselves on Rose's land?

When they reached the front patio, the snow was falling faster and Rose's hands shook as she tried to unlock the door. He reached over and took the keys from her, then opened it himself.

The dogs greeted them as if they'd been gone for days

instead of fifteen minutes. Rose picked up Tsuna and held her to her chest as she went to sit in front of the fireplace.

He knew it was going to be a long night, so he started a fire in the fireplace. Quickly, the room was heated, and he went back into the kitchen and put on a pot of coffee.

This time, when the doorbell chimed, Rose was tucked under a blanket on the sofa with both dogs snuggling against her, a hot cup of coffee in her hands.

"I'll get it," he said, standing up.

"I'm supposed to be watching you, not the other way around." She started to get up, but he stopped her.

"I can open a door." He touched her shoulder. "Stay." He smiled down at her.

She nodded, and he walked over. The chief was standing on the other side with Carson and Brown.

"Come on in."

"The coroner just arrived. We've got the scene marked off and they're out there taking pictures and looking for any sign of foul play."

"Do we have an ID yet?" Sawyer asked.

"The wallet." Carson moved closer to the fireplace to hold out his hands towards the warmth. His partner had been outside in the falling snow for more than an hour already. "Belonged to Nat Willis."

"The construction worker?" Rose asked. "The guy who might have been the one who attacked Sawyer? Who would kill him?"

Deter broke in. "Rose, do you think you can get us some coffee?"

"Oh, sure." She jumped up and made her way back to the kitchen.

Deter turned to him. "Carson says you didn't see another set of footprints, is that correct?"

"Yes, but it had just started snowing harder. Another set, maybe say, coming from another direction, could have been covered by the time we made it out there. We could barely make out the first set."

Deter nodded. "How long after you heard the shot did you discover the body?"

"Ten minutes, tops," he answered.

"I hate to ask it, but, are you taking your pain pills? They could have distorted time."

"No, I'd just gotten out of the..." He stopped himself from saying bath. "Out of the shower. I was about to take them then head to bed. Besides, I called Carson right after we heard the shots." He turned to his partner, who nodded in agreement.

Deter sighed, then turned back to him. "How are you feeling?" he asked as Rose carried a tray of mugs and a pot of coffee into the room.

"I'll manage," he answered truthfully. He was in pain, but nothing he hadn't experienced before.

"Good." Deter took a cup and waited while Rose poured the hot coffee into it. "We'll try to finish up quickly, so you can get some rest."

"Sugar? Cream?" Rose held up a small jar.

There was a quick knock on the door. The dogs barked, and Rose rushed to gather them.

Sawyer wasn't surprised to see Detective Anderson walk in.

"I heard you had some excitement tonight," he said, walking in.

"I'll get another cup." Rose rushed from the room. Sawyer could tell she was uncomfortable around the detective and knew that most people were. The man's job was to question people, not be their friends.

Sawyer filled the detective in. When he was done going over the details, he sat in the chair by the fireplace. His head felt heavy and his eyes were burning from lack of sleep.

"Sawyer needs his rest." Rose stood up, gaining everyone's attention. "If you're done with him, I'll help him upstairs to his room. He needs to take his pills." She walked over to him, her eyebrows up as she waited for him to argue with her. Instead, he surprised her and everyone else in the room by standing up.

"She's right, I'm not one hundred percent at the moment. If you have any questions, you know where I'll be for the next few days."

"He'll be here for the next week," Rose corrected. "Doctor's orders."

He wanted to roll his eyes, but he was dizzy from the excursion and was pretty sure that if he tried it, he'd end up on the floor.

"We'll get out of your way," Deter said quickly. "However, we will keep a car stationed at the end of the drive to watch the place and be close if you need them." The men set their mugs on the tray and started towards the front door. Rose followed them while he stood at the mantel, waiting for her to help him up the stairs again. He doubted he could even walk across the room without blacking out.

When he heard the door shut and the lock slide into place, he bit the inside of his lip to try to keep himself conscious. His stubborn pride caused him to make his way slowly towards the base of the stairs. "I would help you clean up, but..."

"I'll do it after I put you back to bed." She took his arm. He felt like an invalid, but he let her lead him back to his room. Once again, she tugged off his shoes, putting them back in place. He pulled off his jeans, too tired to care if she saw him in his boxers and then sat on the bed and waited as she took the wet towel he'd set on the back of the chair back into the bathroom. When she came out, she glanced at him.

"I need help with the shirt," he said.

She slowly pulled the shirt over his head. "Where did you put your gun?" she asked, glancing around.

He pulled it out from behind him. "Can you put this in the top drawer?" He asked and nodded to the nightstand.

"Yes," she moved to touch it, then pulled back.

"The safety is on." He added.

"Good." She sighed and set the heavy weapon in the top drawer. "I feel better knowing you're here."

She lifted his legs up to the bed, and he crawled under the sheets, watching her once again disappear into the bathroom. She came back holding a glass full of water and a handful of the pills he'd been prescribed.

Without complaint, he swallowed them, and she set the glass down on a coaster on the nightstand.

"If it's okay with you, I'd like to keep the doors open," she said, and he thought he saw her shiver.

He nodded, already feeling his head grow heavy. "Night."

She reached down and turned off the light and left the room.

He didn't hear her go back downstairs and clean up. Hell, a semi truck could have run through his room and he wouldn't have stirred again.

When he did open his eyes, it was too bright sunlight coming through his window.

He moved and winced. He must have slept in the same position all night. His left arm was asleep and when he sat up, he was pretty sure there was drool on her fancy pillowcase.

He set his feet on the floor and cringed at the coldness of the hardwood flooring as he made his way towards the bathroom.

He'd had Rose pack a few button-up shirts since he couldn't pull T-shirts over his head himself. Pulling on a fresh pair of jeans and a flannel shirt, he carefully tugged on his wool socks and made his way down the front stairs.

Halfway down, he smelled something amazing and his stomach growled loudly. When he stepped into the kitchen, both dogs jumped up from the dog bed and greeted him.

"Morning," Rose said from in front of the oven.

"Whatever that is, it smells wonderful." He looked over her shoulder.

"Breakfast quiche." She smiled over at him. "You're looking better this morning."

He'd noticed the same in the mirror, but when he'd pulled on his clothes, he knew that looks could be deceiving.

"I feel a little better too." He leaned against the counter since the walk down the stairs had caused a little shortness of breath. "Can I help you with anything?"

"No." Her eyes ran over him and he could tell she was seeing his labored breathing. "Sit, I've got this. The quiche is almost done." She walked over and set a cup of hot coffee at the table near the back windows. "I thought we'd eat in here this morning, so we can watch the snow fall."

He glanced out the large windows and sighed. "I heard we're supposed to get a foot of the stuff. Our first major snowfall this season, and it's going to be a doozy."

She smiled. "I love it." She frowned as he sat down and sipped his coffee. "I am going to have to do something about Tsuna, though."

"What's wrong with her?" he asked, glancing over at the small dog curled beside Ozzy by the heater.

"She won't go outside in the snow. Ozzy even tried to get her to go with him, but it appears she doesn't like to get her feet wet."

He chuckled. "When she has to go, she'll go." He took another sip. "Ozzy was the same way when he was younger."

"Really?" She walked over when the buzzer on the oven went off.

"Yeah, Tsuna will get used to it."

Wonderful smells flooded the room when she opened the oven door, and his stomach growled loudly again. She glanced back and chuckled.

"Do you always cook like this?" he asked when she set what he thought of as a piece of artwork in front of him.

It was like a beautiful pie, the top decorated with squash, tomatoes, and bacon. The crust was twisted and there was even a flower-shaped piece of flaky crust on the top.

"No." She frowned down at him and he could see sadness fill her eyes. She took two plates from the cabinet and set them on the table, along with silverware and napkins.

She sat down and started cutting into the quiche.

"I used to cook a lot, for Isaac, but after... It took me a while to get back at it. Even then, it wasn't like before." She shook her head. "I guess I enjoy cooking for someone else instead of just cooking for myself." She set a slice of the quiche on a plate and handed it to him.

He waited until she had her own plate in front of herself before digging in. The first bite was like heaven. He'd imagined it would taste a lot like other quiches he'd had—a whole lot of egg and not a lot of seasoning—but this one had a bite to it.

"This is amazing." He took another bite. "Is that... jalapeno and green peppers?"

She nodded. "I hope you like spicy." She took a bite and smiled.

"I love it." He took more. "You could probably toss in a dozen jalapenos and I'd still be happy."

She was silent, and he could tell she was thinking about something he'd said. Wondering if he'd offended her, he jumped in.

"Did I say something to upset you?" he asked.

She shook her head. "It's just... Isaac couldn't stand spicy foods. I once made chicken enchiladas and he didn't even take a bite."

"His loss. I bet they were amazing. Just like this." To make his point, he reached for another piece but grunted when pain shot up his ribs.

"Let me." She scooped him another slice of the quiche.

"This is going to drive me crazy," he said as he sipped his coffee.

"What? Being waited on?" She smiled slightly.

"No, not being able to move."

"You'll just have to fill your time with other things. We have a lot of books in the library."

He thought of spending the next few days lying around and sighed. "I guess I was due a vacation. I had hoped to spend it someplace tropical. You know, scantily clad women in bathing suits and a tropical drink in hand." He smiled at her as she chuckled.

"We can crank up the heat and I can make us some margaritas," she suggested.

He wiggled his eyebrows. "Got any sexy swimsuits?"

She laughed this time and he enjoyed the sound and the sight of her relaxing. His phone rang and when he saw the chief's number, he sighed and stood up. "I'll take this in the other room."

Her smile and the laughter behind her eyes were gone as he left the room. He knew that all the memories of last night and the body they'd found rushed into her mind, just as it had his own.

"Morning," he answered once he was out of earshot. "What's the news?"

"Positive ID on Nat Willis. ID confirmed by a tattoo he had. The coroner has ruled out suicide, even though the gun was found in his hands."

"How did he do that?" he asked.

"Willis was left handed, the gun was in his right hand," Deter explained.

Sawyer sighed. "Murder." He turned back towards the kitchen. He could hear Rose cleaning up after their breakfast. "Any clue who wanted him dead and why they were on Rose's land?"

"None. You're sure you were with Mrs. Clayton at the time of the shot?" Deter asked.

"Yes." He knew Rose was still on the suspect list in her husband's murder, but the chief had too many unanswered problems with her involvement.

Even Deter thought Rose should be cleared of Isaac's murder. After all, his plane had taken off from the small airport on the morning of the seventh, and the workers confirmed that Rose had been at the house that morning, watching them pour the cement for the wall that would enclose her husband's body for over a year.

The other questions weren't so simple. The plane was reported going down over the Atlantic on the eighth. If Rose was the one flying it, she had plenty of time to jump from the plane during the storm, but unless she had a boat waiting for her, there was no way she would have gotten back home in time for her to be home when Carson and Sawyer had shown up at her door to inform her of Isaac's death.

Unless Rose was working with someone else, the chief and the detective had already ruled out her direct involvement with Isaac's death. Still, more questions flooded his mind with the new death. From the sound of the questions, Sawyer wondered if Deter was checking *his* whereabouts. After all, they were pretty sure it was Willis who had attacked him.

"Then we'll have to assume Willis was on her land to meet someone else and that meeting turned deadly." The chief was silent for a moment. "You said the guy that jumped you was big?'

Instantly, Sawyer's mind jumped to the same place. "Yeah. I'd like to see another picture of Willis if you can send me..." His phone beeped.

"Just shot one to you." Deter said.

"You're quick." He flipped his phone out and looked at the man. The height and weight matched Sawyer's general impression of his attacker. Even though he hadn't seen his face, the man in the mug shot could have easily been the man who'd jumped him. "I can't be certain, but yeah, he fits the description."

"I'll have the guy's check for steel-toed boots, see if we can swab them for your blood. I'll get back to you soon." The chief hung up.

"Was it Willis?" Rose asked from the doorway.

He turned, then nodded. "Yes, and we're pretty sure he was the one who jumped me."

"Why?" She shook her head. "Why attack you then..." She frowned. "It was suicide, right?"

For a moment, he thought about keeping the new information from her but then decided against it.

"No." He sat down in front of the fire she'd built earlier that morning. "The gun was placed in his right hand. Willis was left handed."

She sat down next to him. "Who would want him dead?"

"Maybe someone who was pulling the strings? How much did you know about Willis?"

She shook her head. "I didn't even remember his name until you mentioned it last night." Tsuna jumped on her lap, and she pet the small dog absently. "There were about six workers that used to help around here. The only one I ever talked to was RJ. Mostly, before the wall was built, Isaac dealt with them. After... I only talked to RJ. Who would murder someone on my land?" she asked, looking over at him.

"That is the question of the day." He hated to say the next part but knew that it needed to be spoken. "My guess is the same person who murdered your husband."

FIFTEEN

A VISITOR...

Sawyer's statement kept playing over in Rose's head as she got ready for Julie's visit. She freshened the sheets on the bed and made sure there were fresh towels and plenty of soap in the bathroom.

When she was done with that, she climbed the stairs and double-checked the artwork she wanted to show her. After almost an hour of fretting over it, she gave up and went downstairs to make a quick lunch for her and Sawyer.

For his part, Sawyer had been resting in the library. He'd built a fire there, curled up on the sofa with the dogs, and had fallen asleep reading a book. When she woke him for lunch and to take his pills, he told her he was contemplating taking a walk with the dogs after lunch.

Deciding to go with him, she pulled on a jacket and her snow boots. Two steps out of the back door, Tsuna whined and she bent to pick up the small dog.

"You baby her too much." Sawyer chuckled. Ozzy ran around the backyard, playing in the new snow. At one point, the top of his head disappeared under the fresh powder.

"See, Ozzy's having fun," she told Tsuna, who only shivered in her arms and tried to bury her head in her scarf. "Maybe I should buy her a sweater," she wondered when Tsuna's shaking continued as they walked away from the house. Sawyer picked the path that led towards the cliffs that overlooked the beach area and the boathouse she hardly ever used. Isaac had purchased a sailboat only weeks after moving in. He'd paid the men extra to get the boathouse fixed up for it and, since Isaac's death, the sailboat had sat, dry docked and forgotten.

Willis' body had been found in the opposite direction of the path they were on and she was thankful that Sawyer had picked the path to avoid the area. It had been hard to get the image of Willis' dead body out of her mind last night. She'd spent a few hours trying to flush it from her memory.

"How are you feeling?" she asked when they stood over the hillside looking out over Lake Erie. The snow was still falling, but not as hard as it had been earlier that morning. The grey sky caused the waters to darken. She could see that another storm was coming towards them and would probably hit later that evening.

"Tired. Like a child ready for another nap." He sighed and turned back to the house. "I hope your friend makes it here okay," he said as they began to head back. "It looks like we're in for another storm."

"Julie left early this morning." She glanced down at her watch, shifting the small dog, who was now tucked inside her heavy winter jacket. Ozzy was still racing around like he was having the time of his life. "She texted me about an hour ago and told me she was two hours out. She said that she had rented a large SUV with four-wheel-drive, so she should be okay. She lived in Alaska for a few years in high school. Her dad was stationed at a military base up there." She smiled, remembering the pictures Julie had shown her from the small town near Anchorage. "I always wanted to go up there to visit."

"What stopped you?" he asked as they approached the house.

She shrugged. "Isaac was too busy, and he didn't think it was wise for me to take the trip up there by myself."

He was silent, and she could tell he wanted to say more. Before he had a chance, they saw the patrol car parked in the front of the house.

"The chief wanted to fill me in on a few things," he assured her.

She could tell he was slightly out of breath and the short walk in the deep snow had probably exerted him too much. "I'll start a pot of coffee." She stomped the snow from her boots on the patio and greeted the chief.

Setting the tiny dog down inside, she removed her boots, scarf, and coat, placing them all in their designated locations. Then she disappeared into the kitchen to start some coffee. She placed some cookies and crackers on a tray and carried them out to the great room. When she noticed the men standing by the fireplace, she was reminded she needed to put all her furniture back in place. Sawyer had built another fire and the men were warming themselves against it.

Setting the tray down, she poured them each a cup of coffee and motioned towards the sofa. "Do you have time to sit?"

"No," the chief said with a sigh. "I have just enough time for a cup and maybe a few of those cookies."

"Well?" she asked. Both men turned towards her. "Any news?"

The chief looked at Sawyer. "I'll let him fill you in on what we found out about Willis. As far as your husband's case..." He took up a cookie she offered and bit into it. She waited as he swallowed and took another drink of the coffee. "We're looking into a few leads."

"Such as?"

"There are five people who knew or worked with your husband who have their pilot license," he answered.

"Five?" She shook her head.

"Your father-in-law, your stepbrother, your neighbor Boone Schneller, a coworker of your husband's at the office by the name of Ray Gardezi, and..."—the chief glanced between them—"Kristy Owens." Rose stiffened.

Isaac's mistress hadn't had anything new to say lately. All the interviews she was taking had the same questions and answers as if she'd run out of new angles or stories to tell. Rose knew she was still in town, which is why she was having her groceries delivered. Still, the woman's face was all over the news. So much so that Rose hadn't turned on the television in days.

"She... can fly?" Rose asked.

The chief nodded. "She learned for a part in a movie called *Bleached*, where she was an undercover pilot in Hawaii."

"Wasn't that for helicopters?" Sawyer asked.

"Yes, but she underwent both small engine and helicopter training, not to mention parachuting," the chief answered. "We're looking into all five of the suspects deeper, looking for proof of where they were the morning of your husband's disappearance."

"What about RJ?" she asked.

The chief shook his head. "He was cleared; the man had shown up the morning the cement was poured half an hour late. Plus, he can't fly."

"So, does that mean I'm off the list of suspects?" Rose asked. Her mind was still whirling slightly from the list of names.

"Not officially, but you're off my list, if that counts for anything." The chief smiled at her.

She smiled back. "It does, thank you." She handed him the plate of cookies and he took a few more.

Then he surprised them by saying. "Now, I've got to get back out there. Miss Owens is leaving town today."

Rose felt a huge relief wash over her. "She is?"

He nodded. "The media has died down since the storm hit and a new Hollywood scandal broke last night, so she's flying back to New York and we get to babysit her trip to the airport. I miss the old days when the biggest call we had was for an illegally parked car."

"Or the Goldstein and Tibbs feud," Sawyer added. The chief chuckled and pointed at him with his half-eaten cookie. "How did that one turn out by the way?"

"Tibbs doesn't remember a thing other than walking into his house and getting stabbed. The Goldsteins are denying any part in it and claim it was probably a drug deal gone bad." The chief sighed. Then he glanced at Sawyer again. "How are you feeling? Is she taking care of you?"

"I'm getting there. If Rose keeps feeding me like she is, I'll be coming back to work ten pounds heavier than before."

The chief chuckled. "Enjoy it while you can. You won't get cookies like this at the station."

"I can pack you up some. I made two dozen the other night and have a bag of them in the freezer."

"I won't say no to free cookies." He set his mug down. "You two stay warm. We're supposed to get more snow tonight, possibly even another foot."

As the chief left, she thought about everything he'd said. Turning away from the door, she took the empty plate and coffee mugs back to the kitchen.

"I hate to say it, but I think I'm going to head upstairs and rest," Sawyer said. She noticed that he was still out of breath, his eyes were a little red, and he was looking pale again.

"Go, and take Tsuna and Ozzy with you." She nodded to the two sleeping dogs. "I'm going to start prepping for dinner."

Sawyer nodded and then snapped his fingers and both dogs followed him out of the room.

She waited until he was gone before walking back into the living room. Glancing around, she imagined a new way to decorate the room with some of the furniture she already had.

Instead of the sofa sitting in front of the fireplace, she pulled it a few feet away and turned it. Then she rolled out a cream and burgundy hand-knotted rug from Finland in the space in front of the sofa, directly in front of the fireplace. She carried two cream-colored wing-back chairs from the office and faced them towards the sofa. She set one of the two end tables between the chairs. The other one went on the right of the sofa, away from the fireplace. She had to drag in the heavy matching coffee table and set it over the rug, between the chairs and the sofa.

Then she tossed two throw blankets over the arms of the chairs and a larger one over the end of the sofa.

Standing back, she smiled at the functionality of the room. Now several people could sit in front of the fireplace and enjoy its warmth while they all could see one another.

Glancing at her watch, she pulled out her phone and checked for messages from Julie. Seeing none, she texted quickly.

-Hope you are safe, take your time, it's supposed to snow more.

She was surprised when she got an instant reply.

-I'm an hour out. Stopped for gas. Driving is going well, I'll see you soon.

-Okay, don't eat, I'm cooking.

-Duh! I can't wait to have another Rose Clayton homemade meal. Getting back on the road, adios.

One hour, Rose thought. She'd already planned a meal for tonight but hadn't pulled out the wine yet.

She glanced at the basement door as she passed by. Nope, not ready yet. She veered into the kitchen and started meal preparation.

Tonight's dinner was a caprese chicken breast. She took her time cutting the vegetables and making the basil pesto sauce. Once the chicken was in the oven and the wild rice and steamed vegetables were ready to cook, she turned her attention to the avocado salad, making the dressing and adding in the fresh ingredients.

While she waited for everything to finish cooking, she threw together a three-layer brownie trifle. She'd made the brownies earlier that day while Sawyer had been napping and just had to put it all together in a glass container, making sure that each layer was perfect, like a piece of artwork. She topped it all with chocolate shavings and placed the container back in the refrigerator to chill.

She went into the formal dining room and set the table. She threw a few more logs onto the fireplace and, once again, as she walked by the basement door, thought about going downstairs to find the perfect wine.

This time, however, instead of feeling defeated, she thought about how many times she'd gone downstairs over the past year.

She'd spent almost a full week down there, clearing out all the clutter that the previous owners had left—furniture that had been rotted, old belongings that someone had treasured once.

The entire time she was down there, Isaac had been there, and she hadn't known it. It hadn't bothered her then, why was it different now that he was actually gone? Would she ever feel comfortable going down there alone again?

She refused to be a prisoner in her own home. Reaching for the door handle, she took a deep breath and twisted it. Once again, the cold air hit her, reminding her that the glass sliding doors the new contractor had ordered hadn't arrived yet. James Dylan, her new contractor, was hopeful the large glass doors would be there sometime this week. Once they arrived, he could install them, snow or no snow.

She took the first step down, then the next, all while holding her breath. The light flickered slightly when she hit the bottom stair, causing her to jump.

She avoided looking across the room and, instead, focused on the wine closet. Opening the door quickly, she stepped in and took her first breath since coming downstairs as the door closed behind her.

She took her time picking out a bottle of wine that would complement the meal. She chose a sauvignon blanc that someone had given them as a gift and reached for the door, ready to head back upstairs.

Her eyes traveled past the glass door and her hand on the door handle froze when she spotted the snowy footprints just inside the massive plywood piece that hung over the open spot in the wall.

The bottle of wine slipped from her hand. The glass shattered, and wine rushed over the pants and socks she'd been wearing.

Without thinking, she rushed from the wine closet and ran up the stairs.

She slammed the basement door and turned to run to get Sawyer. When she bumped into a solid chest, she screamed at the top of her lungs.

"Easy," Sawyer said, his hands going to her shoulders to hold her steady.

"Some... someone was down there." She pointed to the basement.

"What?" He shoved her behind him. "Now?"

"N-n-n-o, s-snowy footprints." She couldn't control the shaking.

"Did you see someone?" he asked.

She shook her head, too afraid to speak. Her throat had closed, and her head felt light.

"Stay here." He took hold of the door handle just as the front doorbell chimed.

"Julie." She took a step back and glanced around. Why had she thought it was a good idea to invite her friend into this madhouse?

"Hang on." He took her hand and started walking. He glanced down.

"You're bleeding," he gasped. She looked down and realized that she was getting wine all over her floor.

"No, it's wine. I dropped the bottle." She bent down and pulled off her socks and tossed them on the tile floor.

Sawyer picked her up, and she scolded him when he winced, but he shushed her as he carried her to the living area and set her on the sofa. Then he marched past her and opened the front door.

"Hi." She heard Julie's voice go from friendly to sexy. "Is Rose home?"

"She's in the living area." He motioned. "Come keep her company. She's just had a shock."

"Rose?" Her friend's voice turned to concern.

"In here," she called out, feeling stupid. Her feet were sticky with wine, which was also dripping off her pants onto the new wood flooring.

"Are you okay?" Julie dropped her bags inside the room and rushed to her side.

"Yes." She filled her friend in as Sawyer made his way down to the basement to check on the footprints. When he came back up, she interrupted her story and asked him. "Did you find anything?"

"Footprints, men's size ten."

"How do you know that?" Julie asked. Her friend's dark eyebrows went up.

"I wear size eleven, and I'd wager they're a size smaller. I took pictures and made sure the board was secure again. I added a few more screws. Whoever got in, won't be doing it again. Unless we get some warmer weather, I think they'll keep until the chief and the detective get here. Are you cut?" he asked, getting down on his knees in front of her and checking her feet.

There was a small stinging in her heel and she winced when he pulled out a piece of glass.

"I'll get the medical kit." He turned to go.

"Who is tall, dark, and sexy?" Julie asked when they were alone again.

"Sawyer," she answered. "He's a friend."

"A friend or a... friend?" Julie asked, drawing out the last word.

Before she could answer, Sawyer walked back in, carrying the small case she kept in the pantry. She didn't know how he'd known it was there when she'd completely forgotten about it.

He gently cleaned the small cut and put a bandage over her heel.

"You may want to change out of those pants." He nodded to the wine still dripping from them.

"I'll be right back." She looked over at Julie. "I can show you to your room, so you can freshen up before dinner."

"Something smells wonderful." Julie jumped up and helped her to her feet. "During dinner, I expect a full report of what the heck has been going on in your life."

She chuckled and nodded.

Since the wine had soaked her pants and feet, she jumped in the shower quickly to rinse off. Then, instead of pulling on another pair of pants, she tugged on a pair of black leggings and a large cream sweater to go over it. She put on a thick pair of wool socks, tied her hair up in a loose bun, and reapplied a little makeup.

When she walked downstairs, Julie and Sawyer were sitting in the living room talking. Julie had a glass of wine in her hand and Sawyer jumped up when he spotted her.

"I hope it's okay, I grabbed another bottle of whatever you dropped. I tried to clean up, but... I didn't know where your mop was."

"Thank you." She smiled. "Dinner will be ready soon."

"The chief says he'll stop by first thing in the morning. There was a hitch with Owens," Sawyer added.

"What kind of hitch?" she asked.

"He wouldn't say, told me he'd fill us in tomorrow." He shrugged.

She nodded, and Julie stood up and hugged her.

"Hi." Her friend smiled at her. She'd changed from her travel clothes and had pulled on a pair of cream-colored leggings and a black sweater. "Look, we match," she joked.

Rose hugged her again. "It's so good to see you." She sighed and took in the feeling of holding onto her friend.

"Let's go eat. Dinner should be ready by now and I'm sure you're hungry." She took Julie's hand and led her out of the living room.

They all sat around the table, enjoying the meal she'd made, drinking the wine she'd picked, and making small talk. Julie filled her in on her trip up there, how she'd enjoyed driving in the snow, and how it had reminded her of her time in Alaska.

She asked Sawyer a few basic questions—what he did, where he lived, how he was injured.

When Rose set dessert and a fresh carafe of hot coffee on the table, the talk turned towards Isaac's and Willis's murders.

"Another man was murdered here?" Julie glanced around. "Yesterday?"

Rose sighed and nodded.

"A few hundred yards from here," Sawyer added. "We have no idea if that murder has anything to do with Isaac's. It could be simply a—"

"What?" Julie jumped in. "A different murder? You mean, instead of one murderer, there might be two running around?" She turned to Rose. "That's it, you're packing up and coming back to the city with me."

Her friend was serious, but Rose knew she couldn't

leave. This was her home. Just like she needed to conquer the fear of her basement, she had to stand her ground.

"I appreciate the offer"—she reached over and touched Julie's hand—"but I can't. I belong here."

Julie's eyes turned to Sawyer. "Tell me you're sticking around here, and I'll feel better."

"I am." He nodded.

Rose knew that it was on the tip of his tongue to tell Julie that he was only here for a week, but instead, he looked over at her and asked for more dessert.

SIXTEEN

THERE'S ALWAYS A FIRST TIME...

After dinner, they all headed back into the living room. She poured herself and Julie another glass of wine as they made themselves comfortable in front of the fire.

"My god," Julie said, relaxing back and putting her socked feet up. "That meal was worth the long drive up here. Like I've always said, you could go into the culinary arts and make a lot of people happy."

Rose chuckled.

"I'm going to let the dogs out," Sawyer said before sitting down. She moved to get up, but he stopped her. "I've got this. Stay, enjoy some time with your friend. I'll probably head up and get some rest. I'm feeling tired and wonderfully full now."

"Thank you." She set Tsuna down on the floor. The little dog rushed after Ozzy and Sawyer.

Julie turned to her once they heard the back door open and close. "Okay, dish."

She smiled. "He's just a friend."

"Right, girl." Julie sighed. "I wish I had a friend that looked at me like that man looks at you."

"How does he look at me?" she asked.

"Like Rhett Butler looked at Scarlet."

Rose laughed. "You can do better than that," she joked.

Julie thought about it for a moment, then added. "He looked at you like Noah looked at Allie in *The Notebook*." Julie frowned.

Rose tilted her head and raised her eyebrows.

Julie thought about it for a second. "He looks at you like he's Christian Grey and he wants to drag you to the red room." Her friend's smile turned wicked.

Rose laughed. "I like that one." She thought about doing all the things with Sawyer that the book had described and giggled.

"Girl, you need to lock that in." They grew silent when the back door opened, and they could hear Sawyer talking softly to the dogs. Then she listened as he took the back stairs up to his room. She was sure that both dogs followed him up to bed.

"Tell me, at least, that you've kissed that man?" Julie asked.

"What is this? High school?" Rose laughed.

"No, but if I drink enough wine, we can pretend and braid each other's hair." Julie held up her wineglass.

"I'm so happy you're here." She picked up the bottle and poured more wine for the both of them.

Half an hour later, after filling Julie in about everything that had been happening to her over the last few weeks, they emptied the bottle of wine.

"How about some more wine?" Julie asked.

Rose's eyes turned to the basement door. "Come downstairs with me?"

"Of course. I want to see those footprints and that wall myself." Her friend tugged her up from the sofa.

Once again, she had to take a deep breath before reaching for the door handle. Her friend placed her hand over hers and together they turned the knob.

"Brrr." Julie shivered. "Is it always this cold?"

"Until they put in the glass doors, it's as cold inside here as it is outside," Rose answered.

Julie took her arm and they made their way down the stairs together. This time when the lights flickered, they both jumped, then giggled.

"The wine closet." She nodded towards the glass door.

"Closet?" Julie gawked. "That looks more like a bedroom that your wine sleeps in." She chuckled. Then Julie dropped Rose's hand and made her way across the large room.

Rose stayed where she was. "Don't mess the footprints up," she called out.

"I won't," Julie said back. "This room is bigger than I thought."

Rose nodded and glanced around. At one point, she'd thought of turning the space into a game room or breaking it out into several different rooms. She held in a shiver. Now she didn't care if she cemented the entire thing in.

"You know," Julie said as she stood next to the cement wall. "I didn't always like Isaac, but I didn't think he should end up like that." Her friend made her way back over to her side and took her arm. "Even if he was cheating on you. Maimed and castrated, sure, but not rotting in a cement wall."

"Thanks, I think." She sighed.

"How about we liberate some more of that trapped wine?" Julie nodded towards the glass door. "Then dig into some more dessert as we talk about sexy men with green eyes?" Julie wiggled her eyebrows.

ROSE WOKE the next morning with a hangover. Keeping her eyes closed, she made her way to the bathroom and turned on the shower, then waited until the water heated before stepping in.

She dipping her head under the spray and stayed there until she felt halfway normal. She could sleep in, but she wanted to make banana oatmeal muffins for the chief's visit that morning. Besides, she knew Sawyer and the dogs would already be up by now.

Dressing in an outfit much like last night's, she made her way down the stairs and wasn't surprised when the smell of coffee greeted her. Both dogs rushed to her side when she walked into the kitchen. Sawyer was sitting at the table, a cup of coffee steaming beside him as he worked on his laptop.

"Morning," she said, passing by him and heading to pour herself a cup of coffee.

"Morning." He shut the top of his laptop. As his eyes ran over her, his smile grew. "Did you have fun last night?"

"Yes." She smiled and leaned against the countertop, sipping the coffee. "It's been almost a year since Julie has visited." Julie had been there for Isaac's funeral, but Rose had been too far in a haze of emotions to remember most of the short visit.

"Deter should be here soon." He glanced down at his watch.

"About that. I was going to make some muffins, so he could take them into the office."

"You don't have to do that, but I'm sure he and the gang will enjoy them," Sawyer answered.

She walked over to the refrigerator and pulled out the container with the batter in it. After heating the oven, she busied herself adding the bananas and nuts.

"Do you always have things pre-made like that?" he asked.

She smiled. "I like planning ahead." She put the first pan into the oven. Glancing outside, she realized that it had stopped snowing. Walking over to the door, she smiled at the blue sky. The sight made her want to spend the day outside, painting on the small balcony off her studio.

She hadn't heard Sawyer move, but suddenly, he was behind her, his hand resting gently on her shoulder.

"In case I forgot to say it last night in my zombie state, thank you for dinner. It was amazing."

She turned, her eyes meeting his. "You're welcome. It's nice cooking for others again."

"I like your friend Julie," he added.

"She likes you." She smiled.

"Yeah, I gathered that when she called me McHottie over dinner."

"She did not..." Then Rose remembered and chuckled. "Okay, she did."

He smiled. "She's just what you needed." His smile fell away. "I thought I'd be in the way."

As an answer, she reached up quickly and covered his lips with her finger.

"Don't. I don't think I would be able to sleep without you here. Seeing those footprints..." She shivered.

His arms came around here. "I'm here," he said softly and she melted against his chest.

"Morning," Julie said cheerfully from the doorway.

"Morning." Rose jumped away from Sawyer's warmth and smiled over at her friend.

"I didn't mean to interrupt anything." Julie's eyebrows rose and fell quickly.

"You didn't," Rose answered. She walked over to the oven and checked on the muffins just as the front doorbell rang.

"That will be the chief." Sawyer walked from the room.

"Wow." Julie pounded her hand over her heart. "Straight out of the movies." She sighed as she leaned against the counter.

"Seriously." Rose sighed. "I hate to say it, but Isaac never did that to me."

"What? Make eyes at you in the kitchen?" Julie asked.

"Make my knees feel weak and my heart race a million miles an hour," Rose answered.

"No man has done that to me, yet." Julie sighed heavily. "Can I help you with breakfast?" She glanced around.

"No, you're my guest. Grab a cup of coffee. The muffins will be out soon."

Her friend gave her a friendly salute, then went and got a mug down.

"Oh, grab two. Chief Deter will want a cup."

"Yes, he does." The chief walked into the kitchen, following Sawyer.

"I figured we'd head down first, then talk." Sawyer opened the basement door.

"Coffee first." The chief took the cup from Julie.

"Black?" she asked.

"Yes, thank you." He nodded at Julie. "Matthew Deter." He held out his hand.

"Julie Cromer." Julie shook the man's hand.

"The agent from New York?" he asked. When Julie

looked surprised, he shrugged. "We had to look into Mrs. Clayton's past."

"Rose. I think we're at the point of using first names," Rose chimed in.

The chief nodded. "We don't really do that, but I will start calling you Clayton if that's okay?"

She nodded and smiled.

"Is Sawyer your last name?" Julie turned and asked Sawyer.

"Yes, Royce Sawyer."

Julie nodded. "Royce." She said the name and Rose mentally said it again as well. She liked it but still thought of him as Sawyer.

"We'll head down." Sawyer opened the door and a blast of cold air hit the room. Then the men disappeared quickly.

"When are the men going to put in the glass doors?" Julie asked.

"Tomorrow, if all goes well. My contractor texted me early this morning. It's why I woke up."

"Still can't handle your wine?" Julie joked.

"A glass, two maybe. But two bottles? No one can handle that much." She pulled the pan of muffins from the oven and inhaled the wonderful scent.

"Wimp," Julie said under her breath.

She glanced over her shoulder at her friend. "You weigh about ten pounds more than me..." she started with a smile.

"Oh, we're going there," Julie jumped in, laughing.

"No, it's just..." She chuckled. "You live in the city and probably have drinks with people every night. I've been living here." She motioned around after setting the pan down. "I'm lucky if I remember I have a wine closet."

"Bedroom," Julie added.

"Whatever." She chuckled. "I'm not used to drinking that much."

Julie walked over and wrapped her arms around her. "That's why I love you."

"Why?" She laughed. "Because you can drink me under the table?"

"Yes, and you have the best muffins." Julie squeezed Rose's butt cheeks. Rose laughed and pushed her friend away playfully.

The men walked in and stopped dead when they saw the women hugging.

"At ease men. I was talking about Rose's banana nut muffins." Julie saluted and stepped away from Rose as Sawyer and the chief chuckled.

"She's trouble," Rose added with a smile as she set a plate of muffins on the table. "I've made enough so you can take some back to the office."

Just then the doorbell rang again. "That's Detective Anderson," Sawyer said before disappearing again.

"Wow, these are amazing," the chief said, after sitting down and biting into a muffin.

"Thank you," she sat down and took a muffin for herself.

Detective Anderson walked in behind Sawyer. "I'm going to take him downstairs," Sawyer said before disappearing through the basement doorway.

For the next hour, the detective and the chief went up and down the basement stairs many times. Pictures were taken, molds were made of the snow prints in the basement. She wanted to see the process but couldn't stand to go into the basement again. Instead, she and Julie headed upstairs to her studio while Sawyer dealt with the basement matter.

"This is some of your best work," Julie said, as she stood

over the artwork that Rose had chosen to show her. "But I know you, so I want to see the rest." She nodded towards the wall that held the paintings Rose hadn't chosen.

"Go ahead." She sat back while her friend went painting by painting.

She was surprised as she pulled out a few pieces.

"Wow," Julie said, holding up a painting. "Yeah, smoldering and sexy." She turned the piece around and Rose stared at Sawyer's face.

She smiled, remembering pulling out her paints for the first time since Isaac's death. She walked over and took the painting from her friend and set it on the easel.

"If it wasn't for him, I would still be sleeping in front of the fireplace wearing sweats," she said softly.

Julie moved next to her silently. "You'd gotten that bad? I should have stayed longer." Her friend wrapped an arm around her waist.

Rose shook her head. "No, I needed to go through what I did in order to come out on the other side."

Her friend's arms wrapped around her waist. "I'm only a call and an eight-hour drive away."

Rose chuckled. "Thanks,"

That evening, Julie helped Rose cook dinner. Julie was in the mood for margaritas, so Rose cooked enchiladas.

She made sure to add extra jalapenos and seasoning, making them spicy.

After, instead of heading up to bed, Sawyer stuck around and enjoyed talking with them while they sat in front of the fire. They told him stories of how they met in college and how they had become best friends.

Rose hadn't laughed that hard in years.

She'd met Julie at one of the first art showings she'd gone to in California. She'd walked in expecting one thing, but as she stood in front of the first piece of art, she had no idea what she was looking at.

"I swear it was a V-J," Julie blurted out.

"That's what you said when you stopped by me that night," Rose added.

"It was true. I had no idea the art show was sex-themed." Julie laughed.

"We'd never laughed so hard," Rose added. "We both had been invited, but the flyer didn't say anything about what kind of art show it was. So, we spent the night being embarrassed together and laughing hard."

"Then we ended up grabbing dinner after and that was that." Julie smiled. "Friends ever since."

"What about you, Royce?" Julie turned to him. "How did you end up here? In Twisted Rock?"

He glanced at Rose quickly before answering. "I lived in Cleveland most of my life and after a divorce, I needed a change of scenery."

"Understandable. Divorce sucks." Julie said.

"Yeah, Ann decided my best friend Nick was better suited to her lifestyle," he answered.

"Which was?" she asked.

"Jet-setting to far-off places and spending every dime on fancy clothes and fast cars."

"Are you a penny pincher?" Julie asked, gaining a tap on her toe from Rose.

"It's none of—"

Sawyer laughed. "No, but a cop's salary isn't much compared to the salary of one of the top cosmetic surgeons in Cleveland."

"Oh," Julie said slowly. "Ouch,"

"Yeah. It's for the best." Again, Sawyer's eyes moved over to hers. "On that note." He stood, and Rose heard him groan, then he stretched slightly and shifted his weight. "I'm heading up. I'll let the dogs out, then check around before I head up to bed."

Rose frowned. "Check around?"

"The chief thought it might be best if I had a look around each night. You know, make sure all the doors are locked."

Rose could tell he was trying to act nonchalant about it.

She glanced over at Julie, who just shrugged. "I... I'm going to go..." Rose started.

Julie nodded. "I'm heading up now. I've got to drive back tomorrow and need an early start."

Rose nodded, then followed Sawyer into the kitchen.

"Is there a reason the chief is worried about securing the house each night?"

He opened the back door and glanced back at her as both dogs took off outside. Tsuna darted out after Ozzy, assuring Rose that Sawyer's training sessions earlier that day with her dog had helped.

His green eyes met hers and he touched her shoulder. "Nothing for you to worry about."

"Sawyer." She crossed her arms over her chest. "We haven't known each other long, but I know you well enough to tell when you're hiding something from me."

He sighed and leaned against the doorway. "The chief thinks that whoever came in through the basement might come back," he answered.

"Why? Why would someone come back?"

Sawyer's eyes held hers.

"Me?" She was shocked. "Why would someone..." Her breath hitched, and her hands shook as she covered her heart. "You think that someone, the same someone who killed Isaac and Willis, is after me now?"

Sawyer shrugged. "The chief wants me to stick by you, which means I'm here until they find the murderer. Babysitting duty." Her eyes narrowed as anger replaced fear. "I didn't mean..." Sawyer started quickly, then sighed and ran his hands through his hair.

But it was too late. She turned and marched from the room and took the back stairs two at a time. She felt like slamming the bedroom door but knew that Julie might already be in bed. After all, her friend had drunk three margaritas.

She paced for a while. When she heard the dogs scratching at her door, she opened it for them. She hadn't expected Sawyer to be standing there, his fist raised as if he was about to knock on her door. The dogs rushed past them and jumped into the dog bed. Seeing them circle around and curl up together was heartwarming.

"I..." he started to say, but she moved to close the door. "Rose." He stuck his foot in the door and held out his hand to stop the movement. "Give me a chance to explain." She moved slightly, opening the door a crack.

His eyebrows rose. She sighed loudly and stood back then motioned for him to come in. She shut the door behind Sawyer and motioned for him to start talking.

"I shouldn't have said... It's a term we use..." He sighed. "I'm sorry."

"I don't need a babysitter," she said clearly.

"No, of course, you don't." He reached out to touch her. "I'm just... on edge."

"Why?" She felt the anger drain from her when she saw worry flash behind his eyes.

"If something were to happen... to you." He shook his head and closed his eyes.

"Hey." She touched his shoulders. "I'm right here."

His eyes opened and caught with hers. "I don't think I could bear it if something happened to you." He reached up and touched her face. "I'm falling for you," he said softly. His fingers cupped her face as he brought his lips down to hers. "Don't make me worry about you further. Let me protect you."

She nodded and swallowed. "Yes, of course." She reached up on her toes and kissed him and was pleased when he took the kiss deeper.

He surprised her by quickly picking her up in his arms. She heard him groan with pain, but he shook his head quickly, signaling that he was okay. "This time, there's no stopping," he said against her skin.

"No." She smiled. "Stay with me tonight."

He laid her down gently on the bed, then reached for her. She sat up and unbuttoned his shirt, running her nails over his skin. She avoided the bruised areas and focused only on his pleasure and hers. Her mouth moved over his skin as his moved over her neck. He pulled the sweater over her head and groaned when he realized she hadn't put on a bra that evening. Then he dipped his head and licked circles around each of her breasts.

Pulling back, his eyes ran over her, taking in everything about her as hers did to him. He started to tug her leggings off her legs and she helped him. He sighed with pleasure when he noticed she wasn't wearing anything underneath those either. His eyes heated her skin, and she felt on the verge of exploding.

When she reached for his jeans, he covered her hand and stood up to quickly tug them down himself. Then he was back beside her and their mouths joined again as their skin pressed together, everywhere.

"There. Drawer," she said breathless, as she pointed to the nightstand. "Condom."

He quickly pulled out a package, then was back next to her, raining kisses over her as he opened it.

When he settled between her legs, she quaked with want and didn't think she could hold off. Her body ached for him, from the nights she'd spent dreaming of him, just like this.

Having Sawyer inside her, over her, filling her, she realized she'd never been truly pleased before. She'd never felt as much as she felt with him and when they joined together and fell at the same time, she knew exactly what she'd been missing her entire life.

SEVENTEEN

THE PLOT THICKENS...

For the next couple days, Sawyer took it easy and recovered, but the evenings he and Rose spent locked in each other's arms, tangled together in the best sex of his life.

The construction crew had finished installing the large glass doors in the basement and the new high-tech cameras and had even repaired the gate at the end of the driveway, so now the house was very secure.

Even now, however, he was still concerned that someone was after Rose and remained on guard as much as possible.

He even went with her into town to deal with her daily chores. Taking Tsuna to the vet to get her nails clipped or shopping for groceries, he never left her side.

They ate at a small restaurant in town and he realized everyone he knew had known her for longer. People she'd gone to school with stopped and talked to her about Isaac or the murder of Willis on her property.

He expected that most people thought that he was only there for Rose's safety, since the chief had spread it around town that Rose was under police protection twenty-four seven. The chief had told him that getting that information out would help keep Rose safe. It also gave them some cover, so they didn't have to explain to anyone about their relationship.

The chief's first inclination had been to stick extra cameras and triple protection on Rose, then spread the rumor that she was staying at the house by herself. Sawyer had knocked that idea down quickly. He was not okay with using Rose as bait and, in the end, the chief had agreed with him.

They went an entire week without an incident, then the chief called with some news he wanted to break firsthand.

They waited for him to show up as they speculated what it could be. Rose hoped it was to tell them that they had caught Isaac and Willis's killer, but Sawyer was sure he would have heard something first if that was the case. Besides, something was just feeling off lately.

When the chief rang the doorbell, they answered it together.

"Well?" Rose said as soon as she shut the front door. "What's the news?"

"How about you sit?" The look on Rose's face told him that she wasn't going to wait. "Okay, stand then. We've arrested your father-in-law."

"For...?" Her hand went to her throat.

"Not for the murders, but for a slew of other things including racketeering, bribery, extortion, misappropriation, and even tax fraud."

"What?" Rose walked away from the entrance and sat in the chair closest to the fireplace. The chief and Sawyer followed her into the room.

"The proof was all there, in Isaac's files, the ones we

took from his office, here." Deter nodded towards the office across the hallway.

"Isaac?" she asked.

"From what we can tell, your husband had nothing to do with any of it. There were several communications between father and son where Isaac urged his father to stop the illegal activities. According to the string of lawyers going through all of the evidence, your husband's accounts were all on the up-and-up. His company, however, for now, is shut down."

Rose relaxed slightly. "What will happen to Sean?"

"His license to practice law in New York has been suspended. He'll be tried, and if convicted, he could face disciplinary action including jail time. The federal courts have seized all his assets in the process as well."

Rose leaned back and closed her eyes. "What a mess."

"This opens another door into the possibility that Sean Clayton had something to do with Isaac's murder. If we can find proof that Isaac threatened to go public with his knowledge of his father's illegal activities, there's a possibility that a man in your father-in-law's position would do anything to keep his secrets."

"But... kill his own son?" Rose asked.

"It's happened before," Deter said. "I'll let you know when we know anything further. We have a lot more data to go through. Mr. Clayton's flight records are now in our possession along with his travel itineraries. If we can prove that he was the one flying your husband's plane that day... then we've got him."

"What about Willis? Why would he want to kill a construction worker?" Rose asked.

"He could be covering his tracks. According to RJ,

Willis was the first man on site the day they poured the cement and he was the one handling the cement pump."

They were walking Deter to the front door when Sawyer finally got a moment alone with him.

"What about Kristy Owens?" he asked.

"What about her?" Deter turned towards him.

"You mentioned there were issues with her flight?"

"Oh." He took a deep breath. "Yeah, apparently, she lied to us. She told us she was flying out on a private plane, so we followed her, thinking we were going to the small airport. Instead, she had booked a commercial flight out of Buffalo." He groaned. "We had to follow her all the way up to damn Buffalo."

Sawyer chuckled. "I told you that woman was trouble."

"And then some. She demanded that you be the one to drive her. After arguing with her that you were off for medical issues, she finally agreed to drive herself."

"Thankfully the town is getting back to normal."

"Yeah, Twisted Rock had its five minutes of fame, I suppose." He settled his hat back on his head. "Until we get confirmation, do you mind sticking around here longer?"

Sawyer smiled. "No,"

"Yeah, I didn't think so." Deter winked. "Don't forget, you're still on the job. Well, at least until the doc clears you for active duty again."

"Right." He nodded and leaned against the front door as he watched the chief drive away in the snow. When the car was gone, he motioned for the dogs to head out and do their business. Both dogs had taken to the hand commands quickly. Tsuna was over her fear of snow and rushed out after Ozzy.

"You're amazing with the animals," Rose said as she came up behind him.

"She just needed a little coercing. Besides, Ozzy showed her the ropes, mostly." He wrapped his arm around her as they watched the dogs playing in the falling snow. "Do you think your father-in-law had anything to do with the murders?" he asked once the dogs were back inside. He had just laid another log on the fire and turned to study her as she thought about it.

"Part of me wants to deny it right away, but another voice somewhere in my head says there's a possibility." She sighed slowly. "What do I know? I had been with Isaac for years and never would have thought that he would cheat on me."

He nodded. "It's a hit below the belt." He sat next to her. "When I found out about Ann, it was as if my entire world, everything I'd believed in, was turned upside down."

She turned slightly so they were facing each other on the sofa. "Right. I mean, somehow, him dying wasn't as bad as finding out that he'd cheated on me and lied to me. How is that even possible?" She shook her head.

He took her hand in his. "Deceit is harder to deal with. It's the fact that you put your trust in someone, only to find out after the fact that they swindled it from you. When I think back on all the times there was a question in my mind about Ann, and how she soothed those fears of mine away..." He turned and looked into the fire, remembering some of those moments and still feeling the hurt and pain of it even after almost three years. "That's what's hardest. It took me a while after the divorce to start trusting people again. I still struggle with it at times."

"I wouldn't even know how to begin to lie to someone." She leaned back. "My mother always told me you can read my lies in my eyes." She smiled. "Jenny and Hunter always agreed with her. I suppose Jenny always knew when I was lying because she was older, but Hunter..." She chuckled. "He has never fallen for anything I tried to put past him."

"It must be nice to have siblings."

"Sometimes." She smiled. "It was just me and Jenny for a long time. After our father died, Mom had to work two jobs, so Jenny was more of a babysitter than a sister. Our mother met and married Hunter's father, Bill, when Hunter and I were nine years old. Because we're the same age, we just sort of grew closer than Jenny and I ever were." She smiled as the memory of finding out she was getting a brother surfaced.

"You're still close now." It was a statement instead of a question since he'd witnessed firsthand how they acted around one another. Almost like twins instead of stepsiblings.

"Yes." She smiled and propped her feet up on the sofa. He picked them up and started rubbing her toes, which caused her to moan softly with pleasure. "Sometimes I wish he lived closer, like he used to. Moving to Buffalo was a smart move for him, though."

"He went to the same school that Isaac had?" he asked, trying to remember the details in the file Deter had given him about Rose.

"Yes." She frowned slightly. "It was a big campus though, and Hunter told me that he only ran into Isaac a few times in the years they were both there. Hunter was a year behind. It took him a few tries to pass the bar." He could tell she was remembering the night they had celebrated Hunter's accomplishment, the same night Isaac had disappeared.

He decided to switch gears. "So, what happens now that your agent has taken away the paintings?"

She blinked and smiled again. "Most likely, she'll put them in a show in New York City."

His eyebrows shot up. "Will you travel there?"

She nodded, then frowned. "Isaac used to fly me up there. I haven't been back to the city since..." She dropped off and sighed.

"Did he used to fly you to other places?" he asked.

"Yes." She shifted, moving the sleeping dog to a different spot on her lap. "One of the first trips we took in the new plane was to wine country."

"Isaac had a thing for wine?" he asked, and she nodded quickly.

"Yes, everywhere we went, he'd buy up a case or two and have it shipped back here." She looked into the fire as if she was remembering. "We went to New York City a few times for shows or events." Her eyes moved back to his.

"Did you ever stay at the apartment he rented?" he asked, curious.

"No." She frowned. "Both times, we stayed at hotels instead. The first time, the apartment was getting fumigated. Isaac had said there was a bed bug outbreak on his floor. The second time he said that the hotel was close to where my showing was, so we could walk back afterward."

"Did you question it?" he asked, remembering the times he'd questioned Ann's excuses.

"No, I didn't. I was too trusting, I guess."

"What about Hunter or your father-in-law? Did they ever fly you anywhere?"

"Hunter, yes," She smiled again. "We took a trip to Canada once. He borrowed Isaac's plane since Isaac had flown on a business trip with his father to the UK. Now Hunter has his own plane. Not as new or as nice as Isaac's was. He needed it for trips to the city for court dates."

Sawyer nodded. "Is he a good flyer?"

Her eyes moved to his and narrowed slightly. "Why?"

He shrugged and covered quickly. "Maybe he can fly you up for your showing in New York."

"You're like me." She laughed. "You suck at lying."

He chuckled. "Okay, I was just thinking of the list the chief gave me of their suspects. The people who could have flown Isaac's plane into the ocean and survived."

Her chin went up. "And your first thoughts were of Hunter?"

"No. But he was the first I could figure out a way to ask you about."

She nodded. "Okay, if we're going to do this, let's do it right." She nudged the dogs aside and got up, then quickly disappeared down the hallway. A minute later, she was back with a binder. "I started this shortly after... we found Isaac. It's everything I know." She sat next to him and laid the binder between their laps.

He was impressed with her organization. Everything in the binder was clear and precise.

There were pictures of each potential suspect, an explanation of their whereabouts the night in question, and even a list of motives. The only thing missing was a full chart of the timelines.

They spent an hour scouring over every detail she had written down and added a few new things Sawyer knew about.

"Where does this leave us?" she asked. They had moved into the dining room and had laid out each suspect's information. They had written all the motives on a separate piece of paper and had stacked them next to that person's information.

"The person with the most motives..." He glanced at the

stacks. "It's a tie between Kristy Owens and Sean Clayton. Kristy's motives are in question. Why would she kill Isaac and wait a full year to present herself, framing you for Isaac's death? Sure, she has financial motives now, if she can successfully sue and win back any of Isaac's money for child support. But that's not a motive to kill him. Besides, so far, she hasn't lawyered up. Sean's motives, well... I think there are even more than we have written down." He nodded to the stack of papers.

"What about Boone Schneller? Maybe we aren't giving my neighbor's temper enough weight? Isaac could have been leaving that morning and found Mr. Schneller on our land. Maybe they argued."

He nodded, agreeing. "I think we can rule out Ray Gardezi, Isaac's coworker."

"Wasn't there a statement..." She flipped through her binder and pulled out a piece of paper with her handwriting on it. "Yes, from the news report. Cara Stephens, Isaac's secretary, claimed that Isaac and Gardezi had a huge fight the week before."

"Yes, but Gardezi's alibi is strong. He was in New York, actually, in the courtroom, when Isaac's plane disappeared."

"He could have flown..." She stopped herself. "It is a little far-fetched to think that he jumped from the plane and made it back to the city in time to go to court."

"So, who isn't accounted for when the plane disappeared? We've been looking at Isaac's time of death. What we should also be looking at is the time of the last ping from Isaac's plane. After all, the chances of the murderer hiring..." He stopped talking when a new thought jumped into his head. Without saying anything, he reached for his phone.

He punched Carson's number and cringed when his partner answered with a yawn.

Glancing at his watch, he winced. "Sorry," he said instantly.

"This better be important. I've got an early morning." Carson groaned.

"Nat Willis, have you checked his finances?" he asked. Rose's eyebrows shot up.

"Yeah, sure, why?" Carson answered.

"Any big deposits shortly before or after Isaac Clayton went MIA?" Sawyer asked.

Carson was silent for a while and Sawyer grew concerned the man had fallen back asleep.

"Yeah," he said slowly. "How did you—"

"Deduction. Do we have any idea where the money came from?"

"Not yet. We picked up on the lead shortly after you were attacked. We're still trying to track down the cash deposits into his accounts."

"How much?" he asked.

"Close to ten thousand, each time," Carson answered quickly.

"Each...?"

"The day after Isaac's death, and the day before you were attacked. But, until we clear them, those payments could have been for other jobs he was doing, or, hell, I don't know, an inheritance. We have to dot every "I" at this point," Carson added.

Sawyer felt some sense of justice, knowing the man who'd attacked him wasn't around to harm anyone else. But still, he'd been murdered... Sawyer didn't finish his train of thought.

"Hired muscle?" he asked his partner.

"That's the angle. Which means that whoever was behind him is doing a little house cleaning."

Sawyer sighed and nodded. "Why didn't the chief..."

"He didn't want it leaked. Only the three of us know about it." Carson shuffled around. "Someone in the station is calling the press with every move we make."

Sawyer nodded again and quickly ran over who had been working on the case. Most of the station had touched a part of the investigation at some point. "Have you looked at Anderson?"

"Yup, clean so far," Carson answered.

"How about... Madsen and Brown?"

Carson was silent for a while. "I know you don't like them, but they've been on the force—"

"Just check. We'll chat again in the morning."

"I'll swing by and fill you in further if you can convince Rose to make some more of those muffins."

He smiled. "I'm sure she'd be happy to." Rose's eyebrows shot up in question. "See you around...?"

"Ten. I've got to have some time to look into all this," Carson answered.

"Ten," he agreed. He hung up and filled Rose in on the new angle.

Rose pulled out a stack of sticky notes and wrote a big question mark on one, then stuck it on the table and moved Willis's picture from the newspaper clipping about his murder to a pile underneath it. "If we assume Willis is a pawn, who here has enough money to pay ten grand twice and doesn't have an alibi for the night Willis was shot?" She glanced around the table. "You don't think someone would hire someone else to kill a killer, do you?" She frowned and shook her head. "Even I'm confused at that."

He sighed and stood up. "It's past midnight." He pulled

her out of the chair and held her in his arms. "We're both foggy brained. Let's head upstairs and get some rest, then we can look at this with a clear mind in the morning."

She nodded and smiled up at him. "My mind may not be working, but other parts of me are..."

He chuckled and bent down to kiss her softly. "I think we can come to some sort of arrangement." He picked her up easily, only noticing a slight twinge in his kidney and back this time as he moved towards the stairs with Rose in his arms.

EIGHTEEN

Y*OUR MOVE*...

The next morning, Sawyer sat at the table moving pieces of paper and sticky notes around like he was playing a board game. Rose was making a batch of blueberry muffins in the kitchen for them and, he was sure, for the entire station.

As he looked down at the mess on the table, Sawyer couldn't see an answer in the papers. Even though he'd had several good hours of sleep, his mind refused to see any sort of pattern. He rolled his shoulders. His body felt relaxed, and he was pretty sure he would be back to one hundred percent by the end of the week. He had thought briefly about seeing the doctor early to get cleared for active duty, but he didn't like the thought of leaving Rose here in the house all by herself again. He decided to keep his mouth shut about his speedy recovery.

Even though Willis was gone, he doubted that whoever was pulling the strings was going to stop anytime soon. At least until all of the murderer's tracks had been erased.

Instead of finding answers, Sawyer just kept thinking of

new questions. Did Rose know something more about her husband's murder? Why had Willis attacked him?

He thought back to what he'd been doing that day, what questions he'd been asking. The fact that Willis hadn't attacked Carson or any of the other officers weighed heavy on his mind. He had been the only one getting close to Rose. Did that mean something?

After all, he'd spent most of the day he was attacked with Rose. She had even eaten over at his place just before the attack. Could that mean that someone was stalking her?

He thought about the destruction of her back deck. He was still convinced that it was Boone Schneller who'd torn up her deck and had punctured his tires. The sneakiness fit the man's MO.

Taking sticky notes out, he wrote down each event as it had happened to create a timeline that he could move around.

"What's this?" Rose asked, looking over his shoulder.

"A timeline of events." He moved a sticky note with 'Ozzy's attack,' written on it into place.

"What does Ozzy getting attacked have to do with Isaac's murder?" she asked.

"I'm not sure, but it's an event and..." He shrugged. "Something tells me to put it down here."

She nodded and then sat next to him.

"Do you really think that the destruction of my deck has something to do with the murders? I thought you said it was just Schneller getting back at me..." She fell silent.

"If Schneller had anything to do with all these... murders"—he motioned to the timeline— "then, yes. We won't know until we find the murderer."

Just then the doorbell rang.

"I'll get it. It's probably Carson." She moved a few notes around as he made his way towards the door.

Instead of letting his partner in, he stepped outside to have a private chat with him.

"Well?" Sawyer asked.

"The cash could have come from anyone on the list. We're looking into it... But, from the news I heard this morning, I'd move one name up on the list."

"Who?" he asked.

"Kristy Owens. Apparently, she has just talked with her lawyer and they are ready to—" They both turned as a black sedan drove up the driveway. Carson sighed. "I'd hoped to beat him here by a few more minutes."

"Who?" Sawyer asked, but when the man stepped out of the car, Sawyer had a feeling he knew what was happening. "Damn it." He looked back inside and wished he'd prepared Rose for the possibility of what was about to take place.

"Morning." The lawyer stepped up onto the front porch. "Is Rose Clayton home?"

"And you would be?" Carson asked, crossing his arms over his chest.

The man's eyebrows rose slightly. "This isn't an issue where the police should be concerned." He handed a card to Carson and another one to Sawyer.

The card read 'Jeffrey Taylor, Attorney at Law.'

Just then, Rose opened the door. Her smile fell away the moment she noticed the lawyer on her doorstep.

"Can I help you?" she said sweetly.

"Mrs. Rose Clayton?" the man asked, stepping past Sawyer and Carson.

"Yes." She leaned against the door and Sawyer noticed that her knuckles were turning a little white.

The lawyer pulled out a large manila envelope and handed it to her. "You've been served. Have a nice day." He nodded, then moved quickly back to his car.

"Damn it," Sawyer said under his breath as he turned to Carson. "Tell me this isn't Owens."

Carson shrugged. "I guess we'd better call that brother of yours back down here," his partner said as he stepped inside the house.

Sawyer reached over and took the envelope from Rose. She'd just been staring down at it like it was a snake. "Let's see if we can figure out just what Isaac's mistress is trying to get from you."

Before Hunter arrived, Rose stashed all the sticky notes and stacks of paper from the dining room table in her binder and hid the entire thing on a shelf in the library. Hunter walked into the house two hours later and sat down with Rose to go over the lawsuit Kristy Owens had filed against her.

"Wrongful death?" Rose shook her head as she frowned. "Why is she suing me for all this? I didn't have any control over Isaac's death."

"That's not the way she sees it," Sawyer said, earning him a glance from Hunter. He shrugged quickly. "You have to have seen some of her TV interviews."

Hunter sighed and nodded. He turned back to Rose. "Most likely this will all be thrown out, since she technically wasn't related to Isaac, but..."

"What about her son?" Rose asked, her voice sounding small and weak.

"Unless she can prove, with DNA, that the boy is Isaac's..."

"She can," Sawyer jumped in. "She filed the paperwork less than a week after Isaac's body was found." Again,

Hunter gave him a look. "Sorry. Police information isn't always on the news or available to suspects or their stepbrother lawyers at the time."

"Okay." Hunter sighed. "Still, you haven't been arrested for Isaac's death. At this point, they still aren't sure who murdered him."

Hunter had watched Sawyer and Rose closely and Sawyer knew the man had questions about why he was staying at the house. Still, Rose hadn't said anything to her brother about them or their new relationship yet, and he wasn't going to either. His private life was just that, private. What was between them should remain so for as long as possible.

"What does this all mean?" Rose asked.

Hunter pushed the paperwork away from him, his eyes moving between them quickly. "Worst case, it goes to court, but most likely it won't since there isn't any evidence you had anything to do with Isaac's death. Like I said, we're probably looking at the judge throwing it out before it heads to court."

"What if it does go to court?" she asked.

"Then we simply have to prove you had nothing to do with Isaac's death." Hunter smiled over at Rose and took her hand in his. "Trust me."

"What happens if she wins?" Rose asked.

"If she wins, she can recover any expenses, get a settlement for pain and suffering caused to her, and possibly even punitive damages."

Just then, there was another knock on the door. "I'll get it." Sawyer stood up, but Hunter stopped him.

"Better let me. I'm Rose's lawyer and brother. Besides, this is probably just the beginning." He stood up. "If Miss Owens is in this for fame, I doubt she'll stop at one lawsuit."

Sure enough, there were two more visits that day before Hunter headed back home for the night. He had pulled Rose aside privately before he left. Sawyer knew he shouldn't eavesdrop but couldn't stop himself.

They had talked about why he was staying in the house. Hunter had made it very clear that he didn't like that there was a cop staying with her. Rose told him about his attack and that she was taking care of him, and that he was also there to protect her, and he seemed to quiet down.

Hunter took the legal paperwork with him, but not before Rose scanned them into her computer system. New lawsuits for pain and suffering and libel and slander were added to the mix.

"Why is she filing these lawsuits? I've never said a word publicly about her." He could hear the weariness in her voice.

"Attention," he guessed. "Like your brother suggested. Besides, Hunter will be filing several suits against her on your behalf in return. She went on several interviews calling you a murderer."

She sighed and nodded. "I hate using the law."

"I have to side with your brother on this one."

They moved back into the kitchen, and he watched her make dinner. The way she moved around the kitchen was almost like a dance.

Her cell phone rang, and he listened to her side of the conversation. It sounded like she was talking to her agent, Julie.

When she got off the phone, Rose had a huge smile on her face. She did a little booty dance, which got him just as excited as she was, only in a different way.

"So?" he asked, feeling his heart race at how beautiful she was when all the worries of the day disappeared.

"Julie has set up an art exhibit for this weekend." She did a little dance again. "This weekend! She snuck me into another showing. When she called them... well, it appears that all this news has caused quite a demand for my art. She says that several of the pieces I gave her have already sold."

"Do you think it's wise to play off the publicity at this time?"

"I didn't do anything wrong. I can't stop my life and wait around for the killer to expose himself." She glanced over her shoulder as she worked on making dinner.

"Or herself," he added, thinking about Kristy Owens.

Rose nodded. "Julie seems to think that striking while the iron is hot—her words, not mine—could bring in almost double what I made at the last show."

"What did you make?" he asked.

"Enough to pay for my car." She nodded towards the back door. "Isaac wanted to get me a present for my last showing, but I wanted to pay for something for myself. I chose it, went down to the car dealership, and negotiated the deal myself. Isaac was in New York that weekend." Her smile fell slightly.

"Not bad." He thought about the last price tag he'd seen for the BMW SUV she drove and realized it was more than he made in a year.

She danced again as she went back to work. He was so busy watching the way her butt wiggled in the tights she was wearing that when she stopped and turned around, he was slow to move his eyes back up to hers.

"Come with me," she said, causing him to smile.

"Now?" His eyebrows moved up and she laughed at the look he was giving her. He didn't bother trying to hide the lust that was in his eyes.

"No, to New York," she answered.

His first inclination was to say no. After all, he had work and Ozzy. But he did still have a few days before he was going to see the doctor. He was past the two-week mark in his recovery. From the slight twinges he still got in his left kidney, he doubted the doctor would let him get back to a full work schedule before that weekend.

"I can see if Carson can watch the dogs."

"Really?" She smiled. "You'll go with me?"

His mind quickly ran through everything. He was pretty sure he could convince the chief that someone needed to watch over Rose in the city. Especially now that it was clear that someone had hired Willis to do the dirty work.

"Yes." He walked over and wrapped his arms around her, then kissed her.

"How will we get there?" She turned back around to the stove when the timer went off.

"We can drive."

She frowned over at him. "Seven hours?" She shook her head. "I'm nothing like Julie, who absolutely enjoys long road trips. Are you?" she asked.

He shook his head. He hated sitting in a car or a plane for more than two hours unless he was staying wherever he was going for more than a week.

"I can ask Hunter to fly us up," she suggested.

That would allow him to see Hunter's piloting expertise firsthand. "It's up to you." He walked over and kissed her on the cheek. "I have to make a few calls before I commit fully."

She nodded. "Dinner will be done soon."

He snapped his fingers and the dogs followed him out onto the back deck while he called the chief and ran his idea by him.

"I doubt the doc will clear you by then, so it's up to you what you want to do on your free time. Since there hasn't been a move on Clayton's life, I can't justify police protection, so the moment you're cleared, you're back at work."

"Sure thing." He glanced around the frozen yard. They'd had lots of the white stuff, enough to make the ground gleam white. "Did you find any fingerprints on the keys?" he asked. He had a list of questions he'd wanted to run by the chief since their last meeting. Seeing Rose's notes had made him realize there were some answers he hadn't gotten yet.

"Other than hers and Isaac Clayton's, no." The chief sighed. "She's still not sure how they ended up back in the house?"

"No," he answered.

"Who had access to the place? Besides her?" Deter asked.

"The workers were still here." He remembered when they had finished up with the basement door. "The basement was wide open, so anyone could have come and gone. Hell, we found a set of footprints, remember? They could have been coming and going as much as they pleased before it started snowing. The stepbrother has a set of keys. I'd have to check with Rose, but I think that's it."

"I didn't get my keys back from RJ yet," Rose said from the back door. He turned and realized she was leaning against the doorjamb, listening to him.

"RJ?" Deter asked, obviously he'd overheard her.

"Yeah, sounds like Gamet still has a set of keys to the house. He didn't turn them in after he stopped working here," Sawyer relayed.

"We'll head over there and collect those for her," the chief said quickly, then he hung up.

"So?" She stepped forward and wrapped her arms around him to keep warm. "What's new?"

He filled her in over another amazing dinner.

"I should have remembered that RJ still had a set of house keys before tonight. I've been so..."

"Preoccupied?" he supplied.

"Distracted." She smiled over at him. Tsuna was curled up at her feet and Ozzy was at his, begging for scraps. "Have you made up your mind about New York?" she asked.

"I'll go."

"Wonderful!" She jumped up from the table and took the empty plates to the sink. "I'll have Julie arrange everything."

He took his glass to the sink and wrapped her in his arms. Her arms came around his shoulders as she smiled up at him.

"I've never been to New York," he said. Her eyebrows shot up.

"You haven't?"

He shook his head. "I know, it's so close, but... I never had a reason to go."

"You'll like it. I did, at first, after we moved there." She dropped her arms and walked over to get a cup of tea.

"What changed?" he asked, following her into the living room.

She sat down on the sofa and he bent down in front of the fireplace to stoke the fire.

"Isaac was so involved in his work, he was gone almost all the time." She sipped her tea. "Now, of course, I know that he was leading a double life. But I was alone most of the time. The city was so large and so... full of people I didn't know. I even took an art class locally, just to make friends."

"And?" He moved over and sat next to her. The dogs both settled between them.

"And the only friend I had was Julie. And she was spending so much time trying to get her career off the ground, she was traveling all the time as well. Most of my time I spent locked away in our apartment, painting. Which is why I had so many dark pieces." She nodded to the piece she'd hung on the wall in the living room.

He looked up at the stormy ocean scene. He'd loved the piece when he'd first seen it. He hadn't realized it was one of hers until he was staying there and had walked around and looked at the art that she had hanging up everywhere. Every piece on her walls was hers, and he'd been more impressed than ever. The piece in question was a lot darker than those hanging around the rest of the house.

"Then you moved here?" he asked.

"Yes, Isaac bought this house, Stoneport Manor, as another gift—"

"Did he always buy you things?" he interrupted. She tilted her head and he could tell she was thinking about it.

"Yes. I used to think it was because he loved surprising me, but now I wonder if it was his way of justifying his deceit."

He nodded. "Guilt gifts. Ann used to do that as well."

"I've never heard it called that before, but yes. Looking back now, I'm sure that was it. Every time he would have to leave or stay out of town longer, he'd come back with something small, a piece of jewelry, or even the flowers..." She stopped suddenly. Her entire body froze.

"Rose?" He reached over and touched her.

"The flowers." She turned to him. "Who sent me those last flowers?"

"What flowers?" he asked.

"The ones that were delivered the day before you and Carson showed up on my doorstep. If Isaac was already... in the wall, then who sent me the text and the flowers? I get the killer sending me a text, if he took Isaac's phone, you know, to throw everyone off and make it seem that Isaac was still alive, but why send the flowers? How would the killer know that Isaac sent me flowers when he was gone? How did the killer know Isaac did that?"

"It has to be someone close to you," he supplied. "Let's look at that list again." He stood up and walked over to where they had stashed all the sticky notes and stacks of papers.

For the next hour, they laid everything out again, this time, setting two names to the side. He suggested they take Boone Schneller off their main suspect list altogether since he doubted the neighbor would know about the flowers.

"Maybe he noticed the flower delivery van arrive all the time," Rose suggested.

"What about Ray Gardezi?" Sawyer asked.

She shrugged. "Isaac wasn't too private of a person. Maybe he overheard him making a call or even talked to the man about it. But it is highly unlikely."

"Okay, so we move these two down the list, but not off of it. Owens?" he asked.

"A mistress would know, wouldn't you think?" she asked. "I mean, I would think that if you got into a relationship with a man and stayed with him when he marries, you'd know that he sends flowers to his wife each time he's with you."

He nodded, then moved her to the top of the list. "Hunter?" he asked.

"You know how I feel about his name even being on here. But"—she sighed loudly— "he's been here several times when the flowers arrived. Plus, he's known us and our relationship pattern for as long as I've known Isaac."

He nodded and kept Hunter's stack where it was.

"Your father-in-law?" Sawyer asked.

She nodded. "Yes, I remember Sean mentioning something about it when Isaac was here. They seemed to think it was a great joke. Now that I know everything, I'm sure Sean knew about Kristy all along."

Sawyer moved the father-in-law's pile next to Owens's pile. They both had financial motives. He crossed his arms over his chest as they both looked down at the list. "Our top two suspects."

NINETEEN

Treachery...

When the weekend came, Rose couldn't contain her excitement as the three of them loaded onto Hunter's plane.

Since Sawyer wanted to witness Hunter's flying abilities firsthand, he sat up front with him. She'd flown with Hunter plenty of times and didn't mind relaxing in the backseat of his Cessna 172S Skyhawk.

Their luggage was crammed in the seat next to her, but she still had plenty of room to relax. There was still a light snow falling as they took off, and she smiled when Sawyer's knuckles turned white as he gripped the overhead handle when Hunter took off.

"Have you flown in a small plane before?" Hunter asked, chuckling.

"Yes, but not in bad weather," Sawyer replied.

"This isn't bad weather. We once flew to Montreal in a blizzard, remember that, Rose?" Hunter glanced back at her.

She laughed. "Yes, what fun we had. He took me

skiing." She touched her brother's shoulder. "We had a blast."

"Where was Isaac?" Sawyer asked.

Her smile fell away.

"Stuck in the city," Hunter supplied. "Now, I suppose, we all know why." He glanced back. "Sorry, sis."

"It's okay." She smiled up at him. "I'm just thankful you didn't know about it before I did."

"Why?" Sawyer asked as the small plane continued to climb.

"I probably would have killed the guy," Hunter said easily.

Sawyer nodded. He seemed to relax a little when the plane leveled off.

"You went to school with Isaac, didn't you?" Sawyer asked.

Rose leaned back. Sawyer had talked about using the flight time to ask Hunter a few questions he still had. She'd tried to talk Sawyer out of grilling Hunter during the flight but understood that he wanted to get some answers for himself. In her mind, Hunter being on the list of suspects was ridiculous.

Still, she knew she was biased and Sawyer needed to look at all possibilities. For the record, her money was on Kristy Owens. After all, it hadn't taken the woman much time to jump in after they found Isaac's body.

The only question that weighed heavy on her mind was why the woman hadn't made herself known after Isaac had supposedly died in the plane accident almost a year ago? Why now? Then again, she wasn't sure that Kristy Owens had been in financial difficulties a year ago. Sawyer had mentioned that Owens had signed a large movie deal shortly before Isaac's death, so maybe she hadn't needed the attention or money then. Did that mean the woman hadn't had anything to do with his death?

She leaned her head back as Sawyer and Hunter talked and before she knew it, Sawyer was shaking her awake.

"We're coming in." He smiled back at her. She noticed the change in him instantly. He was relaxed and actually looked like he was enjoying himself. "Your brother let me fly for a while," he said with a smile.

"Oh?" She smiled. Hunter had let her fly several times and she had at one point even thought about getting her own pilot's license. Before Isaac's death, that was. "How did he do?" She leaned forward and touched Hunter's shoulder.

"Not bad," Hunter answered. "Most people already have the basics down, steering, and all that. It's the takeoff and landings and what to do when you're caught in a cross-wind that are harder."

"What would it take to fly one of these into the ocean?" Sawyer asked.

Hunter looked over at him, his eyebrows shooting up. "Isaac's you mean?" Sawyer nodded.

"I mean, in the movies, they tie something to the steering wheel." Sawyer nodded to the two small wheels on either side of the cockpit. "But I doubt it would cause this to take a nose dive into the water."

"Yeah." Hunter thought about it. "I guess, someone would have to be able to jump out."

"Mid-flight?" Sawyer asked.

"Sure. A lot of people who parachute use small planes to take a few people up. Of course, they always have a trail of forms they have to fill out beforehand. You know, flight patterns, legal release forms." He tilted his head. "They don't usually jump out of the front of a plane; the doors aren't easy to open against the wind. But, it can be done.

Or," he shrugged. "the door could have been removed before flight. If whoever flew it kept it low."

She could tell he was thinking about the logistics of it all. From what she was hearing, however had dumped her husbands' plane in the ocean, would have had to have been an expert.

"Have you ever parachuted?" Sawyer asked.

"Sure." Hunter smiled. "Plenty of times. Isaac and I used to go all the time."

"I didn't know that you had been skydiving or, for that matter, that Isaac had." Rose leaned up as the plane started heading downward.

"Isaac got me hooked on it back in college. He was going up with a few buddies and invited me along." Hunter turned the plane.

"What about Sean?" Sawyer asked.

"Yeah, I mean, sure. Isaac told me Sean used to take him up all the time. I guess he got him hooked when he was a kid."

"Did they ever take you up?" Sawyer turned and asked her.

"Me?" She shook her head as she laughed. "Jump out of a perfectly good plane? Nope." Just the thought of it made her head spin.

They landed without any issues, even though the snow was falling harder here than when they had left. Hunter had called ahead and arranged to have the plane parked and housed in a hangar until they left in two days.

Julie had sent a car for them and the three of them piled into the black sedan. Sawyer tried to lift her bag, but when he winced with pain, she berated him and took the bag from him.

"How much longer are you going to be off work?"

Hunter asked when they were heading towards the hotel Julie had arranged.

"I go to the doctor early next week," Sawyer answered. "It's been driving me crazy, not working. The food is good though." He reached over and took Rose's hand, and she smiled over at him.

Since Hunter was in the front seat of the sedan, he didn't see the move, or the smile Rose gave Sawyer in return. Still, she knew that she had to tell Hunter soon that she was seeing Sawyer, since he was so determined she steer clear of him.

He didn't seem mad about the idea. The last time they'd talked about it, he'd stressed how important it was that she keep her nose clean in the eyes of the police, so they had no reason to suspect her. But after she'd explained the several issues she'd had with her back patio and told him about the murder on her land, Hunter had been concerned enough that suddenly police protection hadn't looked so bad.

She'd made a point to keep it secret how close she and Sawyer had become. It wasn't any of Hunter's business whom she dated.

Close. Is that what they were? They hadn't officially gone out on any dates, and his items were still in the guest room across the hall, even if he did spend every night in her bed.

Julie had arranged for three hotel rooms at the Ritz-Carlton. She was a little surprised when Hunter and Sawyer were given rooms on the third floor and she was put on the top floor.

They had arranged to meet Julie in the lobby in the bistro and bar for dinner at eight, which gave her almost four full hours to gawk at the view of Central Park from the Royal Suite.

The last time she'd come into the city for an art showing, Isaac had picked a hotel down the street from the gallery. It had been top dollar, but nothing this nice. She had almost two thousand square feet to herself for the next two nights.

She took her time and hung up her dresses in the larger of the two rooms in the suite. She'd packed several dresses but now she was worried that what she'd brought along for the event wasn't nice enough.

Picking up her phone, she texted Hunter.

-I need to shop. Wanna come?

-Sure, are we ditching the cop? he replied back almost instantly.

She chuckled, then replied.

-He can come if he wants to spend time in the lady's dress department. I'll ask...

She texted Sawyer, who replied back quickly.

-Is Hunter going?

-Yes

-I'll pass, stay safe, stick to your brother's side.

She smiled and typed.

-Did the two of you bond on the trip up here?

-Let's just say, I feel confident that he has your best interests at heart. I'll see you for dinner.

-Okay

She texted Hunter again.

-Nope, he's skipping. Meet in the lobby in five?

-Okay

She freshened up, grabbed her purse, and made her way to the lobby. Hunter was already there waiting for her.

"You should see my room." She hooked her hand in his arm. "The penthouse," she added.

"You deserve it. After all, you're the star of the show."

They walked out the front door and glanced around.

"Where to?" he asked.

"I have no idea." She frowned and glanced up and down the street.

Hunter turned to the doorman. "We're looking for shopping." He turned to her. "Dresses?" he asked, and she nodded quickly. "Women's dresses for a special event."

The doorman pointed them to the left where there was a shopping center with plenty of high-dollar stores. The man assured them that they would be able to find what they were looking for there.

They walked arm and arm down the street and chatted about how exciting the trip was. She could tell Hunter was avoiding talking about all her legal worries and the murders.

For the next two hours, she laughed and had fun with her brother as she tried on more dresses than she could count. In the end, he convinced her to spend a little extra and purchase two dresses, a long formal celadon dress with a low plunging neck for the art showing and a shorter silver and gold floral lace dress for dinner that evening. Since she had already purchased new shoes for the event that would go with both dresses, they made their way back to the hotel.

They had stopped and bought a cinnamon roll on the way to the shops, but by the time she let herself back into her hotel room, she was starving.

She showered and started getting ready for dinner. She had just pulled on the dress when there was a knock on her door. Zipping the dress up, she opened the front door and smiled at the massive bunch of roses meeting her.

"These were delivered to the front," the bellhop said. "Would you like me to set them down?"

She stood back and watched as he replaced the ones on the dining table, then left.

"Thank you," she called after him as she touched the soft yellow petals and smiled. She opened the note and froze.

"Thinking of you. Always yours... IC"

Her throat tightened, and her eyes teared up as she reread the note. With shaky hands, she pulled out her cell phone.

"Hey, I'm almost ready," Sawyer said.

"I... need you up here," she managed to say.

"What is it?" She could hear him rushing around.

"Someone sent me flowers."

"What?"

"There's a note." She set the paper down and stared at it. "It's from Isaac."

"Rose?" When she didn't respond, he asked, "What room are you in?"

"Top floor," she answered.

"I'm in the elevator. Open the door for me."

She walked over and opened the door. When the elevator opened less than a minute later, she dropped the phone as he gathered her in his arms.

"Show me?" he said after she felt a little more stable.

"There." She pointed to the note. He read it and then frowned.

"I don't understand."

"Isaac, the flowers..." She shook her head. "He used to always say that when he sent flowers to me. Plus, those are his initials. He always signed the cards IC. It was kind of his thing."

"Are you sure?" He checked the roses for more notes.

"Yes, it's his handwriting." She closed her eyes and leaned against the door. "The day before he... or rather, the day after..." Her hand was covering her heart. "I received flowers just like this, yellow roses. The note was identical. I gave it to the police."

He set the note down and walked over to her. "Hey, we'll figure this out."

She nodded and looked into his green eyes. "It's got to be a joke, right? Someone's sick idea?"

"Let's find out." She sat on the sofa while he called the front desk. He asked who had delivered the flowers, then asked for the phone number of the floral shop. Then he called and repeated the questions to the florist. When he hung up, he came and sat next to her.

"A man came in about half an hour ago. He paid cash. No photo ID or credit card. No name." Sawyer took her hand and wrapped his arms around her. "We'll find the SOB."

She closed her eyes and sighed. "At least we can mark a few more names off the list."

He leaned back and frowned at her. "Why?"

"It was a man, not Kristy."

He sighed. "She could have paid someone," he suggested.

"Right." She rested her forehead in her hands. They remained silent for a while. When she looked up again, she realized he was already dressed for dinner. The black suit, green shirt, and silver tie looked amazing on him.

"Wow, look at you." She stood up and he followed. "You clean up nice."

He chuckled. "You're not bad yourself." He brushed a finger down the sleeve of the dress. "Pretty amazing, actually. Don't worry about the flowers. We'll get to the bottom of it. I'm sure whoever it is, they're just toying with you."

She knew he was trying to make her feel better but there was still concern behind his eyes.

He moved closer and wrapped his arms around her. "You know, we still have half an hour before we're supposed to head downstairs." His smile grew. She leaned up and, a breath from his lips, she asked, "Whatever shall we fill the time with?"

He chuckled and walked backward with her until her knees hit the sofa. He frowned down at it, then glanced around.

"Wow, what a room." He whistled.

"It's a suite."

"Where's the bed?" He turned around.

"In there." She pointed. He took her hand and she followed him until he stood at the foot of the bed.

"Now, where were we?" he asked softly as his hands ran up and down her sides.

"I think you were trying to take my mind off of... things." She nudged his dinner jacket off his shoulders and started unbuttoning his shirt, slowly.

Her hands ran over his chest and she moaned as his muscles twitched under her fingertips. He groaned when she reached for the snap of his dress pants.

"You're killing me." He reached for the zipper on her dress.

She held still while he turned her around and slowly unzipped her dress. The material landed in a pool at her feet. She stepped out of it and stood in front of him in her lacy black underwear set. His eyes ran up and down her slowly.

"My god," he whispered, "you're amazing."

She stepped closer to him and nudged his pants down his legs. They joined her dress on the floor.

"We're going to end up going to dinner all wrinkled," he joked.

"It's just Julie," she reminded him. She stepped closer, wrapping her arms around him as their lips met. "I need you," she said.

"Yes, god yes," he growled out between kisses as he walked her a step backward towards the bed.

His hands moved over her slowly at first, then as the power and need built, she demanded more, and he provided.

His body pressed against hers and when they fell onto the bed, she laughed as he covered her. When he entered her, she cried out in pure pleasure.

She'd never experienced anything like the unadulterated delight she felt in the closeness she shared with Sawyer. Or how he made her feel when he was touching her, looking at her as if she was the most beautiful thing he'd ever seen.

She couldn't keep herself from falling for him even more or control the emotions that followed after she'd given him everything she had, leaving her raw. All she could do now was hold onto Sawyer as the power of everything he'd done to her, for her, washed over her and consumed her.

They lay together, breathing hard, as their hearts settled back down.

"Okay, now I'm thinking of calling off dinner and staying right where we are for the rest of this trip," he said against her skin, his breath causing goose bumps to rise.

She laughed. "Me too." He rolled back to look at her.

"How about a quick shower?" he asked.

"You read my mind." She rolled over. "You thought my room was nice. You should see the shower." She wiggled her eyebrows at him.

Tying her already curled and styled hair up, she turned on the shower and stepped in and he followed her. "This is amazing." He glanced around at the large shower. "My room is nothing like this." He turned towards her and wrapped his arms around her. "It's nice, but not this."

"I know, right? I'm thinking of redoing my own bathroom," she joked.

The hot water hit them, and she felt renewed once more. "We're going to be late," he warned as she rubbed her body against his.

"Like I said, it's just Julie and Hunter." She kissed him and enjoyed the way his body responded.

They walked into the dining room downstairs less than five minutes late. Julie and Hunter were standing at the entrance to the restaurant waiting for them.

Her dress was slightly wrinkled, as was Sawyer's dinner jacket.

She hugged Julie. "So, tell me all about the show," she asked as they were being seated at their table.

While Julie talked about the art showing, she tried to avoid eye contact with Sawyer, but the man was like a magnet. Julie must have noticed because she leaned closer to her and whispered while Sawyer and Hunter talked about something else.

"Things have changed between you and Sawyer." Julie touched her hand.

"What?" She shook her head, but her friend's smile told her that she'd guessed. She couldn't stop the smile or keep her eyes from moving to Sawyer's green ones. "Yes, they have."

"Chat later." Julie nodded as the waiter delivered their food.

"So, I know it's short notice, but the party is a formal affair. If you two need tuxes, there's a place just down the street. I've already called them. You can stop by anytime tomorrow before the showing to be fitted."

"I have my own," Hunter broke in.

"Since when do you have a tux?" she asked.

"Since I realized it was more cost effective than renting one every time I had a black-tie event." Hunter smiled at her.

"What about you Sawyer?" Julie asked.

"I'll make sure to stop by the shop. Can you text me the store name?"

"Sure." Julie reached into her purse and pulled out her phone.

"I am curious if you know who else knew we were coming into town," Sawyer asked.

Julie's eyebrows shot up and she set her phone down. "Well, I'd hope everyone would. I've spent a fortune getting ready for this show."

"What do you mean?" Rose asked.

"Well, to capitalize on the show, I've spread the word all over the city that you'll be in town." Julie smiled. "Shortly after I did that, the show sold out and I actually had to move the show to a larger art gallery."

Her friend seemed very proud of herself and Rose hated to burst her bubble, but she really didn't want all the attention.

"The media?" Sawyer asked.

"Well, sure, they've been talking about it for the past few days." Julie reached over and touched her hand again. "You're the talk of the town."

Rose felt her stomach roll and pushed her half-empty plate aside.

"Do you think that's wise?" Hunter asked. "There is, after all, still a murderer out there."

Julie's smile shifted slightly. "They're not after Rose." Her friend's eyes moved to hers. "Are they?"

"Someone sent her flowers today," Sawyer said.

"They did?" Hunter shrugged. "I bet she gets them—"

"It was from him," Rose added, feeling her stomach roll again. "The note was the same one that I'd received the day after Isaac went missing. It had his initials on it."

The table was silent. "Did you check to see who sent it?" Julie asked.

"A man, and he paid cash," Sawyer answered. "I'll look into it further tomorrow, but for now, I'm thinking of changing rooms or better yet, sleeping on Rose's couch for the night."

"There are two bedrooms in my suite," she added, knowing full well he wouldn't be sleeping in the other bed.

"I think that's a great idea," Julie added.

"I could always..." Hunter started, but the look Rose gave him shut his mouth and he nodded. "Police protection." He sighed. "But if you need anything, I'm just a few floors down."

"Thanks." She smiled over at him. "Honest, I'll be fine."

"Of course, you will," Julie jumped in. "You're the strongest woman I know. Now, let's talk about what you're wearing to the show."

Rose laughed and filled her friend in on her new outfit.

TWENTY

A SWARM...

The following morning, Rose woke to the sight of Sawyer getting dressed.

"Where are you off to this early?" She propped herself up on her elbow.

"Flower shop first, then I'm getting fitted for the tux after. Want to meet for lunch?" He glanced at his watch. "How about one o'clock?"

"Sure." She rolled out of the bed and walked over to help him pull the shirt down over his head. He was still having problems pulling on T-shirts and hated that he didn't have full mobility back yet. "I saw a little café just down the street. We can meet there," she suggested.

"Okay," he said when he was freed from the tangled shirt. "What are you up to this morning?"

"I was going to do some more shopping."

"Didn't you do that yesterday?" How much shopping could a woman do while she was in the city?

Rose laughed. "Yes, but I'm not sure when I'll be back

in the city. Besides, I need a clutch purse for tonight and some jewelry."

"Is Hunter going with you?" he asked, worry filling his eyes.

"Of course." She leaned up and kissed him.

He nodded his head. "Then, go, have fun. I'll see you at one." He pulled on his shoes with minimal pain.

"We were going to hit a few of Hunter's favorite spots after we have breakfast together."

He leaned down and kissed her. "I wanted to have breakfast with you, but I want to get there when the flower shop opens."

"I understand. We can have breakfast tomorrow before we head home." She kissed him back.

"I like the sound of that. Home." He sighed. "We need to talk about what's going to happen after I feel better." He rested his forehead against hers. "At least until this thing is over, I was thinking of staying put." His eyes met hers and when she smiled, he relaxed.

"I'd like that." She kissed him again. "Go, play cop."

He hated getting in the elevator and leaving her but trusted that Hunter would keep an eye on her. He stopped by her stepbrother's room and knocked before leaving.

Hunter answered in a towel still wet from the shower.

"Hey." He leaned against the door.

"I'm heading out to see what I can learn from the flower shop. You've got your eyes on Rose today?"

"Sure thing." He smiled. "We're doing breakfast then shopping."

"We'll meet for lunch around one at the café she mentioned." He glanced at his phone. "Let me know if you think anything is off or if your plans change."

"Will do." Hunter saluted him with a smile. "Keep us posted, will you?"

"Sure." He turned to go.

"Sawyer," Hunter called, and he turned back around. "We'll have a chat about you and Rose soon." Sawyer's stomach dropped, but he nodded to the man and left.

So much for personal life being private, he thought as he stepped out onto the sidewalk. The snow was coming down even faster and it took him almost an hour to get to the flower shop that was supposed to be less than half an hour from the hotel.

After wasting almost an hour talking to the manager and waiting for the owner to show up, he realized that the reason the man who'd sent the flowers to Rose had chosen that flower shop was because it was stuck in the early eighties. They didn't have a security system, which meant there were no cameras in the place. He even went to the store across the street and the one next door. It appeared that the entire block was a black-out zone without any cameras or security. The closest camera was at the ATM on the corner. Still, he took down the information and figured he could have Carson contact the bank. He sent his partner the information and made his way over to the tux shop.

He arrived almost ten minutes late for the appointment that Julie had set up for him. He thought moving was hard with his bruised body but standing still for almost a full hour was absolute hell.

His muscles screamed at him and he felt a bead of sweat roll down his back as the man took his measurements. Still, he was thankful when he walked out of the store with half an hour to spare.

He thought about what Rose had said, how Isaac used to surprise her with gifts all the time. He had to admit, part of him felt guilty for not getting her anything for the event tonight. So, as he made his way down the street, he stopped in a small jewelry store.

A silver bracelet caught his eye and, after talking to the clerk, he realized how perfect it was for Rose. The silver chain had room for several small charms and he could pick them from hundreds of choices. He chose five charms: a light pink rose with a Swarovski gemstone in the middle, a silver paintbrush, a silver artist's palette, a charm with an R for Rose, and then a clear Swarovski crystal in the shape of a heart.

The bracelet wasn't as expensive as something Isaac would have bought her, but still, it showed her exactly what he thought of her and he hoped she would enjoy it for what it was—his feelings for her expressed on her wrist.

He stuck the box in his pocket and was just leaving the store when the television screen caught his eyes.

Seeing Rose's face on the screen caused his heart to jump. He watched what was happening to her in horror. He pulled out his phone and called her, and when his call went to her voicemail, he tried Hunter's number.

"Hey," Hunter answered on the first ring.

"Is Rose with you?" he asked.

"I just left her in the shoe section of the store while I ran to buy some cufflinks."

"Where are you?" Sawyer asked quickly.

"Why? What's wrong?"

"Kristy Owens. It's all over the news."

"What is?" Hunter asked.

"They're face to face and it looks like Kristy is getting the better of Rose," Sawyer said, starting to run down the street now.

"Damn it, I'm rushing back to where I saw her last." He could hear Hunter running.

"Where are you?" he asked again.

"The mall, just across the street from where we were meeting for lunch." Hunter was breathing heavy. "Damn it, there's paparazzi everywhere over here."

"I'm a few minutes out," he said. "Call me when you have her."

"Okay," Hunter said before hanging up.

Sawyer ran as fast as he could towards the end of the street.

When he reached the outside of the mall, his phone rang.

"We're out of there. Meet us back at the hotel," Hunter said.

"I'm just outside the mall," Sawyer said.

"We're already a block away. I had to get her out of there." Hunter sounded pissed. "They had her cornered." Sawyer could hear Rose crying and it broke him that he wasn't there for her.

"I'll meet you in her room. Take her straight up," Sawyer added.

"Okay, see you there." Hunter hung up again.

Damn it, Sawyer thought, he should have been there with her, to protect her. Julie had told them last night that the news of Rose coming into town was all over. He should have guessed that Kristy Owens would have played her next hand in such a manner. After all, reality TV was popular and what's more exciting than a mistress confronting the wife of her murdered lover?

His phone chimed with a message from Hunter.

-Made it safe to her room.

He was surprised to see a crowd gathering in front of

the hotel. Paparazzi was everywhere and when they noticed him, the cameras turned in his direction as questions were yelled at him.

"Officer Sawyer, what are you doing in New York?"

"What is the Twisted Rock Police doing in New York?"

"Did you follow Rose Clayton to New York to protect her or arrest her?"

Without answering any of the questions, he stormed past everyone and didn't stop until he was in the elevator alone. He tapped his hand impatiently against his leg as he was slowly taken up to the top floor. The doors opened, and he banged on Rose's door. Hunter opened it and he marched past the man to take Rose into his arms. Seeing the lost and hurt look in her eyes made him want to punch something or someone. She held onto him and cried so hard that her body went lax when he wrapped his arms around her.

He turned while holding her and asked Hunter, "What happened?"

"From what I can tell, they, the paparazzi, jumped and swarmed her. That woman..."

"Kristy Owens," he supplied, and Hunter nodded.

"She was nowhere to be found by the time I got there. Rose was backed into a corner as the damn paparazzi took pictures and yelled questions at her," Hunter growled out. "I should have been there."

"We both fell down on the job," Sawyer said.

"I have to move," he said, pacing the floor. "I'll go get us some food downstairs." Hunter stormed out of the room.

"Are you okay?" he asked Rose when they were alone. He gently picked her up and carried her into her bedroom and sat with her on the edge of the bed.

"It was awful," she said against his chest. "That woman... The things she said."

"Did she touch you?" he asked.

Rose looked up at him. "N-no." She shook her head. "I don't think so. Why?"

"You could have her arrested for assault if she pushed you," he suggested.

"No, she didn't touch me." Rose shook her head slightly.

"But she backed you into a corner?"

"Everyone... the paparazzi did. She approached me and accused me of killing Isaac. She said that I'd never loved him like she did and that he only tolerated me because... he felt sorry for me." Her eyes closed, and his heart broke seeing her pain. "She said that he was going to leave me, that he was tired of being around me. She laughed and said that he had no plans of having kids with me and that he was going to tell me the night he disappeared."

"Hey." He brushed her hair out of her face. "She's an actress. She'll say anything to further her cause and to hurt you." He pulled her close again. "Are you sure you're okay?"

She nodded against his chest and wiped her eyes with her coat sleeve. "Hunter saved me." She sighed. "I should have known better than to go shopping today." She looked up at him, then gasped slightly. "You don't think... that sort of thing will happen tonight? That she'll be there?"

"I'll make sure it doesn't." He pulled out his phone to call Julie as Rose watched him. When she answered, he stepped out onto the balcony.

"I saw it on television. I've been trying to call Rose. Is she okay?" Julie asked.

"Yes, for now. We need to know that Owens won't be allowed in tonight."

"Of course not. I've already talked to security and told

them that she's not allowed. I may be playing off the publicity, but I love Rose and would never do that to her."

"Good, what about the paparazzi?" he asked.

Julie sighed. "Well, that's a little different. I can't keep everyone with a camera out tonight, but I have a list of some of the worst offenders and I'll make sure they stay out."

"I'll want to talk to your security firm beforehand," he added.

"Sure, I'll forward their contact information and tell them you'll be calling them."

"Thanks." He started to hang up.

"Tell her I'm sorry," Julie added. "I never expected..." She sighed. "Tell her I'm sorry."

"Will do. We'll see you in a few hours."

"Okay." Julie hung up and he stepped back inside out of the cold.

While he was on the phone with Julie, Hunter had walked in followed by a woman with a cart of food. Now Rose and Hunter were sitting around the dining table.

"Is everything okay?" Hunter asked.

"Yes, security is all arranged for tonight." He took Rose's hand. "I won't take my eyes off you."

"Neither will I," Hunter added quickly.

Rose smiled. "How can a girl go wrong with you two as protection?"

"Eat, then you can rest before the show," Sawyer suggested.

He could tell that the ordeal had worn Rose out. After finishing off her burger, she disappeared into her bedroom.

"What's the plan?" Hunter asked once they were alone.

"Plan?" Sawyer asked. "To have one of us within a foot of her all night long. That's about it."

"What if something like that happens again?" he asked.

"Then we get Rose out of there like you did today." He slapped the man on the shoulder. "Great job by the way."

Hunter's shoulders lifted, and he smiled bigger. "Thanks." His smile fell quickly. "I shouldn't have left her. I had forgotten my cufflinks and thought I could just..." He sighed and shook his head.

"Hey, I wasn't even there. I had my own errands to run." Sawyer leaned back in the chair.

"What are the police doing about finding Isaac's killer?" Hunter asked.

Sawyer's eyes searched Hunter's and seeing only concern, he gave him a vague answer that gave him more information than he would have given anyone else. "We're working hard on it. We have our suspects."

"I take it from all the questions on the way up here that I'm one of them?" he asked.

Sawyer nodded slowly. "Along with a few others."

"Kristy Owens and Sean Clayton?" Hunter asked.

"Yes, on both accounts," Sawyer answered.

"Sean's out, waiting on his trial." Hunter sighed.

"Yeah, I'd heard." Sawyer felt his stomach roll at the possibility he was behind his son's murder and the thought that the man might get away with everything he'd done.

Sawyer could only remember a few things about his own father, but the man had been nothing but kind before cancer had taken him before his thirtieth birthday.

Hunter sighed. "After that stunt today, I'm putting all my money on Kristy Owens. That was a nasty situation, and from what everyone is saying, it was all her doing."

"Have you seen the video?" He nodded to the television, which was turned off.

"No, I don't think I could stomach it." Hunter glanced at the set.

Sawyer walked over and flipped on the screen, making sure to lower the volume to where he had to stand in front of it to hear anything.

Hunter walked over and stood next to him as he flipped through the stations until he found one of them playing the video.

The scene started outside the store. Owens was smiling into the camera, giving an obviously staged interview. Then someone zooms past her shoulder and calls out to Rose. Suddenly, Owens was next to Rose.

"Why don't you save us all some time and confess to murdering Isaac, the love of my life," Owens said, standing a foot away from Rose.

Cameras were turned onto Rose, who already was looking as if she'd been blindsided. Rose's eyes scanned the room, seeking help from any source.

"You know he was leaving you that weekend." Owens chuckled. "He told me you wanted a child." She laughed harder. "Like he would ever want a child with you when he has one with me," Owens sneered. "He couldn't stand you. The only reason he was with you is because he felt sorry for you."

Rose let out a small gasp as tears started falling down her face. The cameras were shoved closer to her face as questions were yelled out. This went on for almost a full minute before Hunter could be seen pushing several men away from Rose, gripping her arm, and pulling her free of the crowd.

Sawyer flipped off the set and tossed down the remote. His anger boiled over and he was pretty sure that Hunter's matched his own.

"Bitch," Hunter said under his breath.

"Yeah, I wouldn't argue that, and I'd wager most everyone who saw that is thinking the same thing now."

"Kristy Owens looked stoned or drunk," Hunter suggested. "Anyway, I'm heading downstairs and calling in a few favors to get a restraining order filed against her. By tonight, that woman won't be able to come within a hundred feet of Rose." Hunter pointed to the dark television set, then spun around and headed towards the door. "I'll see you in the lobby at eight."

"Keep me posted on the restraining order," he called after him. Hunter waved his hand and disappeared out the door.

Sawyer flipped the lock on the door behind Hunter and then moved into Rose's bedroom doorway. Seeing her balled up on the bed fast asleep, he toed off his shoes and crawled in next to her, pulling her close to his side. She sighed in her sleep and snuggled against his chest, and he drifted off holding her tight.

TWENTY-ONE

An evening to remember...

Rose looked at herself in the mirror one last time. Gone were the puffy eyes and the red-tipped nose, thanks to the stylist Julie sent over. Ranald was twenty-something and fabulous. Even Sawyer laughed at his jokes as the man curled her hair and applied her makeup.

Sawyer's tux arrived half an hour before they were set to leave, and he disappeared into the other bathroom to get ready himself while Ranald finished the last touches on Rose. Then she slipped on her dress and shoes and walked out into the main room where Ranald and Sawyer waited for her.

All three of the men's eyes lit up and she smiled.

"Twirl, baby girl," Ranald said, and she obliged. "My work is done." He smiled at her and walked over to kiss her cheek. "Have fun and be fabulous," he whispered before leaving.

"You look amazing." Hunter kissed her cheek. "And we're going to be late if we don't leave now." He made his way towards the door.

"We'll meet you in the lobby," Sawyer said, holding her hand to stop her from heading towards the door.

Hunter shrugged and pulled on his coat, then walked out.

"Sawyer, we'd better go." She smiled up at him, unsure of why he wanted to be alone with her.

"Soon." He pulled out a large square box, and she frowned down at it. "I have a gift to say… congratulations on a successful night, but I couldn't wait until after the evening was over to give it to you." He smiled and opened the box.

The silver bracelet was beautiful. Small charms hung off the silver chain. He helped her clasp it onto her right wrist. "It's beautiful."

"Do you like it?" he asked. She looked up into his eyes.

"It's perfect." She smiled and hugged him. Isaac had always given her things that cost too much or were things that he wanted. She'd never received anything as perfect as this. She ran the jeweled heart between two fingertips and smiled. "Yours?" she asked.

"If you'll have it," he said softly.

She answered him by leaning up on her toes and kissing him.

The limo ride to the gallery was short and when they pulled up outside of the glass building, there were more people with cameras than had attacked her earlier that day.

She must have stiffened because Sawyer reached over and took her hand in his. "Easy, we're here."

"Are you okay?" Hunter asked her.

She took two deep breaths and smiled at them both. "Yes, I can do this. I'm ready."

When they climbed out of the limo, Hunter went first, followed by Sawyer, who reached back and helped her from the low vehicle. The extra material in her long dress snagged on the bottom of her heel, but she freed it just before stepping out onto the sidewalk, which was full of cameras.

Brushing the material of her skirt until it lay straight, she pulled a wrap over her shoulders and then took Sawyer's arm as they made their way down the carpet towards the front doors of the gallery.

Questions were shouted at her, but she held her head up high and smiled as they walked through the light snow and the bright flashes from the paparazzi's cameras.

"You did great," Sawyer whispered as they stepped into the brightness of the gallery. As with most galleries she'd been in, the walls were painted a stark white and it took a moment for her eyes to adjust.

Her wrap was taken from her shoulders. She gripped her clutch purse to her side and looked around while Sawyer and Hunter turned in the coats less than a foot from her.

She smiled, knowing that all evening long, the two of them would probably never leave her side.

"Shall we?" Hunter held out his arm. "Sawyer's going to check security."

"Rose." Julie rushed across the room towards her. Her friend kissed her and gave her a hug. "Hunter." Julie smiled and gave him a light hug as well before turning back to Rose. "I'm so sorry about what happened earlier. I tried calling but..."

"I lost my phone," Rose told her. It was something she hadn't even told Sawyer yet. She glanced over as Sawyer walked back over to them.

"You did?" Hunter and Sawyer asked at the same time.

"Yes." She looked between them. "Just before... I

thought it was in my purse, but..." She shrugged. "I'll get a new one when I get home."

"You should have told us," Sawyer said softly.

"I've lost phones before," she added with a smile.

"Three times before," Hunter offered with a chuckle. "Joan—that's Rose's mother," Hunter said to Sawyer, "used to joke that she was going to staple the next phone to your hand, so you wouldn't lose it."

Rose chuckled and remembered the argument with her mother.

"Sawyer, it's good to see you again. It looks like you're back in full swing." Julie shook Sawyer's hand.

"I'm a quick healer," he said. "Where's the head of security? I'd like to talk to him." He glanced around.

"His name is Cameron." Julie looked around. "There, the man in black who looks like he just stepped out of the FBI." She pointed to a man across the room.

"I'll be back," Sawyer said to her. He looked at Hunter. "You've got this?"

Hunter took her arm and smiled at Sawyer. "Go, we're going to mingle."

Hunter had attended a few other gallery showings of hers before and he knew the drill.

"Let's start over here." Julie took her hand from Hunter's and pulled her towards the side. "Your pieces are..." They passed a divider and suddenly she was surrounded by her paintings.

Dozens of people made their way to talk to her and for the next hour, she stood in one spot and talked. At one point, Sawyer handed her a glass of champagne and whispered, "You're doing great."

Her feet and back hurt, but she continued to smile and answer questions about her art, her style, and her process.

The crowd had died down some and she was in a deep conversation with a prospective buyer when she was tapped on the shoulder.

"I'm sorry to interrupt," the woman said. Rose turned around. The woman looked familiar, but she couldn't place a name or figure out where she'd seen her before.

"I'm sorry." She turned back to the man she'd been listening to.

"No, I've taken enough of your time. I'll just go hunt down Julie. Have a wonderful evening." He kissed her cheek and left.

Rose turned back to the woman and noticed Sawyer leaning on the wall less than five feet away from her. He looked bored, but his eyes were scanning the room as if expecting someone to jump out of the shadows. Placing on her smile again, Rose held out her hand for the woman.

"Have we met?" she asked, her eyes scanning the dark-haired woman in the sleek black dress. She was shorter than Rose but held herself as if she was the center of the room.

"No." The woman's chin went up slightly. "But we have mutual friends." She moved closer and lowered her voice. "Your stepbrother Hunter and I used to date in college. I'm Melanie."

"Oh?" Rose had never met one of Hunter's girlfriends before, but she'd seen a few pictures on his social media. That's where she'd seen the woman before. She'd heard all about Hunter's exes from him, but so far, hadn't met one face to face. Her eyes scanned the room for her brother.

"Yes, he's the one that introduced me to Isaac." Melanie's smile grew, and her eyes turned hard, causing Rose's heart to skip.

Rose's entire body stiffened, and she took a step back.

The woman reached out and gripped her arm tightly. Again, the woman's voice lowered.

"He knew all about Kristy and Isaac. After all, he's the one who introduced them." The woman shoved something into her hand.

Rose looked down at a printed photo of four people in swimsuits at the beach—Hunter and the brunette standing in front of her, and Isaac with his arms wrapped tightly around Kristy Owens's barely covered perfect body.

Rose tossed the image onto the ground. "Why?" She shook her head as tears formed. "Why are you doing this?"

The woman stepped closer. "You took everything away from Kristy. You didn't deserve Isaac, Kristy and Ash did. You murdered him." At this point the woman's voice had risen and Rose felt an arm wrap around her and tug her backward. Feeling Sawyer's warmth, she pushed him away, not wanting to be protected any longer.

"I didn't kill Isaac. I didn't even know about Kristy or Ash. Not until a year after he'd died," she cried out. Sawyer pulled her away once more and the woman was carried out by security.

"Rose." Julie rushed over to her side.

Rose pushed Sawyer away, unable to be touched, not wanting his comfort at hearing the news. Her eyes scanned the room and Julie tugged her towards the back.

"Bathroom," Julie said, and Rose followed her. She was sure Sawyer had followed them but didn't look back to check.

Rose walked in and with her expensive new heels, kicked the plastic trash can once they were alone in the bathroom.

"What happened?" Julie asked.

"He knew." She spun around and marched back and

forth in the small space. "Hunter knew about Kristy and Isaac," she cried out as tears rolled down her face.

Julie gasped. "Son of a..."

"How could he? He lied to me. All these years. He lied to me." She stalked back and forth, needing more space, needing to run, needing to hit something. Since her toes were throbbing from the trash can, she refrained from kicking it again.

"What can I do?" Julie asked, looking helpless.

"I need to get out of here." She glanced around. "I've caused enough scenes today, I can't handle another one."

"I'll handle it." Julie walked over and hugged her. "I'm sorry," she whispered.

Rose hugged her back. "You didn't do anything wrong." She felt the hurt starting to drain her of energy.

"No, but if I hadn't put this together tonight, you'd still be in your blissful mansion locked away with your new prince charming."

Rose smiled at her friend. "Speaking of which..." Just then the bathroom door opened, and Sawyer stepped in.

"I waited as long as I could." He glanced around.

"I was just leaving. I'll clear the back doorway area so the two of you can sneak out," Julie said with a smile before leaving.

Sawyer walked over and stopped a foot from her.

"Are you okay?" he asked.

She could tell that he wanted to touch her but held back.

Walking over, she wrapped her arms around him and rested her head on his shoulder. "Hunter knew about Kristy and Isaac," she said into his chest.

"Yeah, I overheard, so did the entire gallery." He sighed and wrapped his arms around her. "Let's get out of here."

There was a knock on the door. "All clear," Julie said from the other side.

"My coat?" she said as Sawyer opened the door. To their surprise, Julie held up both of their jackets.

"Thanks." She smiled over at her friend.

"Thank *you*. I'll call you tomorrow and tell you how we did." She winked at her and motioned towards the back door. "The limo is waiting."

They ducked out of the gallery's back door and slipped into the waiting limo. She sighed when the door was shut behind them.

"I can't believe Hunter knew." She rested her head back. "He promised me that he didn't know." She sat up slightly and looked back down the alley as they drove out. "Where is he?"

"He went to get some food." Sawyer glanced at his watch. "He told me he'd be back about now." He frowned and less than a minute later, Sawyer's phone chimed.

"It's Hunter." He held the phone up.

"I have nothing to say to him." She pushed it away.

Sawyer answered it, but then she grabbed it from his hand.

"Is it true?" she asked, feeling her temper spike again.

"Is what true? I just got back here with a plate of food for you only to find out that you two had left."

"Did you know Kristy and Isaac were an item?" she asked clearly.

"No," Isaac answered.

"I saw a picture of the four of you," she countered.

"Who?" Hunter's voice changed.

"Melanie." She spat the name out.

The phone was silent. "Rose…"

She hung up and tossed the phone in the seat next to her where it immediately started ringing again.

"I want to go home tonight," she said, looking over at him. "Can you arrange for us to catch a plane?"

"I can check." He picked up his phone and for the rest of the ride back to the hotel, was busy trying to arrange the trip back.

"How about a car?" he asked as they drove up. "There's a storm coming in..."

"Sure," she tossed out. "I just want out of this city." She climbed out of the limo before he could help her out.

He hit a button on his phone and caught up with her. "The car will be out front in fifteen minutes," he added. "Can you be packed by then?"

"Yes," she said as they stepped into the lobby. Sawyer had moved his things into her room last night, so they went straight there. She spent ten minutes packing up and then pulled on jeans, boots, and a long sweater for the car ride home.

"I'll get that." Sawyer picked up her bag and tossed it over his shoulder just as someone started pounding on the door.

Rose walked over and opened it, almost causing Hunter to fall inside on his face.

"Rose," he started.

She held up her hand, stopping him. "No." She shook her head and stepped around him.

"I think it's best if you give her some time," Sawyer said as he passed by Hunter.

"I didn't..." Hunter started. Rose spun on her heels. Her eyes narrowed as she glared at him, causing him to shut his mouth. "I'll fly you home," he offered.

"No." Rose shook her head and punched the button for

the elevator. Sawyer followed her into the elevator, then held up his hand when Hunter tried to get in with them.

"Take the next one," he said softly and stood back as the doors slid closed behind him.

"Are you okay?" Sawyer asked as the elevator started moving towards the lobby.

"No," she said softly, feeling her shoulders sink as tears rolled down her face. "How can I ever trust him again?"

Sawyer dropped the bag and pulled her into his arms. "Hey, I know you don't want to hear this now, but maybe you should hear his side of the story. After all, Owens and her gang are professional manipulators."

She closed her eyes, and the image of the four smiling faces popped up behind her closed eyelids. There wasn't any manipulation about the image. The four people had been on that beach, together.

There could be more to the story, but right now, she didn't want to hear it. The pain from her brother's deceit outweighed any rational thoughts.

The black SUV rental was waiting for them and Sawyer loaded up the luggage. They drove out of the city, guided by his phone's map program.

She leaned her head against the cold glass and watched the snow falling in the dark night as they left the city. If she never returned, she'd be completely content.

She must have fallen asleep at one point, but when the car slowed, she woke and glanced around.

"Sorry," Sawyer said softly. "I'm stopping for gas and some coffee."

She sat up a little. "I can drive." He parked by the gas pump and took her hand. "No, you sleep. I'm good to go."

"Where are we?" she asked, looking around.

"Just outside of Denville." She had no clue where

Denville was, but it didn't really matter. "Do you want anything from inside?"

They were parked at the gas pumps at a brightly lit gas station where people were coming and going. She glanced at the clock and groaned. "It's a quarter past one." She yawned.

"Yeah." He smiled. "That's the reason for the coffee break."

"I'll come in with you." She found her purse on the floorboard and followed him into the store. "I'm going to hit the bathroom." She turned towards the back wall but then froze.

"Sawyer?" She gripped his arm and nodded towards the television as she felt her entire body start to shake.

There on the screen was an image of Kristy Owens, and underneath the picture of the pretty blonde, in bold text, it said, *'Film-star Kristy Owens found dead in her New York apartment.'*

TWENTY-TWO

DROPPING LIKE FLIES...

"Damn it, Deter, there is no way Rose or I had anything to do with Owens's death. You know that," Sawyer hissed into his phone.

"Sure, I do, but the NYPD want her back there ASAP for questioning," Deter said.

"We're holed up in some hotel outside of Clearfield." He ran his hands through his hair. It was a quarter to five in the morning and he hadn't gotten any sleep. Rose was inside the room they had gotten for a few hours, hoping to get some sleep before they hit the road again. They had made it halfway home before he'd needed to pull over for some sleep or they would have ended up in the ditch.

"Well, we need some rest and I doubt that Rose will want to head back to the city anytime soon."

"I'll stall them for as long as I can," Deter said. "Get some rest. I'll expect to hear from you the moment you set foot back in Twisted Rock."

"Got it." He hung up and stepped inside the small hotel room.

"Well?" Rose was drying her hair as she sat on the large king-sized bed.

He set his phone down and lay down in the bed beside her. She'd cleaned her face from all the product Ranald had slathered on her earlier. She was even more beautiful like this and he had a hard time taking his eyes from her face.

"We'll get some rest then continue on home. Deter's going to deal with the police asking after us."

"Are they?" she asked, her eyebrows going up slightly.

"Asking about us?" He shrugged. "They can wait." He flipped on the television. "I know you probably don't want to hear about it, but... I'd like to know what they're thinking."

She nodded as his phone chimed. He picked it up and read the message from Hunter.

"Your brother made it home okay. He asks if you're okay?" Sawyer told her.

"Tell him to stuff it." She lay down next to him with a small bounce.

"Those words?" He started typing.

"Yes, those words exactly." She crossed her arms over her chest.

"Something tells me you had a very fun vocabulary when you were younger. I would have liked to see you pissed when you were five." He chuckled. When she glanced over at him with a glare, he stopped smiling, finished typing, and hit send.

Hunter's response came quickly.

-Get her home safe and know that there is more to the story.

-Will do.

He replied and set the phone on the nightstand. He turned up the set when the story came on.

"B-movie actress Kristy Owens, known for her roles in *Bleached* and *Solid Leads*, was found in her New York apartment, which was purchased by her late lover, Isaac Clayton..."

Rose sat up slightly, her eyes glued to the set.

"She kept the apartment?" she said softly.

"Rose?" He touched her shoulder, causing her to turn towards him.

"Isaac only rented the place." She frowned at him.

"I hadn't heard. Shortly after we found out about Owens's involvement, I was removed from the case and didn't get a look at the file," he explained.

"Isaac purchased the apartment for her?" She frowned and turned back to the screen where the reporter was standing outside of the massive brick apartment building.

"The police seem to believe at this time that Owens OD'd on pain pills. The young mother leaves behind her three-year-old son, Ash, whom she left in her mother's care more than two months ago after losing the legal battle with Fuller Films. Some speculate that—"

Sawyer flipped off the set and reached up to touch Rose's shoulder.

"Looks like her conscience got the better of her after all." Rose turned back to him. Fresh tears were building behind her eyes.

"Her son." She shook her head and closed her eyes and then buried her face into her knees and hugged them. "Why would she do that?" she cried, and he held onto her.

When he felt her body go lax, he pulled her down and tossed the blanket over them, and she cried herself to sleep in his arms.

The next morning, they left just after eleven. After hitting a drive-through for some food, he drove the rest of the way home. When he pulled into her long driveway, he wasn't surprised by the row of media vans parked out front. Deter was also there, leaning against his patrol car with Detective Anderson waiting beside him.

"Carson will drop off Tsuna and Ozzy after his shift is over," he said. "I'll talk with Deter; you can go up and rest."

"No, I want to hear what information he has. After all, we may have just freed ourselves from Isaac's murderer." She took a deep breath.

He must have been foggy brained because he hadn't thought of that angle. Nodding, he pulled the rental behind the patrol car and turned off the engine.

"Deter." Sawyer nodded to the chief as he stepped out.

"I thought I'd save you a call." The man walked over and shook his hand. "And the stress of worrying."

"Let's get inside." Sawyer nodded to the sky as more snow fell around them.

He set the bags down inside the doorway and walked over to light a fire. The heater had been turned to low and Rose turned it up now that they were back home.

"So," Rose asked, "what's the news?"

Deter sat down across from Rose, who had tucked her legs under a blanket. Anderson stood by the fireplace, rubbing his hands together.

"First reports out of New York are suicide. They found more than half a dozen pill bottles around the apartment," Anderson answered.

Sawyer sat next to Rose. "Time of death?" he asked.

"That's the kicker. Apparently, she left you in the department store, rushed home, and took more than a handful of pills," Deter explained.

"Right after..." Rose shook her head.

"I'll need to know where you were after you left the

store." Anderson walked over and sat down, then pulled out a notepad.

"We returned to the hotel, had something to eat, then slept until about six in the evening, when Rose's agent sent a stylist to come and take care of Rose's hair and makeup for the event."

"You were together?" Anderson asked.

"Yes, the entire time," he answered, no longer caring what his admission meant to him or his job.

"It's just covering your butt, but I'll want more details if you have them. The stylist's name, your agent's info," Deter said to Rose, who nodded.

"I lost my phone in New York, but I have Julie's number..." She disappeared into the library and came back with a note. "Julie will have Ranald's information. That was the stylist."

Deter stood up, followed by Anderson.

"We'll get out of your way. I'm sure you're both tired after the weekend you just had."

"Thanks," Rose said, sitting back down on the sofa and wrapping the blanket around her.

"I'll walk you out." Sawyer stood and followed the men out the front door. "You'll let me know if anything changes?" Sawyer asked.

"Sure will, but for now, I'll share this information with the NYPD." Deter looked around, then back at him. "We found some more information about Willis's finances."

"Oh?" He leaned against the door. "Besides the deposits?"

"We've confirmed that he had large cash deposits, one the day after Isaac Clayton went MIA and the second, the morning you got attacked."

"So, you're pretty sure it was Willis who jumped me?" he asked.

Deter sighed heavily. "That's our working theory."

"Who paid him?"

"We had a look at Owens's finances, before... There was no way the woman could afford those amounts. About the only people on the list who could are Sean Clayton and Hunter McDonald."

After spending the last few days with Rose's stepbrother, Sawyer had moved the man down on his mental list. Even after finding out that Hunter had known about Kristy, he just couldn't see the man in the role of murderer.

"Clayton senior seems more likely to me. What's he been up to?" he asked.

"He made bail shortly after being arrested. He's been silent since then," Deter answered.

"Where is he?" Sawyer asked.

"His penthouse in New York. The police have been keeping tabs on him."

Sawyer nodded, feeling his entire body starting to shut down. "I'm going to head in and get a few more hours of rest. Carson's supposed to be here with the dogs soon. If you find anything else out, text me."

"Will do." Deter shook his hand. "When is that doctor's appointment of yours?"

"Two days. Why? Miss me?" He smiled.

Deter chuckled. "We're shorthanded. I know I moved you to the evening shift, but we may need you working some double shifts for a while. Carson's been complaining that he's had to partner up with Madsen, now that Brown walked."

"Brown finally stepped out?" he asked. The man had been threatening to move to the city where he could move up to detective more quickly, or so he'd always bragged. With the man's disciplinary record, Sawyer doubted he'd go far.

"Yeah, he said that after getting a taste of the excitement with all the media in town, he felt the need to move onward and upward."

Sawyer chuckled. "Good riddance." He turned and let himself back into the house.

When he stepped in, Rose was lying on the sofa covered by the blanket, fast asleep.

He tugged off his shoes and tossed a second blanket over her. Then he threw another log on the fire and lay down beside her, pulling her into his arms.

"There isn't enough room on here," she said softly next to his body.

"We'll make room." He smiled and buried his face in her hair. "This is the warmest room of the house right now and I want a few more minutes of sleep."

He woke to the doorbell and dogs barking.

"That would be Carson with the dogs." He sat up, but Rose was already standing and moving towards the door.

For the next half hour, they played host to Carson and enjoyed the happy reunion with their mutts. Rose asked Carson if he wanted to stay for dinner. His partner, being a smart man, agreed.

He and Sawyer sat in the kitchen and talked about the trip and Owens's death as Rose cooked pork chops and potatoes.

"A man could get used to eating like this," Carson said after taking his first bite of food. "No wonder Sawyer is sticking around here." He nudged his arm. "Besides the company, I mean." He winked over at Rose.

"Don't let Bridgit hear you talk like that," Sawyer joked.

"She knows I have great taste in women." Carson laughed. "Besides, she's visiting her sister in California this week. I've got the place all to myself." He smiled and shoveled more food into his mouth. "I enjoyed the solitude at first, but after the first day, I was thankful I had these two to keep me company. I don't know how you do it, living in that small place all by yourself." Carson shook his head.

"I have Ozzy." He smiled down at the dog who was currently begging at his feet.

"Still, nothing beats the warmth of a woman next to you at night." Carson's eyebrows wiggled.

"Matchmake much?" Sawyer asked, causing his partner to laugh.

"Everyone in town can tell you two are good together." He pointed with his fork between them.

"Everyone?" Rose asked, putting another spoonful of food on Carson's plate.

"Yup, even the chief. Course, I knew it that night over a year ago." He shook his head. "Not that you and Isaac..." He cleared his throat. "Well, that was different."

"How?" Rose asked.

Carson set down his fork and nudged his plate away. "Well, the two of you came from different worlds. Isaac was his father's son, born with a silver spoon in his mouth." Carson glanced around the room, decorated with the best furniture and chinaware. "You came from... well, I knew your dad. He was the one who took me under his wing and trained me when I first joined the force after school."

"He did?" Rose asked, leaning closer.

"Sure. That night, when he was killed, I blamed myself for a long time. Even though I hadn't gone out on the call, I wondered for years if I could have stopped it or saved him if I'd gone instead of Brown."

"Brown?" Rose asked.

"Rick Brown?" Sawyer asked.

"Sure, he was Rose's father's partner at the time," Carson told them. "You come from cop's blood. Clayton might as well have come from the other side of the universe. Sure, you kids were cute together, but there was just something about the Claytons I never could put my finger on."

"What do you mean?" Sawyer asked.

"It was their house that your dad was called out to that last night. There was a domestic dispute call out at that fancy place Sean Clayton had purchased the summer before."

"The one Clayton sold shortly after Isaac's death?" Sawyer asked.

"Yeah, that was the place." Carson pulled his plate back towards him and started eating again.

"Whatever happened to Mrs. Clayton?" Sawyer asked Rose and Carson.

"She divorced Sean and took off for Italy," Rose answered. "Or so Isaac had always said."

"No." Carson shook his head. "She never officially moved to Twisted Rock. She came into town shortly after Sean and the boy moved into the house. Then... she never got a chance to leave. That night..." He pushed his food away again and took a deep breath. "That night your father and Brown were called out there, Isaac's mother shot and killed your father, then turned the gun on herself."

"What?" Rose stood up, her hands on the table. "Isaac's mother killed my father?" She shook her head.

"I thought..." Carson frowned at her. "Didn't your mother ever tell you? After you started dating Isaac, surely she mentioned it."

Sawyer stood up and walked over to Rose, but she

nudged him aside and marched into the kitchen. When he walked in, she was on the house phone, staring out at the back door.

"Mom?" she said, and he winced, not sure if he should listen in on the conversation. After hearing her next words, he backed up and went back to sit at the table with Carson.

"I'm sorry, man. I thought... I should have..." Carson ran his hands through his thick grey hair.

"Don't worry about it. Rose has had a lot of shocks in the past month." He followed Carson to the front door.

"I... thank her for dinner, will you?" Carson shook his hand.

"Will do. Thanks for watching the mutts." He nodded to the two dogs sitting at his feet while they waited for him to open the front door.

"Anytime. I think I convinced Bridgit to get another one. We're going to swing by the shelter when she gets back home."

Sawyer nodded. "Night."

Sawyer watched the dogs race around the snow in the front after Carson drove away. When he snapped his fingers, both dogs came rushing inside, shook the fresh snow from their fur, and disappeared back into the kitchen area, no doubt looking for Rose.

He carried the plates into the kitchen. Both dogs were sitting at the back door as if wanting to go out. He glanced out the back window and saw Rose standing on the deck, still talking on the phone.

Putting the dishes in the dishwasher, he kept his eyes on Rose from the window. Her hands were flailing about as if she was arguing, and she paced as the snow fell around her. At least she had pulled on the rubber boots she kept by the back door. He was worried that she hadn't pulled on a jacket, but she didn't appear to be chilled.

By the time she stepped inside, the kitchen was clean, and he was standing at the window, sipping a cup of coffee. When she walked in, he handed her a full mug.

"How is... everything?" he asked.

She took a long drink of the coffee and sighed. "She tried to pull the whole 'I don't want to talk about it' bit again. How could she?" She shook her head.

"How could she what?" he asked, touching her shoulder.

"Keep something like that from me. Why didn't she say something when Isaac and I started dating?"

"When you were what, ten?" he asked.

She rolled her eyes, then set the coffee mug down and pulled a carton of ice cream from the freezer. She grabbed a spoon and sat at the table.

"The least she could have done was tell me before the wedding." She took a large spoonful of the chocolate chip ice cream and shoved it in her mouth.

He grabbed his own spoon and sat across from her.

"Dealing with my mother always makes me binge eat." She took another spoonful. "It's like talking to a child sometimes." She set her spoon down. "I was finally able to get the entire story from her."

"And?" he asked, taking another spoonful of the ice cream.

"Apparently, the story had gone around that Isaac's mother was mentally ill. She'd been in and out of facilities her entire life. My mother said that's why Sean and Isaac moved to Twisted Rock after a messy divorce. Sean wanted to raise his son in a wholesome environment. But Dianna,

Isaac's mother, followed them there and that night..." Rose closed her eyes. "After the 'incident,' as my mother called it..." She picked up her spoon and took another mouthful. "Like my father's murder was a fender bender." She shoved the ice cream in her mouth and stayed quiet until she had swallowed it. "After my father's murder and Isaac's mother's suicide, Sean wanted to keep Isaac out of the spotlight and stayed put, telling his son a lie about his mother moving to Italy. Nice touch." She rolled her eyes. "It wasn't until Isaac was in high school that Sean opened his law practice in the city."

"Why didn't your mother tell you the truth sooner?" he asked.

"She claims that it wouldn't have made a difference. When Isaac and I started seeing one another, she and Sean agreed to keep the details of that night from the both of us. Sean claimed that he wanted his son to fill unhindered in life. Isaac was too young to really remember his mother and he felt that if Isaac knew that she had struggled with mental illness..." She sighed, and he could see sadness in her eyes. She set the spoon down again and rested her forehead on the table. "Okay, I get that. How could you tell your kid that their mother killed herself?" She sat up, her eyes meeting his. "Kristy and Isaac's son. I hadn't thought..." Tears started filling her eyes and he moved quickly and pulled her into his lap.

"You're amazing." He sighed as she cried against his chest.

"Because my life is a hot mess?" she asked.

He chuckled and rubbed his fingers through her hair. "No, because you're the only woman I know who would cry over her husband's mistress killing herself and their bastard son finding out about it someday."

She looked up at him. "Like I said, I'm a hot mess." She smiled.

He brushed her hair away from her face. "Like I said, amazing." He laid his lips over hers.

TWENTY-THREE

The Visitor...

The last thing Rose expected to wake up to the next morning was her mother standing over her and Sawyer's bed.

"Mom!" she cried out. She pulled the sheet up higher since they had fallen asleep in each other's arms after a sweaty bout of welcome-home sex.

"Who is this?" Sawyer asked.

Her mother's eyes narrowed towards Sawyer.

Thankfully, Rose was smart enough to hold his chest down, so that he didn't jump out of bed and shoot or attack her mother.

"My mother," she said to Sawyer.

"How did you get past security and..." He glanced down to the two sleeping dogs. "Them?"

"I have my own keys to the house, and I guessed the gate code." Her mother smiled. "As for them..." Just then the dogs woke up and barked at the newcomer.

"Too late," Sawyer groaned.

"After our talk last night, I figured we needed to come for a visit. Especially since you keep turning us away."

"Us?" It was then that Rose heard laughter and the sound of kids' feet pounding in the house. She groaned. "Jenny and the kids are here?"

"Well, of course." Her mother sat on the edge of the bed and Rose kicked at her.

"Mother," she growled out, "some privacy please." She dragged out the word.

Her mother's eyebrows rose. "Not until you explain to me who this is."

"Royce Sawyer," Sawyer said, sitting up slightly, exposing his bare chest. It took all of Rose's concentration to turn her eyes away from the sexy muscles and back towards her mother.

"He was invited into my bedroom, you were not." She nudged her mother's butt off the mattress again.

At this point, both Ozzy and Tsuna were dancing around happily on the floor, excited about the new visitor.

"Downstairs." Rose pointed. "I'll be down in five minutes." When her mother opened her mouth, Rose narrowed her eyes at her. "Go."

Her mother's chin rose, but she stood up and walked out of the room.

"Dogs?" her mother asked as she held the door open. Both Tsuna and Ozzy escaped the room, and Rose hoped that her mother or sister would have enough common sense to let them outside to do their morning business.

"Mom." She dragged the word out, causing her mother to smile.

"It was nice meeting you, Royce," her mother said before shutting the door.

"I take it that the sound of elephants running through

the downstairs is the kids you mentioned?" he asked, getting out of the bed.

Her eyes were glued to his firm butt cheeks and it took her a moment to process what he'd said.

"Regan, Cole, McKenna, and..."—she sighed— "my sister Jenny are all downstairs, probably making a mess in my kitchen."

He pulled on a pair of jeans and his eyes met hers as she watched his every move.

He bent over, placing his hands on either side of her body as his mouth hovered an inch from hers. "Keep looking at me like that, and we'll be the ones making the pounding noises up here." He wiggled his eyebrows, causing her to smile.

"Maybe that's what I want." She wrapped her arms around his shoulders, allowing the blankets to fall away from her naked body.

His eyes moved instantly to her bare breasts and heat flooded them, turning them a deeper shade.

"My god, how did I get so lucky?" he asked just before he covered her lips with his.

Fifteen minutes later, she walked into her kitchen with a smile on her face. She'd gotten dressed, braided her hair, and put on some basic makeup since she knew her mother would judge her if she didn't at least make an effort.

Sawyer had dressed quickly and explained that he was going to take Ozzy and Tsuna over to his place to check up on it. After dropping off the rental car, he was going to head down to the station and see if he could find out anything more about Kristy Owens's death.

He had snuck out the front door while she debated whether to head down to the kitchen.

Before entering the kitchen, she had taken a call from

Julie, who filled her in quickly on how successful the art show had been. Apparently, they had sold every last piece of hers and there were some high-end art dealers wanting to get their hands on more of her work. Julie made her promise she'd ship the rest of what she had to her as soon as she could.

"You've hit the big time, girlfriend," Julie had gushed. "Just promise me you'll remember us little people when you reach the top."

When Rose entered the kitchen, her sister walked over and gave her a half hug as she kept her eyes glued to the stairs. "Mom says you have a man up there."

"Sawyer had a few errands to run." She took over making pancakes from her mother, nudging her aside by bumping hips. Her mother gladly handed over the spatula.

"I thought his name was Royce?" her mother asked.

"It is, but everyone at the police station calls him Sawyer."

"Oh, he's a cop?" Jenny asked.

Rose glanced back at her sister. "Seriously? Where have you two been? It's been all over the news for the past month."

"What has? Royce?" her mother asked, sitting down at the bar and taking a sip of her coffee.

"Everything..." Rose swung the spatula in the air as she motioned around. "Everything, all of... well, everything. Sawyer, Owens, Isaac..." She shook her head.

She'd talked to both her sister and mother several times after they had discovered Isaac's body. They had even come for a short visit, but Jenny's job didn't allow much time off, and Rose was shocked that her sister and the kids had come along with her mother this time around.

"Why aren't you at work?" Rose asked, changing conversations.

Jenny smiled. "I quit."

"What?" Rose turned and looked at her sister. "Why?"

"She's pregnant again," her mother chimed in.

"What?" Rose felt her heart sink to her stomach.

Jenny covered her stomach as her smile grew. Jenny's youngest, McKenna, was six years old.

"I thought you and Bill were done with kids," she said.

"So did we." Jenny giggled. "Still, we're thrilled."

"Four kids?" Rose felt her heart burst. She'd just wanted one, now her sister was having her fourth.

Setting the spatula down, she walked over and hugged Jenny. "Congrats." She held onto her sister.

"Your day will come," Jenny said softly in her ear. "Maybe even with this Royce guy." She wiggled her eyebrows.

Rose thought about Sawyer and turned back to the stove. They hadn't talked about their future together yet. But he'd confessed in his own way that he loved her, even if he hadn't said the words yet. Then again, neither had she, she realized as she continued to cook breakfast for her family.

"How long are you guys staying?" she asked as they all ate breakfast.

"Only tonight. The kids have to be back at school Thursday. I could only take them out for a few days. But there are a few weeks left until winter break." Jenny sighed. "I'm thinking of homeschooling them."

"Oh?" Rose asked, trying to imagine her sister teaching. She laughed. "If my memory serves me correctly, you had a hard time passing algebra."

Jenny narrowed her eyes at her.

"Mom?" Regan, the oldest broke in. "If you didn't pass algebra, why do I have to take it?" Regan was ten going on thirty. The boy had more life skills than both Rose's mother and sister put together.

"Smart kid." Rose chuckled and handed her nephew another pancake.

"Thanks, Aunt Rose," Jenny said sarcastically. "Maybe I'll just bring them here and you can help them with all the math problems."

Rose smiled. "I'd be happy to. If you remember correctly, I passed the class."

"Can we paint?" McKenna broke in. The girl was wiggling her loose front lower tooth and swinging her legs back and forth as they dangled from the chair.

"Sure, sweetie." Rose smiled across the table. "After breakfast."

"I want to see where they found Uncle Isaac," Cole, the eight-year-old, said, earning him a slug from his brother, Regan.

She sighed, knowing the boys didn't mean anything by it. But she could see the interest in both of their eyes.

"The basement." She nodded to the door. "You know where it is. Don't go outside."

"Outside?" her mother asked.

"The workers put in a sliding glass door where…" She swallowed. "Instead of closing the wall all the way again."

"A light in the darkness," her sister said sadly, reaching for her hand. "Fitting."

She hadn't thought of it like that, but it was a beautiful analogy. Where Isaac had been locked for a year in darkness now stood a large pane of glass that let in the light of each new day.

"Rose?" Her mother took her other hand. "Is everything alright?"

"Regan, could you take your brother and sister up to my studio? You know where the art supplies that I have set aside for you guys are." The boys looked a little let down about not going into the basement yet, but Regan nodded.

The boy stood up and took his little sister by the hand. "We'll draw you a pretty picture." He smiled up at her. "To make you happy again."

She hadn't realized she was crying until McKenna asked Regan, "Why is Aunt Rose crying?"

Hearing the boy's answer caused her to chuckle.

"Dad always says, 'It's a great mystery as to why a woman cries.'" The boy opened the doorway to the back stairs and helped his brother and sister up to her art studio on the third floor.

"I needed that." She wiped her eyes dry. "I needed you guys." She looked to both her mother and sister.

"We've tried being here for you, but every time we call, you say you're fine and not to come," Jenny answered.

It was true. Her sister and mother had called her more than a dozen times since they'd found Isaac in the basement.

Her mother had actually been packing once to make the drive, but Rose had talked her out of driving all the way over from Pittsburgh, thinking that dealing with her mother would be more harmful than helpful. Now that she had Sawyer to lean on if needed, dealing with her mother and sister for one night didn't seem overwhelming.

"Is it true that Isaac had an affair with that actress?" her mother whispered, glancing towards the doorway through which the kids had just disappeared.

Jenny checked the stairs, shut the door, and sat down. "They're upstairs."

"It appears he did. What's more hurtful is that Hunter knew," Rose added.

"What?" Jenny and her mother gasped at the same time.

"Are you sure?" Jenny asked.

"I was approached by one of his ex-girlfriends, Melanie..." She shook her head remembering the photo of the four of them on the beach.

"Melanie Crown?" Rose's mother asked. Both Rose and Jenny turned to her in surprise.

"What? He's my stepson. I know almost everything about him."

"I'm closer to Hunter than either of you, and I had never heard him mention any of his girlfriends' names before," Rose said.

Her mother shrugged. "Hunter and Bill talk, and Bill and I talk."

"What did Melanie say that caused you to believe Hunter knew about Isaac's affair?" Jenny asked.

"It wasn't what she said, but what she showed me. A picture of the four of them on the beach. Isaac had his arms around Kristy Owens as if they were longtime lovers." Just the thought of it made her stomach roll.

"Maybe it was taken when you were away at college. There were a few years back then that the two of you saw other people," Jenny suggested.

Rose had thought of that herself and Sawyer had even suggested it when they talked about it on the long trip home.

"Still, when I asked him if he knew anything, he said no," Rose explained. "Deceit by omission is still deceit."

Everyone was silent for a moment. "Have you talked to Hunter about it?" her mother asked.

Rose shook her head. "We left New York and came home. Hunter's been trying to call Sawyer, but..."

"Why hasn't he called you?" Jenny asked.

"I lost my cell phone in the city."

Her mother instantly went into her standard lecture about losing her vital data and hackers.

"Mom, I had a passcode on it," Rose supplied.

"Still. Have you ordered a new one?"

"No, but Sawyer said he was going to take me tomorrow to get a new one. I called the phone company and filled them in. They say no one has used the phone since." She shrugged. "I probably just lost it somewhere at the store and someone turned it in. It might be stuck in a lost and found box in a store somewhere. Anyway, I've avoided his calls." She stood up and took the plates to the sink and started doing the dishes.

Her mother came up behind her. "He's your brother." She laid a hand on her shoulder. "Go, give him a call. We'll deal with these." She nudged her aside. "Go." She handed Rose her own cell phone.

Rose took the new iPhone out onto the back deck. The snow was still falling but more slowly than it had the previous night when she'd talked to her mother out there.

This time, she remembered to grab her jacket. She stepped out and walked a few steps away from the house.

Her mother had always used a mixture of her and her sister's birthdays as her passcode, so Rose punched it in and unlocked her mother's phone.

Hunter's cell phone rang three times before he answered, a little breathless and sounding like he was in a hallway.

"Hey, Mom, I'm just heading into—"

"It's Rose," she said, breaking in. The phone went silent and she heard the sounds change.

"Hi," Hunter said finally when it was quiet on his end.

"If you're busy..." she started.

"No," he said quickly. "I have a few minutes."

She was silent, wishing he'd start talking. Instead, she blurted out. "Why? Why did you tell me you didn't know about Kristy Owens and Isaac?"

"Because I didn't. Whatever picture Melanie showed you, it was from college. I was trying so hard to impress Melanie that I didn't pay any attention to Isaac and the girl he was with. We drove to the beach together, but the rest of the day I spent with Melanie, alone. Isaac and that girl disappeared. I didn't see them together again. I even gave him shit about being with someone when you two were supposed to be together. He told me you knew and that you had gotten together with someone else too."

"I did," she said softly, "but not like that."

"I'm sorry, I should have..." Someone interrupted him, and he covered the phone. When he came back she could tell he was walking again. "I've got to head into court. Can I call you later?"

"Sure," she said. "Mom, Jenny, and the kids are here."

"Good, enjoy them. I wish I could make it, but I'm in the middle of a case."

"Go." She sighed. "Do lawyer stuff."

"I love you," he said. "I'm sorry I hurt you."

"I love you too," she said before hanging up.

Tucking her mother's phone into her pocket, she looked back at the house. Sawyer was gone with the dogs, the kids were probably making a mess of her studio, and her mother and sister were no doubt already opening a bottle of wine instead of cleaning the kitchen. Wine after breakfast was their thing when they were both on 'vacation' mode.

Turning away from the manor, she looked down at the pathway towards the beach and sighed. She really needed some time to herself, so she started towards the stone steps that led down to the private sandy beach area. She wrapped her jacket around her as she walked down the stone pathway that she had cleared herself last summer.

She had hired a lawn and maintenance crew to clear a few dead trees along the pathway and they had also replaced a few of the larger broken stones, but she'd spent several back-breaking days in the sun herself, working on making the pathway beautiful.

She had even planted a few bushes and flowers along the way that would bloom every spring.

She had purchased wooden benches and beach chairs for several choice spots. Kids had come and carved their initials, surrounded by hearts, into the heavy wood. She wanted to be mad, but so far, no one else had vandalized the chairs. She had found herself tracing the initials and wondering what kind of future the lovers would have. So instead of having them sanded out of the wood, she kept them as a reminder that love can exist.

She was halfway down the steep pathway when she heard quick footsteps behind her.

She turned around just in time to see the butt of a long rifle slam into the side of her head just above her left ear. Pain blinded her as she cried out. She reached for something to steady herself. Then heavy hands fell on her shoulders and pushed. She fell back towards the steep stairs.

Her body connected with the next stair, her hip slamming into the corner of the stone. She continued to grasp for something to stop her from rolling all the way down the hillside to the bottom, but her nails hit only dirt as she rolled and twisted to the bottom. Her head hit several times on the way down and, each time, she cried out in pain.

When her body finally came to rest, she was breathless and disoriented. She tried to move, but there was too much pain. She blinked several times to clear her eyesight, but a grey fog settled in front of her eyes, and she slipped into unconsciousness.

TWENTY-FOUR

Getting dirty...

Sawyer had dropped off the rental car and walked to the police station with Ozzy and Tsuna. He'd ended up carrying Tsuna, who had whined every time he took a step. He had zipped the little girl in his jacket, and she had fallen asleep.

When he walked into the chief's office, the chief had taken one look at him and laughed. "Tell me you're not pregnant?"

Sawyer frowned down at the bump in his jacket and smiled. "No, it's Tsuna." He unzipped the coat and chuckled when the dog tried to bury her head further into his armpit. "I guess I wore her out on the walk from the rental car place." He sat down and let the dog lay in his lap. Ozzy lay at his feet, a little tired himself.

"Before you ask, I don't know anything more yet about Owens's death. The report out of the city is still showing she OD'd," Deter jumped in.

"Can you give me any details?" he asked, feeling like he was wasting his time.

"Only that the place was locked, and she was the only one with the keys. That's why it took so long to find her. Her friend showed up after Rose's event and called security when Owens didn't open up. They had to break in."

"What friend?" he asked.

"The chief glanced down at the stack of notes on his desk. "Melinda Crown."

"That's the woman who verbally assaulted Rose at the gallery. She must have gone to Owens's place after being tossed out of the showing by security. Was it a deadbolt or just a handle nob lock?"

The chief's eyebrows rose. "I asked the same question. Both the door handle lock and a deadbolt were engaged. Which means no one could have gotten in there and made it look like suicide."

Sawyer nodded. "But if we were to go with a theory that it wasn't suicide, who on our list was in New York?"

"Three of the remaining suspects, plus Rose Clayton, if we still count her." Deter held up his hand to stop him. "Yes, I know, she was with you."

"Time of death is still shortly after the incident at the mall?" he asked.

"Yes. Just after noon on Friday."

"Do we know where everyone was?"

"Sean Clayton was unaccounted for or so I'm being told. He was supposed to be in a lunch meeting but never showed. When the police asked him, he claimed he had gotten the stomach flu and was home alone sick." He glanced down at his notes again. "Boone Schneller claims he was home. We do know for a fact that he was in Twisted Rock, since he had a court date for that afternoon, so that leaves Ray Gardezi, who was in the middle of his niece's birthday party, surrounded by more than two dozen of his family and friends." Deter looked up at him. "You were with the stepbrother?"

"Yeah." He frowned. "What did you find at Willis's place?"

"Steel-toed boots. The lab is working on the blood found there, but chances are it'll match yours."

Sawyer nodded. "Yeah, I figured. The more I think about it... I'm sure it was Willis." Then he remembered what Rose had discovered last night. "There's a new angle we haven't looked at yet."

"Oh?" Deter's eyebrows rose. "What would that be?"

"Isaac's mother was the one who shot and killed Rose's father." He was still unable to believe the turn of events.

Deter slowly nodded. "Yes, I remember hearing about it. It was slightly before I took over. I was transferred in from Cleveland, like you."

"Well? Did you know that Rick Brown was Glenn Browning's partner that night?"

"Rose Clayton's father?" he asked and by the look on the chief's face, the man hadn't known that detail.

"Do you happen to know if Brown has his pilot's license?" Sawyer asked.

"You think he's hiding something?" he asked.

"I know that after Clayton's wife murdered a cop and committed suicide, he would have done anything to keep it out of the papers. He started his law firm in the city a few years later."

The chief sighed heavily. "It's worth a look. Brown was transferred to the city pretty quickly last week. I thought the entire ordeal stank of something." The chief turned to his computer. "Get out of here and finish healing. We need you back at full capacity and soon."

Sawyer picked up Tsuna and started to stand, but then

stopped. "Chief, I'd keep this last bit between us. After all, a lot of people in the station liked Brown."

The chief nodded and then waved him off. "I'll let you know when I find something."

Carson drove Sawyer back to the house but had to leave immediately, as he was still on duty.

"Sorry, I've got another call about the Denny's dog barking. If they'd let the poor guy inside once and a while instead of keeping him on that chain, he wouldn't bark so much."

"Good luck with that." Sawyer wasn't envious of his partner, who would spend the next hour trying to convince the two neighbors to get along.

When he walked into Stoneport Manor, it was quiet. He set Tsuna down and went to the kitchen to see where everyone was.

Rose's mother sat at the kitchen table with another woman, who Sawyer assumed was Jenny, Rose's sister.

The resemblance was slight. Her sister looked more like her mother than Rose did. He imagined Rose took after her father's family.

The women were sitting at the table, an open bottle of wine and a half-finished pie between them as they chatted. He couldn't believe they were drinking this early. Then again, it appeared they were both having mimosa's instead of just straight wine.

"Hi," he said, breaking into their conversation.

Two matching pairs of brown eyes turned towards him.

"Royce, we were just talking about you." Rose's mother smiled up at him. "This is Rose's sister, Jenny." She motioned to the other woman.

"Hi." He glanced around. "Where is Rose?"

"Oh, she went for a walk." Jenny motioned towards the back door.

He frowned instantly. "A... walk? Alone?" He moved towards the door.

"Yes, don't worry, she has my cell phone on her," her mother said, waving him off.

"Call it." He handed her the house phone. She shrugged and made the call.

On the fourth ring, the phone went to voicemail.

"Maybe she's out of the service area," she suggested.

"How long has she been gone?" he asked, feeling his gut twist.

"No more than an hour." Jenny glanced down at her watch and gasped slightly. "Closer to two now."

"Damn it." He marched to the back door, calling for Ozzy, who came rushing in. "Keep trying to call," he told Rose's mother, and then he left quickly.

"Find Rose," he told his dog and pointed. They had played hide and seek between themselves, but he didn't know if his dog's abilities were broad enough to handle this task. "Rose," he said again as Ozzy looked up at him questioningly and Sawyer began to doubt his dog's intelligence. "Rose," he said again, not wanting to give up. The dog surprised him by sniffing the ground as if on a mission.

He followed the dog until he noticed a set of light footprints in the snow and started following them. Halfway across the yard, they grew too faint to see. Ozzy sprinted by him, racing towards a pathway that led to the beach. By the time he reached the top of the trail, he was running. He slipped on an icy stone and slowed down.

Ozzy was ahead of him, barking wildly, and when Sawyer turned a corner, he saw a small brown mound at the base of the hill. His hands shook as he raced towards the bottom. He could hear a phone ringing and knew that Rose's mother was still trying to call her cell phone. Sawyer pulled out his cell phone and dialed Carson.

"Carson," Sawyer said into his phone. "I need an ambulance out here. Rose has fallen." He hung up the phone without waiting for a response when he reached Rose. He gently turned her over. "Easy," he told Ozzy who sat down and whimpered.

There was a lot of blood coming from a large gash on Rose's forehead and her skin was so cold. Was he too late? He pulled out a glove from his pocket and used it to apply pressure to the cut. He ran his free hand over the rest of her and determined she didn't have any broken bones, so he gently lifted her in his arms and rushed towards the top of the pathway while Ozzy followed behind.

The cell phone in Rose's pocket continued to ring as he raced towards the house.

When he reached the back door, her mother was standing there and opened it for him.

"What happened?" she cried when she noticed the blood.

"She must have fallen." He rushed her inside and laid her down on the sofa. "An ambulance is on its way. Build a fire, she's freezing."

"I'll do it," Jenny said behind his back. He'd taken both blankets from the sofa and covered her, then ran his hands over her exposed skin to heat her up.

"Here." Rose's mother handed him a fresh towel. "For the cut."

"You apply pressure, I've got to get her warm." He continued to run his hands over her, using his heat and friction to warm her skin.

"I hear the ambulance," Jenny said a few minutes later.

He was rubbing the skin on his hands raw, but he would have gladly gone on until they bled if it meant getting Rose warm.

He picked her up when he heard the ambulance stop outside and carried her towards the front door.

"I'll get the kids." Jenny rushed from the room.

"We'll meet you at the hospital," Rose's mother called after him.

When the ambulance driver saw him, he opened the back door and let him step in to lay her on the gurney himself. He knew both the driver and the EMT and had worked with both on several occasions. He sat down and filled the EMT in on what had happened.

By the time they reached the hospital, Rose's body temperature was returning to normal, thanks to the fluids they were pumping into her arm and the heat blankets.

Still, she hadn't woken up, and in the light from the back of the ambulance, he could see bruises covering her chin and forehead. He stood back as they wheeled her into a room, not taking his eyes from her face and desperately wishing she'd open her eyes.

When he was asked to leave, he flashed his badge and told them that she was under his protection. He didn't care if it was a gross misuse of his power. They told him to stand against the wall and not get in their way as they took her vitals and worked on her.

"You brought her in?" The doctor turned to him.

"Yes, how is she?"

"We've gotten her body temperature back up. Do you know how long she's been unconscious?" the doctor asked him.

"No, but it's possible it's been close to two hours. That's

how long she was gone." The doctor winced, and his worry doubled.

Just then there was a low moan and they both turned to see Rose open her eyes.

Sawyer pushed past the man and took Rose's hand in his. It was still cold, but not as bad as it had been when he'd found her.

"Rose," he said softly. "Open your eyes, honey," he begged.

"Sawyer?" Her eyes opened slightly. "It hurts." She blinked and then closed her eyes again.

"Can we turn down the lights?" he asked and turned back to her. The lights dimmed slightly.

"Where are we?" she asked.

"The hospital. You fell down the pathway," he added.

She shook her head, blinking at him several times. "I didn't fall. Someone hit me with a rifle." She reached up and touched the spot. They had already bandaged it, and he'd heard the doctor say that he didn't think stitches were needed.

"That would coincide with the wound on her forehead," the doctor said behind him. "We're going to move her to a private room, but first, we'll want to do a CT scan to make sure she doesn't have bleeding in the brain."

He stood back to allow them to roll her out and followed them. "My mother?" Rose asked and looked up at him.

"They're probably in the waiting room," he answered.

"Go tell them I'm okay. They must be worried." She squeezed his hand.

"We're going to take her to Radiology," a nurse told them, "and then to room..." The nurse looked at her chart. "Room one-oh-two. Everyone can see her there, after."

He bent down and kissed her. "I'll see you soon."

She smiled and sighed. "I should have known better than to go off by myself."

"You'll never have to worry about that again," he promised. He kissed her again before heading out. He'd lost track of time and when he found her family in the waiting area, he was slightly surprised to see Hunter standing there with Rose's mother and sister.

"You made the trip fast," he said, shaking the man's hand.

"I flew. When Joan called and told me what had happened, I rushed out of court and jumped in my plane." He ran his hands through his thin hair.

Sawyer nodded and turned to Joan and Jenny. "She's awake. She says someone hit her with the butt of a rifle and pushed her down the pathway. I've already talked to Carson, and he's out there looking for clues."

"Can we see her?" Joan asked.

"They're taking her in for a CT scan and then to a private room." They all made their way towards the private room wing and crowded into the empty room to wait for Rose.

"Who would want to hurt Rose?" Jenny asked when they were all settled in the room. Both of her smaller kids were sitting on her lap. The oldest boy was standing next to his mother with a sad look on his face. Sawyer's heart broke a little, knowing that they worried for their aunt.

"After seeing her, maybe you should go back to the house," he said to Jenny. "We'll stay here."

"No, I..." She shook her head.

"Jenny, you can't keep the kids here for too long." Rose's mother nodded to the little girl, who was almost asleep on her lap. "McKenna will need her nap."

Just then, they rolled Rose in. They moved her to the bed and she was quickly surrounded by her family.

"It looks like it's my turn to have a concussion." She smiled up at him. The bump on her forehead was fairly large and the skin around her left eye was already turning purple.

He leaned down and took her hand. "Tell me everything you remember, if you can."

The room grew silent as Rose started talking.

"I hung up with Hunter." Her eyes moved past him to where her brother stood. "He was rushing into court."

"I left after Joan told me during a break what had happened," Hunter explained.

"I'm sorry." She sighed.

Hunter chuckled. "Don't be."

"Go on," he broke in. Rose's eyes moved back to his.

"I wanted to take a walk, to clear my head. The snow had let up some. I reached the pathway that led to the stairs and was thinking about what I could do to the stones to make them better next spring when I heard footsteps. I turned around and..." She bit her bottom lip. "It was a black rifle."

"Did you see who hit you?"

"No, just the butt. I felt the pain and started falling backward. I felt hands on me, on my shoulders, pushing me back towards the hill. Then I was falling." She turned and looked over at Jenny and the kids, who were all watching her.

Sawyer could see that the story had affected the young ones, and he walked over to where her sister sat, holding the little girl. The boys were standing there, holding hands.

Sawyer knelt in front of the oldest boy. "We left our

dogs at the house. Do you think you could go back with your mom and watch after them for me while I'm here?"

The kid looked to his mother, then nodded after she did.

"Good. The white and black one's name is Ozzy. He understands most basic commands and will know that you're in charge. Tsuna is the little brown one. She's younger and sometimes gets lost outside, so when you let them out to do their business, you have to watch her really close. Can you do that?"

"Sure," the kid answered with a smile.

"I want a job too," the younger boy chimed in. Sawyer turned to him.

"There's dog food in the pantry. They each get a scoop of food when you have your dinner. Can you make sure they have dinner?"

"Okay." The boy nodded.

"Me!" the little girl added, clapping as if it was a game.

He smiled and turned to her. "Tsuna will need someone to snuggle and play with.

She'll miss Rose, and if we stay here, she'll need someone to sleep with. Do you think she can sleep with you?"

"I like doggies." The girl smiled and nodded quickly.

"I'll drive you back to the house," Hunter told them. "I have to rearrange a few things. I'll be back later," he said to Rose, who nodded slightly.

"Mom?" She reached for her mother's hand. "Do you think you could go home and bring me some clothes?" She looked down at the gown she was in.

"They cut her out of hers," Sawyer explained.

"Sure." She leaned down and placed a kiss on her daughter's cheek. "Get some rest, we'll be back soon."

Once they were alone in the room, Rose scooted up a little. "How bad do I look?" she asked.

He smiled. "You're the most beautiful thing I've ever laid eyes on."

She chuckled, then winced. "Thank you, but how about some truth?"

"You've got a black eye, a bruise the size of my fist on your chin, and there's this..." He motioned to his forehead. "I think you're growing a unicorn horn up there."

She chuckled again, this time without the wince after.

"I'm one sexy beast." She sighed.

"How are you feeling?" He took her hand up to his lips.

"Like I was hit on the head and pushed down a flight of stairs." She met his eyes. "Do you think it was the killer?" she asked.

"No. They haven't gone after you before, why now?"

She shrugged. "New York changed things? Maybe we're one step closer. Maybe he got spooked."

"Still..." Just then there was a knock on the door. He opened it to see Carson and the chief on the other side. "Come on in. We were just talking about who could have done this." He motioned for the men to enter. "What did you find?" he asked Carson.

"Nothing, other than a few bushes that Rose probably took out on her tumble down the stairs. How are you doing?" Carson asked.

"I'll be okay." She smiled.

"We need to know everything." Deter stepped forward.

For the next ten minutes, Rose filled them in and the four of them went over possible suspects.

In the end, they had determined that Schneller had a black-handled rifle. He also had the most motive to harm Rose. He'd been charged with trespassing when Carson had found the man on Rose's land when they were away in New York City.

"We'll head over there and see if we can find any proof," Deter said. "Keep an eye on her. We'll fill you in as soon as we know anything."

Shortly after they left, a nurse came in to check up on her, followed by a doctor who gave them the results of Rose's CT scan. He informed them that she would be free to head home in a few hours, as long as she was able to stand and move around without falling over.

"You don't want to keep her overnight?" Sawyer asked.

"No, there's no need. She is awake and coherent, and I don't see any signs of a concussion."

"You don't?" Rose broke in. "The radiology tech said—"

"No," the doctor smiled. "I had a look at your films. You're all clear. You'll have that bump for a few days, but it's just that, a bump. You're lucky you were hit where you were; it's one of the hardest spots of the skull." He smiled at her.

Sawyer's concerns weren't eased, and he seriously questioned if Rose should stay longer. But after the doctor left, Rose called her mother and told them the news. She persuaded the rest of her family to stay at the house until Sawyer drove her home later that evening. Hunter was going to bring her a change of clothes.

"Don't complain." Rose took his hand. "It's going to be nice sleeping in our bed tonight instead of here." She glanced around. "Besides, now I have a few hours alone with you." She sighed and yawned.

"Rose?" He waited until her eyes met his. "You scared me."

She nodded. "I was afraid I'd never see you again."

He shifted. "When I saw you lying at the bottom of the

hill, my only thought was that I hadn't told you... I hadn't said the words." He took her hand up to his lips again. "I love you," he said after their eyes locked. "I don't know what I'd do if something happened to you."

"I love you, too." She smiled, and he felt the center of his universe shift.

TWENTY-FIVE

THE BEST MEDICINE...

By later that evening, Rose was wishing her family would leave already. She hated being pampered and treated like she was an invalid. She was propped up on the sofa, and a roaring fire had been built. She had been brought an endless supply of hot tea, and her sister was even sitting on the end of the sofa, rubbing her feet.

Sawyer had gotten a call and disappeared upstairs with Hunter. She could tell something was up, but the men weren't sharing the news yet. So, she sat back and tried to keep her head from exploding with pain by breathing slowly and trying to relax.

"Really, Jenny, I'm okay." She winced when her sister dug her thumb into the heel of her foot.

"Massage and physical therapy are the best things for a quick recovery, along with lots of fluids. You just need to know where to apply pressure." She pushed on her foot again.

"Jenny, stop. You're going to add more bruises to my

body." She laughed and pulled her foot away. "And I can't afford it right now."

"Fine, but drink." She nodded to the tea.

Rose groaned. "I've had two cups already. As it is, I'll need to use the bathroom for the rest of the night."

"Aunt Rose!" Regan, Cole, and McKenna rushed into the room. Their clothes were splattered with bright paint, and Rose held in a groan at the mess she'd have to clean up in her art studio once her family left. "We painted you some get-better pictures."

"See?" Cole held up a picture that looked a lot like Batman, his current favorite DC Comics character.

"Wow, that's really nice." She took the painting and noticed that the wet paint was still dripping. She quickly leveled the paper, so it wouldn't drip onto the floor or the sofa.

"Look at mine." McKenna held up her picture of what Rose assumed were flowers. "I ufed crayons. I'm not afpofed to ufe paint." Rose chuckled and decided not to correct the little girl's language. Looking closely at the drawing, Rose had to admit the little girl had talent, more so than her brother.

"I colored you flowers too." Regan held up his. It was in watercolors and Rose was even more impressed.

"Obviously, they get their talent from me." Jenny laughed.

"These aren't bad." She held them up. "Batman, daisies, and yellow roses." She nodded to each one in turn.

"Like your name," Regan added, pride showing clearly in the boy's eyes. "Hunter said they were your favorite." He smiled up at her.

"They are." She tapped him on the nose and set the

painting aside. Tsuna was laying in her lap and McKenna walked over to pet the dog.

"Can fhe ftill fleep wif me?" she asked.

It was then that Rose noticed the empty spot where the little girl's tooth had been earlier. "Did you lose your tooth?"

"U-huh. Uncle Fawwwer help me wif it." The girl smiled and showed her the empty space. "It didn't even hurted."

Rose smiled. "You like Uncle Sawyer?" she asked softly.

"He helped us paint," Regan told her. "Uncle Hunter and Sawyer are cleaning up your art room. We made a mess." He frowned. "Sorry."

"Why don't you three go up to the bathroom and clean up for bedtime?" Jenny said. "Mom, would you..."

"Come on, kiddos." Their mother took the hint and stood up. "Let's go jump in that big bathtub Rose has to clean out when we all leave." Her mother glanced back and winked at her as the kids raced towards the stairs.

"So," Jenny said, starting to rub Rose's feet again, this time more gently, "tell me all about you and Sawyer."

"What's there to tell? He was the one who knocked on my door over a year ago and told me that Isaac's plane had gone down."

Jenny winced. "Ouch."

"Yeah." She sighed. "Then a few months later, when I'd turned into a Gollum, he showed up, fixed my power and..."—she chuckled—"saw my underwear." Jenny's eyebrows shot up quickly. "They were all over the living room. I'd been sleeping in front of the fireplace."

"Why didn't you tell us you'd gotten so bad?" Jenny asked.

"I didn't want anyone's help."

"You never do." Jenny stopped rubbing her feet and Rose wiggled them.

"Don't stop, that felt good." She added, "Lightly, though." Her sister started rubbing her socked feet again.

"What happened then?" Jenny asked.

"Then I cleaned up and put everything I had into Stoneport." She looked around and smiled at the transformation of the place.

"It does look amazing. You've changed a few things since the last time I was here. New floor?"

Rose nodded. "Sawyer and Hunter helped."

"When did it change?" she asked. Rose knew her sister wasn't talking about the floor.

"One day, he kissed me in my studio." Her face heated when she remembered that he'd done more than kiss her that day.

"Oooh." Jenny smiled. "Why don't we have chocolate?" She glanced around. "There should be chocolate when we're talking boys." She jumped up, dislodging Rose's feet from her lap, and raced into the kitchen.

When her sister came back, she had two spoons and the carton of mint chocolate chip that she and Sawyer had started binge eating the other night.

She sat back down and tucked the blankets around them. "Okay, finish…"

"What more is there to say?" She took a spoonful of the ice cream.

"When did he move in with you?" Jenny asked.

"He's not…" She frowned. "He's only staying temporarily, until…" Her words fell away at her sister's look.

"Dude, he's totally living here," Jenny said.

"He is," she agreed, but she didn't feel like going into the details. Her head was throbbing and the medicine she'd been given was making her drowsy. "He is." She took another spoonful. She was feeling warm and the cold on her throat was soothing.

"Are you okay?" Jenny asked. She reached up and touched her cheek. "You're burning up." She set the ice cream carton down and took her spoon.

"Mom?" she called out. Rose winced at the volume.

Instead of their mom coming down the stairs, Sawyer and Hunter rushed down.

"What's wrong?" they both said at the same time.

"Rose is burning up." Jenny was standing over her at this point.

"The doctor said it was a possibility. She'd been out in the cold so long." Sawyer walked over and touched Rose's forehead. "Do you have a thermometer?"

"My bathroom." She sighed when Sawyer picked her up.

"I'll watch after her from here on. She's probably tired," Sawyer said.

"Take her tea."

Rose groaned.

"If she wants some more, I'll come down and get a fresh cup. Night." He started towards the stairs.

Hunter watched them walk by. "Will you be here tomorrow?" she asked.

"I'm due in court again first thing in the morning," he replied. "I'll have to leave at eight. I'll knock on your door before I go."

"Night," she called out since Sawyer hadn't stopped walking. "Where are you taking me?" she asked, resting her head on his shoulder.

"I'm putting you in a cool bath, then hovering over you like a mother hen." He smiled down at her.

"Mmm, we haven't bathed together. Showered, yes, but not bathed." Her head was heavy, and she enjoyed resting it against his chest. She could hear his heartbeat and enjoyed the soothing sound.

"Rose?" Sawyer's voice shook her out of the trance. She must have fallen asleep, because when she opened her eyes, she was in the bathtub, naked.

"How did..." She shook her head slightly. "Woah, time travel." She smiled.

"Honey, you need to drink this." He held a cup in front of her.

She sipped and spit the sour tasting fluid out. "What is it?"

"Something to bring your temperature down." He put the cup to her lips again. "Swallow it all."

She did as he asked, wishing she could spit it out. But the liquid warmed her from the inside and she rested her head back against the bathtub pillow.

"This is nice." She sighed, wiggling her toes.

"How are you feeling?" he asked.

"Relaxed." She sighed, then opened her eyes. "Why don't you come in here and scrub my back?"

He smiled, then felt her forehead. "Next time, I promise. You're still too hot. I hate doing it, but I've got to add a few more ice cubes to your water."

She frowned and looked down. Sure enough, there were ice cubes floating around. She would have sworn the bath was borderline boiling. She watched as if in slow motion as he dumped a bucket of ice into the water. Then suddenly her body started shaking, and her teeth chattered, and she tried to climb out of the water.

"What the..." She shook her head.

"Rose? Stay with me, honey." He gently rubbed her arms.

"It's freezing." She wrapped her arms around herself and he felt her forehead again. "How did a few ice cubes do that so quickly?"

Sawyer frowned down at her. "That was over an hour ago. You've been in and out of consciousness since then." He reached in and picked her out of the water. The move soaked his shirt and jeans. He set her on the edge of the counter and wrapped a large towel around her.

"An hour?" she said as her teeth continued to chatter.

"Yes." He was looking at her with worry. "You were a little delirious for a while."

"I was?" She didn't remember anything other than him pouring ice into the tub. "What did I say?" she asked, reaching for her bathrobe.

"Things."

"Like?"

"Later." He pulled off his soaked shirt, and she smiled as he reached for the snap of his jeans. She ran her eyes over every part of him. He really was something to look at. Not that Isaac hadn't been, but Sawyer was taller, leaner. His chest and stomach were full of long lean muscles. He had that sexy V in his hips that pointed down to below his jeans, making his hips and flat stomach a playground she wanted to enjoy every day for the rest of her life.

When his jeans lay in a wet pile on the floor next to his shirt, he picked her up and carried her into the bedroom. He laid her gently down on the bed, slid under the blankets with her, and pulled her close to his chest.

He was warm and, listening to his heartbeat, she immediately fell asleep again.

She woke to a light knock on the door. Remembering

Hunter wanted to talk to her, she climbed out of the bed and moaned as the world turned.

"Rose?" Sawyer touched her shoulder.

"I'm okay, it's Hunter. I wanted to talk to him..."

"Go slow," he suggested and laid back down. "If you need me..."

"I'm okay." She smiled back at him.

Taking his advice, she slowly stood, holding onto the bed frame. When her head settled, she wrapped her terry cloth robe around her, slipped on a pair of fuzzy socks, and left the room.

She found Hunter in the kitchen, sipping on a cup of coffee.

"How are you feeling?" he asked, his eyes scanning her face.

"Better." She took the mug he offered her. After sipping she turned to him.

"I'm sorry," he said again. "God, I wish I could go back and..."

She shook her head and stepped into his arms. "It's not your fault."

"I should have told you about that day, at the beach. I didn't think anything..." He sighed and looked down at her. "I didn't think."

"That wouldn't be the first time," she joked, getting him to smile back down at her.

Just then his phone chimed. "I'm going to be late." He sighed. "I'm booked for the next week straight. Will you be okay?"

"Yes, Sawyer's here now."

Hunter sighed and nodded. "Get a new phone. I hate not being able to talk."

She nodded. "Sawyer is taking me today."

Hunter frowned. "Wear a hat over that." He nodded to her forehead. "And maybe some dark glasses. And a ski mask." He smiled.

She groaned. "That bad?"

"Haven't you seen it yet?"

She shook her head. "I'm too afraid."

He sobered. "Go back to bed. Rest. Get better." He kissed her cheek. "I love you."

"Fly safe." She hugged him.

"See you soon." He set his mug in the sink and walked out the back door.

After she heard Hunter's rental car disappear down the driveway, she let the dogs out, as they were both whining at the door.

When the dogs came back in, they were both a little muddy since the snow had started melting sometime in the night. The sun wasn't even up, and she could tell it was going to be warmer today than yesterday.

Using a towel, she wiped both of the dog's paws and thought about heading back up to crawl into bed with Sawyer. Then her stomach growled, and she decided breakfast was more important than sleep.

An hour later, Sawyer, her mother, Jenny, and the kids came padding downstairs, all drawn to the kitchen by the smell of bacon.

Sawyer looked freshly showered and shaved and was dressed in clean jeans and a black T-shirt. He looked as sexy and as dangerous as he had the first night she'd met him on her doorstep.

"What's all this?" he asked, leaning in for a kiss.

"I slept so much yesterday, I wanted to cook."

"We're not complaining," Jenny said as she scooped more eggs onto her plate.

"Jenny, don't you think you've had enough?" her mother added.

"Hey, I'm eating for two here," her sister joked.

Sawyer's eyebrows shot up.

"Oh, yeah, my sister is pregnant again," Rose whispered. He turned to her and gave her a funny look.

"I'm... going to let the dogs out." He walked to the back door and stepped outside.

Rose wondered if it was something she had said, but then the timer on the oven went off and she forgot about it as she served up some more bacon.

"We've got to head out soon if we're going to make it back home in time for dinner," her sister remarked.

"It's only about a three-hour trip," Rose said, setting down to her plate of food.

"Not with these three." Jenny motioned to the kids. "Besides, Sawyer mentioned that he had a doctor's appointment this morning and that he was going to run you by the phone store to get a new phone for you."

"And I'm sure you want to rest. You still look tired," her mother added, reminding Rose that she could only take about twenty-four hours of her mother at any given time.

Sawyer stepped back in with the dogs and she watched him closely as he filled a plate of food for himself and sat next to her. "We have about an hour before we need to leave if you still want to get your new phone."

She nodded up at him. "I'll go shower." She took her plate to the sink.

"We'll do the dishes, honey," her mother said. "You go. You'll probably want to take some extra time to fix your face." She walked over and hugged her. "Stay safe," she whispered.

Without another word, she walked up the stairs slowly, suddenly feeling every ache and sore muscle in her body.

Stripping off her clothes, she turned on the shower. She happened to get a glance of herself in the mirror and gasped.

Walking over to it, she ran her eyes over her face.

The left side of her forehead was double its normal size. Reaching up, she peeled the bandage away from her face and winced at the butterfly bandages holding her skin together.

Her chin and her left eye were black and purple with hints of green. Even her lip was swollen. Glancing down at her body, she took stock of every bruise, every cut, and feeling slightly depressed about the fact that Sawyer had seen her like this last night in the bathtub, she climbed into the hot shower.

Maybe that was why he was acting so strange this morning. Was he disgusted at her body now that it was bruised and swollen? No. She shook her head. Sawyer wasn't that shallow. Then what could it be?

He'd mentioned that she had been in and out of consciousness and that she'd been talking to him. Had she said something? Suddenly, she remembered. She'd been talking about kids and her desire for children.

Oh god, had she said something to Sawyer about wanting his kids?

Feeling her face heat, she turned off the water and groaned.

"Are you okay in there?" Sawyer asked from the other side of the glass.

"Yes." She straightened up and reached out for a towel. He handed her one and she quickly wrapped it around her body, suddenly feeling embarrassed at the bruises.

"Feeling better?" He was leaning against the countertop like he'd been there a while.

"Yes, much better." She smiled and walked into her closet to find some clothes. When she came out, dressed in a pair of jeans and a cream-colored sweater, he was still in the same place.

"Do you want to talk about last night?" he asked.

She closed her eyes and leaned against the counter. "I don't know what I said, but I hope you understand that whatever it was, it was fever-induced stupidity."

He chuckled. "I meant about the attack, but now that you mention it..." He turned to her. "My answer is three," he said clearly.

"Three?" she said slowly.

Sawyer nodded. "Yes, I've thought about it and three is the right amount. Why just have two when one more is just as easy?"

"Okay," she said slowly. "Three..." She waited.

"Kids," he supplied, and she let out the breath she'd been holding. "You asked me last night, and now I have an answer." He smiled.

"Is that what..." She shook her head. "It took you that long to answer?" She was a little shocked that he was so easily talking about having kids with her. Every time she'd brought up the subject of kids with Isaac, he'd evaded the topic.

Sawyer chuckled lightly and wrapped his arms around her. "This isn't something that someone should make a quick decision about." He kissed her slowly, rubbing his lips over hers. "After all, we'll be dealing with these kids the rest of our lives." His smile grew.

"We will?" she said, her eyebrows going up as she looked deep into his green eyes.

Images of three mini Sawyers running around the house quickly flooded her mind, causing her to smile.

"Man, you must have really been out of it last night." He shook his head, then he took her hand in his. "Come on, we're going to be late for my appointment. We can talk about it on the way."

TWENTY-SIX

MIND MAZE...
After his doctor cleared him for light duty, they stopped off at the cell phone store and replaced her lost phone.

Then they ate lunch at a local sandwich shop while she configured her new phone. Luckily, she'd saved all her contacts to her log-in and it didn't take long before she was back up and running.

They had talked briefly about everything she had said the night before when the fever had taken over her. He'd been a little shocked and surprised at how much she'd confessed to him.

She had told him things about her relationship with Isaac that he doubted she would admit to anyone else. He wasn't even sure if she knew how she felt.

She'd said that she'd never really trusted him. Shortly after they had gotten back together, after going their separate ways for college, she'd believed he was cheating on her. Even if he wasn't, it was something she could see him doing in the future. He'd acted as if he were a different person sometimes.

He'd be hot one moment, then that evening when he'd come home, he'd be cold.

She confided in Sawyer that Isaac had told her that he wasn't impressed with her career choice, but since he made all the "real money," it didn't matter to him what she did in life, so long as it was a respectable career and didn't hinder him in any way.

When she'd talk to him about it at other times, he'd act as if she wasn't making sense, and tell her he was incredibly proud of her for her work.

She'd also shared that she had always felt like she had to be perfect around Isaac. He wanted her to elaborate but was unsure how to approach the topic. After lunch, he decided a short walk through town would be a good way to get some time alone together.

She'd applied makeup to cover the bruises on her face and wore a knitted stocking hat to cover the bump on her forehead.

She had wrapped up in a thick jacket, a knitted scarf, gloves, and dark sunglasses, and was wearing her snow boots even though the sun was out and most of the snow was melting.

He'd removed his own jacket altogether and left it in the car before heading inside to eat lunch. She hadn't removed hers even during the meal.

"Are you warm enough?" he asked as they started walking.

"Yes." She smiled up at him. "I just don't want to take a chance. I'm still a little... wobbly."

"We could..." He nodded back to the car.

"No, I'm good. Besides, I wanted to stop in the bookstore for something new." She nodded to the building at the end of the street.

Taking her hand, he started walking.

"You mentioned last night that you felt you had to be perfect around Isaac." He glanced sideways at her.

When she stopped walking, he turned and looked at her. She was frowning.

"I did?"

He nodded. "You said, and I'm quoting here, 'I would make sure every piece of hair was in place, my lipstick was perfect, and that I was wearing an outfit I knew he'd like.' You mentioned Stepford Wives." He shook his head and she sighed heavily.

"Yeah. She started walking again and he fell in step with her. "Sometimes I felt like one."

"Isaac wasn't abusive, though?" The question had been burning in his mind all morning long. He'd been so preoccupied by it, he knew Rose had gotten the idea he was upset about something.

"No."

"You do know that abuse is more than throwing punches, right?" he asked.

"Yes," she said quietly.

"Did he ever yell at you or tear you down?" he asked, unsure of why he wanted to know.

"Not really," she said after a moment. "Sometimes, he liked things to be a certain way. I mean, who doesn't? Other times..." She shrugged. "He acted like he didn't care. He'd never been like that before..."

"What do you mean?"

"Before he left for college."

He stopped her and put his hands on her shoulders. "You know, with me, you only have to be yourself. Always. I don't expect or want perfection." He removed her dark sunglasses and she blinked a few times until her eyes adjusted.

Her left eye was so black now, even the makeup she'd put on earlier couldn't hide it.

"I mean it. I'm not perfect, and I would never expect anyone I'm with to be."

She nodded slowly. "I'm over that part of my life." She bit her bottom lip. "I think after realizing everything... Isaac and Kristy." She sighed. "I'm not... I can't... That's the old me."

"Good." He bent down and kissed her softly.

"Rose?" someone said from behind them. They both turned to see a woman about their age rushing over to them. A small child was clinging to the woman while another was trying desperately to stay next to her.

"Nikki." Rose turned, and he felt her entire body stiffen.

He'd seen the woman around town before and knew that she was married to the manager down at the local bank. Ken. Or was it Kirk?

"Corey and I were just talking about you," the woman said, stopping in front of them a little breathless. Nikki's eyes ran over him quickly and then locked on his hand still holding Rose's.

"Oh?" Rose slid on her glasses again and Sawyer could tell she was feeling self-conscious.

"Yes, I'm sorry we haven't been by the house to check in on you. You know how it is with kids..." The woman chuckled, and Sawyer narrowed his eyes at her. There were some people you could tell hadn't meant to offend when they said something that upset someone. Nikki wasn't one of those. She knew full well her statement would affect Rose and it did. Her body went even more rigid.

"I'm just fine," Rose recovered.

Nikki leaned closer, her eyes narrowing. "We heard about your little fall yesterday. You really ought to be more careful walking down those stone steps. Maybe have them replaced with something a little newer and more practical in this sort of weather." She shifted the kid on her hip and held the baby closer. "I just don't know how you do it, living in that old drafty place all by yourself. I mean, there's something to be said for having a new house built." The woman's smile brightened. "We've so enjoyed the custom home we had built a few years back."

"Yes, I'm sure you have," Rose said dryly. "I rather enjoy classic things," she added, but it didn't matter. Rose could have said anything. Nikki was beyond hearing or caring.

Nikki's eyes once again went to him. "I'd heard that you two were... an item?" The last part was meant as a question.

"Yes," he answered for Rose.

"You're a police officer?" Nikki asked.

"Yes," he answered again.

"Oh, that's just great. I always said..." Sawyer tuned out when the woman started talking about other couples in town. She went into a string of gossip that kept him and Rose glued to the sidewalk for the next five minutes.

Finally, when he felt Rose shiver next to him, he wrapped his arm around her and interrupted Nikki. The woman's own kids looked cold and bored, but that hadn't been enough to stop her from chatting about everyone else in town.

"I'm sorry, Rose still hasn't quite recovered from the attack yesterday. I need to make sure she gets inside someplace warm." He started to walk.

"Attack?" Nikki asked.

He turned back quickly. "Someone hit her over the

head with a rifle and tossed her down the stairs, where she lay in the snow for almost two hours until I found her." He added quickly, "Or didn't that bit of gossip spread around town yet?"

Nikki gasped. "Oh my god, I had no clue." The woman touched Rose's shoulder. "I had only heard you fell."

"I'm okay," Rose assured her again, but he had turned and started walking towards the bookstore.

"I hope you feel better," Nikki called after them.

"Thanks," Rose said back.

"Tell me that's not one of your close friends," he said softly.

"No, she was my arch enemy in school. She wanted Isaac, but I had him." Rose smiled.

"At least there was that." He opened the bookstore door for her.

A wave of hot air hit them as they stepped in. He'd been in the store plenty of times himself and had met the owners, Debra and Rick, shortly after he'd moved into town.

"Hi, Sawyer." Debra waved at him as they walked further into the warmth.

"Hi, Debra," he called out.

"Is that Rose?" Debra blinked a few times. "Is it that cold outside?" The older woman moved around the countertop.

"No, it's actually nice and warm," Rose answered. "I'm just... recovering from a fever."

"Oh, I'd heard about your fall." The woman stopped a foot from them, a frown on her face. "Obviously, the rumors were greatly understated. You look like death." Then Rose removed the sunglasses and Debra gasped. "Oh, honey." The older woman closed the gap between them and took Rose into her arms.

Sawyer was a little surprised when Rose burst out crying and held onto Debra.

"There, there, child. You've had it bad for a while now." Debra stroked Rose's hair and held onto her.

Sawyer felt useless and wished he was the one holding Rose instead of the bookstore owner. Finally, Rose's tears slowed down.

"I've known you since you were yay high." Debra held her hand to her waist. "You come on back here and have a cup of—"

"Don't say tea," Rose added with a groan. "Jenny almost drowned me with it last night."

Debra chuckled. "How about some hot cocoa?"

"Yes." Rose wiped her face and then looked at him and mouthed. "Sorry."

He nodded, then walked over and hugged her. "Go sit down, relax. Enjoy yourself. I'll get us some books."

"Thanks."

"What kind of books?" he asked.

She shrugged. "I'm not picky. I love all books equally." She smiled slightly, then turned and followed Debra to the back room.

He spent the next fifteen minutes wandering around the bookshelves, looking for something Rose would like. He decided that if it sounded like something he would like, she would as well. After all, they practically had the same taste.

By the time he set a large pile of books on the counter, Rose was walking out of the back room, a big smile on her face. Her eyes seemed brighter and she was even laughing.

"He took a deep breath. "Feel better?"

She nodded and walked over to wrap her arms around him. "Thank you for being patient."

"Anytime." He kissed her and turned as Debra walked out, smiling at them.

"We should stop by the store on the way home. I need chocolate." Rose smiled.

"I could go for some chocolate." He held onto her tightly as Debra rang up the bill.

They left the bookstore with two large bags of books weighing him down and walked back to the end of the street.

They stopped off at the local grocery store and bumped into a few more people they both knew. They quickly filled everyone in on what had happened to Rose and then made their way back home.

"If it's alright with you, I have to stop off at my place and pick up a few things," he said before the turnoff.

He'd stopped by yesterday, but he hadn't been cleared for duty yet, so he hadn't picked up his uniforms.

"Sure," she said. She'd been resting her head back and he was pretty sure she was too tired to care either way.

"Why don't you rest, I'll just be a few minutes," he suggested when they arrived at his place.

"Sure," she said again, and she closed her eyes and leaned back against the seat.

He reached over and touched her forehead. "You're still a little warm."

"That's funny because I feel cold," she countered.

"I pushed you too hard today." He frowned at her and could see that she was tired. Her eyes were dull, and she was still a little too pale.

"No, I needed to be out. Thanks."

He got out and rushed to gather the items he'd need, making sure to take all three of his uniforms and his service weapon, which the chief had signed back over to him.

When he walked back out with the duffle bag, Rose was asleep.

When they got back to her house, he carried her in and laid her gently on the sofa and covered her with the blankets before carrying everything into the house.

After letting the dogs out and taking a short walk with them, he wandered the big mansion and somehow ended up in Isaac's office.

He found himself wondering more about the man who'd won over Rose so unconditionally. Walking around, he frowned at the law books that filled the shelves. Most of them looked like they had never been handled, let alone opened.

The large wooden desk that sat in the middle of the room screamed of superiority, quality, and wealth with its massive size and ornamental decorations.

He sat down in the large leather chair and opened the top drawer.

They had already been through Isaac's things, removing anything that they believed would serve as evidence, but he was hoping for some insight into the man, not the murder.

Most of the files in the lower drawer were legal paperwork that, if Sawyer had to be honest, didn't mean anything to him. Nor did they give him insight into Isaac Clayton or his relationships.

He found an old photo book in the middle drawer and pulled it out.

There were pictures of Isaac and Rose. Sawyer leaned back in the chair and scanned through each one, enjoying the ones of Rose when she was a child. Still, seeing her with Isaac, he could tell that the two had been devoted to one another when they were young.

Then, as the subjects grew older, something in both of

their eyes dimmed. He'd seen it many times in relationships. They were working on autopilot. The spark that had once been there was long gone by the time the last picture, which happened to be a wedding picture, was taken.

The love was still there—there was no doubt about it, seeing the way they looked into each other's eyes—but something major was missing in Isaac's eyes and Sawyer could tell that it had nothing to do with Rose, who looked up at the man she's married with nothing but love.

Setting the book back in the drawer, he continued through the drawers. When he didn't find anything further, he stood up and walked over to the window. From here, he could see the basement wall and the new glass door that had been installed. Tilting his head, he thought about the logistics of hiding a man in a cement wall.

He'd helped remodel a few places himself in his life. Nothing as big as adding a load-bearing cement wall with steel footings and rebar, but he had the basics down and knew what materials were used: rebar, steel beams for support, aluminum studs to hold the extra weight. It wasn't rocket science, but still, how would someone go about hiding a one-hundred-seventy-pound man?

RJ Gamet had claimed that when his crew had arrived that morning, the large plywood forms and the plastic coverings were already in place, which would have kept Isaac's body hidden from view. The only way someone would have been able to spot him was to stand on a tall ladder and use a flashlight to look down between the two plywood forms before the cement had been pumped in to the area.

RJ had sworn that the outer support hadn't been in place the night before, since Nat Willis had planned to arrive early the next morning to install the last piece, which was the size of the entire cement wall.

Someone would have had to push Isaac back on the protruding rebar, which punctured his left lung and sliced his heart, killing him immediately, then install the framework over him, closing him in and allowing the cement to be poured from the top so that the body near the bottom of the wall was hidden completely.

He could see it all clearly in his head, now that he was looking at the outside wall.

Was it Willis who had hidden the body? It could account for the large deposit into his bank account. Had the second amount been a payment to attack him? Or had he, like so many others before, gotten greedy and demanded more for his silence? Maybe that was why he'd been killed.

Then why kill Kristy Owens? If she had been killed, that was, and it wasn't a suicide like everyone still believed. Something in his gut told him that the woman he'd met hadn't seemed overly depressed. Then again, he'd only meet her twice.

Walking back into the library, he pulled out the folder they had put all their notes in and started rearranging the sticky notes.

They had agreed to keep it a secret, which meant putting it all away after each use. He laid everything out and stared down at the notes for more than an hour.

He even took to pacing the small library area while he thought about every angle. Ozzy whined to be let out and when he walked towards the door, a thick book caught his eye.

Here, in the library, the shelves were full of books Rose enjoyed—mystery, fantasy, romance. So why was there a law book sitting on the top shelf?

Reaching up, he pulled the book down from the shelf over the doorway. The shelf was easy for him to reach, but

Rose would have had to stand on a stool or a chair to reach it.

Setting it on the table, he let the thick book fall open and frowned at what he found inside.

"What's that?" Rose asked from the doorway, causing him to jump slightly at her voice.

Too late, he tried to shut the book and hide the stack of images that someone had hidden inside. But he heard her gasp and knew that, once again, Isaac Clayton had broken her heart.

TWENTY-SEVEN

THE ANSWER TO LIFE, THE UNIVERSE, AND EVERYTHING...

Rose looked down at the images of Isaac and Kristy with the newborn baby they shared and felt her heart break once more. Seeing the family that they were together, the family she should have had with him, broke her. Tears started filling her eyes, but before they could fall, Sawyer was there, his hand on her shoulder, comforting her. Then something amazing happened. Before the misery of Isaac's betrayal could consume her completely, she looked into Sawyer's green eyes full of concern, and it disappeared.

"Hey." His soft voice broke into the haze of self-pity that always came when she thought about Isaac and Kristy together. "Are you okay?" he asked softly.

"I am." She took a deep breath as she felt her world shift to a new center. Him.

The way Sawyer looked at her, his light touch, the way she knew and trusted him made all the betrayal and deceit in her past seem mundane. She took another deep breath and, this time, when she exhaled, let all the pain leave her body with her breath. She smiled up at him. "You're not him," she said clearly.

"No," he agreed and smiled back at her. "And you are no longer the Rose you used to be with him."

"No, I'm not." Her chin went up slightly and she leaned up to kiss him.

"Don't touch anything," Sawyer said as he stepped back and pulled out his phone. "I'm calling the chief." He took a step back and she got a better look at the pile of things on the table.

"About the pictures? Why would he need to know about them?" It was then that she noticed the note. It was simple, yet to the point.

"End the affair or suffer the consequences."

It was written in red under the snapshot of Isaac and Kristy Owens in an embrace with their three-year-old son. Everyone looked so happy together, so... family.

"You think the note is..." She turned but realized Sawyer was busy talking to the chief.

Taking another step forward, she picked up a pen and, with the tip of it, moved the top image aside, to see the next picture underneath it.

"There are more," she said to the room.

Sawyer was off the phone and moved to stand beside her again.

"From the looks of it, he'd been getting these for a while. The boy is younger in these pictures." She showed him. "See?"

He took the pen from her and moved them all, so they were in chronological order. "Six of them," he said.

"Are there envelopes? How did he get these?" She tilted her head towards the book.

"I'm not sure." Sawyer picked up the book and shook it

as if expecting something else to fall out.

"We'll have to assume they were delivered by hand and left where Isaac would find them."

"You think whoever killed him did it because..." She paused then gasped. "This makes it look like I..." She felt all the blood leave her face.

"Hey." Sawyer took her by the shoulders again. "This means nothing. Anyone could have threatened him about the affair. This does not make it seem like you're the one who killed him."

She nodded slightly, but in the back of her mind, she knew the guilt meter was pointing back towards her.

"The chief needs me to come in and wants me to bag them and bring them in, including the book." He picked up the bag from the library and nudged everything in it. "I won't be long. He needs me to fill out some paperwork since I'm cleared to work again." He groaned. "Night shift. I hate night shift."

She nodded, still not trusting her voice.

He set the bag down and took her shoulders. "I won't be long."

She nodded again, then he leaned in and kissed her until her body relaxed.

"I'll lock the door behind me," he said. She followed him to the front door and watched him pull on his jacket then tuck the bag under his arm. "Set the alarm."

She nodded. When he opened the door, she realized that it was raining lightly.

"Drive safe," she called after him. He walked back over to her, his finger going under her chin.

"I can bring us back something for dinner," he suggested.

"No." She shook her head. "I feel well enough to cook

something. It's my way of relaxing." It was also her style of therapy. Besides, Debra had given her a new recipe she wanted to try out. It had been handed down from her great-grandmother, who smuggled it out from Russia after defecting during the cold war.

"If you need anything, call me." He nodded to her phone. "Keep it with you."

She nodded and waved as he walked out and then set the alarm. Since it and the cameras had been installed, she felt safer in the house. Still, it was the first time she had been left alone since Sawyer had moved in.

Half an hour later, she and the dogs were in the kitchen putting the beef stroganoff into the oven along with another loaf of bread.

She poured herself a glass of wine and imagined what it would be like to have her and Sawyer's kids here. She imagined the sound of children's laughter echoing through the home she'd built.

There were still things to be done to the place, but she'd put it all on hold after Isaac... She shook her head. She scanned the kitchen and started building a mental list of items that still needed to be done. When the list got too long, she pulled out her notepad and started writing it down.

When the dogs whined, she pulled on her boots, disarmed the alarm system, and took out the umbrella, since she knew Tsuna wouldn't go out unless she was protected from the rain.

"Let's go," she called out to the dogs. Ozzy took off quickly after she opened the door. Tsuna whined until she picked her up and carried her out under the protection of the umbrella.

When they reached the grass, she set Tsuna down and

waited while the little girl did her business. She called out for Ozzy, but the dog didn't come back. Snapping her fingers, she picked up Tsuna and set her inside the house, since the dog was shivering.

She called Ozzy several more times, and when he didn't come, she took the flashlight from the kitchen drawer and wrapped her jacket around her more tightly, making sure the phone was tucked into her pocket.

"Come on, Ozzy," she called. "Daddy's going to be home soon."

The bushes near the driveway shook and Rose walked towards them, thinking that Ozzy had gotten stuck.

A dark figure stepped out instead, and Rose froze. It felt as if all the blood from her body had just drained out.

There, standing across the driveway in the dim glow of the porchlights, stood Isaac.

Her joy spiked then quickly turned to fear as the man moved forward.

Shaking her head, she backed up. Her hand covered her heart as she blinked a few times.

"I...Isaac?" She continued to shake her head. "But you're..."

"Not Isaac," the man said, moving closer as a slow smug smile curled his lips upward.

From the way he walked and the tone in his voice, she knew instantly it wasn't her husband, couldn't be her husband. Still, he was wearing Isaac's face.

"Who are you?" she managed.

"Ian." He smiled. "Isaac was my twin," he spat out. "Bet they didn't tell you about me." He was less than a foot from her, and she realized it was too late to retreat. He reached out and gripped her shoulder.

"W...who?" She tried to pull her arm free, but she was

weak from fear.

"Our dear old dad," Ian spit out.

Rose felt her blood pumping quickly through her body and tried to force her heart to slow, but she knew there was no way she could. When her eyesight started fading, she tried to fight it, but she slipped into darkness as she fainted.

When she woke, she was lying on the sofa in her living room. Or so she thought. It wasn't until she sat up that she realized it wasn't her living room or her sofa.

Instead, she was in a smaller room, furnished similarly to her own. So much so that as she looked around, she had to reassure herself that she wasn't seeing things.

"Do you like it?" The warm tone was so much like Isaac's. Jerking her head around, she saw him standing near the doorway, a tray of cups in his hands.

"Who are..." She shook her head. "Isaac didn't have..."

His laughter stopped her.

"Yes, so everyone was made to believe." He set the tray down in front of her on the coffee table that matched the one she and Isaac had picked out together.

"You were twins?" she asked, finally allowing it to sink in.

Ian sighed and tilted his head to look at her instead of answering. His gaze ran over her body and, even though his eyes matched Isaac's perfectly, the way he looked at her made her very uncomfortable.

He'd removed her boots and jacket so that all she wore was the tight pink sweater shirt that covered her black leggings.

"Where... are we?" she asked, glancing around slowly.

He handed her a cup of tea. "I tried to make it as comfortable as I could for you." He smiled when his blue eyes landed back on her. "Just like our place."

"You've... been in my place?" she asked, taking the tea but not taking a sip. She didn't trust the man, not with the looks he was giving her. There was something different in his eyes, something she'd never seen in Isaac's before.

"Yes, many times. Isaac's keys were helpful until that cop moved in. I left them there on the fireplace, for you to find." His expression turned dark.

It was then that she remembered the cell phone she'd shoved in her jacket pocket before she'd stepped outside to let the dogs out.

Glancing around, she scanned the room for any sign of her coat.

"Did you..." She turned back to him when she didn't see the coat or her boots. "Did you kill Isaac?"

He took a deep breath. "An unfortunate accident when we first met face to face." He smiled. "Apparently, he'd gotten wind that something was wrong. He kept his eyes out for me and that night caught me sneaking around the house. Paying off the worker who had showed up early that morning was easy. I simply told him I'd killed a wild dog and shoved its body into the cement wall. I still had plenty of money our mother had left me."

"You..." She shook her head.

"Our mother had set up accounts for both of us before she was murdered by our father," he sneered.

"What?" She set the cup down, and when his eyes narrowed, she decided to quickly take his mind off the fact that she hadn't drank any of the dark liquid. "Your father murdered your mother?"

"Yes, and your father." His smile was back. "I bet my dear old dad didn't tell you that one either."

She shook her head, unable to breathe or talk.

"Why don't I start at the beginning? Shall I?" He leaned

back and crossed one leg over the other, a move Isaac had done so many times before.

She nodded, then tried to appear more relaxed, even though she was still scanning for a way out of the situation. After all, Ian had just admitted that he'd killed Isaac and had paid Wallis off, which meant, he could be the one who'd killed the worker as well.

"Our parents divorced when we were two. Since neither one of them wanted to give up guardianship of us, they settled on each taking one of us."

"Isaac with Sean and you with your mother?" she asked.

He laughed. "You would have thought so, but no. I actually went with our father and Isaac with our mother. Sean and I moved to Twisted Rock to escape the clutches of my mother's very large and wealthy family. It seems, however, shortly after we moved here, my true nature was revealed." His smile widened, and she was reminded of Jack Nicolson in *The Shining*, which caused a shiver to rush down her spine. "My parents set up a meeting, here at our home. That evening, our father demanded they switch sons. Our mother, you see, had been in and out of institutes all her life." His eyes turned darker and she guessed that he was remembering something unpleasant. "Apparently, it runs in the family. Anyway..." He shook his head and focused again. "When our mother wouldn't agree to the exchange, dear old dad pulled out a gun and killed her, shot her point blank in the face. One of the staff members heard the shot and called the police, but by the time your father and the other officer arrived, Sean had set it up so that it appeared our mother had committed suicide. Our father claimed that she had shown up, desperate to take him back, and when he wouldn't agree, she shot herself."

He bent down, took his tea and sipped, then nodded to

her tea. "Drink." It wasn't a question or a suggestion, but rather a demand.

"No, thank you," she said softly. "What happened next?" She tried to convince him to go on.

His eyes narrowed, but he continued.

"Your father, apparently, didn't buy it. The other officer, however, was easily paid off after my father shot your dad. My father has been paying the man off, chunks at a time, over the past twenty years."

"And? Where have you been?" she asked.

"Just like my mother, my father decided I was too much of a risk and had me locked up." His spooky smile was back. "Shortly after I turned eighteen, I was able to check myself out, finally emancipated. It didn't take long to find Isaac at school and to sneak into his life here and there." He laughed. "Messing with him was easy. I knew which classes he was in and since he never skipped a class, it was easy to make sure I was never seen in the same places." He shrugged. "A trip to the beach with an old friend, or even going skydiving and taking flying lessons." He shrugged and laughed. "Sleeping with beautiful women who think you're someone they've wanted was so easy, so fun."

Her heart skipped. "You... and Kristy?"

His smile turned, and his eyes grew darker. "Yes, she was all mine, her and Ash." His smile returned but was different. "My son. Not Isaac's."

She thought about the woman's death and he must have seen her questions.

"She was making a mess of things." He sighed. "She had a weakness for pills. I still had my keys, so I let myself into our apartment." He shrugged. "I saw what she did to you, at the mall."

"You... were there?" He laughed and nodded. "You

killed her?" Once again, her eyes darted around the room. The fireplace was the only light in the room, and she couldn't see beyond the glowing light.

"Less messy than killing the worker. I had paid him not to ask questions about the body."

She shook her head. "But Willis must have seen Isaac that morning."

Ian laughed. "No, I was smart and covered him with plastic before the worker arrived that morning. But when they found Isaac's body a year later and then I showed up shortly thereafter, the worker knew instantly that I wasn't Isaac and demanded more money. So, I paid him, with the condition he kill the cop who was sniffing around you. But the man botched that up, so he had to die." He shrugged and picked up the tea and handed it to her. "Drink."

"I'm not..."

"Drink!" He slammed his fist on the table, sending the other cups dancing.

She held the cup up to her lips and pretended to sip. The tea smelled sweet, too sweet, but she must have been convincing since he nodded and went back to his story.

"Why tell me all this now?" She played with the heart on the bracelet Sawyer had given her, afraid of his answer. She wondered if she'd ever see Sawyer again, if she'd ever have a chance to tell him how she felt. They had said the words, but did he know just how deeply she had meant them?

"I should have had his life, it should have been me! Not him!" Ian screamed, then he quickly settled back down. "I was the one who sent you those roses, the yellow ones." He sighed. "We will have to have an open and honest relationship unlike you and Isaac had. I'll need to know everything, all the time." He sighed and relaxed back. "You'll see, things will be just as wonderful as they were before."

Her stomach twisted. "Have you ever... have we..." She felt her entire body convulse as his eyes heated.

"It was so easy, after Isaac graduated college, filling in for him every now and then. Only the once, when he was away on that long business trip. I flew home to my wife." He reached over and took her hand. "Then, that last night, after Isaac lay in the wall, I returned to you, made love to you." He smiled. "You must have known. I had dreamed, hoped you would know it was me and not him making love to you."

She leaned over and emptied the contents of her stomach on her favorite rug and her mind blurred as she remembered it wasn't really her rug, but Ian's. The man who'd filled in for Isaac, her husband. How many times had he returned home, played the role of her husband? How many times had she made love to Ian, instead of Isaac? He said twice, but suddenly, everything made sense and her mind cleared.

Isaac had never been the one to demand perfection from her, he'd never complained about her art. Several times before, she could remember Issac doing so, now, realizing it had always been Ian. Ian had been the one who was controlling, the one demanding she be something she wasn't. Knowing everything she did, where she was. So much made sense to her now and her stomach rolled again. A bucket was shoved under her face.

"There, there." Isaac's voice soothed her, and she relaxed as memories blurred with the present.

"Isaac?" she cried.

"Yes, I'm here, I'm right here, sweetie." His hand soothed her hair away from her face. "You'll get better, then we can start on that family we've always dreamed of."

She glanced up, her eyes filled with tears and, for a moment, she allowed her mind to convince her that it was Isaac sitting next to her, soothing her. Then Ian smiled and broke the trance.

She gathered all her strength and pushed him, causing him to fall off the sofa and land on his butt on the rug she'd just soiled. Without thinking, she rushed from the room down a long hallway and through the door at the end. It led to the kitchen and, when she didn't see another door, she looked around for a weapon. She froze when she saw an outline of a man sitting at the kitchen table. The lights were off, so she couldn't see who it was, and she didn't know what to do next. She could hear Ian calling to her, searching the large home for her. He opened each door in the hallway and she knew it was only a matter of time before he found here there.

Squinting, she took a step closer to the figure. Her eyes adjusted, and she realized it was Boone Schneller sitting at the table. When she reached out to touch his shoulder, his head fell back, and she noticed the large gash from ear to ear. His eyes stared up at her in the darkness and dried blood covered the man's shirt.

She screamed and screamed, her mind going completely blank as Ian walked into the room, a gun pointing at her chest. In his other hand, he held a mug.

"You see, I will protect you." He nodded to the body of her neighbor. "He was the one destroying your deck, the one who attacked you. I saw what he did to you." His eyes turned dark as he stepped closer to her. "I'll always protect you." He moved closer, the gun going down to his side. "You haven't finished your tea, wife." Ian held the cup towards her as she once again felt her world go black.

TWENTY-EIGHT

Full disclosure...

"What do you mean she's not there?" Carson said into the phone.

Sawyer felt another wave of panic wash over him as Ozzy danced around his feet. "I mean she's not here. Ozzy was locked out of the house, Tsuna was in, and Rose is nowhere to be found. Get your butt over here and bring anyone else you can drag out here as well." He reached up and flipped off the oven.

The bread and the dinner she must have made were beyond help, charred to blackness. It was a wonder they hadn't caught fire.

He hung up the phone and rushed to the back patio. The door was unlocked, and he followed Ozzy outside.

"Find our girl," he bent down and told the dog. "Find Rose again."

Ozzy whined and glanced around, then without any more prompting, took off like a bullet across the driveway and through the brush with Sawyer fast on his heels.

He'd grabbed his gun and kept his phone tucked in his pocket as he ran as fast as he could through the muddy yard.

The dog lost him several times, but when he whistled, Ozzy would bark and give away his location, then wait for him to catch up.

They crossed Rose's land, through acres of trees and brush, and even crossed a small stream that drained into Lake Erie.

He was soaking wet when he snapped his fingers and forced Ozzy to sit outside of the house he had led him to. It was almost a quarter of a mile from Rose's. Pulling out his phone, he called Carson.

"Where are you? We're at the house," Carson said.

"Ozzy followed her scent to a house, her neighbor's place, the closest house to the left. About a quarter of a mile away. Can you call it in? Do a quick search and see who owns the place? Then meet me here, quiet like. I don't want to spook whoever has her," Sawyer added.

"Are you sure she didn't just hike over there to deliver some cookies to the neighbor?" Carson asked.

"Pretty damn sure." He sighed as the rain started falling faster.

Carson sighed. "I thought not. Stay put, I'll call you back soon."

"My phone is on silent," he said, before hanging up.

Ozzy and he waited in the dark, under the shelter of a large maple tree whose leaves were already gone, giving him little shelter from the cold rain falling from the sky.

Ozzy whined, and Sawyer pulled him closer and tucked him under his rain jacket. "Shhh, we'll get her back, buddy," he promised the dog, who seemed to understand and settled in the warmth of his jacket.

When his phone buzzed, he answered.

"You're not going to believe this." It was the chief instead of Carson. "We're heading up your way. Carson should be there on foot any minute, but..."

"Who owns the place?" he interrupted the chief.

"The house is owned by Clayton." Sawyer could hear as he turned on his sirens.

"Sean?" Sawyer frowned at the dark home. It was smaller than Rose's mansion, but then again, every house in Twisted Rock was smaller than Stoneport Manor. It looked as if it had been built within the last thirty years and had been updated more recently.

"No, not Sean. At one point, yes long ago, but it was transferred into Isaac's name shortly after his death."

"What?" Sawyer's eyes narrowed. "How did that skip under our radar?"

"Because we weren't looking at the finances of a dead man. Why would we? He's been dead for over a year."

"So." Sawyer heard a twig snap behind him and grew silent.

"Sawyer?" Carson called out lightly.

"Here," he whispered, and his partner stepped out from the darkness. Just then, a shot rang out. Sawyer grabbed Ozzy and flattened their bodies to the muddy ground.

He heard Carson cry out in pain a few feet away from him and knew that his partner had been hit.

"Ten-seventy-one. Shots fired. Officer down," he yelled into his phone as the gunfire rang around him. Tossing his phone aside, he crawled behind the tree trunk, holding Ozzy next to his body. The dog started to squirm in his hands and he lost his hold on him. The dog darted away from the house, heading directly towards Stoneport Manor. Smart dog, Sawyer thought as a bullet hit the bark a few inches from his own head.

Sawyer flattened his body tight once more and crawled through the mud towards where he'd seen Carson.

"You okay?" he asked his partner when the night grew silent again.

"Yeah, got me through my calf." He was holding his leg. The man had already removed his belt and had a tourniquet wrapped around his thigh as he leaned against the thick trunk of a tree, his back to the house.

Sawyer checked the wound, tightened the tourniquet, and made sure Carson was out of the line of any more fire before starting to crawl towards the house.

"You're not going in." Carson laid a hand on his arm.

"Rose is in there." He shoved past his partner.

"Wait for backup," Carson called out to him.

Sawyer couldn't voice it, but he knew that it might be too late by the time backup got there.

He made it about ten feet from the house before floodlights flashed on, blinding him. He was momentarily stunned at the brightness, so stunned that he didn't realize that he was fully exposed until a bullet landed less than an inch from his hand. Dirt and mud spit up, splattering him before the night grew silent again.

Not waiting for more bullets, he jumped up and rushed towards the house, zigging and zagging, as he'd been taught back in the academy. Bullets landed at his feet, several times whizzing by him close enough that he could feel the burn and crackle from the air as they zipped by him.

"Sawyer?" Carson called out.

"Yo," he replied back. "Take care of the dogs," he said, unsure of why that had been his first thought.

"My god! Are you hit?" Carson yelled.

"No, but either I'm bringing Rose out alive, or..." He let

his statement die in his throat as he heard the sirens approaching.

He crawled around the house until he found a back door that was boarded up with an old piece of plywood. He circled the house once and determined it was the best way inside.

Taking a chance, he stood to the side of the door and knocked.

"Police!" he called out loudly. "Come out of the house with your hands up..."

He thought he heard Carson chuckle from the darkness as the patrol cars grew closer.

"Worth a try," he said, then knocked again. Just then, shotgun bullets tore through the back door, splintering the wood into a million pieces. Sawyer had to fling himself into the mud once more to avoid being hit by the second round of shotgun fire, which shattered the rest of the plywood like glass.

He listened and heard the telltale sounds of a shotgun being reloaded then tossed onto the ground as someone threw out a soft curse.

Taking a deep breath, he pulled out his weapon and stood up, putting himself in the line of fire. Within a split second, he stopped himself from shooting as he watched a man in the darkness move forward.

Rose was tied and gagged. Seeing her held in front of the man's body like a shield caused his blood to boil.

"Why don't you come in?" the man said calmly from the darkness.

It was then that he saw the gun pointed at Rose's temple.

"Come on, don't be shy Officer Sawyer," the man coaxed him.

Sawyer stepped in through the splintered door, pushing some of the wood aside to make room for him.

When he stepped into the dark room, his eyes met Rose's and he saw the tears flowing down her cheeks.

"Are you okay?" he asked Rose, who slowly nodded. Then his eyes went past her, took in Schneller's body, the slit throat, and winced. Then for the first time, he got a look at the man who was holding Rose and frowned.

"Isaac Clayton?" He shook his head and wondered if he'd hit his head sometime in the past fifteen minutes.

The man laughed. "Close." He motioned with his gun. "Go ahead, drop your gun outside the door." He nodded to Sawyer's gun.

Sawyer did what he asked, knowing he'd tucked his personal gun in the back of his jean's waist, just in case he needed it.

"Good, now, why don't you step in further?" the man asked.

"Let Rose go," Sawyer said calmly.

The man laughed. "Oh no, you don't get to make the demands here. I'm in charge!" the man screamed the last.

Sawyer had gone through a course in hostage negotiation, but at the moment, he couldn't remember a damn word from the lesson. Not when the gun kept going back to Rose's head.

"Okay." He held up his hands. "You're in charge." He agreed. "Tell me what you want."

The man smiled. "We want to leave here, without being followed."

Just then, he heard his chief's voice over a bullhorn and groaned.

"Police! Drop your weapons and come out with your hands up. We have the place surrounded."

"Tell him." The man waved the gun in his direction. Sawyer felt relieved when it was no longer pointing at Rose.

"They won't let you walk out of here with her. Why don't you take me instead?" Rose shook her head.

"It's not you I want," the man said calmly.

"Why don't you tell me what it is that you do want?" he asked. Rose raised her hands and tugged the gag out of her mouth.

"He's Isaac's twin, Ian," she said before the man shook her and she shut her mouth.

"Ian?" Sawyer tested the name. "Is it true? You and Isaac were twins?"

The man's eyes narrowed at him, pointing the gun at his chest.

"I'm walking out of here with my wife." He pulled Rose closer to his chest.

"Rose isn't your wife." Sawyer took a step closer while the man's eyes were on the door behind him. "She was Isaac's."

He stopped when Ian glared up at him.

"She should have belonged to me! All of this should be mine. I was the one dad chose, not Isaac!"

Sawyer could tell by the tone in his voice that the man was growing more unstable and they were running out of time.

"Ian," Rose said softly, "why don't we sit down and have some more tea? Then you and I can talk." She stopped talking when he jerked her.

"Don't talk in that tone," he growled in her ear. "You're just like them. All of them. Talking to me as if I'm deranged." Suddenly, Ian pushed her towards him and Sawyer caught her before she hit her head on a table. Then, he shoved her behind his body and took a step backward, towards the door. The man's gun centered on his chest.

"You're just like the rest of them," Ian continued as if he didn't know he'd just given up his last game piece. "You want him, not me."

As if in slow motion, Sawyer watched the man's finger twitch over the trigger. With all of his might, he pushed his body backward, sending both him and Rose falling through the splintered remains of the back door just as the gun went off.

Falling through the air, he felt the bullet rip through his flesh, but he was focused on twisting their bodies around so that when they landed in the mud outside, he took the brunt of the force. The impact caused the breath to burst out of his lungs.

"Run," he told her when he could get his breath back, then he shoved her up, off of his chest. "To the house," he said quickly.

Thankfully, she did as he asked and after slipping in the mud a few times, quickly disappeared into the darkness.

He reached around and pulled the gun from the back of his jeans. His hands shook as he pointed it at the door. He waited a heartbeat, then another. After five, he decided Ian wasn't going to come bursting through the doorway, shooting at them.

He rolled into the darkness, away from the doorway, and disappeared into the trees again.

"Sawyer?" Deter called out.

"Here." It came out as a groan.

When the chief and Madsen reached his side, he was staring up at the house, his gun still pointed at the dark hole in the building that had been the doorway. Now, as he watched, a spark caught and, starting deep inside the darkness, a fire grew.

"He's lit the place on fire," Madsen said.

"It was Isaac's twin," he said and was surprised that his voice sounded as if it had come from someone else.

"Officer's been hit," Deter called out, ripping Sawyer's shirt open wide.

"Damn, I just got that shirt cleaned." He looked down and saw the blood oozing slowly from the perfect hole in his left side. "Not again." He looked up at the chief. "Third time's a charm. I quit." He smiled when the chief laughed.

"You can hand in your resignation later. But for now, let's get you out of here." The chief turned to Madsen. "Secure the building."

"How?" The officer shook her head and looked at the house, totally engulfed in flames.

"Just watch the damn door and make sure no one comes running out," Deter said. "Haffner is watching the front.

The chief pulled Sawyer up and helped him around the front of the building.

"Rose," he said. "She ran back..."

"She's here," Deter said, nodding towards the ambulance where they were loading Carson into the back.

"Boone Schneller was in there." He nodded to the house, which was totally engulfed now. "Throat slit."

Deter sighed. "No wonder we couldn't find him." They walked slowly around the building, avoiding the heat of the flames. "Looks like I'm going to be short on officers for a while," Deter said when they approached the front of the building where all the lights and cars were. "Why couldn't the two of you just dodge bullets? Just this one night." Deter sighed as Sawyer chuckled.

"Sawyer!" Rose cried out when she saw him and rushed across the muddy yard to wrap her arms around him.

"Easy." He hissed with the pain.

"You've been shot." She frowned down at his blood-covered shirt, which Deter had put over the wound and was using to apply pressure.

"Yeah, it's just a flesh wound though." He laughed at the old Monty Python joke, then felt his entire body tilting at an odd angle. "Don't be upset, but I'm going to pass..."

Everything went dark.

He woke in the ambulance. Rose was leaning over him, concern flooding her eyes.

"Hey." He smiled up at her, suddenly feeling like he could fly if she asked him to. "You look amazing." He tried to reach up and touch her face, but his hands wouldn't move.

"Easy." She wiped a tear from her face. "They had to strap you down. They gave you some pain meds. You were trying to fight them."

"I was?" He frowned and shook his head. "I don't want to ever fight again. Not when I have you." He smiled again. "You're so beautiful. I'm so happy you're going to marry me."

Her eyebrows shot up. "Am I?" she asked, causing him to frown.

"Sure," he said. "We're going to have kids together."

"It's just..." She glanced around, then moved closer. "You haven't asked. I assumed, but..."

"I haven't?" He frowned. "Damn, I can't even do that right. The ring." He tried to feel in his jean pocket. "It's here somewhere."

She chuckled and helped him search his jeans. "No, nothing's here."

"Hmmm." He closed his eyes. "Oh, that's right. I gave it to Ozzy." He smiled up at her.

"What?" She frowned at him. "You gave my engagement ring to Ozzy?"

"Sure, he was supposed to give it to you," he answered, feeling even more light-headed. He worried he'd fall asleep again without hearing her answer.

She laughed. "Sawyer, you're delirious."

"No." He shook his head, causing a wave of dizziness to wash over him. "It's on his collar, you were supposed to see it..." He frowned. "Sometime."

"Shh, we'll talk more about it when you're better."

"Answer me," he said softly.

"Ask." She smiled down at him.

"Marry me? Please?" He sounded as if he was begging. Still, her smile and the tears in her eyes smoothed his fears away.

"Yes." She leaned down and placed a soft kiss on his lips. "Of course, I'll marry you."

A WEEK LATER, Sawyer was propped up on the sofa in the living room with both dogs lying on his lap. He'd put in his resignation and had officially put the ring on Rose's finger.

She was already planning a day next spring to host their wedding in the garden on the grounds. She wanted something small and, to be honest, he was happy to marry her anywhere, anytime.

Carson had left the hospital the same day but had gone through a few more surgeries than he had due to the bullet hitting a major artery. His old partner was looking at months, maybe even years of rehabilitation, which meant he was being forced to take an early retirement. Carson wasn't complaining though. He'd been threatening to retire for years. This gave him the perfect excuse to do so, and to get that dog he'd always wanted. He'd persuaded Brigit to get him a yellow lab to help him out. He'd called it Frank.

Rose had filled him in on the inner twisted mind of Ian Clayton and explained how the man had filled in for his brother all those times after being released from the institute.

In the city, he'd been the one who had stayed with Kristy Owens, even purchasing her apartment. Ian had only filled in for Isaac's life with Rose when he knew Isaac was away on travel.

For years, he'd been filling in for Isaac when he could, even flying his own plane up there, staying in the house next door, which he'd purchased under Sean's name and later transferred to Isaac's name, with money their mother had left him.

Then that night over a year ago, he had fought with Isaac after Isaac had discovered Ian outside of the house when Isaac had gone to check on the progress of the wall shortly after dinner. Isaac had known something was up because of the pictures someone was sending him. He knew it wasn't him in those pictures, but he didn't know about his twin. Ian had murdered Isaac and it had been Ian who'd returned upstairs to Rose.

That next morning, Ian had gone out to deal with Isaac's body, and Willis had shown up to install the last forms. Ian had covered the body with plastic and told the man he'd killed a wild dog. The man had promised to remain silent for a large wad of cash, and Ian had paid him off quickly.

Then Ian had filled Isaac's shoes and had left for New York that next morning on Isaac's planned trip back to the city. He'd hoped to take over the life of his twin.

The next bit they had learned from the police interview with Sean Clayton.

The day after Isaac's death, Sean had caught on to Ian instantly when Ian had tried to fill in for Isaac during a business meeting. Ian had always filled in for Isaac's personal life but had never tried to fill in for his work life. After all those years of school, Isaac had been a great lawyer. Ian knew nothing about law.

Sean had known almost instantly what had happened and had convinced Ian to meet him after work to discuss his other son's new role in the family business. Instead, Sean had had Ian committed to a private institute upstate, the same one where Ian had been committed during his youth.

Sean hoped everything would go back to normal. He'd flown Isaac's plane over the ocean, jumping out and meeting a friend in a boat, then returning to work the next day like nothing had happened, playing the role of a distraught father who had just lost his only son.

Ian had been released from the institute a month after Isaac's body had been discovered in the basement wall. He'd taken up residence in the house next door, so he could stay close to Rose once more.

He'd murdered Willis when the man had asked for more money after a botched attempt to kill Sawyer.

Ian had drugged Kristy after Kristy's mother, the legal guardian of their son, Ash, had called Kristy that day after Kristy had confronted Rose at the mall. She told her that she had just seen Isaac watching his son play at the park. The entire time Kristy and Ian were together, she'd believed him to be Isaac, a married lawyer and heir to his father's fortune.

Kristy had rushed home and Ian was in their apartment. There, he'd drugged her and left her to slowly die of an overdose, locked in the apartment that they had shared together.

"So, Isaac never cheated on you?" Hunter asked.

Her brother, her sister, her mother, and her mother's husband, Bill, Hunter's father, all sat around the living room, along with Sawyer's mother, Gloria, who had made the trip from California to check up on him after hearing about the entire mess. Jenny's kids were back home with her husband since they couldn't take any more time off school until the winter break.

"No," she sighed. "He really was on work trips. Apparently, he was going behind his father's back and taking other clients of his own. He was trying to start his own law firm, one away from his father's powerful influence and criminal activities." Rose took Sawyer's hand in her own. "We may have had issues in our marriage, but disloyalty wasn't one of them." She smiled at Sawyer.

He knew she was happy to hear it, and he was happy for her.

"Still." Her smile fell away, and she turned back to her family. "Ian had filled in for Isaac a few times in this house." She looked around. "Which now, in hindsight, makes so much sense. There were times Isaac would question some of the work we'd done together around here. Like, he didn't remember helping me clean the fireplace." She turned her head towards the fireplace, where a fire was heating the room. "Ian is the one you went to the beach with you that day, the one who went skydiving with you," she told Hunter.

Her brother shook his head and sighed.

"He had me fooled." He sighed. "I'd always wondered why Isaac never wanted to talk about skydiving and a few other things with me. We did, eventually, go later, I'm sure it was him." Hunter frowned, then looked up, his eyes searching. "Wasn't it?" He shook his head.

"He filled Isaac's shoes a lot over the years," Rose added.

Jenny set down her cup of tea. "He filled in... filled in."

Sawyer felt Rose shiver. "Yes," she said softly. "Still..." Her chin came up and she glanced at him. "It helps me to think about the good times I had with the man I loved, Isaac. No matter who he was when we were together, he was Isaac, my husband. He loved me, and I loved him." He smiled and squeezed her hand. "I will remember nothing but kindness and love from him." She shook her head. "Them, both of them. Even though Ian and Isaac were different, to me they were just... Isaac." She sighed, and he took her hand to his lips and kissed it.

"From now on, you're a one-man woman." Sawyer smiled over at her.

"So," Rose frowned, "if it was Ian killing everyone, who sent Isaac the images and the notes?"

"What notes?" Jenny leaned forward.

"I did." Everyone gasped and turned towards Hunter.

"You sent Isaac the threatening notes?" Rose asked. "You promised me you didn't know about the affair."

"Threatening?" He frowned. "If you mean I was going to expose him and tell you, yes. I'd gone to the city to see Melanie a few times. We've had this on and off kind of relationship since college." He ran his hands through his hair. "Anyway, I saw Isaac with Kristy. Well, who I thought was Isaac, anyway. I asked Melanie to take a few pictures of them. She sent me those pictures and I... well, I confronted Isaac. He promised me that he wasn't having an affair, convinced me that he would get to the bottom of it and that it would stop. I believed him." Hunter turned to Rose. "I'm so sorry I didn't tell you. I should have... after New York. But I forgot about them. It was almost two years ago." He shrugged. "I've had a crazy schedule and... I forgot. I'm so sorry."

"You're going to owe me," Rose scolded. But then she reached for his hand. "You were just looking out for me." She smiled at her brother.

"Isaac must have known, looking at the pictures, that it was Ian. Maybe he thought his brother had moved on, had his own family. Why didn't he just tell you it was his twin?" Jenny asked.

"Sean Clayton gave us the answer to that one," Sawyer added. "Isaac didn't know he had a twin."

"What?" everyone in the room said at the same time.

"What do you mean?" Hunter asked.

"Well, it seems that when Sean had Ian committed, it was because he'd attacked Isaac. He'd knocked him over the head with his little league baseball bat. Isaac was in the hospital for almost two weeks," Sawyer said.

"I remember him telling me how he'd got hit over the head playing little league." Rose frowned. "I always thought..." She shook her head. "My god."

"Sean said, after that day, he'd convinced his five-year-old son that his twin, Ian, had been an imaginary friend instead of a real brother. Sean believed it was best for Isaac growing up to not know about his crazy twin or his crazy mother. Since no one in town had seen the two boys together, he convinced everyone that Isaac was his only son."

"But it was Sean who killed Glenn, my husband?" Joan asked.

"Yes, Sean shot his wife, Dianna, and then Glenn that night when your husband didn't believe Dianna had committed suicide. Sean paid off the other officer, Rick Brown, to keep it all quiet. Brown is rotting in a jail cell, right next to Sean Clayton," Sawyer explained. "Then, years later, when Isaac confronted his father about the images, Sean knew Ian was free from the mental institute and began looking for him. When Ian showed up at the law firm, pretending to be Isaac, he knew that Issac was dead. Ian had told him that he'd killed himself. So, he quickly and quietly had him committed again, making sure to cover his tracks by firing anyone who had seen him that day. Before taking care of Isaac's plane. The sad part is, Sean Clayton must have known all this time that Ian had killed Isaac. Now Sean Clayton is being charged with murdering his wife all those years ago, as well as all the other charges, and Brown is being charged with accessory."

"Where does this leave you?" Jenny asked Rose.

Rose leaned slightly on him and smiled. "Well, we're planning our wedding for the spring." Jenny and Rose's smiles grew. "Which leaves us..."—Rose glanced over at him and he nodded— "about six months to come up with a wedding dress that will fit my large belly."

"Large..." Jenny said, then her eyes grew big. "You're..." Her hand went to her own growing belly. "We're pregnant together?" Jenny jumped up from her spot and rushed over to hug Rose.

After all the excitement died down, Rose snuggled against his chest. "We didn't plan this, this early," he told Rose's mother.

"Some of the best surprises are like that." She smiled.

"Rose wasn't planned either, but she was just as loved as Jenny." Then she turned to Hunter. "You weren't planned either. Bill and I... we didn't mesh at first." She smiled over at her husband and took his hand. "But, it was right, and you and Rose were like..."

"Two peas in a pod?" Jenny added, earning her a laugh. "What? That's what we always called you."

"Like twins," Rose added, taking Hunter's hand in hers.

"But not the kind of twins where one's evil and the other is normal," Hunter said. When everyone groaned, he smiled. "What? Too soon?"

This is a work of fiction. Names, characters, places, and incidents either are the product of the author's imagination or are used fictitiously, and any resemblance to actual persons, living or dead, business establishments, events or locales is entirely coincidental.

TWISTED ROCK

DIGITAL ISBN: 978-1-945100-00-0

PRINT ISBN: 2370000753793

Text copyright © 2018 Jill Sanders

Printed in the United States of America

All rights reserved.

Copyeditor: Erica Ellis – inkdeepediting.com

No part of this book may be reproduced, stored in a retrieval system, or transmitted in any form or by any means, electronic, mechanical, photocopying, recording, or otherwise, without express written permission of the publisher.

ALSO BY JILL SANDERS

The Pride Series
Finding Pride
Discovering Pride
Returning Pride
Lasting Pride
Serving Pride
Red Hot Christmas
My Sweet Valentine
Return To Me
Rescue Me
A Pride Christmas

The Secret Series
Secret Seduction
Secret Pleasure
Secret Guardian
Secret Passions
Secret Identity
Secret Sauce

The West Series
Loving Lauren
Taming Alex

Holding Haley

Missy's Moment

Breaking Travis

Roping Ryan

Wild Bride

Corey's Catch

Tessa's Turn

Saving Trace

The Grayton Series

Last Resort

Someday Beach

Rip Current

In Too Deep

Swept Away

High Tide

Sunset Dreams

Lucky Series

Unlucky In Love

Sweet Resolve

Best of Luck

A Little Luck

Silver Cove Series

Silver Lining

French Kiss

Happy Accident

Hidden Charm

A Silver Cove Christmas

Entangled Series – Paranormal Romance

The Awakening

The Beckoning

The Ascension

The Presence

Haven, Montana Series

Closer to You

Never Let Go

Holding On

Coming Home

Pride Oregon Series

A Dash of Love

My Kind of Love

Season of Love

Tis the Season

Dare to Love

Where I Belong

Wildflowers Series

Summer Nights

Summer Heat

Summer Secrets

Distracted Series

Wake Me

Tame Me

Stand Alone Books

Twisted Rock

For a complete list of books:

http://JillSanders.com

ABOUT THE AUTHOR

Jill Sanders is a New York Times, USA Today, and international bestselling author of Sweet Contemporary Romance, Romantic Suspense, Western Romance, and Paranormal Romance novels. With over 55 books in eleven series, translations into several different languages, and audiobooks there's plenty to choose from. Look for Jill's bestselling stories wherever romance books are sold or visit her at jillsanders.com

Jill comes from a large family with six siblings, including an identical twin. She was raised in the Pacific Northwest and later relocated to Colorado for college and a successful IT career before discovering her talent for writing sweet and sexy page-turners. After Colorado, she decided to move south, living in Texas and now making her home along the Emerald Coast of Florida. You will find that the settings of several of her series are inspired by her time spent living in these areas. She has two sons and off-set the testosterone in her house by adopting three furry little ladies that provide her company while she's locked in her writing cave. She enjoys heading to the beach, hiking, swimming, wine-tasting, and pickleball with her husband, and of course writing. If you have read any of her books, you may also notice that there is a love of food, especially sweets! She has been blamed for a few added pounds by her assistant, editor, and fans... donuts or pie anyone?

- facebook.com/JillSandersBooks
- twitter.com/JillMSanders
- amazon.com/Jill-Sanders
- bookbub.com/authors/jill-sanders
- goodreads.com/Jill_Sanders
- instagram.com/jillsandersauthor
- youtube.com/JillSandersAuthor
- pinterest.com/jillmsanders
- snapchat.com/add/Jillsandersbooks

Made in the USA
Columbia, SC
24 January 2022